Praise for John David

"It is, in one word, a masterpiece! The best book I've ever read, and I've read thousands."

"*The Harvest* is amazingly written, intriguing, very different and fascinating, deep…highly recommended reading."

"*Time Cursor* was amazing! What a great read from start to finish. I could hardly bear to put it down. I can't wait to read it again so I can pick up on all the little clues I missed the first time around. And, thank you! It's been too long since I have read a novel and not guessed nearly every element and twist of the plot from chapter one."

"It is amazingly brilliant, right there with some of the best I've read. In terms of science fiction, it's up there with greats like Heinlein; definitely a book I'm going to make sure stays in my possession."

"The only thing I can say is **WHAT A RIDE!!!!!!!!!!!!!!!!!!** Far exceeded my expectations. I've been reading SF since Asimov & Bradbury started, and this was a treat and a blast. Thanks again for a great run."

"In short, it's amazing and I could not wait to finish it."

"*The Harvest* had me completely enthralled from beginning to end. I never wanted to put the book down, being one of the most interesting reads I have ever had the pleasure to experience. I have difficulty expressing in words how much I truly loved this book."

"Not only is *The Harvest* the best book I've ever read, it is very likely the best thing I'll ever read!"

"I loved your books! They took concepts that I've been trying to reconcile for quite a while now and combined them into an excellent, well-told story with internal consistency and a unique perspective on their applications within the real world. Thank you for a fantastic read. I can't wait to read more!"

THE
AEGIS
SOLUTION

JOHN DAVID KRYGELSKI

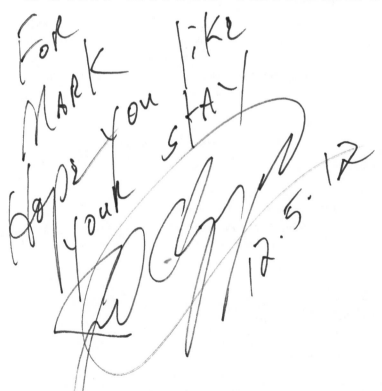

For Mark
Hope you like
your stay

12.5.12

STARSYS PUBLISHING COMPANY

The Aegis Solution

WWW.STARSYSPUBLISHING.COM

Cover art - Michael Nolan.
Art Direction - Michael Nolan - www.michaelnolanart.com
Editor - Jean Nolan Krygelski

Published by Starsys Publishing Company
WWW.STARSYSPUBLISHING.COM
526 N Alvernon Way
Tucson, Arizona 85711

ISBN 10: 0983052840
ISBN 13: 9780983052845
Library of Congress Control Number: Pending

First Edition - November 2011
Printed in the United States of America

Dedication

This book is dedicated to Jean, without whom *The Aegis Solution* could not have been written. There is no warmer heart, kinder soul, sharper mind, or brighter light.

Acknowledgments

First and foremost, I must thank my editor, Jean. So much more than an editor, she has become my writing partner as we go through this process together. Thank you, again, to Michael Nolan for another breathtaking cover. I'd also like to thank Tim Sweezea, Michael Hutson, and Jay Crabill for their invaluable contributions in the areas of ordnance and jargon. A thank you to Erin Christiansen for helping me to understand surface obs, variable winds, and anemometers. And, of course, all that is accurate in these areas is to their credit; any errors are solely mine.

Anarchy is craved by the best among us for what it affords – and by the worst for what it allows.

PROLOGUE

Neve Walker stared out her bedroom window at the darkened landscape, tears streaming down her cheeks. Her hand, almost involuntarily, clenched into a fist, crumpling up the sheet of paper containing her handwritten note, as if a part of her mind wanted to prevent the chaos her words were certain to cause.

Drawing a deep and shuddering breath, she attempted to force at least a degree of calm into her agitated mind. Reluctantly, her eyes shifting away from the window view, Neve looked down and noticed the balled-up note she held tightly. With exaggerated slowness, her fingers opened and she dropped it onto the bed. It was ineluctably a symptom of her mental state that the wad of paper assumed the characteristics of a wrecking ball as it crashed into the quilt which had been handmade for Neve by her mother.

Focusing what remained of her dwindling reserve, with deliberate motions, Neve meticulously peeled open the wad and, with her fingertips, gently smoothed out the paper, mindful of the poignancy as a tear fell from her cheek onto the page.

Satisfied, she turned to the nightstand to stare at the one and only picture placed there. Clipped into a cheap frame, which she had purchased with her allowance years ago, was a badly taken photo of herself, sitting between her mother and father. Although, in the time since, she had been given many posed portraits taken by professional photographers, this shot, snapped by a tourist who had happened by, was still her favorite.

As she gazed at the picture, her mind traveled back, as it had so many times before, to that wonderful day. She and her parents had gone to the Renaissance Festival. It had been her idea that they dress for the occasion. Her mother was resistant to the idea at first, but her father prevailed, as he always did. She still vividly recalled their stifled laughter as the stranger asked if he could join them at their picnic table while they ate, their mirthful reaction caused by the unlikely juxtaposition of images he presented.

"It's not every day," he said to them, sensing their amusement, "that you see a Vietnamese guy dressed as a court jester from Olde England."

The four of them laughed, and he joined them at the table. This was, she reflected wistfully, back in the period of their lives when such a thing was still possible.

It was then, just as he sat down, that Neve decided she wanted a picture. She dug the disposable camera out of her maroon velvet Victorian satchel and handed it to their new guest, asking if he would mind taking a shot of the three of them. He cheerfully agreed and stood up from the table, backing away as he stared through the plastic lens, trying to capture the group within the frame. Satisfied, he stopped and, rather than asking them to say "cheese," remarked, "You realize that I am Vietnamese, not from Japan, so no guarantees about how this picture will come out."

They all burst into laughter, and he snapped the picture.

Neve stared intently at the photograph, trying to burn the image into her mind. Her father was to her left, his face stretched in a broad guffaw, a massive turkey leg hovering in front of his chin. Because the stranger was also laughing as he snapped the shutter, the camera had jiggled and he had cropped off the top of her father's head, concealing the leather hat with the flamboyant purple plume affixed.

To Neve's right, sat her mother, wearing the green velvet dress of a noblewoman, with a lace parasol perched upon her shoulder. She had not yet noticed the large gravy stain on the filigreed bodice, acquired as she had just previously eaten beef stew from a bread bowl.

Neve's eyes then fixed upon her own face in the picture. Despite her objections earlier that morning, her father had prophetically insisted that she dress as a princess, rather than the Robin Hood-esque character she had planned. A beautiful rhinestone tiara was clipped into her tousled hair, cocked at a slight angle and looking as if it would soon fall off. Around her delicate neck hung a matching necklace, which disappeared into the open neckline of the pink chiffon gown. Her eyes were squeezed tightly shut, her mouth wide open in mid-laugh, and Neve...even on this day...was still able to recollect the total joy she had felt at that moment.

But it was only the memory of joy which came, not the feeling itself. Such had been the case for quite a long time.

Tearing her eyes from the photograph, she looked down at the pistol on the bed.

How unfeminine! she thought to herself, knowing that most females kill themselves with pills.

Neve had considered that option during the agonizing stages of planning she had gone through and decided that pills were too uncertain. The available resources at her father's disposal were so overwhelming; she did not want to take the chance of being discovered early and a miraculous intervention occurring which might save her putrid life.

The steel butt felt cold as her fingers wrapped around it. The barrel tasted of gun oil. With one final glance at the nightstand photo, she pulled the trigger.

Almost before the reverberations of the gunshot died down, the bedroom door was kicked open and two Secret Service agents burst into the room, skidding to an awkward stop as their trained eyes instantly absorbed the horrendous scene.

⊙

William Walker stood at the podium, his eyes not focusing on the faces before him, his mind reticulating out the whir and hum generated by the jumble of recording equipment all aimed in his direction.

He began to speak and found that his throat was tightly clenched. Pausing, Walker took a small sip from the glass of water which was ready for him next to the microphone stand. It took three attempts before he succeeded in swallowing. Tentatively, he cleared his throat and began. His voice was not of the timbre and vibrancy this group and the whole nation had become accustomed to. Many of the broadcast reporters witnessing the speech would later comment, as they made their on-the-air analyses, that William Walker, President of the United States of America, sounded weak, tentative, even beaten.

"I want to begin by thanking the millions of Americans, and our friends around the world, for the prayers and expressions of sympathy that my wife and I have received over the past weeks. I cannot tell you how much they have meant to us during these very dark days.

"The loss of our only child, Neve, is an experience no parent should ever endure."

Walker paused and stared into the distance at some unseen vista, causing a silence which quickly grew uncomfortable for the reporters and technicians in the room.

With multiple blinks of his eyes, the President refocused and continued, "Only God can possibly explain the reasons for her decision. And those answers will be kept from us until the day we join Him...and, I pray, once again see our beloved daughter."

Walker hesitated a second time, but only for a moment. His back visibly stiffened and, as he began to speak, his voice revealed a trace of its former power.

"Many of the religions of the world, including my own, believe that suicide is a sin, an offense punishable by an eternity in...in a place other than Heaven. In the days since this horrific event occurred, my wife and I have prayed to God that this not be the case...or, if it is, prayed for lenience from Him.

"During these prayers...during the long days and nights which have passed since Neve's death...I have come to a conclusion."

Walked paused once more. For the first time, rather than falling into another absent gaze, he directed his eyes to the lens of the lone camera, shared by all of the television networks for their video feed.

"I would like to place before the American public the idea...the belief...that no civilized country can consider itself such without offering an alternative to those who have lost all hope. I am proposing that we build a place...a sanctuary...open to all who may need it, where they may go when they have nowhere else to go. It would be a haven for the desperate, a refuge for those who cannot see another way."

Walker paused to take another sip of water before resuming. "For this concept to serve its intended purpose, the sanctuary must be free from any and all judgment of those who may enter. And it must be a place where one can go to escape the consequences of his or her own actions, no matter how extreme...no matter how heinous...those actions may have been.

"Over the next days, weeks, and perhaps months, I will meet with my friends and colleagues in the House and Senate. Together, we will attempt to forge the necessary legislation to effectuate the creation of this new place – an establishment which will operate under our aegis, to guarantee that each and every person, if faced with the most dreadful of choices, has a new, and I believe better, final alternative."

$\odot$

Matt Clements watched the county electrical inspector as he replaced the screw securing the cover of the main breaker panel.

"Everything look all right, Ben?" he asked.

Ben Barnes tucked the screwdriver into the back pocket of his jeans and nodded, making a note on his inspection sheet.

"What else do you have on your list?" Clements asked, anxious to wrap up the final inspection and finally get home to his wife.

Barnes looked at him and grinned. "Don't tell me you're in a hurry to get out of here."

Matt laughed and glanced around at the cavernous main electrical room, deserted except for the two of them. "I think twenty-three months in this place is long enough."

The inspector, a retired general contractor who had built more than a thousand buildings in his career, set the clipboard on a transformer and slowly looked around the room. "This is a first for me. I'm sure for you, too."

"What do you mean, Ben?"

"Have you ever built anything, especially anything this massive, knowing that after you walk out, you'll never see the inside of it again?"

Chuckling, Matt quipped, "I hope I don't."

Barnes did not join his former general superintendent in the laugh, a somber expression remaining on his face. "I just don't know about all of this. I'm not sure it's right."

Pulled down into his former employer and mentor's mood, Clements fell silent.

Only moments passed before Barnes snapped back to the here and now. Picking up his clipboard, he scrawled a large *X* on the box next to "approved," separating the bottom sheet from the two-part form and handing it to Matt.

They walked without the banter they normally shared, exiting the electrical room and turning down the main corridor toward the entrance. Their footsteps echoed back at them, amplifying the unease they both already felt as they made their way to the elaborate door system, which was currently secured in the open position.

For the last time..., Clements thought to himself, as he and Barnes passed through into the sunlight. Squinting against the brightness of the day, he saw the four members of the U.S. Marshals Service clustered around their point of egress, sweating. *The Arizona sun is unforgiving enough this time of year*, he thought, *without compounding it by wearing black.*

He was about to inform them that the final inspection was complete, when Barnes, without slowing his pace, announced, "That wraps it up, boys. It's all yours."

Stopping by the marshals, Matt called out, "Ben...."

Not breaking his stride, Barnes looked back over his shoulder at his old friend and said, "I'll catch up with you later. Call me after you get home to Lisa."

Matt watched as his friend climbed into the white truck with the county emblem on the door, started the engine, and promptly drove off.

One of the marshals – Clements had not bothered to learn their names – turned to him and inquired, "Is that it?"

His eyes still on the receding truck, he barely nodded, noticing that the rising heat from the pavement was now causing the shimmering effect known as a mirage. Barnes' truck seemed to be suspended a foot or two above the asphalt, as it disappeared into the distance.

He looked away from the horizon and focused on the federal officer. "Yeah, as he said, it's all yours," he answered, holding up the final inspection.

"Well, you beat most of them," the marshal said.

"Most of whom?"

"The other countries who followed Walker's lead. According to the news, there are at least three other versions of Aegis going up overseas. The only country to get theirs built quicker was Japan."

One of the other marshals tilted his head in the direction of a large temporary tent, which had been set up a hundred yards from where they stood. "I guess these folks will be happy to hear that the place is ready for them."

Matt glanced at the tent. His tone somber, he commented, "There are even more here now than when I went inside this morning."

"Yeah," answered the marshal, "they just keep coming."

Squinting once more in an attempt to see the faces of the gathered, Matt said quietly, "It feels like a funeral."

"In a way, it is."

The marshal turned to his men and instructed, "Okay. Go ahead and let them know. Escort them."

The three men began to walk toward the group, when the lead officer cautioned, "Remember, all of you stop at the door. No one takes a step inside – unless you want to stay, that is."

One of the three departing men turned back and gave their supervisor a look expressing his surprise at the last comment. One glance at his boss's expression dissuaded him from any sort of a comeback remark.

As Clements and the marshal watched, the federal entourage reached the group. The assembled strangers immediately surged forward.

"My God," Matt gasped, "they're acting as though it's opening day at a new shopping mall."

His companion was silent for a time, before finally saying, "I guess I was wrong."

"About what?"

"I didn't think anyone would take us up on this…whatever it is."

The group, numbering more than a hundred, moved rather quickly in their direction. The two men had to step off the concrete walk to give them room.

Now getting a better look at their faces, Matt saw that they were all staring forward at the yawning maw of the entrance as they hurried past. They were a mixture of almost all ages, from teens to octogenarians.

He remembered his wife, Lisa, telling him that it had been decided there would be no formal ceremony for the opening and that all media coverage was banned. As he watched the strange group file past him, he decided this was probably a good idea. His mind visualized a gamut of broadcast reporters lining the walkway as these people entered, shoving microphones in front of their faces and shouting the usual tasteless and insensitive questions.

With a slight nod toward one of the members of the group, the marshal, in a near whisper, asked, "Why would someone that old be going in? It doesn't make any sense."

Letting out a sigh, Matt answered, "My wife has been following this pretty closely during the months I've been out here building it. In addition to being on the news, the story has been all over the Internet. I guess some people are opting to move in here because it's a better alternative than what they've got."

He stared at the face of the woman as she passed. She was clearly in her late seventies or early eighties, using a walker to help her stay upright and stable. As she slowly proceeded up the walkway, he added, "She has probably lost her husband…run out of savings…either doesn't have any kids or at least doesn't have any who are inclined to help her. I'll bet she's thinking this is her best option."

"Either that," the federal officer began, his voice betraying an emotional secret he was not going to share, "or her kids wanted to take her in and she prefers this to placing that kind of burden on them."

Clements nodded. His eyes suddenly connected with those of a young girl who was the only one in the group not staring expectantly at the entrance, but glancing all around. She noticed that he was looking at her, and smiled. It was a half-hearted smile.

She couldn't be any older than my daughter, he thought to himself.

"Maybe sixteen or seventeen at the most."

He did not realize he had spoken the last thought aloud until the marshal responded, "What was that?"

Snapped from his reverie, he answered, "I was just noticing that young girl. She can't be more than seventeen. What the hell is she doing going in there?"

Following Matt's gaze, the officer found her in the crowd and shrugged. "Do you know how many kids that age kill themselves?" he asked rhetorically. "Too many!"

As they talked, Matt noticed that the girl's eyes never left his and she was slowing her pace, letting the rest of the group pass her. As she came even with the two of them, she had managed to make it to the back of the crowd.

As the other new entrants proceeded through the door, she paused near the threshold, looking undecided. For some reason, she was still looking at him. As if drawn by her stare, he stepped toward her, immediately feeling the grip on his arm from the federal officer.

"I wouldn't do that."

Clements turned and looked at him, his normal urge to rebel against authority waxing without encouragement. In a motion slightly more violent than he intended, he jerked his arm free from the grip and insisted, "We were told that through the doorway was the point of no return. She hasn't gone in yet."

The man shook his head. "That's not what I mean. It's a no-win deal for you."

Matt took a quick look over his shoulder and saw that she was still standing and waiting, apparently for him.

"What do you mean?"

"Since we've been posted out here, I haven't let any of my men talk to them."

"Why?"

The marshal's expression softened, and his eyes shifted to some point off in the desert, as he said, "Think about it. Only two things can happen. If you talk to her and don't change her mind about going in there, you are going to wonder about her for the rest of your life…with absolutely no way of ever finding anything out. She will keep popping into your head when you least expect it, and you'll want to know if she's okay…what her life is like in there…if she's even alive."

Matt thought about his words for a moment before saying, "I understand. I can deal with that. But what if I talk her into not going in? That'd be a good thing."

Shifting his eyes back, the marshal persisted, "Would it? You have no idea why she's doing it. You don't know what a mess she's made of things. And if you throw her a lifeline, you might as well adopt her because she is going to attach herself to you like a tick on a hound dog."

He started to respond again, but was cut off. "And what if you do talk her out of going in there and a month from now, or six, or a year, she decides to take the other way out? You're going to feel as if that's your fault. You are going to have to deal with the guilt of knowing that if you'd let her walk through those doors today, she'd still be alive."

The two men stared at each other for almost a full minute before Matt shrugged and said, "I hear you. But it won't hurt to just talk to her."

Before the man could respond, Clements turned and walked over to the young girl. As he crossed the fifteen feet between them, he noticed that she was painfully thin, almost anorexic. Her red hair was shaggy; either it was the result of the latest in youth hairstyles or she had hacked at it herself in front of a mirror. As he came closer to her, he saw that her eyes were a deep green, almost aquamarine color and her face was covered with freckles.

"Hi," she greeted him as he arrived.

"How's it going? My name's Matt." With that, he reached out to shake her hand.

Tentatively, she took his hand. "I'm Tillie."

Smiling at her, he asked, "Short for Mathilda?"

Grinning back, dimples tucking themselves deeply into her freckled cheeks, she replied, "Yeah! Not too many people get that. That's cool."

He released her hand, and she reluctantly lowered it back to her side, as she said, "It's an old-fashioned name. I happen to like old-fashioned."

"I do, too. Matt is short for Matthias."

She smiled, and they both fell into a brief silence until he began, "I walked over because it looked as though you wanted to talk."

Tillie dipped her chin closer to her chest and looked at him through her top eyelashes. The move was too coquettish to be natural in his mind. He waited for her to speak.

"I did. I mean, I do."

Letting one side of his mouth curl up in a half smile, he remarked, "Here I am. But why me?"

"You...I guess you remind me of my dad."

It was Matt's turn to grin. "As I watched you approaching, I thought to myself that you were about the same age as my daughter. How old are you?"

"How old do you think?"

"Sixteen, seventeen maybe."

She jerked her head in a rapid shake, making even the shortened hair twirl back and forth. "I'm almost twenty."

"You don't look it."

"I get that. All the time."

He drew a deep breath, letting it out slowly, before asking, "What did you want to talk about?"

The lightness on her face disappeared. She looked down at the edge of the walkway and motioned. "Can we sit down?"

"Sure." He dropped onto the curb next to her and waited.

His patience was quickly rewarded as she began to speak. "It's not like I'm not sure about this whole thing. I am. I really am. It's such a major thing, you know, and I saw you there and realized that you reminded me of my father. I thought, I don't know, maybe we could just talk it through."

"Okay."

"Plus, I don't have my dad anymore."

"What happened?"

"He died when I was thirteen."

"How?"

"Heart attack. At the time…to a thirteen-year-old, he seemed so old. But, you know, I realize now that he was really young for that kind of thing to happen."

"I'm sorry."

"Thanks. I think, no, I know that if he hadn't died young, I wouldn't be here today. I wouldn't be in the mess I'm in today, that made me come here."

Matt chose his words carefully, still thinking about the marshal's warning. "Want to tell me about the mess? Is it really bad enough to warrant this?" With his last comment he gestured vaguely in the direction of the interior of the complex next to them.

She twisted around on the curb to face him. "I don't know if I want to talk about all of that."

"Then what?"

Tillie hesitated for a moment before blurting, "I want to know what you think of this place."

Surprised, he rocked back on the curb and stared at the bright-blue desert sky, trying to gather his thoughts. "I assume you aren't asking me about the construction but, if you are, I built a damn good complex here."

"You built this?" Tillie asked excitedly.

"Well, I'm the general contractor. All of my crews built it."

"Wow! I knew there was something about you. My dad was a contractor." Tillie's eyes sparkled briefly with excitement.

Matt suddenly felt uncomfortable. The Fed's words about a possible attachment came back to him clearly. Trying to shift the subject, he said, "I guess you want to know what I think about this place...about the concept."

Her face still flushed with residual emotion, Tillie nodded.

"I don't know," he admitted. "I've had almost two years to think about it. My wife and I have talked about it a lot. But I still don't know."

He paused, hoping she would speak, but she remained silent, waiting.

"I understand why Walker did it. That's for sure. If I lost my daughter, I don't know how I'd react, especially if I were the President. But when I start thinking beyond the day a person shows up at the front door...when I focus on what it is that he or she is actually committing to...it just seems beyond the pale."

Tillie's eyebrows arched with curiosity. "Beyond the pale? I've read that phrase before, but I've never known what it means."

Matt Clements smiled, glad the conversation had assumed a more mundane course. "It's an Old English phrase."

"Yeah, I guessed that."

Continuing, he explained, "The king would send out his men to delineate the boundary of the kingdom...the outer edge of his domain and influence. They carried casks of water with them, and as they used up the water, they broke down the wooden casks and used the stakes from each one to mark the line. The stakes were also called pales. So if someone was venturing outside the boundary of what was considered to be the civilized world, it was said that the person was going beyond the pale."

"Cool!" she exclaimed. "That is awesome."

As they were speaking, the four marshals passed them, and Matt could not help but notice the meaningful stare from the lead man. Ignoring it, he said to Tillie, "So I guess this whole thing, checking in at this place, feels like that to me."

Her enjoyment from a moment ago was gone. Her face, as well as her entire body language, reverted back to a mode he could only describe as resignation. Picking up a pebble, Tillie tossed it across the concrete walkway and stared into the distance. He kept quiet, allowing her the time to think, hoping she would come to the right decision for her, whatever that might be.

As they sat in silence, Matt observed one of the men turn the key that actuated the hydraulic pump, closing the massive steel entrance. The symbolism evoked of a vault or tomb being sealed, as the portal thumped into its frame, did not escape him. He could only speculate about the psychological effect it had on Tillie, as her face remained impassive.

The officer he had spoken with earlier then opened the access to what would be the permanent entrance, the one that would be used from today forward. Considering what went into the rest of the facility, the entrance was amazingly low-tech. It was basically a series of modified subway turnstiles which allowed entrance but not exit, altered only to strengthen and fortify the components to deter tampering. One of those modifications was adding a redundant system to ensure that each turnstile could only rotate in one direction. In addition to the usual clutch mechanism, a heavy-toothed rachet module was attached to the bottom of the shaft, buried under the concrete of the floor. This served to create a loud *clack-clack-clack* as the person walked through, adding, in Matt's opinion, an additional sinister feel to the process.

Tillie suddenly sighed, and Matt snapped his attention back to her, eager to hear her decision and dreading it at the same time.

She wiped her hands on her jeans and stood. He stood also and continued to wait for her to break the silence.

She stepped closer to him. It was too close, he thought, feeling a twinge of nervousness. It was the kind of proximity between him and a female that would bring an instant reaction from Lisa, if she were here. Despite his tenseness he did not take a step back, but continued to wait.

Her aqua eyes stared intently into his and, in the bright sunlight, he could see an additional shimmer on their surface. She blinked rapidly several times, and the shimmer went away.

"I guess…. I guess I'd better get in there. I bet you want to get home."

Matt did not know if he was relieved or saddened by her choice. He was startled when his voice broke as he said, "Are you sure?"

Not trusting her own voice, she simply nodded.

Finally, drawing a ragged breath, Tillie asked, "Can I ask a favor?"

Uncertain what to expect, he tentatively replied, "Sure."

Her facial muscles tightened as if she was holding back a sob. "Before I step in, before I leave this…world, I guess, I feel like I need to say good-bye. To somebody. You know, like I have someone seeing me off."

As she said this, her eyes widened, conveying the urgency of her request.

"I…," he began.

Before he could continue, she interrupted, the words rushing out of her. "My mother doesn't give a damn about me. Hasn't for years. I don't even have a father. No one."

The pathos of the picture she painted struck him more powerfully than he anticipated, and he was speechless. Unable to find words, he only nodded.

No sooner had Matt indicated his assent than she stepped toward him, wrapping her arms tightly around his neck, her frail body shuddering with the release of the pent-up emotions. Instinctively, he put his arms around her and let her cry. Over Tillie's shoulder he saw the lead officer, who had warned him earlier, watching.

They stood locked together like this for minutes until the racking sobs subsided.

He loosened his embrace, normally a signal to the other to do the same, but she held him tightly, even pulling him harder against her. He found he was unable to refuse her the solace she was seeking, and reciprocated.

Neither knew how much more time had passed before Tillie finally relaxed, her arms dropping from around his neck. They stepped apart, and as Matt looked at her, he saw something that was not there before, although he was unsure what it was.

"Thanks," she murmured, a feeble attempt at a smile causing the deep dimples to reappear on her cheeks.

He smiled back and said, "Thank you."

With a faint look of surprise, she asked, "For what?"

His smile broadening, he answered, "For picking me, I guess."

"I don't understand. All I did was lay my trip on you."

Chuckling, he reacted, "Lay a trip! I haven't heard that phrase in a long time."

She joined him in the laugh. "I like old sayings."

"Well, you didn't lay any trip on me. You picked me to connect with. I am glad to meet you, Mathilda."

She took his hand and shook it, the simple motion conveying her sense of the irony of his words. "Yeah, glad to meet you too, Matthias. Wish we had met a long time ago."

The implication of her comment clear to him, he chose not to acknowledge the message and only said, "Same here."

Tillie looked as if she would say something more. Instead, she shrugged her thin shoulders and tilted her head toward the entrance.

"Well," she began in a voice with a forced tone of normalcy, "I'd better get in there."

"I'll walk you to the door."

They turned together, when suddenly he exclaimed, "Dammit!"

Tillie stopped. "What's wrong?"

He started to answer but, before he spoke, noticed that the marshal was still hovering nearby. He leaned closer to her and whispered something in her ear.

Hearing his words, she instantly remarked, "Cool! Okay!"

They finished covering the short distance to the turnstile, and Matt turned to Tillie and softly said, "You take care of yourself in there."

Her eyes swept across the panorama of the desert which surrounded them, as she answered, "You take care of yourself out here."

He leaned forward and they again hugged, this time with much less intensity, and parted after only a few moments.

Tillie turned and stepped into the opening, gripping the horizontal bars of the gate. She looked back over her shoulder and smiled at him. As she walked through, pushing on the bar, he heard, over the clacking of the ratchet mechanism, her final comment to him. "Be seeing you."

Feeling saddened and a little empty, he turned and walked over to the officer, who simply stated, "Told you."

Clements studied the man's face for a moment before swinging his gaze back to the now empty turnstile and answering, "No. You were wrong. I'm glad I did it."

By the time they turned and began walking to Matt's truck, the other marshals were already walking to their guard posts.

"What did you whisper to her at the last minute before she went inside?"

Shrugging, Matt replied, "Nothing. I just told her where I hid some candy bars."

The man's stare showed his doubt regarding the veracity of the answer, but he said nothing. They arrived at Matt's truck and shook hands.

Then the officer, sensing something in the contractor, assured, "You did a good thing…building this, I mean."

With a sigh, Clements responded, "If it hadn't been me, it would have been somebody else."

Realizing he had not touched the right nerve, the marshal opened the door to Matt's truck and said, "Take it easy."

"You, too," he answered, and the man walked away. Before climbing into his vehicle, Matt turned and took one last look at the huge complex he had built, his mind visualizing all of the nooks and crannies, all of the dorm rooms, kitchens, gyms, and the myriad other components within the confines of the walls. He also conjured, in his mind, the image of Tillie wandering through the cavernous public areas, and he wondered how she felt.

As he stood next to his truck, he suddenly felt a fresh gust of wind coming out of the west, seeming to push him away from the turnstile entrance. Although it was a hot day, he felt a chill in his spine. Shaking it off, he gave one last look at the complex and climbed into the truck. The engine roared to life, and as he drove away from what had been his project and his home for almost two years, his mind focused on his wife, Lisa, and he pressed down harder on the gas pedal.

Tillie had no idea where the other people had gone. She assumed they must have immediately fanned out to explore their new permanent home, since not even one person was in sight all the way down the long entrance corridor. She continued walking, following the directions given by Matt, until she found the main electrical room. Opening the door, she quickly found what she was looking for, glad that no one else had yet bothered to check out this area. She grabbed it and returned to the main hall. It only took a moment for her to orient herself before she struck out to find the dormitories.

"Time to pick my new place," she said out loud, her voice echoing back at her.

CHAPTER ONE

Elias watched the first accumulation of snow on the window sill. His eyes took in the intricacies of the slowly accreting pattern, but his mind was several thousand miles away, in a place where snow was as rare as the basic tenets of civilization. That corner of his heart, which once felt the almost childlike tinge of joy at the sight, was now empty. No, not empty. Filled. Replaced by a dense, dark sludge which allowed nothing like joy or happiness or mirth.

Such was his condition: a status which had stubbornly cohered to him for more than two years, like a disease with no known cure. In a sense it was a disease, a pernicious malady with vile symptoms and pervasive effects. Yet this blight was not brought about by some malignant, microscopic organism, but by a single man, a man who had shared the nameless, faceless anonymity of an abominable mutated virus. But that was all they had in common, for a virus, no matter how execrable its influence, was unthinking, non-sentient. No conscious motive could possibly be ascribed to its actions. This man, on the other hand, coldly plotted the most flagitious of acts, knowing fully and relishing the tragedy his deeds would bring down upon others.

Obsession was far too temperate a concept for describing how Elias felt about this wretched beast. Hatred, too savorless. It could truthfully be said that he was utterly consumed with the desire to find this abomination of a human being. Diminished not in the slightest over the past two years, Elias' thoughts had constructed scene after scene where he identified him, hunted him down, and patiently, arduously meted out...not justice, for that would be impossible...not revenge; in fact, nothing he could conceive of would satiate that thirst. No...his efforts would be bent solely upon restoring a minuscule increment of balance to the world, correcting an asymmetry precipitated by the never-ending succession of vile deeds perpetrated by this *lusus naturae*.

There were others, to be sure. For he had recently learned the identities of the others who played a part in this horrific act, others who had an, as yet unscheduled, appointment with Elias Charon. But they must patiently wait their turns.

With a sound more closely resembling the bleating of a goat than what it was, the ringing of a telephone, Elias was shaken from his fugue.

"Yes," he answered, his tone flat.

"Elias, Faulk."

"What it is, Richard?" Elias was aware that his question conveyed irritation, but did not care.

"I need to see you. Can you come in?"

"For what?"

"It's" – Faulk paused for a moment, clearly attempting to phrase his next statement carefully – "a special project we need you to do."

"Who's 'we'?"

"Well" – Elias' erstwhile friend tried a soft chuckle to break the obvious tension – "me."

"Why did you say 'we,' Richard, if you meant it was your idea?"

Ignoring the question, the man stated, "Elias, this job is perfect for you. I can't think of anyone better."

"So you still have to pitch it to somebody?"

The voice on the other end paused momentarily, again in an effort to best frame his answer. "In a manner of speaking. Look, Elias, they want me to take care of this…issue. I simply need to get them to bless my choice, and my choice is you. There are no other candidates, as far as I'm concerned."

Elias cradled the receiver against his shoulder and looked out at the snow, taking his time before he said, "Richard, you know what I'm working on. I don't want any damn projects. I just want to be left alone."

His tone deepening, Faulk began, "I know, my friend…."

"I'm not your friend!"

"You've made that clear before. I'm sorry. Bad choice of words. Hear me out, will you? I think this is something you'll want to do."

Closing his eyes to block out the whitening vista outside, Elias swiveled in his chair to face the desk. "What is it?"

Seeing the opening, Faulk rushed his words. "I don't really want to go into much detail on the phone, but it is about Aegis."

Although he hated to admit it, Elias was startled by the last word spoken. "What about Aegis?"

"There's something wrong there."

"No kidding. There's been something wrong there since the day it opened."

"I know. I mean, I know that you've been against it since it was first proposed when Walker was in the Oval Office, but something new has come up. Something that changes things."

"What?"

"Elias!" Faulk almost barked, sensing that he had succeeded in hooking his former friend. "Not on the phone. If you don't want to come in, I'll come there."

Holding the handset away from the side of his head for a minute, Elias stared down at the black blotter on his desk before saying, "No, I'll come in. What time?"

"Now. I'll send a car."

"No. I'll take the Metro. Pick me up at the station."

⊙

The snow was falling faster than the taxi's wipers could brush it aside.

Cutting through Elias' reverie, the cabbie asked, "So, do you think they'll ever finish the Silver Line?"

Without turning his gaze from the side window, Elias answered, "That would be too convenient."

"It'll sure cut down on my fares if they do."

"Well, there is that," Elias commented, reflecting on how different things might look to an individual depending upon his personal, selfish perspective.

The cab driver tried to continue the conversation, but the monosyllabic answers from his passenger soon dissuaded him, and silence filled the taxi. Even with all of his years of experience in this weather, Elias thought, it still intrigued him how even heavy snowfall could arrive with only a whisper of sound. Were this rain, the inside of the cab would sound like a snare drum played during a performance of "Taps."

Thankful for the quiet, Elias thought about Aegis. It had been over fourteen years since President Walker's daughter had killed herself, approximately twelve since the place had opened. Walker had received the gift of a second term from the electorate, partially out of sympathy but primarily because the unemployment rate had fallen to 4.6 percent during his first term.

His successor, now in his second term, was definitely not the same kind of President or the same kind of man. Where Walker had gone through his entire public life seeming to wear his heart on his sleeve, Jeffery Collinger, the former governor of New Jersey, was a hard-nosed, pragmatic politician who made a point of never displaying his personal beliefs in public. In several statements, mostly in response to questions about the institution, Collinger had consistently made it clear that such a place as Aegis would never have been built on his watch. Yet, he acknowledged the commitment that its very creation and existence implied and had vowed to keep his hands off.

Until now, apparently, Elias thought to himself.

His mind drifted back over the past twelve years and tried to recall a month or even a week that Aegis was not a part of the public dialogue. Americans had never been very good at being kept in the dark; this was no exception. It was obvious that the general public, and especially the members of the press corps, could not tolerate remaining ignorant of what was happening behind those walls. Speculation was ever present. The supply of so-called experts, who were plopped in front of a camera to give their opinions on the facility, its inhabitants, and the various legal and moral issues associated with it, seemed inexhaustible. Some of them appeared so often they might as well be drawing a weekly paycheck from the cable networks.

All of this attention spiked to new and dizzying heights whenever it was discovered that another famous singer or Hollywood celebrity had checked in. Each time, there would be renewed cries for "access" into Aegis. The public begged the government to allow television camera crews to go in – if not cameras, at least microphones; if not that, then a removal of the Internet blockade which encapsulated the facility so that emails could flow in and out. One of the entertainment cable channels had filed a civil suit in federal court, hoping a judge would order the Feds to open the floodgates. When the wife of a movie heartthrob checked in, he persuaded the L.A. county attorney to file a writ of habeas corpus, claiming that she was being held against her will and that Aegis was, in effect, kidnapping her. The writ was dismissed.

Davis-Monthan Air Force Base in Tucson and Luke in Phoenix provided air support enforcing the no-fly zone over the facility and, more than once, their pilots were forced to chase off helicopters hired by various media outlets. Some of the interdictions came perilously close to escalating into a messy situation.

No, Elias thought, *people can't stand not knowing something.*

As if the ongoing media circus were not enough, not one or two, but three "reality" shows were broadcast on different channels. The theme for all three was the same: what would it be like inside Aegis? The respective networks dedicated huge budgets to building sets and creating partial replicas of the real compound for their casts to live within. The broadcast network aired an edited, two-hour version seven nights a week. The two cable channels also showed daily condensed programs but, in addition, offered live coverage, twenty-four hours a day, over the Internet. The networks all proclaimed that their casts were completely isolated from the rest of the world during the lives of the shows, but persistent rumors had continued to surface that some of the actors had been spotted at various restaurants and clubs in Hollywood. Of course, all of them were allowed a brief reprieve from the alleged sequestration so they could don their tuxedos and gowns for an evening at the Emmy Awards. And what was the popularity of these supposedly realistic depictions of life inside Aegis? The three shows occupied the first, second, and third spots in the ratings.

A few months ago, a sixteen-year-old girl, who lived in Racine, Wisconsin, left a note for her parents, telling them that she could not live in a world without her idol, some television actor whose name eluded Elias at the moment. Apparently, the news of the object of her teen crush checking himself into Aegis, because he could no longer cope with the fact that his show was being cancelled, caused her to buy a bus ticket to Arizona and follow him in.

Both of these incidents, of course, stirred up new rounds of demands from the public. The loss of the Racine girl did have an effect. Collinger proposed and Congress passed a provision which would build a new structure at the entrance to Aegis. The addition would be, essentially, a hotel – a hotel with a difference. All of the rules of Aegis would apply with one exception: new arrivals could not enter the main complex for thirty days. At any point during that time, they could change their minds and leave, essentially providing a cooling-off period. Construction on this staging area, as it was called, was just now beginning. A moratorium on the entrance of minors under the age of eighteen into Aegis was established and quickly ceased after two teens killed themselves, blaming the moratorium for their decision.

So lost in thought, Elias did not notice they had arrived until the cab came to a stop and the driver turned around and announced, "Here we are, West Falls Church Station."

Elias took some bills from his wallet, paid the driver, and climbed out of the back seat, pulling his coat tightly around his neck to keep out the snow.

The Metro ride into D.C. was fairly smooth, the only jostling occurring as the train rode the rails laid on the original, 150-year-old Washington & Old Dominion track bed. Although recently reset and refurbished, that part of the line, which once carried passengers beginning in 1860, seemed determined to reassert its hard-earned antiquity.

Elias once again focused his eyes on the view through the plexiglass window. The initial portion of the route did provide some scenery. But as it neared the nation's capital, the train plunged underground for the balance of the trip. Despite the absence of a vista, Elias continued staring blankly, lost in his own thoughts, comforted by the steady stream of warm air surging from the slot vent integrated into the window frame. Not once during the duration of the trip did he glance around at his few fellow passengers, a corner of his mind thankful that he had boarded the train after the crush of the morning commute, leaving the adjacent seats vacant.

The train abruptly emerged from the semidarkness of the tunnel and entered the brightly lit D.C. station. Elias had occupied a window seat on the side opposite the platform, and the bank of upward-cast fluorescent lighting nestled between the tracks stung his eyes, causing his pupils to rapidly contract.

He exited the train, his gait neither hurried nor leisurely as he passed the SmarTrip proximity sensors. As was his tendency, his mind, acting autonomously from his conscious thoughts, subtracted the fare from his account balance as his eyes gazed upward. The concrete groin ceiling of the station, with its repetitive, rectilinear design, had been called neoclassical and brutalist, but to Elias it felt as if he were walking through the interior of the honeycomb fabricated by a new, mutated species of giant bee.

The long escalator, which took him from the bowels of the subway system, was always a trustworthy barometer of his mood. In good times – in other words, when he and Leah had been together – the trip up had seemed like an exit from an elaborate amusement park ride. At others times, such as this trip, it felt more like a conveyor between Earth and hell.

The interminable ride to the surface completed, he was surprised to see Faulk waiting for him personally.

"I'm honored," Elias uttered sardonically. "I assumed you'd send a driver."

Faulk tried to overlook the barb and reached out for a handshake. "It's good to see you, Elias."

Elias fleetingly considered ignoring the outstretched hand, then thought better of it. The handshake was brief and perfunctory.

"What is this about, Richard?"

Faulk's irritation with the cold greeting poorly concealed, he snapped, "We'll talk during the drive," and turned toward the exit.

They walked without sharing another word. Outside the station, a black Escalade with government plates was idling by the curb directly in front of a "no parking" sign. A uniformed officer from the Metropolitan Police stood by, ensuring that it was not towed away. Faulk gave a curt nod to the cop, then entered with Elias into the warm interior.

Elias, again surprised that there was no driver, waited patiently as Faulk negotiated the traffic in front of the station. He did not have long to wait.

"We all know how you feel about Aegis."

Faulk paused and waited for a response. Getting none, he continued, "Do you think you can be objective?"

Instead of answering the question, Elias asked, "Why would *I* need to be objective?"

Glancing over at Elias for a moment, Faulk tried to read his expression. Failing that, he said, "We need you to investigate it."

The comment grabbing his attention, Elias blurted impulsively, "Investigate it! How? Peek over the wall?"

Faulk calmed a bit, knowing that he had piqued Charon's interest. "No, the old-fashioned way. By going in."

Twisting around in his seat as far as the seat belt would allow, Elias faced his former friend and remarked, "Now that's a clever way to get rid of me."

A brief, mirthless laugh burst from Faulk. "Elias, we're not trying to get rid of you."

The SUV stopped for a red light.

Richard Faulk took a deep breath, looked at his passenger, and explained, "You would be an envoy…a representative of the White House. You would be the first person allowed to enter and, after your job is done, leave Aegis."

This stopped Elias dead in his tracks. It was not the answer he had expected, and the implications of what Faulk was saying to him tumbled through his mind in a kaleidoscope of thoughts and images.

The traffic light changed to green, and Richard accelerated.

Finally breaking the silence, Elias asked, "What is the job? Specifically."

Keeping his eyes on the traffic, Faulk began to fill him in. "There would be two separate and distinct assignments. We need to know what is going on inside Aegis. Some of the intel we've received has the administration concerned."

"I've seen enough of it on the news."

Shaking his head, Faulk continued, "That's only the tip of the iceberg. We'll show you the rest when we get to my office. But there is one element which never hit the media."

"What is it?"

"Rudy Kreitzmann went in."

A sudden shiver crawled up Elias' back at the sound of the name. "Kreitzmann! How did he ever get back into the country?"

"We don't know. The FBI tried to figure that out but failed."

"How do you know he went in?"

With a heavy sigh, Faulk said, "This isn't public knowledge, but we've had a camera at the entrance since the day Aegis opened. Facial-recognition software flagged him as he entered. It has been validated."

"A camera at the entrance? Kind of a violation of the privacy everyone was promised, isn't it?"

"Yes," Faulk answered casually, "I suppose it is. But we wanted to know if any of the people we were looking for waltzed into Aegis; then we could, at least, stop looking for them. The names of the individuals we spot have always been kept classified."

Elias again fell into silence. Faulk left him to his thoughts for the rest of the drive. They parked in the underground garage and rode the elevator up to the top floor. They continued to not speak to each other as they approached the corner office.

"E.C.! How are you?"

The greeting came from Marilyn, Faulk's aide. She had been a fixture there for years and had worked in the same position for Elias at the time he had occupied the office.

"Hi, Marilyn. I'm okay."

She stood and came around her desk to give him a hug and a brief kiss on the cheek. As she did, she whispered in his ear, "You look like hell."

Elias allowed himself a brief chuckle and replied, "So do you."

She did not, of course.

As they separated, over her shoulder Elias caught a brief glimpse of irritation on Faulk's face. Although he had become something of a hermit since his abrupt departure, there had been enough communication between Elias and Marilyn to know how she felt about her new boss, her dislike amplified, no doubt, by her very detailed inside knowledge of the incident leading up to Elias' abrupt exit.

"I hate to break up this reunion," Faulk interjected, using words perfectly consistent with a friendly jab at the two of them, his tone conveying the opposite. "But we've got quite a bit to do, Elias."

Her back still turned to her boss, Marilyn rolled her eyes, a sour smirk curling her lips. Elias had to struggle to suppress a smile at her as he said, "Let's go."

"Marilyn, we're going to need some coffee, and maybe some muffins."

"Yes, sir." She looked at Elias and asked, "Your usual?"

This time he did allow himself a smile as he answered, "That would be great. Thanks."

The two men entered the large office. Instead of moving toward the desk, Faulk sat at the medium-sized conference table positioned adjacent to the windows. Taking the seat at the head of the table not only placed Faulk in the natural power-position, but also gave him access to a keyboard and control panel. Elias followed and dropped heavily into one of the side chairs.

Mounted on the closest wall to the table, a flat-screen came to life, instantly displaying the agency logo. With a few keystrokes, Faulk summoned up the video he had described to Elias during the drive.

"There he is," he indicated unnecessarily, the camera clearly capturing one of the most notorious faces on Earth, as the man emerged from the inside of the last turnstile.

Faulk had already paused the image when Elias suddenly urged, "Keep rolling."

"What is it?" Faulk asked as he resumed the video.

Rather than explaining, Elias questioned him. "Who are those two?"

Leaning forward in his chair, Faulk stared at the two men who had entered Aegis behind Kreitzmann.

"I don't know. I would guess they are just two more new entrants. Why?"

"Pause it."

Faulk froze the motion on the screen.

"Look at Kreitzmann. Look at the body language. It looks as though he's waiting for them, as though they're together."

Faulk noticed that Kreitzmann was still in the frame. After entering, he had turned to wait for the others.

"Do we have any video of them farther in?"

"No. No interior cameras. Only the entry."

"Don't snow me, Richard. This camera was there while I ran this agency, and I didn't know about it. What else do we have?"

Sighing, Faulk said, "Elias, I didn't know about the camera until Ft. Detrick was ordered by the White House to bring this to me. If there are any other cameras, they haven't told me about them, either."

"Play it again."

With a few clicks on the keyboard, Faulk re-cued the video and started it. This time both of them stared silently. As it finished, Elias inquired, "Did facial-recognition come up with anything on either of them?"

Faulk shrugged. "It wasn't in my briefing. I'll check. But as far as those two guys, they could have merely arrived at the same time as Kreitzmann and, you know, struck up a conversation on the outside. It could be nothing."

"I don't think so."

"Why not? Simply because Kreitzmann turned to wait for them?"

"No. There's something else. Something in the way those two move."

"What do you mean?"

"Not sure. But it doesn't look right."

"I'll double-check with Detrick to find out if they ran any recognition on their faces. But, in the meantime, there's one more thing I want to show you."

"What's that?"

Rather than immediately starting another video, Faulk explained, "Kreitzmann checked in three months ago."

"Three months ago! And you're just now asking me to go in? That's a slow response, even for you. Why did you sit on it so long?"

Without a touch of defensiveness in his voice, Faulk answered, "We didn't."

Understanding instantly, Elias snorted. "Who have you already sent in?"

"Stone. He went in two weeks after Kreitzmann."

"You sent Eric in? What happened?"

Faulk's voice was subdued. "We don't know."

It was obvious that Faulk expected a string of questions. Instead, Elias sat back in his chair and stared at him, waiting.

Stammering slightly, he continued, "We had two elements in place, communication and extraction. The first was a method the tech department came up with so that we could communicate with Stone once he was inside. Every twenty-four hours at a prearranged time, the black-out shield, which prevents anything electronic from entering or leaving Aegis, would blink off for a moment, allowing him to send a flash transmission."

"Like the subs."

"Exactly. We didn't want to take down the curtain for a period long enough to allow anyone else access. Eric was supposed to record his report each day. He carried a device, no bigger than a smartphone, which would encrypt and compress the report. It was synchronized with the blink-off to automatically upload whatever was in his queue and download any information we might want him to have, all in less than a second. No others could use the interruption unless they were perfectly synched, also."

"What did he report?"

At that point, Faulk hesitated for a moment. "We never got a single report."

Faulk watched as Elias' jaw muscles tightened. He expected an outburst. None came. Slowly, Elias clamped down his emotions until he was able to say, "I repeat, why the time lag? Especially since you now had a missing agent."

Speaking quickly, Faulk explained, "We still had our extraction date. That was two weeks ago."

Faulk let his breath out slowly and finished, "Stone was a no-show."

Elias turned away from Faulk and stared at the image on the screen of the two men and Rudy Kreitzmann. Faulk did not interrupt his thoughts. After a full minute, Elias turned back and said, "I'll leave today."

Not surprised by his decision, Faulk added, "As I said, there's one more thing I want to show you."

"There's more?"

"Yes."

His fingers again touched the keyboard, and the image on the screen changed. Whatever Faulk wanted Elias to see was from the same camera inside Aegis, because it seemed as if the three men suddenly disappeared.

"What is this?"

"Watch."

Elias stared impatiently at the flat-screen – when, suddenly, something black and completely opaque rose from beneath the camera lens, fully obscuring the view.

"What happened?"

"Not any sort of a malfunction. According to the technicians, someone covered the lense with a black object."

"Who could do that? Did anyone inside know about the camera?"

"Supposedly not. Micro-lens integrated into the mechanical systems at the entrance. Essentially impossible to spot."

"When did this happen?"

"Two days ago."

"So it could have been Eric. He knew about the camera, didn't he?"

"Yes. At the time I briefed him, he saw the same video of Kreitzmann that you just saw. But I don't think it was Stone."

"Why not?"

"Keep watching."

Minutes passed with no change to the picture. Abruptly, whatever was blocking the camera was removed. Directly lined up with the camera angle, affixed with duct tape to the inside of the turnstile, was a large cardboard square.

Someone with a heavy felt-tip marker had created a sign. Scrawled on the cardboard in large, jagged lettering were two words:

HELP US!

CHAPTER TWO

Elias sipped his vodka tonic and watched the lush countryside slide gracefully past the window of the *Crescent,* a wry grin on his face as he recalled the tail end of the conversation between himself and Faulk. After Faulk showed him the cardboard sign, the briefing continued for another hour, as they discussed the details of what was expected of him and the logistics of the operation. He had, of course, accepted the assignment, and Faulk obtained the approvals, if any were actually necessary, within minutes. Predictably, Faulk asked Elias which agent he wanted as a partner. The conversation descended quickly into an argument when Elias told him he was going in alone. Elias had prevailed.

The tech arrived with the communication device, gave Elias a quick lesson, and hastily departed, clearly uncomfortable with the tension level in the room. The final disagreement arose, as it inevitably did, over the subject of transportation to Arizona. Faulk was in a hurry, as he always was, and told Elias that a jet was already standing by at Andrews Air Force Base. As Elias demurred, telling Faulk that a perfectly good train traveled the route, Faulk exploded, his ranting interrupted by Marilyn, who tapped twice on Faulk's door and entered.

Acting as though she were oblivious to her boss's suspended tantrum, she handed an envelope to Elias and said, "You're all set. You leave on the *Crescent* tonight at six-thirty."

Hearing this, Faulk sputtered before saying, "Elias, it's going to take you *three days* to get there. I can have you on the ground at Davis-Monthan in three hours!"

Elias thanked Marilyn and turned to Faulk, a hint of a smile on his face. "So?"

Marilyn winked at him and left.

"This assignment was requested from the very top. I'm supposed to go tell him you hopped on a slow-moving train to Arizona?"

"Honestly, Richard, I don't give a damn what you tell him. You picked me. You know how I travel. If you want someone there in three hours, send someone else."

The images of the unpleasant discussion still lingered in his mind as Elias saw the first hints of the lush swamp lands which would be his view for the balance of this leg of the journey. The club car was nearly half full with passengers, mostly refugees from the coach cars: a group of four men placidly sipping their drinks and playing cards, a family with several small children who were running up and down the center aisle, whooping and shouting, the cacophony they raised no doubt dampening the reverie of an elderly couple who were seated side by side, facing a window. Other than Elias, the couple seemed to be the only occupants who were attempting to experience the minutiae of a train ride through the bayou.

He returned his gaze to the window and tried, once again, to visualize what he was going to encounter inside Aegis. No one really knew how many people were in residence. Actually, Elias realized, that was not completely true. With the existence of the entrance surveillance camera, which was divulged to him only yesterday, he surmised that there probably was a head count, at least a tally of those who had entered. That number was somewhere in the briefing papers he had yet to fully read. There were two variables which would affect the reliability of that number as any sort of a basis for the current population. The first, of course, would be deaths. The second, and this was one of the many things William Walker never contemplated in his emotional rush to open Aegis, would be births.

It seemed obvious, in retrospect, that if you put men and women together anywhere, offspring were going to result. However, the enabling legislation creating the institution did not acknowledge this reality and failed to address what to do with these children. It was presumed that the parents understood the ramifications of what they were getting into when they checked in. They knew that one of the inviolable terms of entrance was that it was a one-way ticket. But the children...were they to spend their entire lives inside the walls of Aegis? They had no voice in the decision.

This, along with a multitude of other issues, was grist for public debates, position papers, and think-tank studies. The public was constantly reminded that the core concept of Aegis was that the net effect of choosing to enter was, from the perspective of society, equivalent to death. There could be no contact, no communication; in no way could anyone who was inside have even the slightest effect on the external world.

So, in the twisted logic of the current proponents, it followed that those children would have never been born, because their parents would have chosen the act of suicide rather than checking in. And, therefore, if one were to follow the fundamental premise of Aegis, society had no obligation to even acknowledge their existence.

While Elias occupied his mind with thoughts of the bizarre construct he planned to enter, a part of him was aware of the train attendant who corralled the clamorous youngsters and seated them in a circle of chairs. He placed a game of some sort on the table before the children and softly cajoled them to join in, serving the function neglected by the parents who were oblivious to the mayhem their progeny were causing.

Multi-tasking, a portion of his mind continued its attempt to conjure an image of what the world inside Aegis would be like, while another part dwelled on the question of what kind of parents he and Leah would have been, had they been given the chance. Both of these avenues were dark and murky, offering nothing but an inexhaustible source of depression and angst. It was down these two shadowy paths his mind doggedly wandered throughout the remainder of the trip into New Orleans.

Elias stepped down from the train onto the covered platform of the New Orleans Union Passenger Station. The *Crescent* had arrived on time, and it was close to 7:30 in the evening. He was not hungry, having eaten in his bedroom compartment almost two hours earlier. The *Sunset Limited* was scheduled to depart New Orleans shortly before noon the next day. Elias went through the routine of a cab ride, an overnight stay in the nearby Windsor Court Hotel, and the ride back to the station, without indulging in even a moment of sightseeing. He was not tempted by Harrah's Casino, Morton's, or the shops along the Riverwalk Marketplace, all within short walking distance of his room.

The following morning, Elias arrived at the station at a few minutes after ten, immediately found a Red Cap, and showed him his first-class ticket. The baggageman greeted him pleasantly, "Good morning, boss. Hop in," and took the one suitcase Elias was carrying, placing it onto the rear deck of his cart.

Elias was barely settled into his seat when the Red Cap floored the pedal and the electric cart shot forward. With a series of long beeps on the horn, the man expertly maneuvered the cart, weaving through the maze of people and luggage, scooting blithely past the long line of passengers waiting at the gate for permission to board the train.

"What's your name?" Elias asked, shouting over the whine of the cart and the noise of the terminal.

"Barton," he answered without turning his head. "Willis Barton."

"I'm Elias Charon."

"Mister Charon," Barton yelled as he swerved the cart into an access tunnel at full speed, missing the concrete wall by mere inches, "a fine and proper French name. It is a pleasure to make your acquaintance, sir."

"If you don't mind, I'll shake your hand after you're finished driving." Elias was gripping the edge of the canopy above his head to stop himself from sliding out of the vehicle.

Barton tilted back his head and barked out a laugh. "Fair enough, Mister Charon. Fair enough."

They exited onto the platform next to the blue and silver train. Barton swerved to make room for another Red Cap to pass, the tires of the cart coming so close to the edge of the concrete that Elias was certain they were going to plunge down onto the empty track. Successfully completing the slalom maneuver, Barton continued heading toward the front of the train, passing the observation car, the club car, and the dining car, and coming to a stop at the first sleeper.

Barton slid off his seat and grabbed the single suitcase from the back. "Here we are."

Elias swung around and planted his feet on the concrete, standing slowly. "Is this my sleeper?"

"Yes, sir, it is. You got the best car on the train."

"Why is that?"

"It's the closest one to the dining car and the farthest from the engine. Bedroom E is six inches bigger than the others on the car. And, best of all, your attendant is my brother, Napoleon."

Elias, a frequent train rider, was accustomed to the pervasive nepotism in the ranks, at least in the service roster of the train employees. Frequently, the attendants, once called porters, were third- or even fourth-generation employees, their grandfathers working for the railroads then owned by Santa Fe, Burlington Northern, Union Pacific, or the fallen flag of the Southern Pacific, and many times bringing the entire family into the profession.

"I'll go fetch him," Barton promised, disappearing through the open door of the car.

As he waited, Elias took in the sights, sounds, and smells which had always brought him pleasure: the throbbing hum of the engines, the smell of the diesel exhaust, and the look of the train itself poised on the track. Despite his ever-present malaise, Elias detected a faint tremor of excitement as he contemplated climbing aboard for the second leg of his journey.

He was shaken from his pleasant meditation when he heard Barton emerge from the sleeper car. "I found him, but he's still trimming himself up. I'll take you up to your room."

Elias smiled at Barton. "Thanks, but I know the way and I think I can still handle my suitcase."

The baggageman paused and asked, "You sure? It's no problem. Besides, I've got to earn that generous tip you're going to give me."

Elias reached into his pocket and pulled out a twenty, handing it to Barton. "You already have, my friend."

The bill disappeared instantly, and Barton snatched up the suitcase, carried it up the two steps, and placed it on the stamped-steel diamond pattern of the deck inside the car.

"Thank you, sir. And you have a wonderful trip. Are you heading to Tucson to see folks?"

"No. I'm afraid it's business."

Either the tone of Elias' voice or the change in his face signaled to Barton that he had touched a nerve with his innocuous question. He stuck out his hand and said, "I'll take that handshake now, sir."

Elias gripped the baggageman's hand. The handshake was firm as Barton looked into Elias' eyes and cautioned, "You be safe, okay?"

There was something in the delivery that gave Elias pause. He returned the stare, replying quietly, "I will."

Elias navigated the narrow, twisting staircase and turned left, spotting the sliding door for Cabin E. He had to turn sideways to go in while carrying the suitcase. With his one piece of luggage safely stowed on the overhead rack, Elias dropped down into the seat by the window.

Within minutes, Barton's brother arrived, standing in the narrow doorway and leaning his head into the compartment. "You must be Mister Charon."

Elias confirmed that he was and handed the attendant his ticket.

"Can I get you anything, sir?"

"No, thanks. But I would like to go ahead and give you my order for lunch. I'd prefer to eat in here."

"No problem at all, sir. Do you need a menu?"

"No. I'll have the cheeseburger and fries, with a couple of Diet Cokes. And make that cheeseburger well-done."

"You got it, sir. One well-done cheeseburger, fries, and two Diet Cokes. Now you know we won't be serving until after we leave the station, don't you?"

"I know. That'll be fine, Napoleon."

The attendant smiled. "Napoleon is what my kid brother calls me. On the train I go by Barton."

"Barton, it is."

Barton backed out into the passageway and left, returning a moment later with two small bottles of water and a cup of ice. "Here you go, sir, in case you get thirsty before we start rolling."

Elias thanked him, and the attendant left.

Within minutes, Elias fell back into the imaginary world his mind had constructed of the interior of Aegis. He realized that he had never entered a situation where he knew so little going in. Buried in his thoughts, he was unaware of the passage of time until he noticed that the train was beginning to pull out of the station, providing the brief illusion, as he watched from his cabin window, that the station platform was moving and he was immobile. The New Orleans cityscape quickly gave way to a dense, green vista just as Barton arrived with his lunch.

The afternoon passed unnoticed as Elias continued his pondering of the unknown that awaited him. At some point, he had retrieved from his suitcase the file given to him by Faulk. There were several papers clipped together, revealing all the government knew about Kreitzmann. He placed them on top and began to read. The facts and opinions assembled by the analysts painted a picture of a completely amoral researcher who fully embraced the concept that the ends justified the means.

Elias set aside the stack detailing the scientist's offenses and re-reviewed his early history, focusing on the academic career. Kreitzmann had obtained his Bachelor's and Master's at Stanford before transferring to Johns Hopkins for his PhD. Top of his class in each arena, he had published several papers in peer-reviewed journals prior to obtaining his doctorate in biomedical research. Apparently, he had exhibited no signs of his later proclivities at either of these universities, garnering nothing but positive, if not effusive, comments from his fellow post-doctoral students and professors. There was even a paper written by the distinguished geneticist Doctor Logan Reed, which had appeared in the *New England Journal of Medicine*, lauding Kreitzmann for his dissertation and predicting that his young protégé would, one day, have a profound effect on the field.

Elias chuckled at the irony of the comment. "Little did you know what kind of an effect he would have."

Elias finished reading the last page of Kreitzmann's *curriculum vitae* and placed it facedown on the adjacent pile, when he noticed that next on the stack of papers was a printed screen shot of the anonymous plea for help affixed in front of the supposedly hidden camera. Marilyn had obviously decided to include this disturbing picture in the file, but Elias was not sure if it had been included merely for completeness, or to elicit an emotional response from him. Regardless of her intent, Elias, upon once again seeing the hand-scrawled letters, felt the muscles in his back tighten.

He filled the remainder of the thirty-six-hour trip with studying the file, wandering to the club car for a few breaks, and crawling into the lower bunk for some sleep. He awoke briefly in San Antonio as they appended the cars from the *Texas Eagle*, which had arrived from Chicago many hours earlier, to the rear of the train.

Elias arrived in Tucson late in the evening. He tipped Barton and stepped onto the low asphalt platform, carrying his own suitcase. Within minutes, his rental car procured, he drove the few blocks to his hotel. Following a fitful night's sleep, he skipped breakfast and began the three-hour drive west to Aegis.

⊙

Erin Stephenson sighed with frustration. She was now saddled with the third intern this year, Amber, and rather than providing any real help, these earnest college students tended to be time wasters. She now had less than an hour to prepare for the ten o'clock broadcast, and instead of sitting at her desk working, she was following the twenty-year-old to the intern's cubicle to answer a question.

Trying hard to disguise the irritation in her voice as they arrived, Erin asked, "Tell me again what it is."

Nervously, Amber answered, in a rush of words, "Check out this surface ob," referring to the surface observation map on the screen.

Erin's eyes hastily glanced over the barbs, as she noted, "Okay, it's windy."

"I know," Amber replied, succumbing to her hallmark giggle, which Erin found extremely unpleasant. "At first I thought it was just variable wind, but look at all the wind barbs around this area…look at the direction…or I should say directions."

Drawing a deep, calming breath, Erin examined the screen more closely, this time paying attention to the little flag on each barb in the region where Amber had pointed.

"This doesn't make any sense at all," Erin muttered under her breath. Without tearing her eyes from the screen, her right hand reached out and snatched up the telephone. After punching in a number she knew by heart, she heard a voice answer on the other end.

"National Weather Service. Rusty."

Thankful that the meteorologist-on-duty was someone she knew, she blurted, "Rusty, Erin Stephenson. I think you're having a problem with your wind anemometers."

$\odot$

Elias parked the rental car and stared through the windshield at the entrance to Aegis. The contractor working on the addition, which would create the "cooling off" residence outside the point of no return, had built a temporary safety tunnel that, Elias knew, would lead him to the turnstile. The slab-on-grade foundation was already in place and a few of the tilt-up concrete panels were standing, braced by steel struts installed diagonally and bolted to the new walls and the floor. Elias hoped the braces were up to the task of withstanding the current winds.

When it was finished, new arrivals would be required to register within the receiving facility where they would each obtain an RFID card. As a part of the project, the outermost turnstile was to be modified so that it would only move if an authorized card was carried by the person entering the cage. The card would not allow the bearer access before thirty days, giving the new arrivals an opportunity to change their minds. To prevent the buying, selling, stealing, or swapping of cards among those in waiting, a biometric scan would be recorded at the time the new arrival received the card. The biometrics had to match the cardholder at the end of the thirty days or the card would be voided.

But, Elias knew, none of that was yet in place. At the end of the 2x4 and plywood tunnel was the turnstile, and that was it.

A gust of wind violently rocked the car, and Elias' view of Aegis was briefly obscured by dust. He decided there was no point in delaying any further, and he grabbed his suitcase with his right hand while firmly gripping the door handle with his left. As Elias tripped the door release, the wind instantly pulled the handle from his grasp and slammed the door all the way open, wrenching the hinges in the process. The interior was instantaneously filled with tan-colored powder even though he quickly climbed out and fought the force of the wind to slam the door of the car. Due to the now sprung hinges, the car door did not fully close, making it impossible for him to lock it.

Hunched forward, Elias walked/trotted to the mouth of the safety tunnel and gratefully took a few steps in, glad for the modest respite from the gale. Although he was tempted to again pause, the severe shuddering and creaking from the wooden tunnel prompted him to proceed through the wobbly, makeshift structure before it collapsed on top of him. The turnstile, lighted from behind, loomed ominously at the end. As he neared it, his familiar goulash of emotions returned. Dread, fear, anger, and frustration were but a few of the feelings elicited by the sight of the steel entrance.

Though it was a chilly day, as his fingers touched the bars, he involuntarily jerked them back; the horizontal metal rods of the turnstile felt substantially, almost irrationally, colder than the ambient temperature. Indicating impatience with himself by a shake of his head, Elias firmly grasped the bars and pushed forward. The loud *clack-clack-clack* of the ratchet mechanism reinforced his already present feeling of foreboding.

All of his speculating, all of his contemplating, wondering, and even dreaming as to what he would find inside was about to be answered. In his mind, he pulled up the floor plan of the entry. After navigating the entrance turnstile, which was actually a series of three turnstiles, each positioned around a corner from the previous, the first area he would see would be a wide corridor, which, he recalled, was one of many spokes on a wheel. He remembered thinking, as he had studied the layout, that Aegis reminded him of a science fiction space station. It was designed with concentric rings, served by arcing passageways, each of those accessed by wider corridors radiating straight outward from the center common area.

This entire thought process transpired in the few paces it took him to pass through the final turnstile. He reached the interior opening where the horizontal bars of the turnstile passed through the fixed set of bars, which precluded the entrant from simply staying inside the revolving door and proceeding back out again. This prevented the turnstile from being used as an exit, since the bars would only travel in one direction.

Unbeckoned, the melody and lyrics of the Eagles song "Hotel California" filled his mind as he stepped from the turnstile and surveyed the room. The entire facility was designed to minimize electrical and water usage and, in fact, was completely off the grid. Daytime lighting was accomplished utilizing integrated solar collectors, reflective tubes, and diffuser lenses to capture the maximum amount of sunlight on the exterior and carry it inside to the corridors and rooms of the complex. Most of the roof surface was covered with solar panels, to convert sunlight into electricity. Water came from a primary well and a secondary, or backup, well. The pumps on both of these wells ran only during the day, when the solar panels were generating electricity, each of them maintaining the water level of two elevated tanks, which provided adequate water pressure due to simple gravity. Hot water was also created during the day, again by use of the sun and a crisscrossing web of insulated black pipes leading from the roof areas. These pipes were fed by the water tanks. The sun heated the water within them during the meandering journey through the latticework, until the water was diverted down into the building where the pipes were chambered in another insulated raceway and tied into the plumbing system for general use. Sewage was handled by an extensive septic system installed in the desert adjacent to the facility. All garbage was to be dumped in a massive, lined excavation with a powerful ram assembly at the top. The debris was first compacted and then dropped into the pit.

Other than the water from the aquifer and the limitless sunlight, Aegis took nothing from society and gave nothing back. Zero impact was the goal of its state-of-the-art design.

As Elias stepped into the entry corridor, the first image which greeted his eyes was also the first answer to his volume of questions. All of the visible walls were covered with graffiti. None of the so-called urban art had been visible on the video he had seen in Faulk's office because the camera was tightly focused on the exit from the turnstile and did not show the adjacent walls. To his uninitiated eye, it was unreadable, communicating contempt rather than any specific message. In one sense, he was not surprised by the vandalism, since Aegis was anarchy in its purest form with no pre-existing governance or law enforcement. One of the many problems Elias had with the establishment from its inception was the concept of creating an environment where people, who were already at the end of their ropes, would wander in and then be expected to create a viable society from scratch.

The entry corridor, lined with several doors, was easily spacious enough to accommodate hundreds of people, yet it was empty. Despite the lack of an audience, Elias resisted the urge to wave at the camera, knowing that Faulk was watching and had been impatiently waiting for his arrival. He did make a point of ensuring that the lens received a full-frontal view of his countenance.

"I wasn't expecting a welcoming committee anyway," Elias said aloud, his voice echoing back to him from the various hard surfaces.

On the train ride, he had found the tally in the files: more than eleven thousand people had entered Aegis since it opened. There was, of course, no way for him to know the current population.

Elias shifted his suitcase to his left hand and reached into the pocket of his windbreaker with his right, gripping the butt of the 9mm Beretta but leaving it concealed. With his feeling of self-confidence bolstered, he walked forward into the corridor.

Knowing from his memorization of the plans that he had a nearly one-half-mile walk to the center of the complex, he paced himself at a steady but not quite brisk stride. He did veer to the side so that he walked near the right-hand wall, rather than down the center. The silence and emptiness was unsettling, creating the illusion that Aegis was completely unoccupied and abandoned.

Elias had traveled approximately one hundred yards, he guessed from counting his paces, when he approached the first of the intersecting hallways. This would be the outermost ring of residential units. The graffiti was as dense on the walls as it had been at the entrance. Just as he entered the intersection, two young men stepped into his path from the right side, coming to a halt directly in front of him. Before he could react, he noticed two more emerge from the hallway to his left, supplementing the impromptu blockade. Elias stopped and said nothing, wanting them to make the first move.

The tallest of the four, the top of his head covered with a black stocking, declared, "This is where you stop."

Elias took a brief moment to size up the stranger and his three accomplices before speaking. "Why is that?"

The young man shook his head as if Elias had asked him a foolish question. "Cuz this is where you decide."

"Decide? What?"

The leader had obviously expected the newcomer to be frightened. Since he did not hear a satisfactory level of fear in Elias' voice, he took a step forward, clearly intended to intimidate, and menaced, "Whether you belong to us or die."

As the man spoke, Elias heard a shuffling from behind and glanced over his shoulder to see that two more punks had approached. They had, no doubt, been hiding behind one of the closed doors he had passed. He was now surrounded.

Turning his head back to the front, Elias also took a step forward, bringing himself within inches of the apparent leader, and while staring directly into those dull eyes, in a low and steady voice answered, "I don't think so."

Angered by the response, the leader bit his lower lip for a moment before barking out, "What you mean, you don't think so? You don't *have* a choice!"

Elias grinned at him, his expression anything but mirthful. "But you said it was my decision. I've decided to keep walking."

He took a quick side step, and the leader moved to block him. Expecting this, in a series of movements which were almost a blur, Elias dropped his suitcase and reached up to grip the front of the stranger's shirt while pulling the 9mm from his pocket. He jammed the barrel of the pistol into the neck of the leader and ordered, "Tell your other punks to walk away."

The tall one's eyes showed white all the way around the irises as the reality of his predicament sunk in. But before he could speak, a gunshot rang out in the corridor, and Elias felt the body of the one he had thought was the leader go limp. Almost instantly, the thug's shirt blossomed with blood. Elias released his grip, allowing the stranger to drop limply to the floor, and looked around to see that all of the others had pistols drawn, all aiming at him.

From his detached perspective, Elias pondered the foolishness of their positioning as the five remaining young men stood in a circle, guns drawn; their clear intent was to aim at him, but their unacknowledged result was to have drawn a bead on each other, with only the bullet-stopping ability of his body as the buffer.

Elias was not sure if he was witnessing the field promotion of the former second-in-command or if the youth now dead at his feet had ever been the leader, but another member of this small gang stepped forward, his only true distinguishing characteristic being that he was the widest among them. From his position and the direction of the shot which had taken out the tall one, Elias realized that this was the thug who had fired. Taking care to not place himself within Elias' reach, he halted and threatened, "Drop the gun or die."

Elias slowly bent forward, and gently placed the Beretta on the concrete. He then straightened, his arms hanging loosely at his sides.

"Kick it away."

Placing the side of his right foot against the pistol, Elias slid it to his side, toward the wall on his right.

His eyes never leaving those of the gang leader, Elias asked, "What's this about?"

The slightest smile curled one corner of the thug's mouth as he said, "I got no problem explainin'. Every place needs jack...money...even this place."

"I didn't bring any," Elias answered, his tone conversational, as if he were oblivious to the fact that he had five guns, in the hands of obvious amateurs, aimed directly at him.

The smile spread on the face of the thug and he shook his head hard, as though he were trying to dry his hair. "You don't get it, dude. In here the currency is you."

As he heard this, the second piece of the Aegis puzzle fell into place for Elias. In the anarchy which would prevail within these walls, paper money would be essentially worthless. Yet every society, even the most chaotic, would need a medium of exchange.

It would have to hold an intrinsic value. With a steady stream of people walking through the front door, the obvious choice would be slavery.

Elias shrugged. "Okay. I understand. I'm all yours."

The caricature of a smile left the wide youth's face. "I don't think so."

His eyes darted down to the pistol on the floor, then back to Elias, before he said, "You gonna be too much trouble. Nobody gonna want you."

The thug, speaking to the two standing behind, said, "Unless you want to take a bullet, you better move your asses."

Elias heard the scuffling of feet behind him but did not dare to look over his shoulder, deciding to keep his eyes on the young man in front of him. When the sound from the rear stopped, the youth lifted his gun up and pointed it directly at Elias' forehead. Elias recognized it as a .357 magnum, and his mind calmly ran through the firing characteristics of the weapon, knowing that within moments his head would be vaporized. In an almost detached way, he observed the shooter's thumb pull back the hammer.

With nothing to lose, Elias ducked under the revolver and plunged forward, hoping to overtake his executioner in time. The thug was quicker to respond than Elias hoped, and he felt the butt of the heavy pistol slam into the top of his head. Instantly, his legs crumbled beneath him and he fell to the concrete floor. Somehow he managed to retain a feeble grip on consciousness and, as he fell, rolled to the right.

He now lay on his back, at the feet of the thug, who took a step forward. "See, I told you, you're too much trouble."

The punk obviously knew enough about ballistics to understand that if he shot Elias in the head in this position, the .357 slug would ricochet off the concrete. He aimed at the part of Elias' body which would provide the most resistance to the bullet, the chest, and again steadied for the kill shot. Elias had deliberately fallen to place himself within arm's length of his 9mm, but his mind could not come up with a scenario where he could grab the weapon, aim, and discharge it before the thug could pull the trigger.

Although there was more than adequate light, Elias only saw a dark blur suddenly sweep into his field of vision. The fast-moving phantom, or whatever it was, collided with the punk standing over Elias, causing the pistol to fly from his grip and clatter to the floor, followed immediately by the thug himself, who collapsed facedown.

Even though he had no idea who or what attacked the new leader, Elias took advantage of the sudden distraction to grab his pistol and roll against the wall, bringing the barrel up to bear on the nearest of the other thugs. A split second before applying enough pressure on the trigger to discharge the 9mm, Elias relaxed his finger, seeing that there was no need to fire. The other gang members were running headlong down the side corridor, already almost fifty yards away.

As he shifted his weight and got to his feet, Elias looked around for the source of intervention which had saved his life, but the area around him was empty except for the two motionless thugs at his feet. He tucked the 9mm back into his pocket and reached down to check for a neck pulse on them both and, although not expecting to find one on the first punk who took a .357 slug to the chest, was surprised to discover that the other gang member was also dead. It did not require the skills of a medical examiner to determine that his neck had been broken.

With a final glance around, Elias picked up his suitcase and resumed walking toward the center hub of the complex.

CHAPTER THREE

Elias noticed that the graffiti gradually diminished as he proceeded, until it was all but gone from the walls. Apparently, he was leaving the territory of the gang who had accosted him earlier. Although the attack and dialogue with the gang member had answered one or two of his questions about Aegis, his mind was swirling with the new ones prompted by what he had seen, especially the mysterious dark blur which had passed directly into his view, disarming the thug, breaking his neck, and disappearing without a trace.

As these thoughts entered his consciousness, he mentally chided himself for his florid descriptions, remembering how often, while he had been the occupant of Faulk's office, he would call agents on the use of terms like "mysterious" or "disappearing" in their field reports. And yet, he thought, how else could he depict the intruder or, he should say, rescuer?

He had passed the center hub of the complex and was now walking down the opposite corridor, when he was not surprised to find that there was a blockade which had not been shown on the plans he had reviewed. Nearing it, he saw that it was constructed of salvaged concrete blocks. Obviously, since building materials were not a part of the regular supply deliveries to Aegis, the residents had improvised, demolishing a CMU wall somewhere in the complex and reusing the blocks. As he reached it, Elias noted that there was no door.

Although he had seen the miniature camera mounted high on the side wall of the corridor, Elias decided that since the obvious intent was concealment, he would pretend to be unaware of its presence. There was no point in acting like anything other than a normal entrant to Aegis.

Suddenly, a voice came from a hidden speaker above. "Are you alone?"

Elias nodded and answered, "I am."

Fifteen feet above, a panel in the ceiling slid aside and a rope dropped down, dangling a few feet from Elias. The male voice on the speaker instructed, "Tie your suitcase to the rope."

Aware that in a situation such as the one created within these walls, commodities would have a much greater value than money or gold, Elias asked, "How do I know that you won't just take my stuff and leave me here?"

"You don't," the voice replied flatly. "You can always stay on that side and take your chances."

With a shrug, Elias set down the suitcase and looped the nylon braid through the handle, tying a simple square knot. Before he finished this process, a rope ladder was dropped for him to use. Obviously, whether he would relinquish his suitcase had been some sort of a test. He had passed.

He scaled the rope ladder, following his suitcase up into the opening in the ceiling. At the top there were two men waiting. Both gripped his arms, helping him through. The moment his feet touched the plywood platform, the two strangers pulled up the ladder and slid the cover back over the opening. It fell onto the supporting lip with a solid *thump*.

One of the two men extended his hand and introduced himself. "I'm Will Rogan." Elias shook his hand as he took measure of the man. He was somewhere in his mid-thirties, with a slender build and thick, curly hair.

"And this is Ontewon Johnson."

The other man could best be described as thick and muscular, his head shaved so closely that his black scalp shone in the dim light. The handshake Elias received from him was substantially more powerful, as he smiled and said, "Welcome to Aegis."

The two turned, making it obvious that Elias was to follow them. Picking up his suitcase, he did, and found that at the end of the short platform, oriented just on the other side of the blockade, was not another opening with a rope ladder, but an actual set of stairs descending to the floor.

$\odot$

The courier from Fort Detrick stood at attention at Faulk's desk, not showing the slightest hint of disapproval as the recipient of his delivery violated protocol by opening the pouch in his presence. The flash drive slid onto the desk blotter, and Faulk quickly snatched it up and inserted it into the USB port of his desktop computer. The embedded security program on the drive activated instantly and Faulk was prompted for his password, which he hastily typed. The security gateway instantly disappeared from the screen, replaced with a file list, which contained only one entry. Faulk double-clicked the file and a video clip ran. It was only twenty-eight seconds long.

After watching the video three times, Faulk signed for the delivery and handed the paperwork back to the courier. The man was not fully out of his office before Faulk had completed a phone call on his secure line.

"He's in."

⊙

"Zack, what the hell was that thing?" BQ shouted, the adrenaline coursing through his body and causing him to pace aimlessly.

"I don't know," the tall young man answered, his hand still shaking from their panicked run back to their home zone, or from the terror he still felt. "It musta been what Slate told us about before. One minute Jay-T was standing there with that dude, and the next minute he was on the floor dead! I never saw what hit him."

"Me neither. All I saw was a streak."

Ignoring the chairs and sofas strewn around the room, BQ dropped to sit on the floor, leaning his back against the wall. He pulled up his knees and rested his arms on them, trying to calm his breathing and slow down his thundering heart.

The young man called Zack dropped heavily onto one of the sofas, his head coming to rest on the upholstered arm while his feet remained on the floor. After a minute, he asked, "How are we gonna be able to keep doing business if that thing's out there?"

"Doin' business! What you talkin' about? That's the least of our worries! If that thing wants to come in here and take us out, it can. What we gonna do to stop it?"

⊙

Neither Elias nor the two men escorting him ever noticed the stranger crouched in the shadows above the ceiling line, in the jumbled and darkened mechanical space which surrounded the access platform. They never saw or felt the pair of eyes watching as Elias came up the rope ladder and went down the stairs on the other side of the barrier wall.

The unseen watcher remained motionless for several minutes after the three men departed, before finally retreating into the deeper shadows away from the area.

⊙

Throughout the brief walk down the moderately clean and well-maintained corridor, Elias was mildly surprised at the utter normalcy of the environment on this side of the blockade. He still was not sure what he expected inside this anomalous institution, but to his eyes and ears, it appeared as if he were walking the hallways of some ordinary complex in the outside world, rather than penetrating deeper into Aegis. There were others who passed him as he was being escorted, and they smiled at him and nodded a greeting.

Johnson and Rogan walked casually at his side, not conveying the sense that he was their prisoner, or even their charge, but simply that they were helping him find wherever he might be going.

"I am curious about one thing," Elias addressed them both.

Rogan chuckled. "Only one thing. I would have thought you'd have lots of questions."

"I do, I guess, but that is a pretty serious blockade back there."

Rogan nodded as they walked. "It has to be. There are gangs in Aegis who want to expand their territory."

"I get that," Elias responded. "I ran into some of them on my way."

Johnson faltered for a moment in his gait. "You did?"

"Uh-huh."

"And you're here to talk about it?"

Elias decided to keep the dark, fast-moving apparition to himself and answered, "I guess I got lucky. I outran them and was able to hide until they gave up. Anyway, you have the solid barrier blocking the corridor. I'm assuming you have a camera hidden somewhere near the wall."

"We do," Rogan replied.

"A microphone and speaker system, a rope ladder, a platform above the ceiling – all pretty impressive."

"Thanks."

"But all I had to do to get in was tell you I was alone?"

"Yep" was all Rogan said.

"I don't get it."

Rogan stopped walking, joined a moment later by Johnson. Elias followed suit and turned to face him directly. The man responded matter-of-factly, "The Manager can explain if you're curious."

"The Manager?"

Rogan just nodded.

Elias shrugged. "Okay, let's go meet the Manager."

They resumed the walk and within less than two minutes arrived at an open doorway leading into what looked like a medium-sized meeting room.

Johnson gestured toward the table and seats. "Wait here, if you don't mind. The Manager will be right in."

Elias decided that it was probably a waste of time to ask the two of them any more questions, so he thanked them both, parked his suitcase on the carpeted floor, and waited.

He did not have time to look closely at his surroundings before a door opened at the opposite end of the room from where he had entered, and a woman walked in. It was difficult for Elias to judge her age. Her short hair was completely white, yet her face showed few age lines. She wore a turquoise, loosely fitting dress. He was not sure, but Elias thought some of the girls in his classes had called it a squaw dress in the more politically incorrect days when he was in elementary school. Instead of shoes, she had on leather sandals.

"I'm Mildred Pierce," she announced, extending her hand in greeting as she crossed the room to Elias.

"Elias Charon."

They shook hands. Elias noted the firm yet brief handshake.

"Welcome to Walden."

"Walden?"

Pierce flashed an insincere smile. "That's what we've named our little corner of Aegis."

"Someone's a Thoreau fan."

"That's right," Pierce answered, the phony smile returning. "I think there was talk of the name long before it became an 'official group.' I'm not totally sure who thought of it, but I'm sure it was a 'fan.' It is a nice fit. Please have a seat." She motioned toward the meeting table and chairs, and Elias sat in the closest one while Pierce chose one which left an empty seat between them.

"Would you like some herbal tea, or perhaps some wine? We have a fun Cabernet from Napa Valley."

"That is very kind, but no thanks."

Clasping her hands together on the table, Pierce asked, "What, if I may ask, did you do before coming to Aegis?"

He and Faulk had discussed what Elias' cover would be, so he answered quickly, "I was a forensic accountant."

He noticed her eyes narrow momentarily at his response, but the Manager's voice retained its lightness and conviviality as she said, "Forensic accountant, huh? For whom did you work? The government?"

"At times. I was a freelancer, had my own PC with several clients; the Fed was one of them from time to time. I spent most of my time working for lawyers who were chasing assets on behalf of their clients."

"Your own professional corporation," Pierce repeated, leaning back in her chair and staring at the ceiling grid above her.

"That's right. Why do you ask?"

Pierce returned her gaze to Elias. "I don't know how much time you spent thinking about what it would be like here in Aegis."

Elias shrugged and lied, "Not much."

"Well, in many ways we are like a colony which is assembling itself after some apocalyptic event. Money has no value in here, at least at this time," Pierce said cryptically. "What does have value are certain specific talents, fields of knowledge, or training."

"That makes sense."

"Obviously, doctors and dentists are the most in demand. Certain tradesmen, especially electricians and plumbers. Chefs, definitely. Naturally, the arts – actors, writers, artists, singers, comedians, musicians, and the lot. You see, we don't get the Internet in Aegis. Nor do we receive any television channels. No radio. Nothing from the outside."

"I knew there was no communication between Aegis and the outside world," Elias stated, "but I don't see why they don't allow those things to come in."

Elias, of course, did know. The electronic jamming, which was necessary to prevent any signals from leaving Aegis, also stopped anything from entering. There was always the alternative of cable but, as of yet, there was no such thing as a one-way cable feed. It had been suggested that a communication signal could be embedded in a laser which would be directed at a receiver on Aegis, but the debate as to what would be broadcast had brought this discussion to a deadlock.

"In the infinite wisdom of those who created this place," Pierce pronounced with unconcealed sarcasm, "it was decided. That is all we know.

"The others of value to us are teachers, physical trainers, and therapists."

"Therapists? You mean, like counselors?"

She nodded. "Yes, counselors. But also therapists who specialize in meditation, yoga, tai chi, aroma therapy."

"And I assume you have a need for former police personnel, or those with military training."

Elias once again saw the brief flash of distaste appear. "No. Not at all. Here in Walden there has been no need or desire for that group."

He leaned forward and explained, "If you've established a community with no troublemakers within, I can understand that, but from the reception I almost received before I arrived here, it surely looked as though you could use some protection."

"That is why we established the perimeter you came through," she answered with a hint of smugness in her voice.

Allowing a rueful smile to show on his face, Elias remarked, "I didn't hear accountants anywhere on the list."

Pierce's insincere smile was replaced with an equally insincere expression of sympathy. "I'm afraid not. Without any currency, or any other method of asset accumulation, there is actually no need for someone who can keep track of it."

Pierce quickly continued, as if to placate her guest, "I'm certain that you noticed there are many other professions absent from the list."

"Lawyers, for one?"

"Exactly. Many of them have arrived, and some initially pleaded their case as to the importance of their skills in assisting us to organize a rule-following society. But we quickly found out that their presence was anything but helpful in that direction. We also have no need for stockbrokers, for obvious reasons, bankers – really, the entire financial field."

"I have no way of knowing this," Elias interrupted, "but do you think that since financial problems may be the root cause for many of those who choose to check in at Aegis, there might be an emotional component to excluding that category?"

The bogus smile quickly returned and Pierce replied, "That very well may be, Mr. Charon. But you may be surprised to discover that this same *excluded* list is also populated with many who practiced in several of the engineering fields, with the exception of civil, electrical, and computer engineers."

"Why no engineers?"

Pierce tilted back in her seat. "That can best be answered by sharing a story with you. I was still outside of Aegis and living in Miami Beach. My daughter, who was graduating from college at the time, told me that she, her boyfriend, and two of his friends were going to climb into his twenty-year-old car at nine o'clock at night and drive to Orlando so they could go to the amusement parks the following morning.

"I told her I thought it was a stupid idea. She asked why, and I explained that her boyfriend's car could break down in the middle of the night and they would be stranded. Quite indignantly, she replied that I had no reason to be concerned because, after all, if the car broke down, she would have three engineers with her. When I finished laughing, my comment was simply 'And what will they do if the car stops running, whip out their laptops and design a new car?'"

Pierce indulged in a self-satisfied chuckle as she relished her remembrance of the event.

Elias waited for her to stop before asking, "Did she go?"

"No. She decided not to go, but made it quite clear to me that it was her own decision and had nothing to do with what I'd said. Anyway, back to the matter at hand. Walden is not to the point where there is any value to having engineering experience in our cohort. At some point, perhaps, but not now."

"I see."

Leaning forward and resting her slender arms on the table, she continued once more, "Our careers are not all that define us. Any avocations? Hobbies?"

Recognizing the opportunity to provide the Manager with a suitable answer, Elias knew that if he told her his lifelong hobbies were woodworking and furniture making, he would suddenly find himself on the "right" list; but he simply said, "I'm afraid not. After a long day of crunching numbers, all I wanted to do was go home and watch cable."

Another momentary flicker of distaste flashed on her face before Pierce responded, "Very well."

"I'm sorry."

"Oh, nothing to be sorry about," she remarked airily. "But to change the subject, I understand, as you referenced a moment ago, that you had an altercation with our not-so-friendly neighbors after you arrived."

"I did."

Her eyes narrowed slightly as she proceeded. "Apparently, they are not a particularly conscientious bunch, and many people who enter Aegis make it all the way to our front door, so to speak, without encountering them. You are the first who has and arrived to describe it. If I may ask, how did you manage to elude them?"

"As I told Rogan and Johnson, I guess I was lucky. I don't think they were in position to really ambush me. They saw me. I saw them. It was immediately obvious they weren't intending to offer me herbal tea or a fine glass of wine, so I ran."

Pierce was not completely certain Elias' last comment was sarcastic, so she dampened her momentary irritation and persisted, "You just ran away from them?"

Reading her correctly, Elias answered, "I did omit this earlier. My one off-work activity was running marathons. I found that it was a great way to get the clutter out of my head. I actually planned my vacations so that I would be in various cities during their runs."

"Marathons! Really?" Her entire body language changed as she asked excitedly, "Did you ever run the Boston?"

Elias nodded. "The Boston *and* the New York."

"Well, no wonder you were able to lose them. I doubt that they are runners."

"It was fairly easy to cause them to give up," Elias acknowledged.

The woman they called the Manager paused, her eyes diverting to the blank wall behind Elias, her mental processes so transparent they might as well have been scrolling across her forehead as she stared. The moment of decision came quickly, followed by the first sincere expression to appear on her face, a slight look of sadness.

"Well," Pierce began, her voice subdued, "do you have any questions for me?"

Deciding to maintain his gullible demeanor, Elias replied, "I do. Has there been a relatively recent arrival by the name of Eric Stone?"

"Eric Stone, no."

Since her answer came so quickly, Elias was tempted to ask her if she was certain, but thought better of it. He had already decided that Stone would not have lingered in Walden.

"In that case, no. I don't have any other questions, at least that I can think of right now. I'm sure I'll have plenty for you later."

At his last comment, her eyes flitted away from his. "Very well, then."

She stood and said, "Please come with me."

Rising and fetching his suitcase, he then followed her to the door through which she had entered. He was not surprised to find Rogan and Johnson waiting there. As he and the Manager joined them, Elias almost did not notice the slight shake of her head as Pierce made eye contact with Rogan.

She turned to Elias. "It was a pleasure meeting you, Mr. Charon."

"Thank you," he answered, milking his manufactured image. "I'm looking forward to staying in Walden."

More prepared this time, her gaze remained steadily on his face. The faux smile once again curving her mouth but leaving the rest of her face neutral. "Yes. Well, have a good day."

With that, she turned and walked back into the meeting room, closing the door behind her.

"That way," Rogan indicated.

As Elias followed them, he decided to engage in small talk. "She seems very nice."

Johnson nodded. "She is. She's a good manager for us."

They led him down one of the curving hallways perpendicular to the first corridor. He was now traveling on one of the concentric circles right outside the hub of Aegis.

"Do you both like it here?"

"It's fine," Rogan answered.

"Yeah, I do," Johnson said.

Neither of their responses indicated any interest in continuing the conversation, and Elias was certain he knew why. His suspicions were quickly confirmed when they reached another blockade in the hallway. He saw that this one had a steel plate barred to the center.

Apparently, this border to Walden was not as elaborate as the first Elias had seen and included no cameras on the other side, as Johnson hurriedly peeked through three different peepholes, making certain there was no one lurking. After he gave an "all clear" sign to Rogan, the other man lifted the heavy bar from the steel door.

"Where are we going?" Elias asked innocently.

Rogan leaned the bar against the wall and turned to his visitor. "I'm afraid we are escorting you out of Walden."

"Out?" Elias exclaimed, mustering some degree of shock in his voice. "But why?"

"The Manager decided."

"Come on, now. I like it here. Oh, it's because I'm an accountant, isn't it?"

Rogan simply shrugged and said, "It's up to the Manager. That's all we know."

With that, he gripped the handle on the door and swung it open. Johnson stepped through and checked the hallway more thoroughly. He turned back to Elias. "You have a clear route. It looks okay out here. Follow this hallway to the next main corridor, then turn left. You'll find another group there."

"Another group! But I don't...."

Rogan held up his hand to stop Elias. "Look, Mr. Charon. It's nothing personal, all right? Just please don't argue."

Elias decided he had played out his act as far as it should go.

"All right."

He stepped through the opening and paused. Johnson rejoined Rogan on the

Walden side of the opening, and they promptly closed the door. The sound of the bar being dropped back into place punctuated the finality of the decision.

Charon began his walk down this hallway, mentally adding the new facts he had gained from his interlude with the people of Walden to his picture of Aegis. His pistol still in his right pocket, he carried the suitcase with his left hand and kept a closer vigil on his surroundings. He did not want to be blindsided again, knowing that he could not count on the fleeting apparition to rescue him a second time.

As he slowly proceeded, his mind composed a narrative of his findings thus far. He had suspected that Aegis would, in some ways, become a microcosm of society. That was obvious and inevitable. But *which* society was the question. Would it be a mini-version of the society he had just left? Or something else? An answer was beginning to formulate in his mind, but he knew he needed more information before a final conclusion could be gleaned.

Approaching the first "spoke" corridor since departing Walden, Elias slowed his pace. Determined to avoid another ambush at this intersection, he quietly placed his suitcase on the floor several yards back and drew his pistol, flipping the safety to the off position. He bent his arm, holding his gun at shoulder height and pointed toward the ceiling, and then moved forward while hugging close to the wall. When he arrived at the corner, he took the next step rapidly, half spinning into a shooter's stance and quickly sweeping the corridor for threats from either direction. It was empty.

Retrieving his suitcase, Elias followed the instruction provided by Rogan and took the route to the left. He was, once again, impressed with the size and scope of Aegis. As he traveled the corridor, proceeding cautiously and stopping to repeat his method of entering each intersection, almost an hour transpired before he encountered anything but emptiness.

Ahead of him was another barrier across the wide corridor, yet this one was different from what he had encountered at Walden. It was also made with concrete blocks, but instead of there being a solid floor-to-ceiling and wall-to-wall blockade, there was a full-height wall in front, which began at the right side of the corridor and stopped approximately five feet short of the opposite side. Only a few feet behind it was another wall, attached to the left side of the corridor and disappearing behind the first.

Another difference was that this front barrier also had several narrow slots integrated into the masonry, the purpose obvious as he heard a voice ring out from behind the wall. "STOP WHERE YOU ARE!"

Elias froze.

"PUT DOWN THE SUITCASE AND RAISE YOUR HANDS."

Complying, Elias asked in a voice deliberately shaky, "What do you want?"

Ignoring his question, the man behind the wall authoritatively shouted, "MOVE AWAY FROM THE SUITCASE AND LIE FACEDOWN ON THE FLOOR."

Elias crab-walked two steps to the right and dropped slowly to his knees while keeping his hands raised. Then, slowly, he lowered his arms, and placing his palms on the floor, lay facedown down and said nothing. As soon as he was down, he heard two sets of footsteps approach. Judging by the sound, one of the two stopped several feet away, no doubt positioning himself to guard the other. Elias assumed they were armed.

He heard the other guard circle around and approach from behind, reaching down to begin searching him, and finding the Beretta almost immediately. After taking it from Elias' pocket, he resumed the frisk until satisfied that there was nothing else of concern on the newcomer's person.

"All right. Stand up."

Despite his excellent physical condition, Elias rose from his lying position with feigned difficulty, including grunts and groans as he lifted himself. The two men, dressed in green cargo pants, black T-shirts, high-laced boots, and sporting an assortment of tattoos on their arms and necks, both carried Glocks holstered on their hips. Elias guessed they were in their mid-twenties. One of the two was pointing a 12 gauge shotgun at him while the other was down on one knee, rummaging through the contents of his suitcase.

As Elias stood, automatically raising his arms above his head without being told, he looked more closely at the tattoos on his guard and said, "So, 4-1 or 1st Cav?"

The guard grinned instantly. "Yeah, 1st Cav. Are you infantry?"

"Doc Charon. I was in the 4-1."

"Medical Corps, huh? Afghanistan?"

"Iraq and mostly Germany."

"Attached to which unit?"

"I was with the Big Red One."

The smile broadened. "Pussies. You 'prolly' spent all your time treating STIs."

Before Elias could reply, the second man flipped the suitcase closed and rose, nodding at his partner, who lowered the shotgun and took three steps forward, extending his hand.

"I'm Sweezea. This is Crabill."

Elias shook Sweezea's hand, then Crabill's.

After removing the clip from the Beretta and checking to make certain the chamber was empty, Crabill handed Elias his pistol and said, "Welcome to Madison." He turned over the clip to his partner.

"Madison?"

"As in James."

They turned and walked toward the entrance to the barrier. Elias asked, "Madison, Walden. Do the punks by the entrance have a name for their territory?"

Sweezea laughed. "Yeah, ZooCity. You had the pleasure of making their acquaintance?"

The three men turned to the right as they passed behind the first wall, and Elias saw another man stationed there. He had been watching through one of the view slots and held an AK-47 at the ready, in case his two partners needed help.

"This is Hutson," said Sweezea.

The third man turned to face Elias and, dropping his rifle down to the rest position, stuck out his hand. As he did, Elias read aloud the tattoo on his forearm, "Screaming Eagles."

"Yes, sir."

"Don't 'sir' me. I worked for a livin'. Just a medical corpsman. Charon."

As Elias said this, he noticed the firmness of the grip intensify slightly and the handshake itself become more enthusiastic.

"Good to meet you, Doc."

Hutson resumed his vigil at the slot as the two others led Elias behind him and around the first switchback. The corridor barrier was a series of offset walls with five-foot openings at alternating ends. When they came to the final offset wall, Elias saw that this walkway was shorter than the others, and built into the end of the aisle was another block wall, also with gun slots facing them. He could see the barrel of what he deduced was an automatic rifle of some type projecting through one of the slots and, at the moment, trained directly on the center of Elias' chest.

"Nice defensive setup," he complimented.

"It works," Sweezea acknowledged. "So how'd you snake past the ZooCity denizens?"

Elias shrugged to communicate that it was no big deal. "A little difference in orientation. They seemed to think that sidearms are for pointing at people. I was always taught that guns were only good for one thing."

Both Crabill and Sweezea were amused by his comment, and Crabill added a facetious "Bang, bang."

"So there's a body back there?"

"Two."

"Cool!"

They cleared the defensive maze and entered the wide corridor.

"I'm going to stay on post," Crabill advised.

Sweezea nodded. Crabill held out his right hand to Elias and said, "See you around, Doc." Elias once again shook his hand.

As the two of them set off down the corridor, Sweezea asked, "You mentioned Walden. You met those guys, too?"

Elias kept pace next to his escort as he answered, "I did."

"Man, you get around! Why are you at Madison? From what I hear about that bunch, they would've snatched you like you were the last whore in town."

"My choice. The second I walked in, I realized that I'd have to leave my testicles at the door if I was gonna live there."

His companion laughed again. "Boy, you nailed that, all right. Still, I can't believe they didn't give you the full-court press to stick around."

"I didn't tell them I was a doc."

"What'd you tell them you did?"

"Accountant."

"Good call."

"Yeah, I figured that out pretty quickly. So where are we going?"

"To meet the Chief."

As they walked, Elias noticed that the environment behind their entrance was, once again, different. ZooCity had been a chaotic mess. Walden had appeared neat in comparison, but had a casual, worn look and feel. Madison, by contrast, was spotlessly clean. Where there had been no placards of any kind in Walden, Madison had an abundance of crisp signage everywhere he looked, mostly filled with indecipherable abbreviations and directional arrows. There were also lines painted on the floor, each a different color. Elias determined that the color of the lines corresponded to the font color on individual signs. As they reached each minor intersection of hallways, some of the colored lines continued straight, while others turned to the right or left. *This place*, he thought to himself, *was set up by someone with a bad case of OCD*. The overall feel created was one of regimentation and structure.

As the two of them walked, they passed a man in his late fifties or early sixties, down on one knee, with a drop cloth spread out over a four-by-four area, a bucket of white paint on the cloth, and a paintbrush in his hand as he touched up a small section of wall adjacent to a door. Mounted on the door was a handmade wooden sign, engraved with the legend, "Chief of Staff – Milton Pierce." Sweezea stepped over the drop cloth and knocked twice. A male voice immediately responded, "Come in."

With a slight jerk of his head, Sweezea indicated to Elias that he was to follow, and opened the door, entering. With everything he had seen so far, Elias expected his escort to come to attention and salute the man inside; however, other than a subtle stiffening of his posture, Sweezea acted as if he were bringing a new hire in to meet his civilian boss.

"Sir, this is Doc Charon. He's a newbie."

The man behind the desk was in his forties. He wore a long-sleeved, white shirt, which was crisp and well starched, and he was clean shaven, with hair that was long for a military cut but short for a civilian. Elias decided this compromise was deliberate and contrived to convey a specific message that the man was neither.

"Charon," the man greeted him, standing and extending his hand. "I'm Milton Pierce."

They shook hands, and Elias probed, "Pierce?"

A smile crinkled the corners of the Chief of Staff's eyes. "I see you've met my sister."

"Mildred Pierce is your sister?"

"Yes, she is." He turned and said, "Thank you, Sweezea. You may return to your post."

"Yes, sir."

Sweezea reached into a pocket on his vest and extracted the clip from Elias' Beretta, handing it to Pierce. He then turned to Elias. "It's good to meet you, sir."

Elias shook his hand. "What did I tell you about the 'sir' stuff? It's a pleasure meeting you."

Elias' escort turned and left the office, closing the door.

"Please have a seat," Pierce invited, making a show of placing the loaded clip on the edge of the desk near Elias, and lowering himself back into the leather seat. Elias took one of the two offered chairs.

"If you don't mind my asking, how did it come to be that you and your sister run two of the enclaves here in Aegis?"

The man's smile returned as he leaned back in his chair. "I don't mind at all. I'm sure it's a bit curious. Mildred and I arrived together. Back then, there were no enclaves, as you put it."

"How long ago was that?"

"Coming up on eight years now. The people here hadn't split into distinct communities yet."

"Really!"

Seeing surprise at this on Elias' face, he added, "Oh, the seeds for the eventual segregation, as some might say, were already present. But at that time the size of Aegis allowed for a reasonable amount of buffer space for everyone, so the friction between people with very different viewpoints, philosophies, lifestyles, et cetera, was manageable.

"However, as the population continued to grow at a rapid pace, maintaining anything resembling a peaceful coexistence became more and more difficult."

"Sounds a lot like out there," Elias commented, pointing his thumb in a vague direction over his shoulder to indicate the outside world.

"Precisely," Pierce agreed. "As long as there was open space, unclaimed territory, then people who felt that they didn't fit in could always strike out and establish a new community."

"Or country."

"Or country. You're right. But to continue...even though we were scattered about this facility, we were beginning to clump into groups. The groups were rather fluid at first, in both membership and location."

"What do you mean?"

"Some people have a tough time deciding where they fit."

Elias nodded. "That's for sure."

"Right. They might wish to indulge themselves in an unrestrained, hedonistic lifestyle for a time, then awaken one morning feeling guilty and make up their minds that they need structure, an externally imposed discipline to compensate for the absence of that trait in their character. They would migrate from group A to group B.

"Others might initially embrace the construct of a well-defined, regulated environment, only to suddenly rebel and want to cut loose, as it were. They, then, suddenly would switch from group B to Group A."

"I imagine there was quite of bit of that going on."

"There was. That is why I described that period as fluid."

"What you've depicted so far doesn't sound unreasonable or unworkable. What happened to force the creation of the barriers?"

"Borders."

"Yes. I suppose they would be."

"Of course they are borders. What else would you call them?"

Elias shrugged. "So what happened?"

"As I mentioned, the burgeoning population happened. Previously, individuals could carry on as they wished, hurting no one, and away from the watchful eyes of those who might disapprove of their choices."

"You said 'hurting no one.' There wasn't any crime?"

"No, there was, but surprisingly little back then. You'd be amazed how much of a difference it makes to a social group if there is no money involved. Most of what did occur could fairly be dropped into the category of 'crimes of passion.' Handling those issues as they arose was not particularly challenging."

"And what happened? What was the trigger?"

Pierce leaned back in his chair and stared at the ceiling. "I guess we reached a tipping point. There was no warning. Actually, that's not true. In retrospect there were plenty of clues. There was a breakdown in communication. It was initially subtle but eventually obvious."

What do you mean by a 'breakdown in communication'?"

"People stopped talking to each other. I mean, *really* talking. One day individuals or small groups were able to sit down, discuss things, and come up with a reasonable compromise and, seemingly, the next day they couldn't. Every discussion, every organized meeting quickly degenerated into screaming and name-calling."

"That sounds like the outside, too."

Pierce did not acknowledge Elias' comment. "Then one night, some couple, I don't even know who they were, were having *sex*" – the note of disgust in Pierce's voice was unmistakable – "out in the open…in a corridor instead of in one of their rooms. A woman named Beth Havlichek came upon them while walking with two of her friends, and made a comment about how they should take it to someplace private."

Elias saw the Chief of Staff squeeze his eyes shut, as if trying to block out an image.

"They killed her!"

"What?"

"They beat her to death, both of them, right in front of her friends."

"Her two friends returned to the gathering they had just left and described the incident, painting an especially vivid picture of the pleasure, almost glee, that the couple displayed as they murdered Beth."

"The seven people they told stampeded immediately from the room and ran to the scene, to find that the couple had resumed their activity, right next to Beth's body."

"Good God!"

Pierce opened his eyes and leaned forward, resting his elbows on the desk. "The small, angry mob descended upon the couple and killed *them*."

Pierce paused, giving Elias an opportunity for a comment. None came, and he resumed, "Then it began. It spread like a wildfire through Aegis. Those who associated themselves with the couple retaliated in kind. The other side, so to speak, struck back. And for the following twenty hours, the halls of Aegis were filled with mayhem, bloodshed, and death."

"Who put a stop to it?"

"No one! No one could, I guess. But other than some feeble, half-hearted attempts, no one tried. I, myself, have been filled with shame since that day for cowering in a hiding place instead of doing something…anything."

"Don't beat yourself up. There isn't much anyone can do when something like that happens."

A weak smile played across his lips as Pierce muttered, "Thanks. But to answer your question, I think everyone merely got tired of the rampage."

"It burned itself out."

"Right. And the bottom line was that, after twenty hours of hell, approximately sixty percent of the population was dead, more than three thousand people."

Pierce paused and Elias said nothing. The silence hung heavily in the room.

Shifting his gaze down to the desk, his voice a flat monotone, Pierce continued, "Cleanup parties were organized. The wounded were treated as best we could. The dead were gathered up, using those gray plastic rolling bins that construction crews use to haul material, and taken to the trash compactor."

Pierce hesitated for a moment, looking up at Elias, and said, "You know what was the most surreal aspect of the cleanup?"

Elias did not answer, waiting.

"The crews, who self-organized to do the work, contained members from both sides of the conflict, working side by side. No one mentioned anything. I'm certain it was because no one wanted to trigger another flare-up. But watching it…participating in it…knowing the folks right next to me had committed horrendous deeds…was almost more than I could bear."

"I can't even imagine what that was like," Elias responded quietly.

"After the cleanup...after all the bodies were gone and the damage was repaired, discussions to segregate just happened. There was no doubt that it was necessary or appropriate. Madison was created, as were Walden and ZooCity.

"And to address your initial question, I guess I was selected to run Madison for the same reason Mildred was chosen for Walden. Neither of us had participated in the rampage."

"I'm sure there's more to the choice than simply that."

Pierce shrugged. "Perhaps. On the outside I had been a politician, a mayor. Mildred had been a city manager. We both had training and experience overseeing a populated entity. But I am certain that the first criterion was primary in most people's minds as they voted."

"So each enclave was set up with its own set of rules?"

Pierce nodded. "Its own set of rules. Its own bylaws. In reality, its own personality."

"I'm guessing Madison was modeled after the Constitution."

"The Constitution," Pierce acknowledged, "as well as some of the papers of our Founding Fathers and, of course, the Bible."

"And Walden?" Elias asked.

A sudden snort came out of Pierce. "I'm not sure exactly what Walden was based upon. My sister and I were always at the opposite ends of the political spectrum. From the time we were young teens, she was always 'out there.' I suppose you could say she's a utopian."

"Really?" Elias reacted with a note of surprise in his voice. He had already formed his own opinions about Walden but had decided to play along.

"I don't know how else to capture it in a single label. During our youth, we debated constantly. I had, very early on, become entranced with the beauty of not only the logic of our founding documents, but the wisdom. And by that, I mean the grasp that Jefferson, Madison, Hamilton, and the others had on the realities of human nature. They wanted to create a system where the individual could flourish, but at the same time recognized our frailties and faults, and knew that safeguards – checks and balances – needed to be in place, if the nation was to survive.

"My sister resented the checks, the limits, placed upon the individual and believed that people, given the chance, would self-regulate; that morals and ethics would somehow spontaneously spring into the very fabric of the social consciousness; that they would come from within each person; that there was no need for having them imposed from without; and that, in fact, imposing them created, by the very act of imposition, a *de facto* oppression that withered the soul of the individual."

"Nice thought."

"Exactly!" Pierce almost shouted. "That was what I said to her time and time again.

I always told her that what she described would be wonderful, would be a society which was idyllic, except for one problem…."

"People."

"Right. Maybe, at some point in the distant future, people will be able to handle that kind of structure, but we aren't there yet."

"Didn't she see that obstacle with her own eyes at the time the massacre erupted in Aegis?"

Pierce became subdued. "I would have thought so. But she didn't. She rationalized it. She was absolutely certain that the outbreak was caused by intolerance. If only Beth Havlichek had looked the other way as she encountered the couple having sex in the corridor, if only she had accepted that sex is a natural act, not something to be disgusted by, and not *judged* the couple, the fuse on the powder keg wouldn't have been lit."

Elias shook his head. "So the problem your sister had with the first incident wasn't that the couple killed Havlichek; it was that she made a disapproving comment?"

"Right, if you can believe it."

"The brief period of time I spent in Walden, I didn't see anyone *in flagrante delicto* in the hallways."

With a sound that could only be described as "harrumph," Pierce confided, "You were lucky. I've visited Walden on more than one occasion since the segregation occurred, and I've seen more than I cared to see."

"What about ZooCity? Do they have a defining set of principles?"

"You could say that," he answered sarcastically, "if you are inclined to define the absence of such as a defining set."

"Isn't that what Walden is all about, though?"

Once again leaning back in his chair, this time causing a loud creak, Pierce elaborated, "You have made the same point I've tried to convey countless times to my sister. There is a distinction between the two, but it is, in my opinion, a subtle one. I think that ZooCity is a logical extension of the Walden philosophy – the same concepts and ideals, only taken to an extreme. ZooCity types definitely do not want to be encumbered with rules, limitation, a rigid set of ethics; in that, they are similar to the Waldens. The difference lies in what they are willing and capable of doing to outsiders and even to each other. Even murder is as casual an act to them as swatting a fly would be to you and me."

"I witnessed that during my encounter with them."

"Is that so? What happened?"

"When I was first confronted by the group, I grabbed one of the members as a hostage, hoping they would back off and let me pass. Their response was to simply shoot him. They killed their own man."

Disdain etched itself across Pierce's face at Elias' description of events. "Precisely.

That is quite typical of their actions, from what I've heard."

Elias decided to steer the conversation back to the topic he cared most about. "If I may ask an unrelated question?"

"Of course. What is it?"

"Have you, or your people, come across a man by the name of Stone, Eric Stone?"

"Stone?" Pierce turned to a large, old-fashioned Rolodex on his desk and spun the wheel around until he located the "S" tab. "Don't recall that name. When would he have arrived?"

"Several weeks ago."

Searching the correct section, Pierce thumbed through several of the cards. "I have a few citizens with the name Stone, but no Eric. Nor do I recall a gentleman by that name passing through. Friend of yours?"

Elias kept his tone casual. "More of an acquaintance, actually. He had told me he was checking in at Aegis a while back. To be honest, Eric doing it first sort of helped me to decide. And I don't really know anyone else in here."

Flipping closed the lid of the Rolodex, Pierce returned his attention to Elias. "Anything else you wanted to ask?"

For a moment, Elias almost asked about Kreitzmann but thought better of it. Inquiring about one person would probably appear normal; two might give Pierce pause. "No. That was it."

Pierce folded his hands together on the desk. "You'll be pleased to know that we don't engage in the same newcomer filtering that my sister does at Walden. So long as you understand that we have rules and you have no problem abiding by them, you are welcome to stay. You are, of course, expected to contribute to the community, in whatever way you can."

"Thank you, Mr. Pierce. That's good to know. I'll be honest with you, though. I'm not sure where I want to end up within Aegis."

A genuine look of surprise filled the Chief of Staff's face. "I see. So you are planning on returning to Walden?"

"No. I'm afraid not. Your sister has made it clear to me that I am not what they are looking for."

"Then where? Surely not ZooCity!"

"No," Elias chuckled. "I think I would prefer that my first experience with them would also be my last."

"I repeat, then where are you planning on going?"

"There are no other enclaves within Aegis?"

Pierce shook his head rather forcefully. "Essentially, no. Just the three. There are some small pockets of people who live on the fringes of our communities. From what I understand, there are also some loners, who don't wish to be a part of any group. Other than that, we are the only games in town, in a manner of speaking."

Shrugging, Elias explained, "I guess I'll poke around a little. I do want to try to find Eric. If I don't have any luck, I'm sure I'll be back."

Pierce stood up and Elias followed his cue. "As I said, Mr. Charon, you are more than welcome to stay. From our brief chat I believe that you are the type of person who would fit in quite nicely here. Since you have decided to leave, consider it an open invitation."

Elias shook the man's hand. "Thank you very much. It was a pleasure meeting you, and you are right – Madison is probably the best spot for me."

Picking up the clip for the Beretta and dropping it into his pocket, Pierce said, "I'll walk you back to the checkpoint."

"Thank you."

They exited the room and retraced the route Elias had taken several minutes earlier. As they walked, Elias asked, "What do you think is next for Aegis?"

"What do you mean?"

"Well, the steps so far have been logical. At first there was so much room that individuals were able to live the way they wanted. And then, as people started bumping into each other, conflicts began, until the incident you described which prompted the creation of the enclaves."

"I suppose you're right. It's all been inevitable. I remember reading, before I came to Aegis, about the changes that occur in primates, like chimps, when they are brought in from the wild and caged in groups. The behavior described in that article is strikingly similar to what has happened here. The brutality, the savagery, the wantonness of the acts in many ways have mirrored what I read. But to answer your question, ever since that horrible day of the rampage, it seems that I have only reacted. Everything I've done since then has been a response to that day. And that includes creating Madison. I haven't mentally looked forward. I'm curious – what do you think is in store for us, Mr. Charon?"

Based upon what he had been told and witnessed thus far, Elias had a very clear image of the coming events, but he answered, "I have no idea. I was wondering what you thought."

For a moment, it appeared as if Pierce did not believe him. "Time will tell, I suppose."

They continued walking, and nothing more was said until they arrived at the checkpoint. Pierce extended his hand. "I hope that you return to us, Mr. Charon. It was a pleasure."

"Mine, as well, sir. I'm sure I'll be back."

Reaching into his pocket, Pierce pulled out the clip and handed it Elias. "I hope you won't be needing this. Good luck."

Elias took it from him and dropped it into his own pocket. "Thank you."

Pierce turned and walked away. Elias entered the zig-zag barricade and, after the third turn, saw Sweezea.

"You're leavin' us, huh?"

"Yep. I might be back."

Sweezea grabbed Elias' suitcase from the corner where it was stowed, and turned to join him as he walked. "Why are you going? You don't like Madison?"

Elias grinned at him. "Can't say. Haven't been here long enough to decide. I'm looking for a friend and I understand from Mr. Pierce that he isn't here."

They finished the serpentine route and emerged, passing Crabill who was stationed directly behind the entrance, peering through one of the view slots in the wall.

To Crabill, Sweezea said, "I'm going to walk with the doc for a ways."

"Don't make a run for it," Crabill joked. "You'll be in my cross-hairs."

Sweezea laughed, and they continued out into the corridor.

After they were out of hearing range, Sweezea asked, "Who's your friend? Maybe I've seen him."

"Stone, Eric Stone."

Shaking his head, Sweezea answered, "Don't know the name, but a lot of people who come here use something different. What does he look like?"

Elias described Stone and watched as the soldier processed the information in his mind. After a brief pause, Sweezea concluded, "Afraid not. If he came through here, it wasn't on my watch."

They stopped walking at the first crossing, and Elias changed the subject. "I was wondering about something; maybe you could explain it?"

"Shoot."

"I didn't expect much chatter in ZooCity, but Pierce's sister interviewed me at Walden and I had a fairly good little talk with the Chief, and neither one of them asked me the one question I thought I would get asked in here."

"What's that?"

"Why I came to Aegis."

"You won't. It's kind of an unwritten rule. We don't ask each other or the newbies."

"Why's that?"

Sweezea leaned against the wall in a nonchalant pose. "We just don't. If you want a better explanation, you'd better get your ass back inside and ask the Chief. I'm just a dumb grunt."

Elias grinned broadly. "Save your moron act for the other guys. Do you have a first name, Sweezea? Mine's Elias."

"I do. Tim."

Instinctively, they shook hands with each other to formalize the introduction.

"Tim, as I said, can the 'I'm just a dumb grunt' act. I know better."

Sweezea looked away from Elias for a moment, leaned his head back against the wall, and either composed his thoughts or decided how much of his opinion to share with Charon before speaking.

"There are two reasons, really. The first one is that people are going to lie to you, anyway. Remember, we have no way of checking on anyone or anything from the outside. Somebody could walk through the front door and tell us he was a brain surgeon, a movie producer, or the head of the CIA, and we would have no way of knowing.

"That's the weird thing about Aegis. People who come in here feel like it is their chance to be who or what they always wanted to be. Usually, the real reason for checking in is tied to who or what they were. So...they lie to maintain their story."

"What's the second reason?"

"Privacy. Most guys are ashamed of whatever they did or whoever they were, whatever it was that brought them here. This is a chance for them to start with a clean slate. Why ruin it for them by making them tell us the truth or forcing them to lie to us? Both options are bad deals for them, because then either they haven't escaped what they did, or they are starting out their new chance with a big, fat lie that they'll have to maintain for the rest of their lives. We decided that everybody who joins us should at least be allowed to have a little dignity."

"You said 'most guys.' Do you mean guys, or are you talking about both genders?"

Sweezea laughed. "It's a good thing nobody else is around for this conversation. No, I meant guys. Women, most of them, *want* to talk about whatever the mess was that they made before they came here. They want to talk about it constantly and to anybody who will listen. Now that you mention it, that's probably a good third reason why we don't ask. If they finally do stop talking about it, we don't want to start them up again."

Smiling, Elias shook his head. Another thought crossing his mind, he remarked, "I imagine you get a lot of guys who tell you they were in the service, when they never served a day."

Tim nodded. "Oh, yeah, especially Special Forces."

"I would guess that particular line of crap doesn't last too long."

Sweezea laughed again. "Maybe about two minutes. I had one newbie tell me he was a SEAL, so I handed him my rifle and asked him to break it down. The only thing that broke down was him! Turns out he was an insurance salesman."

"That would have been fun to watch."

Pausing, Sweezea said, "Should have been, but it wasn't. It was sad. He just bit off more than he could chew with his new identity."

"Tim, as long as we're talking, I do have one more thing to ask."

"Shoot."

"There is another guy...came in here a few weeks ago. His name is Rudy Kreitzmann."

"Rudy Kreitzmann is in here?"

"You know who he is?"

"Hell, yes. I haven't been in here that long. While I was outside, I read the news. Are you kidding me? He came to Aegis?"

Elias nodded. "That's the word. I don't know for sure. That's why I'm asking."

"Why would he come here? Did what he was doing finally get to him?"

"I doubt it. I think he came here because he had nowhere else to run."

Sweezea shook his head. "Can't help you. I hadn't heard he was here. Why are you looking for him?"

Deciding to keep his answers vague, Elias only replied, "I have a score to settle with him."

"From what I heard about him, you and about a thousand other guys."

"So you haven't heard any rumors about him, or some new arrival who might be doing some strange things?"

His eyes suddenly widening, Sweezea asked, "You think he might be up to the same stuff in Aegis?"

Elias shrugged and said nothing.

"Man, if he is, I'll hunt him down and cure him myself."

"Cure him?"

"Oh yeah, cure him. I hear he has an acute case of lead deficiency."

Elias chuckled.

"But to answer your question, no, I haven't heard anyth…wait a sec. There is something."

"What's that?"

"I'm not sure this would have anything to do with Kreitzmann. But it's weird. We picked up a new addition to Madison a couple of weeks ago from ZooCity."

"Really?"

"Yeah, it happens. Urban newbies check in, see that there's a gang in here and, at first, they feel right at home and join up. Then, after a little while, they figure out it was that crap they were running away from, so they come to Madison or go to Walden. Anyway, this guy arrives and tells us the damnedest story about a man who arrived about three months back. I'm not sure about the time, but it was close to that. Anyway, he arrived with two other men…."

Feeling vindicated in his suspicions, Elias flashed back to the video of Kreitzmann's entrance and the two men who walked through the turnstile after him.

"Apparently, they watch the entrance for each new arrival, but they don't make their move until the first intersection. Our new guy told us that he was part of a group who jumped the three of them, or at least tried to."

"What happened?"

"I guess the guy telling the story was the one designated to provide cover, so he was twenty or thirty yards back. Five ZooCity thugs made their move – when, according to our friend, the two men who arrived with the stranger just turned into a blur." Sweezea held up his hands and exclaimed, "I know this sounds nuts!"

"No, it doesn't sound crazy at all. I've seen it myself."

Elias' comment got Sweezea's attention. "You what?"

"You asked me how I got past them, and I exaggerated a little. It seems I'm as guilty as the others who come in...wanting to make myself look better. The gangbangers had the drop on me. I was dead meat, but suddenly there was a blur, something, I don't know what. A few seconds later the ZooCity toughs were either on the floor or hightailing it."

"Dead?"

"Uh-huh."

"Yeah, that's what the newbie told us. All of his group were dead. Necks broken. I don't know if this had anything to do with Kreitzmann, but the timing was right and it was strange enough. At first we thought the guy was feeding us a line of crap, but since then, some other people have seen similar things happen. Now you. I guess it must be true. Man, that's a little scary."

"It was."

"But how would this tie in with Kreitzmann?"

"I don't know," Elias answered honestly.

The two were silent for a minute or so, both lost in their own thoughts, until Sweezea finally asked, "If it does, you are going against him with only a sidearm?"

His moment of honesty passed, and Elias said, "Yes."

Standing away from the wall where he had been leaning, Sweezea unslung the automatic rifle from his shoulder and handed it to Elias. "AK-47. Not the latest gear. Not the best, either. I don't know what good it'll do against whatever those things are, but here, take it."

The gesture surprised Elias. "That's nice, man. It really is, and I appreciate it. But aren't you going to need it?"

Sweezea simply shrugged. "We've got a decent stockpile. I can spare it."

"Why me? We just met."

A grin spread slowly across his new friend's face as he explained, "I spent two tours in Iraq, one in Afghanistan, walking down dusty side streets and waiting for some sniper to put one in between my eyes. You get locals coming up to you all the time. Big smiles on their faces. Arms out, offering gifts for saving their country. Sometimes they mean it, and one of them really is trying to hand you some trinket his wife made. Other times they have C-4 taped to their chests underneath all those robes, and if you let them get close enough...*BOOM!* Either you get pretty good at reading their eyes, or you become a pink cloud on that little street."

"That works, huh?"

"I'm here, aren't I? Anyway, I found out the same skill serves me well stateside."

Grinning back at Sweezea, Elias said, "So when you look in my eyes, you think I'm one of the harmless guys with a trinket for you?"

Suddenly turning serious, Sweezea replied, "No, you're anything but harmless. And maybe I'm making a big mistake, but I don't think so. I think you and I are on the same side. So do you want the extra hardware or not?"

Elias reached out and took the rifle, slipping his arm through the loop and swinging it around to ride on his back.

Opening one of the pockets on his fatigues, Sweezea pulled out a handful of magazines. "You're gonna need these."

Elias took the ammunition and put it away. "You think so?"

With a tight nod of his head, Sweezea cautioned, "I don't know what good it'll do against the blurs, but there are some other targets out there. Aegis is not Club Med."

They both fell into silence again until it became awkward. Breaking it, Elias stuck out his hand and said, "It was a pleasure meeting you, sir."

Sweezea returned the handshake. "Sir, the pleasure was all mine. Hope you find your guy."

Elias picked up his suitcase and turned away. As he walked, he heard Sweezea shout, "Doc!"

He paused and looked back.

"If you need anything, you know where to find me."

Resisting the urge to reply, Elias gave Sweezea a curt wave and resumed his walk.

CHAPTER FOUR

The silence of Aegis embraced Elias as he made his way down the corridor. He divided his mind into two processing units: one focused on his surroundings, vigilant and alert for another attack; the other sorting through what he had learned at Madison and Walden, and from what he witnessed at ZooCity.

His question to Milton Pierce has been exploratory. Elias already had a clear idea of what was in store for the residents of Aegis in the near future. In his opinion, the progression was inevitable.

Instead, he turned his thoughts to the probable fate of Eric Stone. He might have been jumped by the punks shortly after entry and had not been as fortunate as Elias. Apparently, he had not made it to Walden or Madison or, if he had, was immersed in one of those enclaves anonymously. Elias doubted that. There would not have been any reason for Stone to operate that way. And if he had quietly melded into one of the two groups, why had he not contacted Faulk, and why had he not shown up at the extraction?

The likely explanation, he knew, was that Stone either had died soon after his arrival, or was being held by someone. And if he was being held, it was probably by a group other than the ZooCity gang. Stone, Elias knew, was too good to be held captive by amateurs.

Elias was satisfied with his progress thus far. Although he had not yet located either Kreitzmann or Stone, he had filled in several blanks in his mind as to the social structure of Aegis, mentally colored-in the sections controlled by Walden and Madison, and assessed their defenses; and a fairly clear sense of the timing of their decline was emerging. The next step was to locate and secure his base.

⊙

Finally recovered from his previous terror, Zack was standing his corner, as he had been instructed to do by BQ. His swagger back, his attitude having returned to him after the interlude with the "streaker," as they had begun to call the bizarre apparitions, he was again cocky and confident. The hallway he guarded was the only entrance to ZooCity.

Since the incident, he had neither seen nor heard anything out of the ordinary. There had been no newbies through the turnstiles, no disenfranchised loners wandering the corridors of Aegis. It was a quiet time, and he was lounging against the wall, his back to the direction of ingress.

It was so quiet that he should have heard the approach of anyone, especially anyone near him, which explained his surprise as he suddenly felt a light tap on his shoulder. Startled, he whirled to see the stranger who was standing alone, directly behind him.

"Who the f...?"

The stranger held up a single finger, intended to silence Zack. For some reason it worked. The man was somewhat shorter, white, clean shaven, with a severe, conservative haircut, resembling the style Zack had seen in old shows on TV Land. He was wearing a gray suit, white shirt, and highly polished dress shoes. Zack remembered that his old man had a pair just like them that he only wore to church. He called them wing-tips.

"Do you have a leader?" the stranger asked.

"What?"

With the tolerant expression one would get when talking to a small child, the man explained, "A boss, a captain. From whom do you take your orders?"

Zack's first impulse was not to give the man an answer, to spout off. Instead, he found himself saying, "BQ."

"Will you take me to him?" Although phrased as a question, it was clear that it was not.

Gathering self-confidence, Zack asked, "What for?"

A smile spread across the stranger's face. "I think I have an offer for him that he will want to take."

Deep in his mind, he knew there was something he should do or something he should say, rather than acquiescing to this man. "Okay," Zack said, and turned to escort the stranger into ZooCity.

⊙

Elias made a show of meandering through the maze of primary and secondary corridors. In his mind, he was following the route which he had developed during the train ride as he had studied the layout of Aegis, his intent being to appear as if he had no purpose and no destination in mind. The circuitous route was only partially necessary, but Elias wanted to make certain he had not picked up any curious, hidden escorts in his travels. He deliberately walked past his intended goal, a service door, and proceeded to the first intersection beyond, casually turning the corner.

He quickly lay on the floor, his head oriented back toward the way he had entered, and waited several seconds. Listening and hearing nothing, he slowly edged forward and peered around the corner at floor level. The hallway was empty and silent.

Suitcase in hand, he returned to the service door and opened it. It was one of many electrical service rooms scattered throughout the facility, and he heard the humming of a bank of step-down transformers lined up against one wall. Elias went all the way in and closed the door. The heat generated by the transformers made the room uncomfortable, and he noticed that he had already begun to sweat.

He made his way to the far end of the room, to the steel ladder affixed to the wall. Still toting his suitcase, and with the AK-47 given to him by Sweezea flapping painfully against his back, he climbed the ladder to the ceiling until he came to the awkward part. Elias had to wedge the suitcase between his body and the ladder to free one hand. He reached into his pocket and pulled out a ring of keys, found the right one, and inserted it into the lock on the ceiling hatch above his head. The master key worked, and he pushed the lid open, immediately shoving the suitcase and rifle through the hatch onto the deck above, before climbing through it himself.

The deck of this level was bare concrete, as were the walls; the structure had been built using tilt-up panels for all of the primary and load-bearing walls. This part of the complex was lit with ceiling-mounted LED fixtures, which provided a dim but sufficient amount of light. He was in what was referred to on the plans as a raceway, part of an interconnected series of passages through which the pipes, or conduit, ran, supplying electricity to all parts of Aegis. The raceways were built to accommodate someone who was there for servicing and repair purposes, albeit not comfortably. He knew from the plans that there were several junctions, where a confluence of the shiny pipes came together from different locations. These junctions were more spacious, and it was one of them that Elias intended to call home during the duration of his stay in Aegis.

Once again he slung the rifle over his shoulder and picked up his suitcase. Relying upon his sense of direction and memorization of the layout from the "E" pages of the plans, he began walking through the passage. The rifle began slapping loudly against the adjacent wall-mounted conduits, creating a sound like the ringing of a bell which reverberated through the piping with each step. He paused to pull the rifle off his shoulder, deciding to carry it with his free hand.

Elias only had to travel approximately three hundred yards before the first junction. From this larger area, the raceways branched off in four directions. The conduits he had walked beside joined with others, some adding to the array of pipes, others merging into pipes of the next size up in diameter. This was not his intended destination, so he turned a corner and continued.

He passed three more junction rooms, once turning to his left, once continuing straight ahead, and once turning to his right, while pausing frequently to listen for the sounds of anyone who might be following him. He finally arrived at the spot which had been predetermined to serve as his base. This particular junction was no larger than the others, but like any other real estate, the appeal it held was its location. It was the most centrally located junction within Aegis, and provided Elias with above-ceiling access to Walden, Madison, and the portion of the complex that he guessed would be ZooCity. From here he could maneuver above each of them and, with the right gear, observe and listen. He still had no idea where Kreitzmann might have settled, but the network of raceways would provide him with access to all areas.

There had been no litter, no markings of any type along his route, so he was hopeful that he had this labyrinth to himself.

Elias leaned the rifle against a wall and set down the suitcase, opening it. Beneath the clothing and toiletries, which had been rummaged through by Crabill, was the smartphone, his lifeline to the outside world. He was certain that Crabill thought nothing of the fact that he had brought a phone inside, even though they were useless in Aegis. People were creatures of habit, and Elias assumed that most of the new arrivals would do the same thing.

He left the phone in the suitcase for now, and removed one other item. It appeared to be a charging base for an electric toothbrush; in fact, it was something else entirely. Tucking it into his shirt pocket, Elias looked around and located a wall-mounted steel ladder which extended up to the ceiling. This time he retrieved the master key before climbing and, reaching the top, unlocked the hatch, swinging it up and open. He was at the roof of Aegis, and the wind was still fierce. It snatched the hatch from his grip and slammed it open as far as it would go. Fortunately, the spring hinges were beefy enough to not snap from the impact, and the lid remained open. The wind, traveling almost parallel to the face of the now vertical hatch, whipped over the open access, and the Bernoulli effect pulled at Elias, dragging air out of the junction room beneath him at an almost gale force and causing a low-frequency sound like a person blowing over the top of a pop bottle.

Concerned that someone might hear the sound or notice the sudden change in air pressure, he scrambled through the opening and, using all of his body weight, pushed the hatch closed. The wind was so forceful that it nearly caused him to lose his balance and fall onto one of the thousands of solar panels mounted to the roof.

Keeping his feet well apart to help him maintain an upright posture, Elias, in the dimming light of the evening, searched around the bases of the solar panels until he found a weatherproof electrical outlet. The outlets had been placed regularly around the roof system for the use of tradesmen during the construction of Aegis and also to be used by anyone who might perform repairs. Since no outside contractors would ever be allowed inside or on the roof once Aegis opened, Elias guessed that the assumption made by the designers of the building had been that eventually a qualified tradesman would check in and might need to plug in his tools.

Shaking his head at yet another of the idiocies of Aegis, he pulled the device from his pocket and plugged it in, careful to orient the top of it away from his eyes. Now came the hard part. He had to find a way to secure the relatively light base so that the wind would not blow it over. Setting it down, he searched the adjacent area, quickly finding that the contractor who had installed the solar panels had left several pieces of steel angle behind. It was a gauge heavy enough to serve as a lintel in masonry work; obviously, they had been concerned about the sometimes violent desert wind, when designing the support structures. He hefted two of the six-foot-long pieces and carried them back to the spot where he had left the device.

Shivering from the cold, Elias first placed the plastic base in the small open area next to the outlet. He set one of the two angles next to it so that it rested upon the power cord, further securing it. Then he positioned the second piece of steel on the other side of the base in order to wedge it firmly between the two.

Stepping back, he checked out the installation, satisfied that it was probably the best he could do with the materials at hand. After taking one last, long look around the vast flat roof, Elias lifted the hatch, more carefully this time so that the wind would not rip it from his grip, and climbed down the ladder, struggling to pull the lid closed behind himself. He locked it and continued down, grateful for the warmth.

The air turbulence, caused by the opening of the roof hatch, had stirred up the dust, and Elias coughed several times, his throat and lungs stung by the acrid powder. He sat on the floor next to the suitcase and pulled out the smartphone and, with his thumb, slid out the mini-keyboard. Quickly, he typed his first message to Faulk, which would be compressed and transmitted automatically in about two hours. His descriptions of Madison, Walden, and the members of the group who resided in ZooCity were brief, but he supplied more lengthy details about the blurred intervention. He also reported that there was, as yet, no sign of Rudy Kreitzmann. After informing Faulk that the beacon was in place on the roof, Elias read the message once over for errors, saved it, and closed the phone.

Leaning back against the wall, he removed two PayDays and a can of Ensure from the suitcase and ate his dinner. Although he was certain there was something else he could yet do this evening, Elias did not move, closed his eyes, and allowed himself to relax. Within minutes, he was asleep.

Whoever it was who had followed him during his journey through the raceway maze was a very patient person. At no point did the stranger get close enough to be heard or seen. Now, as the stuttering sounds of Elias' snores echoed through the concrete passageways, the figure waited. Fifteen minutes, thirty minutes, an hour, and finally two hours passed before the stranger very slowly and carefully moved forward, not making even the slightest sound – until this wraith stood over Elias, taking in all of the details of his face and the visible contents of his suitcase, paying special attention to the automatic rifle leaning against the wall next to his sleeping figure.

Having learned all that could be learned from this visit, the figure receded into the passageway without making a sound. Because the phone was programmed to perform its function silently and without the screen lighting, the watcher had been completely unaware that Elias' message was sent and a message downloaded during the fleeting observation.

⊙

The stealth helicopter, using the laser homing beacon generated by the base Elias had set up on the roof, hovered above Aegis. On command, the sergeant activated the winch and lowered the package toward the clear area adjacent to the roof hatch. He maintained a running stream of instructions to the pilot, who did a masterful job of flying in the buffeting winds and compensating for the wild swinging of the package at the end of the line. Deciding that gently placing it on the roof in these conditions would be impossible, the sergeant stopped the winch from unspooling when the package swung only a few feet above the nearby solar panels, and waited. After feeling that he had a good sense of the timing of the swings, he hit the clutch on the winch, abruptly dropping the load. He grinned to himself at his accuracy as he saw that it landed squarely where he intended, less than three feet from the laser beacon.

Triggering the line release, he spoke into his headset mouthpiece. "It's down. Let's go."

The pilot wasted no time increasing the elevation of the craft, and they canted forward and sped away.

⊙

Erin Stephenson glanced at the Caller ID on her phone, and seeing who was calling her direct line, quickly lifted the handset. "Hello, Rusty."

"Erin, how are you?"

"Busy, overworked, behind schedule, and ready to strangle Len for allowing his wife to have her baby now, instead of on his day off. I'm doing my own shows and his today. What's up?"

The meteorologist-on-duty chuckled. "That's the life of a big TV star. Quit complaining."

"Yeah, right."

"Anyway, I checked out the anemometers. Even sent a tech out to make sure. They're fine."

This was the last answer Erin expected. "Can't be, Rusty. You've seen the surface ob."

There was a brief pause. When he spoke, all of the former levity was missing from his voice. "I have. I know."

"Then what's the explanation?"

She listened to another pause, visualizing Rusty sitting at his console, staring at the map. Finally, he admitted, "Erin, I don't know."

She turned on her swivel chair and, using her free hand, clicked on the surface observation map fed to her computer from the National Weather Service. She had to zoom out from the default location of the Tucson area, select the desert region to the west, and zoom in. As she read the numbers, she gasped. "It's worse."

"Yep. It sure is."

"Rusty...."

"I know, Erin. I know."

"It's...what I'm looking at, from everything I learned...."

His voice was flat as he finished her sentence – "Impossible."

CHAPTER FIVE

Elias had awakened at around 3:00 a.m., his neck and back stiff from his sleeping position against the wall. Shaking it off as much as he could, he climbed the ladder and found the delivery. The materials sent had been specifically packed into a box which would fit through the hatch. A twenty-foot length of rope had been left attached, which he used to lower the parcel through the opening and down to the floor, fighting the winds through the entire process.

Now equipped with the surveillance gear he needed, as well as other materials dictated by the assignment, Elias spent the next three hours roaming the raceways of Aegis, completing various installations, and positioning microscopic cameras and microphones in what he had designated from his brief visits as key areas in Walden and Madison. The electrical raceways and conduits had provided an ideal environment for this work, taking him directly above any room in the complex and providing him with several penetrations where he could piggyback his devices. He had also found the section of Aegis used as a home by the ZooCity dwellers and had positioned monitoring equipment there, choosing the spots as best he could from the available vantage points.

Elias then returned to his base and set up the laptop provided in the drop. Since all radio frequencies were jammed at Aegis, his method for monitoring all of the surveillance devices was elegantly simply and utilized the miles of interconnected conduit in the raceways. The devices sent their data via an FM signal which was transmitted through the conduits themselves. He screwed a conductive clamp to one of the pipes closest to the laptop. The clamp had a wire soldered to it with a converter and a USB plug at the end of the wire. He plugged it into the port of the laptop and opened the monitoring program. After a minute or two of searching and identifying all of the feeds, the program displayed a menu with each microphone or camera listed by number. Elias reached into his pocket, pulled out the sheet of paper he had used to jot down the locations of all of the devices, and edited the feed menu so that it displayed each microphone or camera by location.

Clicking on one of the ZooCity feeds, he heard nothing but silence. The camera associated with this location showed an empty room. He continued clicking from location to location until his ears were rewarded with the sounds of several excited voices shouting at once. Checking the video, he saw one of the young men put his fingers to his mouth and whistle loudly. They all stopped talking. Once silence was established, the whistler, who seemed to be the leader, contended, "We don't have no choice."

One of the others spoke up, his voice confrontational. "I don't like it, BQ. Those dudes are bad."

"You're right. They're bad. Okay. But we hook up with 'em or we die. Which one you want?"

There was no answer.

After a brief pause, as all of the group fell silent, the punk who had expressed his dislike for the situation asked, "So what they want us to do?"

The one they called BQ answered, "It ain't nothin'. They want us to do the same thing we been doin'. They want us to grab newbies right when they come in. Except instead of doin' what we used to do, they want us to deliver 'em to them."

"And what do we get out of it?" one of the others asked.

It was difficult to tell from the wide-angle view on the laptop but it looked to Elias as if BQ smiled and said, "Mostly, we get to live. There be some other good things, too. They be makin' some crystal and some blow over there. We get some of that. We get some booty. You know, the ones they don't want."

"This ain't right! I like it the way it's been. We had our own game. Now we gotta play theirs?"

It appeared from the video feed that BQ glared at the talker. "We play their game or we be dead."

The talker did not look as if he agreed, but failed to respond.

Elias listened to the entire discussion, trying to glean additional insights. Other than what he learned at the beginning, very little came out of what he heard. As the group broke up and scattered, he rocked back on his heels and thought about this new information. His guess was that it was Kreitzmann, or one of his people, who had contacted this group with the intent of putting them to work for him. That was obvious. What was not obvious was why he needed the ZooCity culprits. The other point mentioned which disturbed Elias was the offering of a supply of methamphetamines and cocaine. The effect of distributing deadly drugs of that nature in an environment like this one, already stressed due to the pre-existing mental state of the entrants and the bizarre nature of the institution itself, would have wildly unpredictable results. The obvious question was how Kreitzmann was able to produce drugs while having no access to an outside supply of the materials needed.

The one other fact Elias took away from listening to the discussion was the abject fear visible even in the grainy image of their faces and audible in their voices. This was a group, whose whole social structure was based upon their bravado and generally macho attitude, talking about their own demise as an inevitable consequence of noncooperation. At least from the moment he began to monitor them, there was not even a hint of their opposing or resisting the overture, not a hint of defiance. In Elias' mind, that could only mean one thing. Whoever had proffered the deal to the gangsters in ZooCity, and he assumed it must have been Kreitzmann, must be the same party connected to the deadly show he witnessed upon his arrival: the blur.

He clicked on the configuration menu of the monitoring program and set it up so that the laptop would record the video and audio feeds from all of the sources on a voice- or motion-activated basis, for his periodic review. Next, using another USB cable, he connected the smartphone to the laptop and downloaded the message which was received at the same time his message was uploaded in the flash transmission.

Within moments, the text message from Faulk's office was displayed. Since this message was transmitted to him essentially at the same time as his went out, there was nothing in it referencing his comments or questions. That would have to come tomorrow. All it contained was a list of the drop shipment, a statement telling Elias that they did not yet have any luck identifying the two men who had accompanied Kreitzmann into the facility, and a comment from Faulk that he was glad Elias had made it inside and was able to check in on schedule.

His next several minutes were occupied opening one of the MREs from the drop and eating a tasteless meal, washed down by a bottle of energy drink. Still stiff and sore from his sleeping position, Elias stood and did some stretching exercises before once again striking out.

"At least tonight I'll sleep more comfortably," he said aloud, unpacking the flattened and compressed air mattress included in the shipment. With all of his self-assigned tasks completed, Elias typed a final command into the laptop and a password screen appeared, locking out anyone who might come across his base camp; then he returned to the access ladder.

By now it was late morning. The section of Aegis into which he emerged was still quiet and unoccupied. He wanted to explore the areas and pockets of the complex not occupied by Walden, Madison, or ZooCity. Given the vast scope of Aegis, he had placed his cameras and microphones in the locations he had already identified this morning, or in the case of ZooCity, guessed. But Elias still had no idea where Kreitzmann was set up, and felt that the corridors and hallways would better serve his purpose of exploring, rather than the electrical service-ways above.

Although Aegis had no windows around the perimeter, there was a large center courtyard and, scattered about the layout, several smaller atria to provide the residents with access to fresh air and sunlight. The hallways adjacent to these interior open areas were built with ample windows to allow the sunlight to come in and to provide views.

Recollecting that the plans for Aegis had called for rather lush landscaping with automatic irrigation systems in each of these areas, Elias noted that the first two he passed were barren and dusty. Over the years, either there had been a malfunction in the irrigation system, which none of the residents were able or willing to repair, or the plantings and hardware had been cannibalized.

The condition of the previous two atria contributed to his surprise as he arrived at the third. From the window where he paused, Elias could see no farther than three feet past the glass. The atrium was bursting with life. Trees, ferns, broad-leaf plants, and vines were tangled together, creating the impression of a jungle, rather than the landscaped, open-air commons area which was originally intended.

His curiosity piqued, he followed the hallway to the first door, finding it not only locked but barred on the outside. Now, even more curious, Elias continued following the hallway, turning a corner when he reached an edge, and circled the unlikely jungle. The second door he encountered was secured in the same manner as the first. Turning the next corner, Elias discovered that the door on the third side was also bolted and barred. In his mind, he planned to simply break one of the windows if the fourth door was inaccessible.

It was not. The metal and glass storefront door swung out, instantly colliding with a large cowbell which hung on a rope above the door, announcing his arrival loudly. Elias was immediately struck with the powerful organic smells of a greenhouse. His hand instinctively sliding into his pocket, where he again carried the 9mm, he momentarily regretted his earlier decision to leave behind the assault rifle given to him by Sweezea.

Taking a step forward, he allowed the door to swing shut behind him, triggering another metallic clatter from the bell. There was a path in front of him, albeit a narrow one, penetrating the dense vegetation, and Elias slowly moved forward, leaving his sidearm in his pocket. So thick was the foliage that it took no more than fifteen paces for the door he had entered to become obscured completely, as was the entire perimeter wall around this jungle. The growth was so tall that he could not see the sky above, only indirect sunlight as it filtered through the stalks and leaves of the canopy above his head.

It had been many years since Elias had trekked through a real jungle, but he still recalled the various sounds caused by the sudden darting of animals through the underbrush, the whoops and cries of birds, monkeys, and other creatures. That discordant symphony was absent here. Instead, his ears were filled with the sound of the whipping wind, high overhead, as it twisted and twirled its way down into the open area. The effect of the unceasing turbulence was to set all of the plants in motion. Elias was surrounded by undulating branches and fronds, dragging and crashing against each other, generating a low-frequency din which nearly drowned out the voice.

"Stop where you are!"

Elias halted.

"Take that right hand out of your pocket."

Complying, Elias pulled out his hand, empty, and let it hang loosely by his side.

"Where are you from?" the voice demanded firmly.

"Phoenix," Elias lied.

"That's not what I mean. You don't look like a ZooCity habitant. Are you from Madison or those mush-heads at Walden?"

The voice was coming from Elias' right, but he could see no trace of the man hidden in the dense, green wall.

Elias manufactured a touch of derision in his voice. "No way! I've met them both."

The stranger paused briefly before asking, "What do you want?" His tone was a little less hostile.

"I just got here," Elias explained. "I am trying to figure out where I want to plant myself."

Above the sounds of the wind, Elias heard a chuckle. "You think I'm that stupid?"

"What do you mean?"

"You come into a park that's been taken over by someone obviously obsessed with greenery, and you think that if you employ subtle comments about wanting to 'plant' yourself, I'm simply going to like you?"

Elias grinned. "It was worth a try."

The stranger coming to a decision, the thick leaves of a philodendron to the right side parted, and an older man, probably in his early seventies, emerged, carrying a shotgun, which was not pointed at Elias.

"Aw, rats. I wouldn't mind a little chat, I guess."

The man extended his hand and introduced himself. "I'm Wilson."

"Elias Charon."

They shook hands.

"Let's go sit down. My knees hurt from crouching."

Wilson pointed down the path with the barrel of the 12 gauge and indicated, "That way."

Elias' smile broadened. "I see you're also not so stupid that you let me walk behind you."

"You got that right," Wilson responded with a wink. "Now follow the path. There's a shack dead-ahead."

Surprised, Elias asked, "You built a shack here?"

"Uh-huh."

Intrigued, Elias turned and followed the path. Within forty yards he found an obviously handmade structure, cobbled together from an assortment of salvaged building materials from the inside of Aegis. He noticed that there was even a porch with two chairs, incongruous in these surroundings as they appeared to have been pilfered from a conference room.

Elias stepped up onto the porch, followed by Wilson, who leaned the shotgun against the wall of the shack and said, "You probably want a beer. Well, I don't have any. How about some tea?"

"Sounds good."

"Take a seat, Mr. Death. I'll be right back."

"Mr. Death?"

Wilson, who was already halfway through the front door, looked back and remarked, "You really do think I'm a dolt, don't you?"

He turned without waiting for a response and went inside, leaving the door open. Elias noted that Wilson had left the shotgun on the porch.

Sitting back in the vinyl chair, Elias stared in wonder at the dense foliage all around him. Not an expert in horticulture, he was certain that many of the species were indigenous or adaptable to the dry Arizona climate, but it seemed as if he were sitting on a cabin porch in the Ozarks rather than the Sonoran desert. Over the wrawl of the wind, he could hear the occasional clatter made by Wilson preparing the tea.

The setting of the shack, and the leafy palisade surrounding it, had a calming effect on Elias, despite the wind, and he could understand why this strange man had created and protected this environment.

"Do you want milk or sugar?" Wilson yelled from inside.

"Sugar, please," Elias replied, raising his voice to be heard.

"I'd better put it in before I come out, or that wind will blow it away. How many spoons?"

"One."

Within a minute, he returned with two mugs, handing one to Elias, who noticed that his mug had the phrase "Don't tread on me" above the familiar image of the coiled snake. Glancing over, he saw that glazed on the stranger's mug was the American flag.

"So what brings you to hell?"

Taken slightly aback, Elias asked, "Hell?"

Wilson chuckled. "Hell, purgatory – what would you call it?"

"Aegis?"

Snorting with derision, Wilson came back, "Because you and everybody else call a pig a rose doesn't mean I have to go along. Ever since man quit cowering in his cave, he's been trying to usurp the natural way of things. All the science, all the technology, inventions, you name it…it's all been nothing but an effort to say 'I can do anything you can do better.' That's all this is. That idiot Walker building this place because he was so broken up about his daughter – it was plainly meddling with yet another thing that was already tried and true."

"What's that?"

"Killing yourself!" Wilson exclaimed as though Elias was a dunce for asking. "All the stuff we do has a reason. It's all been fiddled with and tested and the bugs worked out of it for centuries, no, millennia. That's the reason it's all still around. It works! But we can't stop ourselves from tampering with it."

Elias could not help but be amused at the comments. "You're serious?"

"You bet I am. You want some examples?"

"Sure."

"Names!"

"Names?"

"Yeah, names. For hundreds, maybe thousands of generations, when people got married, they took the husband's name. It wasn't perfect. Sometimes, some poor woman with a perfectly fine name like Mary Jones married some guy stuck with a last name of....As my guest, maybe you could suggest what might be a suitably embarrassing name."

"Boner!" Elias chuckled.

"What?"

"You heard me. It's a common name."

Wilson's face twisted in a grimace. "Very well. But I am using it in the classical sense of 'blunder,' as in the dictionary."

"As you wish," Elias consented, smirking at the old man's discomfort.

Wilson glared at Elias.

"Anyway, as I was saying, she married him, and became Mary Boner. I'm sure she wouldn't be happy about that, and I'll bet their kids would all wish that they were little Joneses instead of little...you know what I mean. But that was what society had figured out, and it worked. Yeah, I know it was male-oriented, but don't get me started on that. Anyway, all of a sudden this generation, for the first time in the history of the whole world, decided to change things – only because they cared about themselves and didn't give a hoot about the rest. Self-centered little cusses!

"Now, they hyphenate. So now, Mary Jones gets married and becomes Mary Jones-Boner!"

"That's true. What's the problem with that?" Elias asked, playing along.

"The problem?" Wilson almost barked at Elias. "What do the kids get to call themselves? Are they Johnnie and Susie Boner...or are they Johnnie and Susie Jones-Boner?"

Enjoying the process of following Wilson's train of thought, Elias said, "I think the norm is that they would be Jones-Boner."

"You *think*! See, that's the problem. Suddenly we don't know. As long as civilization has been around, we would have known exactly what little Johnnie and Susie would be called. There wouldn't be any thought, any decision required. It was all worked out long before they were born, and if somebody didn't like it, there wasn't anybody to get mad at; that was simply the way it was. But now, they pick. And, initially, the parents decide; they're required to put something on the birth certificate. So they pick Jones-Boner, and Susie grows up and decides she doesn't like Jones-Boner – she just likes Jones – and then she's mad at her parents for the choice they made. But forget about that part for a minute."

"Okay," Elias said, grinning.

"Let's say that both of the little brats grow up and love the name exactly the way it is."

"Got it."

"What happens when Johnnie Jones-Boner falls in love and gets married to Wendy Kalinsky-Pratt?" Wilson's voice was louder now and more animated as he reached the point of his soliloquy. "Why, I guess they have to become Johnnie and Wendy Kalinsky-Pratt-Jones-Boner."

Elias burst out laughing.

"But wait, making one little change to how things have always been done makes it even more complicated than that. There isn't any custom dictating which of the surnames goes first. So maybe they are Johnnie and Wendy Kalinsky-Pratt-Jones-Boner, or maybe they are Johnnie and Wendy Jones-Boner-Kalinsky-Pratt! So *they* get to decide, which is only right since it is all about them, right?"

"I guess."

"Now, and I want you to think about this, whichever way they choose is going to either hurt or anger one set of parents."

"Because," Elias added, "both sets of parents will want their name to have the better placement."

"Exactly! So somebody's parents lose and somebody's win. Not only that, but either Johnnie or Wendy is a winner – or loser – as well."

"That's true. They can't both get their way. One does, and the other gives in."

"Right! So now this young couple, just starting out, has a resentment brewing and one set of ticked-off in-laws."

Laughing, Elias agreed, "Makes sense."

"Darn right it does. And then, what about the next generation?"

Elias held up his hands in surrender. "I get the picture."

"Do you? I mean, do you really see what I'm driving at here? We took a system, a custom, which had been worked out long before we were born and had functioned perfectly for countless generations, and we *ruined* it. Part of the beauty of the custom was that it worked without cluttering up people's lives with details and extra names. The other important part of it was that it recognized the inherent tendency of certain acts or decisions within a society to cause pain and hurt feelings – like picking a name – and it removed that decision and made it a given…made it a custom dictated by people long dead. So there wasn't anyone around to blame or get mad at. But if it becomes a *decision* made by a living, breathing person, then everyone involved in the situation is watching to see which way he or she will choose. Winners and losers!"

"I never thought about it that way. But what does that have to do with Aegis?"

Wilson paused and took a sip from his mug of tea. "Well, obviously it's a little different from the name thing, but society had sorted out the whole suicide thing, too. Suicide is, or was, what it's supposed to be."

"What's that?"

"Death," Wilson exclaimed. "It's supposed to be death, not this namby-pamby institution."

Although Elias agreed with Wilson, he wanted to hear what the man had to say. "You don't think this was a good idea?"

"Nope. I don't. Let's talk about people who might consider suicide. Before, if people screwed up their lives, they always knew they had the option of suicide. It was an unpleasant thought and a scary one, but people always knew that no matter how bad things got, there was always that back door they could slip out through.

"You know, Mr. Death, I bet you that if you could somehow remove the option of suicide from the minds of people, the whole civilization would grind to a halt."

"Why is that?"

"People would be afraid to do anything...try anything risky. Suicide is the net under them while they go on the high wire. Remove the net, and who would be stupid enough to go up there and learn those tricks?"

"Makes sense," Elias concurred.

"Darn right it does. But the deal is, for the whole program to work, suicide has to be tough; it needs to be scary and final. And what's more scary to people than the unknown? So they all need to be scared to death, no pun intended...."

"None taken," Elias commented sarcastically.

"They all need to be scared to death to take that step. You know, what if they do go to hell when they die? What if, after they die, there is just *nothing*? All that stuff. And what if killing themselves would hurt like blazes?

"In other words, if that option of suicide is truly too horrible to fathom, people have to try harder to get things right, to find a better solution. What I'm saying is that there needs to be a real deterrent, or people would take the option if they stubbed their toes."

"That's what is happening out there now."

"I know," Wilson sighed. "I've been in here watching. Most of the people coming in aren't doing it for the old reasons, not that all of the old ones were good ones. They're doing it for some of the most ridiculous reasons I've ever heard. There was even a young girl who came here because her favorite actor checked in."

"I heard about that."

"Yeah? Well, would she have done that if she knew he was dead?"

"No. Probably not. Maybe it happened, but I can't remember anyone committing suicide because his or her favorite actor or singer did it."

"Me neither. But that's not what I meant."

"What…?"

"He *was* dead! Within minutes of walking through those spinning doors, they killed him."

"Who killed him?"

"Those punks. They did it for the fun of it. They were so happy to have this spoiled, privileged kid just so they could beat the insides out of him. And then when she arrived, looking for her heartthrob, well, I'm not even going to tell you what those animals did to her."

Elias shook his head. "Unbelievable."

"But, see, if we still did things the old way, she wouldn't have come and it wouldn't have happened. She thought she was checking in at a hotel and was going to be able to make google-eyes at the star. She probably thought she could move into one of the apartments here with him and they could live happily ever after. If he had O.D.'d on sleeping pills, she would have felt bad. Might have even thought about doing it herself, but she wouldn't have had any illusions about living in the hereafter with him!"

"I see what you mean."

"Of course you do. You're not an idiot. The point is, we've cheapened everything, even death."

"What do you mean 'cheapened'?"

Wilson took another long sip on his tea as he collected his thoughts for another tirade. "You look old enough to me to remember something pretty special."

"What's that?"

"Tearing open the plastic wrapper on an album."

"A record album?"

"Yes, a record album. I remember wanting to get a copy of 'Peggy Sue' by Buddy Holly."

Elias nodded, encouraging him to continue.

"I took my allowance money from doing chores around the house and went to the Kresge on the corner. That was before K-Mart. It was 1958, and I bought Buddy Holly's latest album, which had the song on it. I cradled that album all the way home on my bike, ran inside the house, and sat down on the floor in front of my record player. Then came the best part."

The old man grinned as his eyes conveyed the joy of this past memory. "I broke the plastic wrapper with my fingernail, right at the opening of the jacket. Then I slid my finger to carefully slice that wrapper open. Didn't want to tear it, you know."

Elias nodded.

"Darned if I didn't get a paper cut under my fingernail from the cardboard edge inside."

"Ouch!"

Wilson chuckled. "But it didn't matter. Careful not to get any blood on the inside liner – you know, that paper sleeve inside – I pulled out the record, with the sleeve still on it. Then I set down the album cover, gently took the record out of the sleeve, and put it on the turntable."

He looked piercingly at Elias. "You remember that smell? The smell of a new record?"

"Oh, yeah," Elias answered.

"Well, then I played it. And I played it and played it and played it. Boy, did I love that album. But the point is the experience. The process. The ritual. We all had record collections, and you could tell a lot about a fella by his records. Or a girl, for that matter."

"That's true."

"Do you think that all of the younger people around today prize any individual song that they have crammed on their iPods, with the eight thousand other songs they've downloaded, as much as I prized that album? I don't.

"Before I came to this place, I was sitting at a coffee shop and listening to a couple of younger guys talking. From what I heard, they had downloaded, between the two of them, about three hundred songs the night before. Three hundred! And most of them were downloaded onto their cell phones! I'll bet there are some songs they have gotten that they'll never even listen to the rest of their lives, much less care about the way I did that one album."

"You're probably right."

The man leaned forward, closing the gap between himself and Elias. "And it isn't just songs, either. Look at pictures! With digital cameras, people come back from *lunch* with as many pictures as a man and his wife used to take during an entire vacation. And books, too, with those cursed e-books."

This stranger obviously had no way of knowing how many times Elias had made the same argument to his friends over the years. "Let me tell you something, Wilson. Do you have any idea how I got here?"

Taken slightly aback by the question, Wilson ventured, "I assume by car."

"Only the last leg. Before that, I traveled from New Orleans to Tucson by train."

Elias' companion slapped him on the knee. "There you go. Traveling in a way that actually makes you feel as though you've gone someplace."

"You got it."

Wilson dropped heavily back into his chair and sighed again. "But you know what, my friend? Anybody listening to us no doubt thinks we're a couple of old fuddy-duddies for saying these things."

"I gave up," Elias mused, "trying to explain to my boss that just walking onto an airplane and a few hours later stepping off, half the world away, gives us a skewed perspective on where we are and what the world is really like."

"Don't I know it! You can't tell them though, can you?"

"No. You can't. But what you said, Wilson, about the other things and about suicide, makes a lot of sense. I never thought of it that way."

"We're cheapening everything and we're making everything all about us, and future generations be damned. The mind-set that causes us to fiddle with the way we name ourselves and our kids, without even mentally extending it out one or two generations, is the same as letting the debt get so high. Either we don't care or we somehow know that it's all going to end soon anyway, so what difference does it make?"

Wilson turned away and stared out at the riot of plants and trees encircling the porch. Without looking back at Elias and with a more subdued tone to his voice, he continued, "And television. Not all that long ago there were only three channels to watch. Now there are hundreds. And most of it is baloney. With the three, there was always something to watch, something you wanted to see. You could watch *I Love Lucy* or *What's My Line?* or the fights, unless they were taken off for an Andy Williams special" – he paused and smiled at some private memory – "but, seriously, you can search through the choices delivered by the little black cable or satellite dish and usually not find a single thing you want to waste your time on."

Returning his gaze to Elias, Wilson remarked, "You think I'm some crazy Luddite, don't you?"

Elias smiled and shook his head. "No, Wilson, I don't. As a matter of fact, I agree with you."

"So that makes us a couple of fools who can't deal with the fact that society has passed us by, doesn't it?"

"No. It doesn't."

Wilson chuckled. "Of course you'd say that, Mr. Death. Fools and crazy people always think they're fine. It's always everybody else who's gone 'round the bend."

Twisting around in his seat to face his host, Elias asked, "What's with this 'Mr. Death' thing? Why are you calling me that?"

"You're kidding, right?"

"No, I'm not."

"You don't know the historical significance of your own name?"

"Charon? The guide from the river Styx taking the souls across the river?"

"Yeah," Wilson said, still smiling. "But either your parents had no knowledge of history and just liked the name, or they had a wicked sense of humor when they tagged you with Elias to go in front of it."

"Saint Elias the Living?"

"See, you did know! Some believed that Elias was the only saint who didn't die. He hopped on his fiery chariot and rode it to Heaven, body and all. Don't ya think that's a bit of an ironic name for someone waltzing into this institution, which is nothing but a spit in the face of death?"

"Hadn't given it any thought."

Wilson snorted his opinion and said nothing. They both fell into a brief silence, listening to the whirl of the wind. After a few minutes, Wilson began speaking, his voice so low Elias had to strain to hear his words. "All this stuff…the names, songs, photographs, movies, and TV shows…if it were merely the logical progression of things, it wouldn't bother me so much."

"What do you mean?" Elias asked, caught up in the old man's sudden change of mood, realizing that the man he had been chatting with on the porch, until this minute, was a manufactured caricature, and the true person was now revealing himself.

Wilson hesitated once again, and Elias suspected that he was not merely formulating his thoughts, but rather was deciding whether to share them with a stranger. With a deep intake of breath, he indicated the decision had been made. "What do you think I did for a living, before I retired…before I checked in to this looney bin?"

"I have no idea, Wilson. How would I? We just met."

Elias' companion stared intently at him, his gray eyes penetrating deeply. "You're a smart man, Mr. Charon. Very smart. I have a feeling that you've made a career out of reading people. When you read me, what do you see?"

Throughout his career, Elias had long ago recognized that there were frequently points in any cover where you had to decide whether to stick with your story or shift gears. Sometimes clinging to your original cover was the best option, regardless of how absurd the act of maintaining it became. At other times, abandoning the pretext, and either adopting another or simply coming clean about who you were, made the most sense, even if the motivation to do so was apparently weak. Occasionally, breaking cover was the appropriate thing to do for purely utilitarian reasons. Elias decided this was one of those times.

Taking a deep breath, he plunged in. "Wilson isn't your real name." Elias paused for a moment to watch for a reaction to his comment. There was none, so he continued, "I'm not exactly certain what you did, but you are well educated, extremely so. My guess would be the sciences."

Again no reaction other than a very slight, wry grin.

"You were successful in what you did. Probably made quite a name for yourself. And you were used to having a lot of people and resources at your disposal. You liked to solve problems but became bored with the day-to-day running of things, and you've developed quite a contempt for humanity."

The subtle grin filled out into a full smile. "Not bad, Elias. Not bad at all."

"Are you going to tell me who you are?"

"Not *are*, *were*."

It was Elias' turn to smile. "Okay, who *were* you?"

"John Wilson Chapman."

The moment he heard the name, Elias recognized his features. The entire biography of the man tumbled into his mind. John Wilson Chapman, thirty years ago, had been at the top of his field in mathematics. In addition, he had won a Nobel Prize for his work in the area of pattern recognition, and he had been the leading and, at times, vicious opponent of Chaos Theory, believing and maintaining at every opportunity that Chaos Theory was nothing but the scientific community putting a fancy title on the fact that they did not understand something.

He became quickly renowned for discerning the most esoteric and subtle patterns in areas theretofore considered to be too chaotic to predict. Whether it was the stock market, Internet routing, ocean currents, turbulence within the human heart, or the weather, he seemed to relish the chance to unravel the apparently hopeless, tangled balls of yarn in a variety of fields and disciplines. As a result he became both famous and wealthy, only to gradually recede from the public view and consciousness.

Elias stuck out his hand and said, "It is a pleasure to meet you, sir."

Wilson accepted the handshake. "Of course, the normal turn of the conversation would be for me to inquire and for you to supply your identity to me. But I am not quite certain that you have reached the point with me where you would be completely forthright in your answer, and I am enjoying this chat too much for it to be spoiled by dissembling."

Elias only grinned, saying nothing.

With a soft sigh, Wilson continued, "All in good time, I suppose. But to continue my thought, when I first began to notice all of the changes in society against which I have been railing, I chalked them off as the normal evolution of technology, à lá Alvin Toffler. But over time, as I observed and, in many cases, facilitated these so-called advances, I began to feel differently."

"How so?"

Wilson's eyes once again swung away from Elias and stared out into the jumble of foliage. "Why do you think I've created this environment for myself?"

Elias shrugged. "Trying to recreate some childhood setting?"

Wilson laughed. "No, hardly that. I was raised in Las Cruces. It's literally the way my mind has always worked. From a very young age I was fascinated with patterns. I remember, as a boy, sitting for hours watching the apparently random ramblings of ants around their hill, until I was able to discern the subtle plan behind their routes and movements. I wasn't happy until I could accurately predict what they would do next. The same was true with everything around me, so much so that I never married."

"I don't understand."

"You don't? It's simple, really. Even as a teenaged, hormone-driven boy, I studied the dating and mating patterns of all of the boys and girls around me in high school, until the dependable chain of cause-and-effect actions became clear. The unfortunate by-product of this was that I developed a feeling for females that was anything but conducive for romance, love, and marriage."

"Contempt?"

"No. Let's call it a distaste for the process. This process, like everything else, has been devalued. I found females to be far too predictable, too easy to manipulate. Not that I intend for that comment to sound as chauvinistic as it does. My comments apply to males, as well. Regrettably, I found it difficult to find a woman I could view as my equal, my partner."

"I think I understand."

"I'm sure you do. But to continue, I never developed an aversion to patterns. Instead I craved them. I sought out more and more complex sets of variables merely to satisfy my curiosity."

"So the jungle you've created around you here is a challenge?"

Rolling his eyes dismissively, Wilson replied, "No, not a challenge. But it is something, as opposed to a void. At least the plants grow and change and interact and die and give birth. At least there is a relatively complex system which, most important, is ever-changing."

"I get it. Living inside the complex, with its static structures, furnishings, and such would bore you instantly."

"*Bore* is far too understated for the effect it would have. You see, what society has called my ability, my gift, is probably an unmeasurably rare and undiagnosed mental disease. If I had to spend the remainder of my time in an apartment, especially one without even a window, I would surely go mad."

Wilson stopped for a moment and looked at Elias, as if to measure the impact his words had so far.

"All of that being said, I am now led to my denouement. I was completely immersed in the progress and the workings of the late twentieth and early twenty-first centuries. As I mentioned, I not only observed, I facilitated the progress. Yet, my mind being what it is, I also studied the underlying patterns, until the conclusions I began to reach were so disturbing, I had no choice but to extricate myself from it all."

Elias realized that his entire body was tense in anticipation. Whether it was the surreal nature of the setting, the nearly hypnotic delivery of Wilson's words, or the almost mythical reputation of the man himself, Elias was certain that he was on the verge of hearing something of the utmost importance. "Please, go on. What did you find?"

The mathematician did not appear eager to deliver his judgment. An expression most closely resembling distaste spread across his face as he continued, "I became convinced that the patterns, all of the symptoms of progress I've criticized and denigrated here, were not merely the serendipitous occurrences of an evolving and advancing society but, rather, were the intentional and deliberate increments of a plan."

As he finished his statement, his eyes were riveted upon Elias, watching for a reaction.

"What plan, Wilson?"

"Why, Elias, I would have thought it would be obvious from my previous comments. The plan is to carefully and systematically devalue every aspect of life itself for all people on Earth."

Elias was unsure as to what his next comment should be. So much of what Wilson had said earlier echoed his own theories and beliefs, yet it had never occurred to Elias that it was all deliberate, that it was some sort of plot.

"I sound like one of those pathetic crackpots, don't I? One of those people who see a conspiracy behind every event."

Smiling, Elias replied, "There is no better way to neutralize the voices of those who are attempting to alert the public than to marginalize them. No, Wilson, I don't think you sound like a crackpot, and you are anything but pathetic. But what is the ultimate purpose of this plan? What's the goal?"

"That," Wilson said with more than a little chagrin in his voice, "I don't know. Maybe you can help me find that answer."

"Why me?"

"Why not? You're as good a candidate as any."

Elias could not help but be charmed by this man. "I don't think I'll be making any analytical breakthroughs that you've missed, Wilson."

"Have it your way."

"Do you mind if I ask a question?"

"Please do."

"I understand that it is *de rigueur* to avoid asking the residents of Aegis why they came, but I can't help but be curious with you."

With a soft laugh, Wilson answered, "You're wondering why someone...as rich and famous as I...would want to commit suicide, or at least the modern version of the act?"

"No, not the rich and famous part. Plenty of rich and famous people do it. But why would someone with your intellect and perceptiveness want to...?"

"Flick it in?"

"Yes."

"I didn't."

Elias started to speak but was cut off. "I did not desire to end it all. I didn't enter Aegis as an alternative to suicide."

"Then why are you here?"

"I saw it as a refuge. If the developing pattern was global, where else could I go? I was hoping, since Aegis was cut off from society in so many ways, that it might offer a haven from the impending...whatever it is that is about to happen. And I am not the only one. I would venture to say that a large percentage of the entrants to this facility have come for the same reason."

Elias glanced around at the lush vegetation and the ramshackle living quarters. With a tinge of sarcasm in his voice, he queried, "And how's that working for you?"

Wilson laughed. "At first, not bad. I've been here for several years, and for quite a time I was left alone. The sheer space of this facility was enough to allow me the privacy I wanted, and the population seemed quite tolerant of the old kook who wanted to live in the atrium. They didn't mind when I transplanted bushes, plants, and trees from some of the other atria into this plot to augment the existing landscaping. There was more than enough finished space for them to not miss the occasional building material I salvaged from unused portions to use for my shack."

"You said 'at first.' What happened to change things?"

"My gurse."

"Gurse?"

"As I mentioned earlier, my gift and my curse…I call it my gurse."

Elias chuckled.

"I couldn't help but begin to see the developing pattern within these walls."

Elias, knowing where Wilson was going with this train of thought, nodded.

"It is not at all the same pattern as the outside world is experiencing. It is something very different and very ugly. And frighteningly rapid."

"I noticed it, as well."

"I'm sure you did."

"What do you see as the timetable?"

The mathematician stared blankly for a while before answering. Elias felt that he was rerunning the equation or simulation or whatever visualization the man used to arrive at his answers. Finally, he concluded, "It's hard to be certain. I am not one hundred percent comfortable I've identified all of the variables, especially the most recent. Weeks. Maybe days."

"Variables? What is the most recent?"

Wilson again leaned back in the conference room chair, tipped back his mug to drain the last of the tea, and replied, "Why, you, of course."

CHAPTER SIX

"Me? Why am *I* a variable?"

A full-throated laugh erupted from Wilson. As it subsided, he said, "I asked you when we met if you thought me a fool. Elias, you are anything but the usual entrant to this place."

"What do you mean? I'm sure there have been lots of guys just like me who have checked in to Aegis."

Wilson stared hard at his porch companion, his mouth tightly pursed in a look of either frustration or irritation. Elias was not sure if the scientist was trying to read him, or simply deciding his next conversational course. "I was right. The pleasantries are instantly spoilt the moment the dissembling begins. Let me make certain that I understand. You wish me to believe that you are some poor slob who couldn't stand life anymore, so you decided to check in at Hotel Aegis because you didn't have the wherewithal to off yourself?"

Elias said nothing, waiting.

"I don't know why you are here, Mr. Charon. And I am certain that if and when you decide to tell me, I'll be either skillfully misdirected or only partially informed, but I can state one thing with absolute certainty."

"What's that?"

"You, my newfound friend, most certainly have what it takes to kill yourself."

The man's statement required no comment, and Elias did not give one.

"And so, since point number one is that you would not have any trouble whatsoever doing the deed, so to speak, and point number two, as it also became clear to me during our discussion, is that you have a great deal of contempt for Aegis, you would not have made the value decision to come here as a viable alternative to death."

Elias still did not respond, waiting to learn exactly how insightful Wilson was.

"That only leaves one possible explanation. You have come here with a purpose. You have not, yet, told me what that might be. But, whatever it is, it is worthy of banishing yourself to this place for the balance of your life so that you may accomplish it. And, frankly, there are very few things in life people find worthy of that kind of sacrifice – God, country, and a loved one.

"Aegis is an abomination. There is no doubt about that. It probably is an offense against the Almighty, but I don't believe that you are an angel sent down from the heavens to right this particular wrong.

"Aegis was created by our government, and I believe that it serves its purposes as it is; therefore, I think I can tentatively drop country from the list, as well. That leaves a loved one."

Wilson's eyes bored into Elias as he spoke. "Be it a rapist, a killer, or some other vile and wretched subhuman specimen, I can easily see that you would follow that person through the 'gates of hell' for your revenge."

Elias struggled to appear as if he were painfully coming to the decision he had reached earlier. "Your fame is well deserved. You're right. I am after someone."

"I knew it!" Wilson exclaimed, slapping the top of his knee. "Who is it and why?" He took a deep breath to stifle his reaction and, in a more calm voice, added, "Not that it is any of my concern, of course."

"Wilson, I think that if I tell you the *who*, the *why* might be evident."

"Very well, who might it be?"

"No doubt you have heard the name Rudy Kreitzmann."

Elias expected a strong reaction, receiving none.

"Of course I have, but that is old news."

"You know he's here?"

"Certainly. We've spoken."

"You've…?"

"Elias, are you telling me that it is Kreitzmann you're after?"

Elias nodded.

"For what purpose? Oh! You've come to kill him, haven't you?"

Hesitating, unsure of Wilson's feelings about his fellow scientist, Elias said, "No."

"You hesitated. Of course, you must be wondering if he and I are friends. Let's just say, if any value deserves to be removed from the equation, it is Rudy."

Shaking his head, Elias grinned. "I surely cannot figure you out, Wilson. I guess that I don't share your Holmesian abilities."

"Who does?" Wilson remarked immodestly.

Laughing, Elias pressed, "You said you've spoken with him. What about?"

"Before I answer, would you care for more tea? I made a full pot."

"No, thanks. I've still got half a cup."

Wilson stood and returned to the interior of the shack, coming out in less than a minute with his mug again full.

"He thought I would be a good addition to his team."

"Team? Kreitzmann recruited you?"

"Attempted to. I declined. He was persistent, though."

"I thought you were living in Aegis incognito. How did he find you?"

Wilson shrugged. "I don't know. As to my past on the outside, you are only the second person I've told. But he did find me. Walked straight in the door, as did you, and invited me to his lab. That was where he first asked me to join him. I turned him down that day, and he continued to arrive here unannounced, not taking *no* for an answer. He finally gave up weeks ago."

Confusion clouded Elias' thoughts. "I'm afraid I don't understand. He has a lab. He tried to bring you into his fold several times. He gave up weeks ago. It just doesn't add up."

"What doesn't add up?"

"That's a lot for someone to accomplish in three months."

"Three months? What is the significance of that period of time?"

Elias stared at Wilson for a moment before telling him, "That's when Kreitzmann came to Aegis."

"No, it's not! You're mistaken. Rudy has been here for at least five years."

Elias was speechless. This piece of news was the last thing he expected to hear. The moment he did, his stomach began to churn. The implications of what Wilson told him created an entirely new set of potential scenarios, none of which were pleasant, and not the least of those was that Faulk had misled him for some reason.

He saw that Wilson was watching him closely, no doubt continuing to gather clues in his probably unbreakable habit of obtaining and analyzing data. Elias found that his paranoia was percolating at a higher level than normal, certain that this strange man could almost read his mind. Deciding to review the available facts at a later time, when the privacy of his own mind might be more sacrosanct, Elias resumed the conversation. "You said he has a lab. What is he doing there?"

"His usual offenses against God and nature."

"Human experiments?"

"Of course! And since he is operating within the cloistered environs of Aegis, he is unfettered in his experiments."

A distinct chill shivered Elias' spine.

Wilson continued, "And operating within Aegis provides him with a solution to a problem he has struggled with for most of his purulent career."

Listening to the words, the pieces fell into place for Elias, and the picture created was monstrous. "Supply," he said simply, his voice flat.

"Precisely. As he developed his field of expertise, nation after nation, at the very minimum, ejected him from their borders and, at the most extreme, attempted to prosecute Rudy for his work. But now that he operates within a setting which is essentially lawless, he is no longer hounded. And, more important, there is an ever-increasing flow of new subjects walking through that revolving door – people who, from the moment they enter, are cut off from everyone and everything. It is almost as though Aegis was created for the sole reason of suiting his insidious purposes."

"No one will miss them," Elias said. "No one on the outside will know that they've become his lab rats."

"And no one on the inside will even be aware that they've arrived and been nabbed, to use the vernacular."

"When I got here, I was jumped almost immediately by a group of ZooCity goons."

Wilson nodded. "That has been a fairly recent development at Aegis."

"Are they working for Kreitzmann?"

"No. At least to the best of my knowledge. They've begun grabbing the new arrivals, stripping them of anything they might consider to be valuable in Aegis, and then using them for, well, rather sordid purposes."

Elias did not share what he had learned from his surveillance. "So they've been interrupting the supply chain to Kreitzmann."

Nodding, Wilson replied, "I guess you could say they have. I hadn't really thought about that. How did you get past them?"

"I had some help."

Wilson's eyebrow arched questioningly.

"They had the drop on me. I'm not sure what I expected as I came inside Aegis; I guess I wasn't expecting an organized attack. But at the point where the punks had me down, some *thing* intervened. All I saw was a sudden blur of motion; I don't know how else to describe it."

As he said this, Elias was paying close attention to his host's face. There was no change of expression.

"I don't know what it was or where it came from. But one moment I was lying helplessly on the floor about to be killed, and the next moment my attackers were either dead or running away."

"However, you were left untouched?"

"Yes."

"Most odd."

"Do you have any idea what that thing was?"

"I suppose that I might," Wilson answered, pausing to sip from his tea.

"Well?"

"During the incessant entreaties to join him, Rudy felt a need to impress me with his work. His arrogance only allows him to believe that awe, rather than revulsion, would be the reaction from a fellow scientist."

The distaste displayed on Wilson's face contorted his features.

"I despise the fact that my training and expertise places me into the same general cohort as that man! In one of his visits to my little paradise here, Kreitzmann brought a companion, a youngish man, perhaps barely twenty years old. I thought it odd, because Rudy didn't even introduce the gentleman and, in fact, didn't even acknowledge his presence until it served his purpose. And doubly odd was the demeanor of the companion."

"How so?"

"He seemed to be…well…*restrained* I suppose would be the best word, as if he had been exerting every ounce of his mental energy to keep himself from moving. I remember thinking at the time that it was not dissimilar to a person doped up on amphetamines, who was being forced to stand in the corner. His pent-up energy was palpable."

Elias' mind flashed back to that day in Faulk's office when he was shown the video of Kreitzmann's supposed arrival at Aegis. He remembered the men who, in his opinion, accompanied the scientist. Wilson's description came close to describing the odd nature of their movements, which Elias could not define at the time.

"Do you think it was the result of a drug? Is that what Kreitzmann is doing in here? Drug experiments?"

Wilson's face broke into a rueful smile as he said, "If it is, it's a drug I've never read about. While we spoke, and Kreitzmann reached the point in the dialogue when he felt it appropriate to display the fruits of his talents" – his face involuntarily puckered, as though he had bitten into a lemon thinking it was a sweet orange – "Rudy gave a subtle sign to the companion, as he would to a trained animal, and the man simply disappeared."

"Disappeared? Do you mean he left?"

"Oh, he most certainly left, but not in any way discernible to the naked eye."

Elias stared at Wilson, trying to read his eyes for any sign of deceit or insanity. He saw neither. "I don't understand."

"Neither did I. One moment the young man was standing before me, and the next he was gone. We were on this very porch, and the companion was no more than three feet from me. It was bright daylight. There was no trickery, at least that I could detect."

"Where did he go?"

"That is what I asked Kreitzmann. Instead of answering me, he just grinned and looked past my shoulder. As I followed his gaze, I saw the young man standing right over there by the railing, about ten feet behind me."

Elias had no idea what to ask next.

Wilson continued, "You mentioned a blur being visible during your altercation with the gang members. In my countless mental replayings of this event, I believe that I did perceive something like that, but I haven't been certain whether I actually had or whether my mind was manufacturing it to help me digest what I had seen."

"Did Kreitzmann explain what had happened?"

"No! That is a symptom of the contempt he holds for others. Instead of sharing the details of an experiment which could produce such a phenomenon, he merely smirked and told me that if I wished to know how it was done, I would have to join his team! He thought that making me curious would do the trick, as if I were some juvenile.

"From what you've described, it would seem that my visitor on the porch and your intervener would be one and the same."

His mind churning to make sense of this anecdote, Elias asked, "What do you think happened?"

Wilson shrugged. "I have no idea. Are we talking about physical translocation? I am not a theoretical physicist, but my meager knowledge of the field causes me to dismiss that possibility. I don't believe that Scotty aboard the *Enterprise* beamed the man from one part of my porch to another. All that I know about Kreitzmann leads me to the conclusion that he has found a way to alter, modify, enhance…I'm not certain what the correct term would be…humans to the point where they have a new ability. And, I might add, a rather frightening one."

Unable to process this piece of information any further at this time, Elias thought back over the whole of the conversation with Wilson. There was one other point he wanted to clarify.

He leaned forward in his chair, moving closer to his host. "Wilson, at the risk of offending you, are you certain of the timetable?"

The corners of Wilson's eyes crinkled as he smiled at Elias. "You are, no doubt, asking me that question because Kreitzmann has been seen in the outside world during the past five years. And, although I have presented you with a conundrum, you have unwittingly provided me with confirmation of a claim I have pondered for quite some time."

"What is that?"

Gently sighing, a sound barely audible in the tumult of the wind, Wilson explained, "During the aggressive courtship, when Rudy made his repetitive visits to me, he made many offers to entice me. One of them, quite frankly, was a stunner."

Elias waited patiently, accustomed to his companion's delivery.

"Naturally, he bragged about the quality of the lab, the superlative staff at his disposal, all of the other resources. But during his final visit, he told me that if I joined his team, I would be allowed to share a very special privilege…access to the outside world."

"What?"

Recognizing the outburst as rhetorical, Wilson sat back and said nothing.

This new packet of information affected Elias more strongly than the description of the disappearing stranger, for it instantly blazed new paths, new possibilities, new explanations. And what was most disturbing was that all of them led Elias to some very unpleasant conclusions.

He had no idea how long he had sat silently in front of his host. But, finally speaking, Elias quietly said, "I…I am not sure what to think."

Sympathetically, Wilson reached forward and placed his hand on Elias' arm. "It is a bit of a game-changer, isn't it? It seems that whoever built Aegis has given this monster a spare key to the door!"

CHAPTER SEVEN

Charon's mind whirled with possibilities as he pondered the information given to him by Wilson. The statements could only be regarded as revelations – facts, if they were indeed factual – that changed the very underpinnings of his reality insofar as Aegis and Faulk's agency were concerned.

The corridor was empty as he walked, having left Wilson to his lush atrium, with the promise of a prompt return. If what he had been told was true, Elias could not imagine an explanation that did not indicate a complicity between Faulk and Kreitzmann, if not in the present, then surely in the recent past. The ramifications of an association between Kreitzmann and the government were unspeakable. If Faulk and Kreitzmann were connected, why did Faulk send him in here with the assignment he was given?

Mentally shifting gears, Elias thought back over the final questions he had asked Wilson. The scientist had no knowledge of Eric Stone's presence or whereabouts within Aegis. He did, however, provide Elias with directions to Kreitzmann's area within the complex, a route he would soon cautiously follow, right after he completed his detour.

Wilson sat patiently on his porch until he heard the clanging of the cowbell as Elias exited his atrium. For good measure, he waited several more minutes, keenly listening for the telltale sounds of a person moving among the foliage. As a final precaution, he quickly toured the grounds. Seeing no one and hearing nothing but the wind and its effect on the branches and leaves around him, Wilson returned to the interior of the shack, walking across the small main room to a door on the far side. His knuckles rapped twice on the door before he opened it, seeing his friend waiting, holding a pistol aimed at his chest.

"He's gone."

⊙

His base camp appeared to be untouched since his departure. Elias checked the laptop to make certain it was still recording the various audio and video feeds, before he grabbed the item he had returned for, the AK-47. He was not at all convinced that this weapon would be effective against the ghosts – as he was beginning to think of them – which he might encounter, but it made him feel better to have it. Shoving the spare magazines provided by Sweezea into his pockets, he struck out for Kreitzmann's lab.

⊙

Frank D was crouched near the first intersection after the turnstiles, at his usual post. He still simmered over the turn of events, angry that he was working for the Man again.

"This ain't right," he grumbled aloud to no one. The other two members of the ambush party were hiding across the intersection, too far away to hear his muttered comment.

His angry reverie was interrupted by the scuffling of footsteps coming from the entrance. Feeling the jolt of adrenaline that always came as they were about to jump a newbie, he leaned forward and peered around the corner, keeping his head low and close to the edge. There, tentatively walking forward through the graffitied corridor, was a girl who did not look much older than seventeen. She was slender and blond, and he thought to himself that she was just his type. The thought of turning her over to the Man, untouched, reignited his furor.

He had to admit that their artwork on the walls had a powerful impact on nearly everyone who entered. From the moment the newbies emerged from the last turnstile, they knew they were in a foreign land, a zone owned lock, stock, and barrel by the ZooCity locals. The newbies realized that they were interlopers. He knew that the effect was intimidation, and the desired result – fear. By the time the newbies arrived at the first intersection, they were already broken, ready to submit. Their minds had conjured the worst during the short walk, and when he and his two men stepped out, the newbies were ripe and ready.

Right on cue, as she entered the center of the intersection, his two partners stepped out from their hiding place. The young girl let out a strange combination of a gasp and a muffled shriek. Frank D came up behind her as she stood frozen in place, like a deer in the headlights. He grabbed her roughly, his hands traveling to parts of her anatomy now forbidden by their new alliance.

"Please, don't hurt me...let me go," the girl begged weakly.

"Hey, Frank! Stop that. You know the rules," one of the others cautioned, a sudden expression of worry on his face.

"Screw the rules," Frank D snarled, talking to his accomplices as if the girl were not struggling in his arms. "I want this one for me."

"We can't," the other insisted, hoping that he did not see the telltale blur, his eyes darting around the corridors.

As the two men hassled, the young girl thrashed feebly, wrapped inside Frank D's powerful arms, a pathetic whimper coming from her lips. Her movements were less than ineffectual. "They ain't gonna miss one little girl. They'll never even know."

The other stared at their captive, and a glimmer of lust appeared in his eyes. "You don't think so?"

"Hell, no. Who's gonna tell 'em? You?"

The other looked over at their companion, a gang member not known for utilizing, or even possessing, any mental abilities. The silent one shrugged, and the second man turned back to Frank D. "I guess you're right."

A wide smile spread across Frank D's face as he effortlessly lifted the girl and walked her into the nearest room, followed by the two others.

$$\odot$$

Elias followed the directions provided by Wilson. Both Walden and Madison had constructed barriers at the entrances to their enclaves. Thanks to Wilson, he knew the configuration of the entrance, but had no idea what he would encounter, in terms of perimeter security, when he reached the boundary of Kreitzmann's area.

In his mind, Elias visualized the layout of Aegis as a clock face. With the entrance at six o'clock, he knew that ZooCity roughly occupied the seven to eight o'clock portion of the face. Walden was basically in the four to five o'clock region, with Madison filling the two to three o'clock space. The route laid out by Wilson placed Kreitzmann's lab and compound from nine o'clock to approximately eleven o'clock.

It was accessible by not only one of the spoke corridors, as the others were, but by two. With no real reason, Elias had chosen the corridor on the left, and was slowly moving forward. His level of vigilance was at its maximum internal setting, his senses so intensified that the sounds of his breathing and heartbeat seemed amplified, and the noise from each careful footfall was almost like thunder to his ears.

The corridors and hallways were still deserted. Elias was relieved he did not encounter some meandering Aegis resident, fearful that, in his heightened state, he might loose a barrage from the automatic rifle without determining if he or she was even a threat.

He neared the point in the corridor where Wilson said the entrance would be, and was reassured to see that it was set up exactly as described. There was no doorless block barrier as there had been at Walden. Nor was there the offsetting serpentine maze with gun slots which Madison utilized. Instead, there was a simple wall across the corridor with a double door in the center. From his current distance, he could see that there were two peepholes, one in each leaf of the double door.

Since his conversation with Wilson, Elias had decided that a direct approach, with a bit of subterfuge, was probably the best tactic for gaining access to the compound and to Kreitzmann himself. With that in mind, he dropped the cautious air of a soldier on a reconnaissance mission and adopted a casual demeanor. Slinging the rifle over his shoulder, Elias walked directly to the double doors and knocked.

Almost instantly, the doors opened. Elias was surprised to see that he was not greeted by some tough-looking guard, but rather by a young woman who could fit easily into the role of a receptionist at a corporate high rise.

"Can I help you?"

Elias smiled. "I'm here to see Dr. Kreitzmann."

The woman eyed the AK-47. "Of course. But I'm afraid you'll have to relinquish your weapons if you wish to come in."

"Not a problem," Elias answered. "I only armed myself because I hit a few rough patches coming through the facility. I shouldn't think I'd need them now that I'm here."

He unslung the rifle and handed it to her. She took it by gripping the barrel with her thumb and two fingers, as if she were accepting his soiled undergarments. Next, he reached into the pocket of his windbreaker and pulled out the 9mm, relinquishing that, as well.

"Please come in," she said, turning away from him and gingerly placing his weapons on a side table.

Elias stepped through the doorway into a large room, the width of the corridor and at least thirty feet deep. Inside were the side table, a desk with two visitors chairs, and three work cubicles. He noticed that the three cubicles were occupied, two by women and one by a man, all of the occupants at work on something displayed on the computer screens in front of them, none of them paying Elias any heed.

"What's your name?" Elias asked conversationally as the woman turned back to face him.

"Anita. And may I tell the doctor who is calling?"

Grinning at the surreal formality in the midst of Aegis, he answered, "Of course. I'm Patrick Brightman."

If she recognized the name, no indication showed on her face as she shook his hand.

"I'll tell the doctor. Please have a seat." She motioned toward the two chairs at the desk. "It should only be a few minutes."

"Thank you."

She turned and left the room. Elias lowered himself into one of the chairs and waited. He was certain that one of the women at the cubicles was watching him, so he made a point of leaning back in the seat, casually crossing his legs, and staring upward at the ceiling, while showing no interest at all in his surroundings or the paperwork on Anita's desk.

At least ten minutes passed before Elias heard someone approaching. Standing, he saw Rudy Kreitzmann entering the room, followed by Anita. Tall and lean, the scientist was wearing a long-sleeved, powder-blue dress shirt and dark slacks. His hair was cut short in a military style, and he had no moustache or beard. Noticeably, he had the air and demeanor of a confident and competent surgeon.

"Doctor Brightman. A pleasure to meet you."

"The pleasure is mine, Doctor Kreitzmann."

"Please, come with me to my office."

"Thank you."

Kreitzmann turned his head toward the woman. "Thank you, Anita."

"Of course, Doctor." She took her seat at the desk, as Elias followed the scientist down the hallway from which he had emerged.

"And please, sir," Kreitzmann requested as they walked, "we are not all that formal here. I would appreciate it if you would call me Rudy."

"Of course," Elias replied, "and I prefer Patrick over Pat."

"Patrick, it is. If you don't mind my asking, what brings you to Aegis?"

Elias had planned out his response. "Several factors, really. I have admired your work from afar for quite some time."

"Thank you. I am a bit surprised. We never communicated."

Even though they were walking at a brisk pace, Elias attempted to convey embarrassment. "Yes. That's true. I must admit I was somewhat...."

"Afraid," Kreitzmann finished the sentence.

"Yes. I suppose that would be it."

"Don't be concerned. I made many more enemies out there than friends. And you wouldn't be the first to keep your support for my work to yourself. Doing so publicly would have been the kiss of death for you or, at the very least, your funding."

Elias nodded his agreement. "I'm glad you understand. That being said, I came upon a roadblock, a rather substantial one, in my own work, and have been struggling to get past it for quite some time. I have suspected that it is a problem with which you could be of some help."

"I'd be happy to do so. But I have a feeling that there is another reason for your sudden arrival here."

They had been following a meandering route through several turns, and finally arrived at an open doorway with the plaque "Director" beside it. Kreitzmann entered and immediately walked to the large conference table, set off to one side of the large office.

"Please have a seat. Can I get you something to drink?"

Eyeing the glass pitcher on the table, rivulets of condensation running down the sides, Elias answered, "Water would be fine."

Kreitzmann turned over two inverted glasses and filled them both from the pitcher. Elias sat down and was soon joined by the scientist, who took a swivel chair next to him.

"You're right. There was another factor in my decision to exile myself, in a manner of speaking, to Aegis."

Kreitzmann waited silently.

"Throughout my life I have had two things which meant more to me than anything else. Not in the order of priority, my work, of course, was one of them – the other, my wife. It was because of her that I chose the lifestyle that I did."

"I don't understand."

Elias borrowed from his true feelings for his wife and allowed his face to reflect a gamut of emotions as he spoke. "We were so much in love. From the day I met her until...well, until just recently, we were one of those rare couples who are inseparable by choice."

"That is quite rare."

"Yes. Most married folks seem to relish getting away from each other in every way they can. Belinda and I wanted the exact opposite. We would have been perfectly happy being within each other's sight twenty-four hours a day."

"Sounds wonderful."

"It was and, as a result, I never took sabbaticals when I taught. Eventually, I quit teaching, refused all invitations for seminars, workshops...well, you know, all of the demands on a scientist's time that draw him away from home."

Kreitzmann nodded.

"My goal, which I attained, was to obtain private funding and establish a lab at my residence. We bought a ranch outside of Albuquerque and turned one of the outbuildings into a lab. I worked there with Belinda as my partner, helper, and companion. As I told you, I attended no conferences or workshops. Nothing. I'm afraid I essentially became a recluse or a hermit, if you will."

Kreitzmann smiled. "I heard that about you. Bit of a mystery man."

"And in the process, my contempt for my fellow man grew. Rather exponentially, I might add."

The smile leaving his face, Kreitzmann asked, "And your wife? As committed to one another as you are, is she with you here in Aegis?"

Somberly, Elias answered, "No, she's not. I lost her. Three months ago. To cancer."

"I am so very sorry."

"Thank you." Drawing a deep breath, Elias continued, "Losing her caused me to do a great deal of soul searching. I decided that, without her, there was no longer any reason whatsoever to remain…out there. My work had reached an impasse. My reason for living had died with her."

"You mentioned that you came to me for help with your work. How did you know I was in Aegis?"

"I didn't. I came to Aegis for the same reason so many others come here. It wasn't until after I arrived that I discovered your presence. The news sparked something in me, and I realized that I did still want to complete my research, if only to give Belinda and myself the satisfaction of doing so."

Elias expected to be asked from whom he had heard about Kreitzmann living in Aegis, but the man seemed comfortable with the fact.

"I understand. And please accept my sincere sympathy for your loss."

"Thank you very much."

"I never married," Kreitzmann continued, without the slightest show of emotion accompanying his statement, "so I never knew the love and connection that you described. I have been a slave to my research since my college days. I envy what you had, even though it ended the way that it did."

"I wouldn't trade those years for anything in the world."

"I can tell that."

Slapping the tops of his thighs with his hands, Kreitzmann changed the subject. "I'm certain that you are eager to discuss your obstacle, as it were. However, I would like to offer you a tour of our facility. Perhaps you will see a niche that needs to be filled by a man of your talent and knowledge."

"I would enjoy that."

$$\odot$$

Elias stood between Kreitzmann and a lab technician with the name Bonillas stitched above the pen pocket of her white lab coat. In front of them was a twenty-foot-long one-way mirror which allowed viewing into a room filled with children. The youngsters, ages ranging up to approximately nine, to Elias' eye, were scattered about the large room, which resembled a well-equipped day-care center. Some sat at desks or at a large table; some were on the floor. All seemed occupied with toys, coloring books, or other objects. At first glance the scene appeared normal to Elias; then he noticed that there was no talking between or from any of the children.

Before he could ask a question, Kreitzmann commenced, "Doctor Bonillas, why don't you explain to Doctor Brightman what we are accomplishing here."

"Of course, sir. This is our language enhancement lab."

"Language enhancement? None of them are speaking."

Elias had turned away from the view to look at Bonillas as he spoke, and noticed a slight grin curl the corners of her mouth in reaction to his comment.

"There are many methods of communication. Speaking is only one of them. We are attempting to utilize the human mind's tendency to adapt as our primary tool for the development of alternate communication skills."

"You're too modest, Doctor Bonillas," Kreitzmann broke in. "I would hardly describe the success you've had here as an attempt."

"Thank you, sir."

"I'm afraid I still don't understand."

"It's really quite simple," she explained. "Years of study and research, which preceded our work, established that if the body is deprived of one sense...sight, for example...the other senses are enhanced, to varying degrees, of course."

"This is true."

"Doctor Kreitzmann theorized that if that occurred with senses, why not with abilities?"

Elias felt a slight tensing of his neck muscles as he figured out the direction of this work. He struggled to maintain his composure, as well as his cover of a disenchanted scientist who held mankind in contempt. "Fascinating." His single-word comment sounded sincere to his ears.

Kreitzmann once again broke in, "As I'm sure you've already discerned, this path of study fits in quite nicely with my overall thesis for the human race."

"I confess that I am not all that familiar with your underlying principle."

The man puffed up, obviously appreciative of the opportunity to expound. "I have always believed that so much of what we are capable of doing – in fact, so much of what we *are* – is conditioned by the environment."

"The Earth?"

The scientist smirked. "No, by 'the environment,' I mean the society, the human beings around us."

"I'm not certain that I understand."

Gesturing toward the group on the other side of the glass, Kreitzmann explained, "This is a perfect example. I have no doubt that our physiology provides for several methods of communication at the point we are born. It is only because we are immediately surrounded by babbling fools, people who exclusively utilize speech as the sole means to communicate, that we opt for the path of least resistance and succumb to it ourselves."

"Of what other forms of communication do you believe we are capable?"

Triumphantly, Kreitzmann proclaimed, "Telepathy, for one."

"You're not serious?"

"Oh, but I am, Patrick. Do you realize how many times nonverbal, and by that I mean psychic, communication has been documented in the laboratory? The incidence of successful communication far exceeds the mathematical probabilities. And yet, the scientific community continues to ridicule the study of the phenomenon, casting any researcher who dares to follow this path as fringe and a nutcase!"

Elias said nothing, waiting.

"Certainly, you are familiar with the work done in the past demonstrating the criticality of exposure to certain stimuli at early ages."

"I am. The one which comes to mind is the study of musical ability."

"An excellent example. If a child is exposed to music and encouraged to play instruments at a very early age, his or her ability to truly master the instruments increases dramatically. And the lifelong ability to learn new instruments is substantially enhanced, as well."

"True."

"And the converse is true. If a child matures without the exposure to music, the part of the brain which would be dedicated to this skill is assigned to other tasks and skills."

"I've read that."

"What we are doing here is developing and encouraging the skill to communicate psychically."

Forcing an expression of neutral interest onto his face, Elias asked, "How are you doing that?"

The smug grin returning to his face, Kreitzmann explained, "We are utilizing the same learning technique for this field that we have perfected in several others. We create a perfect environment for fostering a skill and immerse the child in it from birth."

It took all of Elias' will power to stop himself from strangling the madman on the spot. Instead, maintaining his cover, he painted a smile across his face and remarked, "Immersion from birth? Amazing. And the results?"

"I'll let Dr. Bonillas answer that."

The woman, who had been standing silently beside them through the dialogue, began to speak. "Our progress has been slow, of course, due to the pace at which human children grow and mature."

"Of course."

"But we are obtaining a rather rapid increase in skill levels now that we are in Phase Two."

"Phase Two?"

Elias was astounded by the detachment displayed by Bonillas as she continued. "Phase One, where we began, was limited by the fact that we were forced to utilize a virtual reality. Although this formula has performed well in other arenas of our research, the concept of telepathy did not lend itself as well to the modality, due to the lack of definitive feedback."

"I'm not really up to speed on the virtual reality you mentioned…."

"Of course," she interrupted. "I'm sorry. We created a room where the infants were first raised."

"This room?" Elias asked, pointing at the area beyond the glass.

"No. This is the Phase Two room. In Phase One, the virtual reality which surrounded the newborns contained no spoken language."

"None? So the infants were tended to by adults who were not allowed to speak?"

"Yes, in part. They were not only barred from speaking, they were forbidden to respond to any verbal communication."

"Including crying?"

"Including crying."

"Weren't some reactions involuntary?"

"Very perceptive," Kreitzmann noted. "We noticed that the caregivers were reacting to verbal stimuli against their conscious will, so we corrected this problem by using only caregivers who were completely deaf."

This conversation was becoming more of a test of Elias' self-control than he had anticipated. Unable to say anything at the moment, he merely nodded.

Bonillas picked up where Kreitzmann had left off. "What we were able to accomplish in Phase One was an intensification of the urge within the infants to communicate. We then exploited that urge with an example which, quite frankly, was a wild guess as to how telepathy worked."

"Now, Doctor Bonillas, I think I would call it an educated guess."

Glancing over at her boss, she corrected herself, "An *educated guess* as to how telepathy worked. As it turned out, we were closer than we thought."

Elias found his voice. "How so?"

"We had decided, after reviewing the available research, as well as the anecdotal evidence in the record, that telepathic communication is symbolic, rather than communication which possesses a vocabulary or grammatical rules."

"Graphic or pictographic?"

"Graphic," she replied.

"So," Elias asked, "if little Bobby wanted to convey that he was hungry, he visualized eating."

"Exactly. And, from what we can tell, very specific imagery. He would not only visualize eating, but would visualize what he wanted – an apple, for example. And not just a generic apple, but a very precise image of a green apple."

"Interesting."

"But Phase One was horribly frustrating. We were shooting in the dark, to coin a phrase. We had no idea if we were making any progress."

"Why is that?" Elias inquired dutifully.

"We weren't in the loop. We were observing the subjects as they appeared to develop the skills, but we had no way of monitoring, or listening in, to see if they really were."

"Why didn't you bring in psychics? Wouldn't that have given you an adult who could provide you with insights into their progress?"

"We tried that," Kreitzmann interjected. "I believe the field is filled with charlatans who pretend to possess the skill. Due to the, uhmm, unique issues associated with bringing people into Aegis, we were somewhat limited in our selection. Either way, they were no help at all."

"I see."

With a dismissive wave of the hand, Kreitzmann resumed, "Be that as it may, now that we are in Phase Two, we know that we were on the right track."

"Why is that?"

Bonillas explained, "The Phase One subjects are now old enough to work with the newest additions to the clinical test. By reason of their age and relative maturity, we can now not only observe, we can question and evaluate."

Elias raised a single eyebrow questioningly.

With a slight smile, Bonillas elaborated, "We have taken some of the most promising subjects from Phase One and taught them to speak. Now that they have developed the desired skill, they are learning to communicate with us using speech as a second language, as it were."

"They are your interpreters?"

"Correct."

"With their feedback we are able to determine that our experiment is working. We are succeeding in developing a group of telepaths."

"Amazing!" Elias exclaimed, trying to sound genuinely enthusiastic. He turned his eyes away from Bonillas and looked through the glass. He now realized that on the other side were children, from infants up to the age of elementary school, who had probably never heard a spoken word. As he watched, he noticed that they were, in some ways, behaving normally. They were engaged in parallel playing, coloring, building with blocks, and the other activities so typical of children in this age group.

However, as he watched closely, he saw a young boy, perhaps five years old, who was sitting on the floor in one corner of the large room, assembling what appeared to be a bridge out of wooden building blocks. Elias watched him closely as the boy rummaged through the available pieces piled next to his project. After not finding what he sought, he glanced around the room, his eyes stopping at a location where another boy, slightly younger, was also working with blocks. Almost instantly, the younger boy picked up a long, green, flat board from his assortment of pieces and stood, walking the board to the first child and handing it to him. The entire process was completed without a word spoken.

"Astounding, isn't it?" As Kreitzmann asked him the question, Elias realized that Bonillas and Kreitzmann had also been watching.

Elias nodded without answering.

"We see examples of that every day, and many of them much more complex and definitive than what you just observed."

Elias remained silent, yet his mind whirled with images of kicking down the door which separated him from these children, gathering them up, and taking them out of Aegis, away from this laboratory and these people.

No sooner had the thought formed than one of the oldest girls in the lab, who had been idly playing with a dollhouse, suddenly jerked her head toward the glass, her eyes fixing directly on Elias, and an expression of extreme fear transforming her face. Despite the fact that the glass wall was a one-way mirror, the little girl continued to stare at Elias and raised her arm, pointing her finger directly at him.

Immediately, all of the other children in the lab turned to stare in his direction, their faces running the gamut from concerned to terrified.

"What happened?" Elias asked innocently. He turned away from the accusatory stares and saw that Kreitzmann was watching him closely.

"You must remember, these children are all telepaths with various levels of skill. What were you thinking a moment ago?"

This was all so new to Elias. He was accustomed to concealing his thoughts from normal people, but not a group who could literally read his mind.

Manufacturing an embarrassed grin, Elias concentrated on clearing his mind and said, "Honestly, the boldness of this research put me off for a moment. I was feeling sorry for these children. I'm afraid my mind wandered to a scenario where I would scoop them all up in my arms and take them out of here."

"That is a normal reaction." As Bonillas spoke, Elias noticed that Kreitzmann was still eyeing him skeptically.

"How we treat children in our world is so hard-wired into us that, at first, creating this environment for them seems harsh and cruel. But I think you saw from their reaction that the thought of being removed from here, and being thrust into the society outside, terrifies them."

"I did see that."

"And there are really two reasons for that terror, as far as we can tell. The first is that they are comfortable here. It is their home, and the world outside Aegis is a big unknown for them. Most children are frightened by the unknown."

"And the second?"

Before she could answer, Kreitzmann interceded. "Would you want to live in a world where you could read everyone's mind?"

Elias chuckled. "There would be some upside to it, but no, I don't think I would."

"Neither would they, at least not in a society where people, in the privacy of their own heads, feel free to be as harsh and cruel as they want."

"Aren't you creating a group of people who can never fit in?"

"Fit in? If you're talking about fitting in with the despicable environment outside these walls, I suppose you're right. But what I...we are creating is a new society. Once there are enough of them," Kreitzmann posited while motioning toward the children in the other room, "they can have their own society, a society without the hateful, mean-spirited aspect of humanity that terrifies them. You see, Patrick, that's really the point of all of this. So much of what we simply chalk off as human nature doesn't have to be. It is only human nature due to the paths we've taken in the past. On a different path, a path where *everyone* knows what everyone else is thinking, the world would be a better place; we will have essentially shut down the festering incubator called 'the privacy of our own thoughts,' from which so many evil beliefs and deeds spring.

"I believe that human nature will naturally choose a better course than it has, if we merely remove a few of the self-imposed limitations. With those gone, then our own normal adaptability will cause us to evolve into a more enlightened race."

There was nothing Elias could say and still maintain his cover, so he decided to focus on the details of the experiment. "But haven't there been small children outside the Aegis environment who have been deprived of verbal input in the past, by accident? Did they develop telepathic skill?"

"We wouldn't know," Kreitzmann stated. "If it occurred, they were probably isolated, not in a group who were all going through the same thing. And if they did exhibit the skill, but it wasn't reinforced as they aged, it would be abandoned or lost. The Phase One environment didn't just deprive them of verbal communication, it also set an example that telepathic communication was probably occurring, an example which would not have been present in the outside environment."

Elias' interest was stirred. "Set an example?"

"Yes. Using the same technique we've successfully utilized in other experiments, we created the virtual reality I mentioned earlier. Although we couldn't provide actual telepathic input to the children, we immersed them into interactions between others, actors really, who *appeared* to be communicating nonverbally. The subjects observed this example and came to the conclusion that it was the way to communicate. Their minds took it from there."

"What I don't understand...."

Kreitzmann interrupted. "This is only one of many projects I wish to show you, Patrick. After you get settled in, you may return and spend as much time as you like with Doctor Bonillas."

A brief look of disappointment crossed Bonillas' face as Elias replied, "Of course. It's just that this is fascinating."

Kreitzmann grinned. "If you think so, wait until you see the rest."

CHAPTER EIGHT

After they stepped out of Bonillas' lab and closed the door, Kreitzmann turned to Elias. "What you've just seen is our newest venture, and certainly the most embryonic, insofar as the progress we've made."

As he spoke, he led Elias to a small alcove in the hallway, where he motioned for him to take a seat at a small conference table.

When they were both seated, Elias remarked, "That was quite impressive."

"Thank you. At the time it was proposed, I admit I was a bit skeptical. Although I firmly believe that the human body is vastly underutilized, as a result of growing up and developing with a lowest-common-denominator environment surrounding it, the psychic, or telepathic, facility seemed outlandish even to me."

"I can understand that."

"However, what it demonstrates is our underlying technique and driving philosophy. The presumption of science, and mankind in general, has been that evolution and human development constitute an upward linear path, that each step taken by every organism is a step toward improvement – betterment, if you will – of the species."

"You don't believe that?"

"I don't. Patrick, look around you. Not in here, but the outside world. Does it look to you as if we, as a species, are striving for perfection? No, my theory is that both evolution in the long term, and human development in the short term will always take the path of least resistance. That path is not the route to betterment, but the road to mediocrity."

"So you think Darwin was wrong?"

Kreitzmann laughed, the sound echoing off the walls of the empty corridor they sat beside. "No, I don't. I think he was right. That's the problem. He was too right."

"Then I am really confused."

"As are most, at first. This confusion stems from the fact that almost everyone tends to forget the very basic element of Darwin's work: procreation, pure and simple, the making of offspring. It is the biological imperative to reproduce. That's the cornerstone of his theory. The only mention of our development, our progress toward becoming something better, is if it benefits us in obtaining a mate and successfully having a litter of children."

Elias had to admit to himself that the man was persuasive. His expectation of this meeting was, in his own mind, something out of a cheap science fiction movie, with Kreitzmann playing the role of the mad scientist, not that his cold exploitation of infants for the purposes of his research was not sufficient to firmly plant him in the category of "monster." It did. But Elias found him to be soft spoken, almost gentle in his approach to the topic. There was no psychotic, fanatical fire in his eyes, no imperious air in his demeanor. Elias did not sense a "God complex" from the scientist, simply an attitude of firm conviction.

"Rudy, there are those who do excel in our society."

"Yes, there are, including you, Patrick. But look at your own choices. Immersing yourself in a community which is biologically hard-wired to do nothing more noble than have children...is a distraction, at best. Remember, you felt a need to escape it to be able to focus on your work."

"I don't know...."

"Think back to middle school and high school. When I attended those stellar institutions, I was called 'brain,' as though it was an insult. I'm sure that you, too, were one of the 'brains' in that environment."

Elias nodded that he was; this answer was true both for his cover as well as for himself.

"Did that make you the most popular guy in school?"

It was Elias' turn to laugh. "No. More like the least popular, until exam time came around, that is. Then all of the girls wanted to get together with me. But we are sounding like a couple of whining geeks, complaining that the jocks got the girls."

"Geeks whine for good reason. That's my point. If evolution were a process that pushed or pulled the human race toward higher plateaus, would the females in high school be hard-wired to prefer the male who could throw the football, rather than the male who could calculate its trajectory?"

"I guess that depends on what you view as a higher plateau. Evolutionarily, it would produce better football players."

"I suppose you're right," Kreitzmann acknowledged, chuckling, "but I'm sure that you see my point. All of society is geared to encourage, produce, and even glamorize an act that is one of our most base, an act that essentially every animal and insect on the planet can perform. We eat. We sleep. We void ourselves of bodily waste. And we have sex and make babies. The message to people is basically this: Once that is done, once you have produced another baby, the evolutionary bells and whistles go off, considering that you've won the jackpot. You've accomplished what thousands of years of evolution directed you to do to fulfill your destiny. You're done, other than feeding the children, clothing them, and providing them with shelter – in other words, safely delivering them to the age of reproduction themselves.

"You see, that's the problem, Patrick. Natural selection has worked too well. We are now up to our eyeballs in population. We have geared our entire society toward quantity, not quality. There is no social pressure to become a better human being. There is certainly no biological pressure to do so, either."

"That seems a little harsh, Rudy. There are expectations. There are rewards for excellence."

"There were!" Kreitzmann almost shouted. "Certain segments of the population have made attempts in the past. There was a class system – not perfect, by any means, but an attempt to create a distinction between the rutting rabble and those who were men of letters. Partially as a result of the abuses perpetrated by this upper class, but mostly due to the tremendous social pressure from the lower group, this system, this distinction, is erased and, in the minds of many, a cause of shame and embarrassment.

"Now, it has become out of vogue to place a person such as you, a person who holds a doctorate, in higher regard than one may hold a factory worker, or even a prostitute."

Elias took a deep breath and let it out slowly before responding. "I understand what you are saying, Rudy. We may differ on the degree, but I do see some merit in your viewpoint."

"You'd have to, Patrick. You are far too intelligent to not."

"Are you attempting to counter all of this, here in Aegis?"

"I am. We are. My first attempts were in more normal settings such as universities and privately funded labs. But we could never obtain the lack of interference from the culture, true control over the control group, that we desired. Aegis is perfect."

"Is it your goal to create a mini-culture within these walls? One that reinforces your vision for mankind?"

A boyish grin came to Kreitzmann's face. "You make me sound as though I have a God complex. This is not," he declared, sweeping his arm around, "an attempt to manufacture a race which complies with some preconceived vision. This is an ongoing experiment to discover what those latent capabilities might be. At some point, more than likely without any input from me, a vision for a mini-culture, as you put it, will be reached by consensus. At that point, Aegis can become a seed, an incubator, for a better mankind."

"Why without any input from you? And a consensus reached by whom?"

"I'll answer your second question first. The consensus can only be reached by those who have attained the plateaus, so to speak. And the answer as to why I wouldn't be involved is quite simple. I could no more understand things from their perspective than an ant crawling across the floor could understand this conversation. How could I possibly contribute anything meaningful to the dialogue?"

Elias was, again, surprised by Kreitzmann's candor and almost self-deprecating perspective. "How will you achieve all of this?"

"At first we will break it down into component skills. The telepathy you witnessed...the other experiments you will see soon. Each one focuses on one aspect or one skill of the human experience. The process will have some successes and some failures. The successes will be kept and moved forward...in a sense, graduated; the failures will be abandoned. As we build a pool of subjects who are superior to the norm in each category, we then move on to Phase Three."

"Phase Three?"

Leaning back in his chair, Kreitzmann tucked his hands behind his head in a relaxed pose. "Explaining Phase Three at this point would be premature. I haven't really described the first two phases or our underlying principles."

"Okay."

"We in this complex believe that the body, given a consistent example, will simply not know any better and will follow that example."

"Certainly there are limitations."

"There are, of course. But they are far higher than the level at which we all now operate. Most of our limitations are learned."

With a slight grin, Kreitzmann asked Elias, "Do you know what is used in circuses to restrain an elephant?"

"I would guess a steel cable of some sort, and a substantial anchor point to which it is attached."

The grin broadened. "Actually, they use a regular piece of rope, tied around one of the hind legs of the beast, with the other end fastened to a wooden stake pounded into the ground."

"Any elephant could easily break that or pull it loose."

"Of course it *can*. But it *won't*."

"Why?"

"From the time it was a baby elephant, that is exactly how it has been secured. As a baby, an elephant tugs and pulls constantly at the rope and stake, struggling with all of its might. But it is not able to budge the stake or break the rope. It *learns* that it can't do it. Later, as it grows and becomes strong enough to easily either break the rope or pull out the stake, it *never* tries because it *knows* it can't."

"I didn't know that."

"It's true. Here's another example. Beta fighting fish are natural territorial enemies. Anyone who owns an aquarium knows that if you put two in the tank, they will fight to the death."

"True."

"An experiment was done where two Betas were put into a tank, but they were separated by a pane of glass. The glass was invisible to them, but they could see each other. They would both repeatedly slam themselves into the glass, trying to get at the other, trying to fight, until they both eventually learned they couldn't do it. They stopped trying. At that point, the glass was removed. The barrier was gone. Yet for the rest of their lives, they never once tried to cross that middle point of the tank; they had learned earlier that it was impossible."

"Is that true? They would never cross the line for the rest of their lives?"

"Never. And there are many other similar anecdotes and experiments which contain the same lesson, experiments using all sorts of animals. These experiments have been described by motivational speakers for years, trying to explain to eager salesmen and middle managers that our limitations are self-imposed."

"Did these experiments put you on your path of interest?"

"Actually, no. There were two events in my personal life which set my course, one small and the other quite significant.

"The first occurred when I was a boy of nine or ten. We had a dog, a springer spaniel, which stayed outside in our backyard. The yard was surrounded by a block wall, six feet high; and, for years, Sneezix was perfectly happy in his environment. Then, one day I looked out one of our rear windows into the yard and saw that there was another dog with Sneezix. They were playing and romping together, and I assumed that my sister must have left our gate open. I went out back. My arrival spooked the stray dog, and he quickly ran across the length of the yard, directly at the block wall. I was certain he was going to turn at the last moment, that he was simply panicked and was running mindlessly. Instead, right in front of me, this small dog, perhaps the size of a beagle, scampered up the face of the wall and over the top.

"I had never seen a dog do this before. He didn't jump the wall. He couldn't. With a running start, he just scratched and clawed his way up and over. I checked the gate and it was closed and locked, so obviously the stray had entered in the same fashion.

"I realized later than Sneezix had also never seen such a feat, but he only needed to see it once because he instantly attempted the same thing. He ran. With a sound of his nails against the block wall, he tried to scratch his way to the top. He fell back, got up, and tried it again. I watched, fascinated. He did not stop. He did not rest. Despite the fact that his paws were soaked with blood, over and over again he tried, getting slightly higher each time. Within an hour, he made it over the top.

"From that day forth, we were unable to keep him contained in the yard. His repeated forays into the neighborhood resulted in our having to pick him up from the dog pound twice. We trimmed his nails almost to the quick, thinking it would stop him. It didn't. We chained him with a long chain, only to have a neighbor spot Sneezix hanging on the outside of our wall, his hind paws not quite touching the ground. Our spaniel had clambered over the wall, even while chained. The neighbor lifted him and unhooked the chain, bringing him to us. That poor dog, nearly dead, lay panting mightily for twenty minutes before he got up and scooted right over the wall.

"Eventually, the dog catcher picked him up a third time, and my father refused to pay the fee. I never saw Sneezix again. But what I learned from the whole fiasco was that it only took one example from the stray dog to show Sneezix that something was possible, something he didn't believe was possible a moment before. And once he saw it, he wouldn't rest until he did it himself. That lesson never departed; it was always in the back of my mind, unformed and unfulfilled until I attended university. It was my personal involvement in an attempt to replicate a well-documented feat from the distant past that crystallized my theory."

Elias said nothing, waiting.

"The physical prowess of men from a thousand or more years ago has been recorded in song, story, picture, and poem countless times – descriptions of the rowing of warships, athletic competitions, voyages, battles. The historical record is rich with very detailed accounts which have provided measurable and replicable feats.

"Take the simple act of throwing a rock. Going back as far as cave paintings, there are depictions of hunters who understood the necessity of staying far enough away from dangerous beasts in order to remain alive. It was the desire for distance that eventually resulted in the perfection of firearms. But the primitives used rocks. From the pictographic evidence, we surmised that they would sneak up on tigers or other beasts, perhaps as the animals slept or ate a kill, and the men would hurl a rock, dealing a stunning, if not fatal, blow. Apparently, the vast majority of the human race has lost the ability to throw with the distance, force, and accuracy it once possessed, when that was an integral part of the hunting or defense regimen."

"Vast majority? There are some who can still perform at that level?"

"There are. There are small pockets of primitive tribes who have, within their group, men who possess a throwing ability which far exceeds that of our greatest baseball pitchers today, in terms of speed, accuracy, and distance."

"I wasn't aware of that."

"It's true. The documentation is plentiful. However, it was rowing which truly captured my attention."

"Rowing?"

"Yes. During college, I was quite involved in athletics, including the rowing team. A notice was posted on campus, asking for volunteers to replicate an ancient voyage. A professor studying the Athenian culture had obtained, from several sources, adequate plans so that he could replicate a trireme."

"A trireme?"

"An Athenian warship, thirty-seven meters long, which was propelled by three levels of oarsmen. There are nearly countless descriptions of voyages taken by these vessels, with much detail. A particular voyage the professor wanted to replicate occurred when the Athenians wished to quell a revolt in Mytilene, on the island of Lesbos in the Aegean. At first, the assembly ordered that all Mytilene's males be put to death. They immediately sent off a trireme to accomplish this. A day later they had second thoughts and ordered another trireme to catch the first before it could arrive and carry out the order. The second ship, with 170 oarsmen, would have made the journey in approximately twenty-four hours.

"So, this professor knew the distance and had constructed an exact replica of a trireme. All he needed were the oarsmen – thus, the posted notice. Many of the members of the rowing team, having recently come off from winning a national championship, were enchanted with the prospect of competing with an ancient record, as were several other athletes. He had no problem filling the roster with a group of young men in amazing physical condition. His plan was to transport the trireme to the Aegean and replicate the exact route, but first he wanted to test it out with his new crew.

"Since the size and configuration of the boat was so different from the sleek and lightweight boats to which we were accustomed in competitions, we spent four months training with the replica of the trireme. The regimen was rigorous and was supervised by a team of three Olympic coaches. During the course of our first trial, we were cohesive as a team and at the peak of our performance. The weather was perfect and the sea was calm, ideal conditions to go against an ancient record."

"I'm guessing that the record wasn't beaten."

A short laugh, not unlike the bark of a dog, burst from Kreitzmann. "*Beat* the record? Not only could we not beat it, we couldn't tie it. In fact, we couldn't even come close."

"You're not serious?"

"I am! The best we did was less than half the distance the ancient Athenian ship traveled that day in a twenty-four-hour period."

"Less than half?"

"Less than half! And according to the descriptions of the event by historians of the day, they did it with one crew of oarsmen. Those descriptions must be true; there was physically not enough room on a trireme to accommodate a second shift of men on board. We had a total of 350 oarsmen, enough for two shifts with a few extras in case of injuries. A modern yacht paced the trireme to transfer the two crews. We rowed in six-hour shifts, with six hours to rest. The ancients did it with one crew and, when they arrived at the destination, the rowing crew had to be in a condition strong enough to then engage in battle."

"That's astounding."

"It's more than astounding; it's revelatory. The scientific community began to theorize as to why there would be such a disparity between these men of the past and our best athletes today. The theories have ranged from society coddling us so that we no longer need the same abilities, to actually putting forth the idea that our genetics have changed in a mere few thousand years. Preposterous!

"That event, intended as a pleasant and challenging diversion for me, triggered what would become the focus of the rest of my life. I immediately began researching any and all comparable efforts. Everything I discovered led me to one inescapable conclusion."

He paused. Uncertain if the pause was for dramatic effect, or if Kreitzmann was waiting for a question, Elias remained silent.

"The eternal question among evolutionary biologists and others is – is it *nature* or *nurture*? How much of who and what we are is genetic, and how much is a result of the environment?"

"True. You seem to have opted for nurture."

"We have certainly placed our emphasis on the environment. Saying that, however, does not paint the entire picture. Genetics would only be genetics. It is the canvas upon which we paint our reality, its borders establishing the outside boundaries of what we can do. But to actualize ourselves, we need more than a blank canvas. We need examples, as Sneezix needed the example of that stray dog, in order to discover an ability he did not know he had. This goes far beyond the simple concept of nurture. I call my field *exemplarium* behavior modeling.

"Wasn't the performance of the Athenian oarsman an example?"

"No. Hearing about something…reading about it…any form of learning and awareness other than direct experience does not have the same effect. At least that is my conclusion after twenty-three years of study. It is essential for the behavior, skill, or ability to be directly perceived. Mankind has a nearly boundless ability to deny and rationalize. Remember the repetitive attempts by Sneezix – the painful falls, the bloody paws. Transfer that experience to a man and, if he hadn't seen the deed with his own eyes, he would give up, deciding that it wasn't really possible after all."

"That's probably true."

"Not *probably* true…true. I've proved it in my studies."

"Other than the display of telepathy, what are the applications of your new field?"

"They are almost limitless. Think about it, Patrick. My work has only scratched the surface. There is probably no aspect of what we do, see, hear, smell, or even think that can't be enhanced by immersion in a new exemplarium."

Forcing a look of mild skepticism onto his face, Elias spoke thoughtfully. "I admit, I'm impressed by the apparent strides toward telepathy that you've made. But I have a concern."

Visibly suppressing vexation at Elias' words, the researcher inquired, "What might that be?"

Elias knew he was walking a tightrope. On one hand, he was portraying an ostensibly like-minded scientist who had previously exhibited a dislike or even contempt for humanity. On the other hand, his own urge to shout out his rebuttals to Kreitzmann's positions was practically overwhelming.

Choosing his words carefully, Elias broached the subject. "Have you considered the possibility that, over the entire continuum of human development on Earth, some of what you are coaxing from your subjects has already been tried and rejected?"

It was obvious, by the evasive darting of his eyes and momentary quizzical expression, that Kreitzmann had not considered this point.

"What do you mean?"

"I haven't seen nor have we discussed the specifics of your other projects;

however, expressly dealing with the one I've observed, what if we weren't meant to have telepathic abilities?"

"Oh, not the old 'If God meant for us to fly, we'd have wings' argument."

"Not exactly, Rudy. What I'm saying is that it is possible that at one time humans, or earlier hominids, did communicate with their minds. If the mechanism is already there, why not?"

"Go on."

"What if there was something inherently counterproductive about it? I'll give you an example. Perhaps very early man was a loner, rather than tribal, and perhaps this early man could read minds. In such a situation, I can see how the ability would be quite beneficial and there would be very little, if any, downside. Any other human being he or she encountered would be a territorial threat. Reading the mind of the other to know what was planned would be an obvious positive. The better at it the individual was, the higher the probability would be to vanquish the other and survive.

"But as man evolved and it became obvious that there were numerous benefits to banding together and forming primitive societies, the invasiveness of telepathy might have hindered that direction, might have suddenly become a detriment. Every time a fellow tribesman lusted after another's wife, there would have been conflict and strife within the group. Every time one felt envious of another's cave or tree or food stock, there would have been problems and mistrust. I think that tribal life would have created a need to take the other members at face value, to rely upon what they decided to speak, rather than what they thought. It allowed, in a sense, humans to install a filter between their spontaneous thoughts and urges, and their deliberately spoken words and consciously thought-out deeds. Darwinian selection would have given the tribes without telepathy an advantage of social cohesion, which could have eventually dampened the ability to the point where it is now.

"In other words, maybe it's been tried and the human race decided they didn't like it. You could, in effect, be opening an old can of worms."

Throughout Elias' entire speech, Kreitzmann sat calmly, absorbing his words. With the final comment, he replied, "You could be right. I hadn't considered that possibility. But" – he placed the palms of his hands flat upon the table – "it isn't our purpose to second-guess. The point of our research is to uncover the buried or underdeveloped skills and bring those out. It will be up to them to retain or discard as they see fit."

"Them?"

"The beneficiaries of our work."

CHAPTER NINE

The discussion ended, Kreitzmann once again led Elias through a maze of interconnecting hallways. As they walked, the scientist, sounding more like a tour guide than an amoral monster, pointed out each of the labs they passed, and what work was being conducted in each.

"This is our computer interface lab. In this module, we are immersing subjects in computer code, rather than English."

"What is your goal here?"

"Our goal with every one of our projects is the same. Just as a chemist creates compound after compound, testing each one until he finds a formula with the desired properties, we make no value judgment with regard to each possibility. We merely develop every conceivable skill which has the potential for benefiting from exemplarium immersion, and then we throw it into the mix. We only attempt to discover if a skill, ability, or talent is possible. Once that is done, it will be up to the group to retain or discard the newly uncovered ability.

"In this project, we are taking a different approach from the human/computer interface labs, as well as the artificial intelligence labs. They are all struggling to make computers adapt and comply with us. Where they continue to run afoul is with the sloppy nature of our thoughts and languages. The very nature of the computer is that it is logical and precise. Everything is black and white, on or off. With humans, everything is gray. Attempting to create a true bridge between them is not possible as long as those two facts are true. Computer engineers have gone further and further afield in an attempt to make computers more like us, with fuzzy logic and so on. We are approaching the same problem from the other side. Here, we are raising a group of subjects who know only the logical and precise language of the computer. They also live in an environment where only black-and-white, logical behavior and criteria in their day-to-day living are rewarded. Patrick, you will be astounded at the ability these subjects have to interface with the computers."

"As you are doing in the telepathy lab, are you teaching them English once they have mastered code as their first language?"

"No need. There are a variety of off-the-shelf software programs that accomplish that for us."

"Word processing?"

"Exactly. That is the beauty of humans communicating in code. With a viable human/computer interface, which we've already perfected, all that is needed is to open a word processing program, and we can talk directly to the subjects and they can answer. With text-to-speech programs, we can easily converse with them."

"The interface? What type of terminal do you utilize?"

"Not a terminal. No keyboard. No mouse. The interface is direct."

"Direct? Do you mean...?"

"Implants with connect/disconnect jacks. The subjects can plug in or unplug as they wish, although we've noticed that their desire to unplug is quite rare."

They had walked well past the computer interface lab. The door had been closed, so Elias' mind, without benefit of a glimpse inside, was free to run rampant, creating a surreal scene of these young children with shaved heads and USB ports embedded in their skulls, wires dangling. He felt, once again, the surge of adrenalin which would normally be the precursor to a violent physical attack on Kreitzmann. With a monumental exertion of will power, Elias tamped down his furor and continued walking beside this soulless being masquerading as a man.

"We just passed the strength enhancement lab, and coming up on the right is our math/physics lab."

The door to the room Kreitzmann called the strength lab was closed, but the math/physics lab was open, and Elias cautiously peered in, afraid of what bizarre tableau he might witness. He was relieved to see only a normal classroom, filled with desks which were occupied by children who all appeared to be no older than first- or second-graders. In the front of the room were two teachers, both standing by dry-erase boards filled with complex equations. As he passed, he noticed something odd.

"Both teachers were talking at once," Elias remarked.

"Yes. One of the human abilities we accidentally discovered along our path is that the human mind, if exposed to the technique from the very beginning, can easily absorb and comprehend two separate inputs at once."

"Unbelievable!"

"Ah, here we are. The speech lab."

Elias followed Kreitzmann into the room. Immediately, one of the staff stood up and hurried to greet them.

"Doctor Boehn, this is Doctor Brightman."

"Patrick Brightman? My God, a pleasure to meet you, sir."

This lab was staffed with approximately fifteen people, most of whom were seated at terminals, paying no attention to the visitors.

Boehn, a lean man, wearing what appeared to be the mandatory uniform of

Kreitzmann's group, a white lab coat, and clutching an iPad instead of a clipboard, said excitedly, "I read many of your papers. I've never dreamed you would join us."

He suddenly looked self-conscious. Glancing at Kreitzmann, he added, "I mean, here in Aegis."

"It's my pleasure, Doctor Boehn."

"Doctor Boehn heads up our linguistics enhancement team."

"Linguistics enhancement? Are you exploring the multilingual capabilities of the subject?"

With a quick darting of his eyes to glance at Kreitzmann, Boehn replied, "No, not multilingual abilities. We actually enhance the fundamental speaking and comprehension-through-hearing abilities of the subjects."

"I'm not sure I understand."

Kreitzmann explained, "I first showed you the most recent addition to our body of work, the telepathy lab. I thought I would bring you here to give you a sense of the path we've traveled thus far. This was our first field of study. I actually began this study at Johns Hopkins, using volunteer students. The concept is quite basic, really. We've all heard those few talented people who can speak at what to us seems an incredible rate of speed. Yet, with recording and playback analysis, their individual word pronunciations are very good. Surprisingly so, actually.

"As the beginning concepts of exemplarium behavior modeling began to take shape in my mind, it seemed a natural to see what we could do in this area."

"You teach people to talk faster?"

"Simply put, yes. Not only do they talk faster, but they are able to understand the spoken word at a greatly advanced rate. I started with the volunteer students who came to my lab for two hours a day, five days a week. In the lab, we exposed them to computer-modified speech that had been accelerated, as well as to those rare rapid speakers. It was a very primitive protocol compared to our techniques today – periods of what I considered at the time to be immersion, followed by tests to determine our success rate."

"How well did it work?"

"Quite well, considering. Over the period of a semester, we were able to speed up their rate of speech an average of twenty-two percent. And that was inclusive of both modes of speech: normal, conversational speech and speech in which the subject was instructed to talk as rapidly as he or she could – what I called *verbal sprints*."

"Excellent results!"

Kreitzmann shrugged off Elias' compliment. "What that first experiment actually taught me was the importance of true immersion."

"True immersion?"

"As I said, we only had the subjects for two hours a day, five days a week. We were able to measure the gains we made in the time period of a single session, and then measure the same subjects again upon their return for the next session. After exposure to the barrage of so-called normal speech in their classrooms, lecture halls, dorms, et cetera, we would lose nearly all of the gain we had experienced. It was almost as if we were starting over every day. And on Mondays, our frustration level was even higher."

"Well, that is the reality of behavioral work on campus."

"I know, believe me. But I kept wondering what we could accomplish without those limitations."

"Having subjects you control all the time?"

"Exactly."

Elias watched the man as he spoke and was amazed at the indifference he displayed for what he was saying. There was not a moment when he appeared to grapple with the thorny ethical implications of his words, not even a perfunctory lip service excusing it. He might as well have been relating a lab experiment with fruit flies, rather than human beings.

"I decided that as long as I was doing my work on campus, there would be no real opportunity to move closer to my goals. I waited patiently until I was away from the academic environment and had secured my first private funding. It was then that we saw, for the first time, the true potential of the technique; and that was by utilizing only adults as subjects, those who had progressed far beyond the critical formative years. We have now reached a point where we are probably very near the structural limits of the vocal components. Would you like a demonstration?"

"Of course."

Kreitzmann nodded at Boehn, who turned away to sit at a monitor. With a few key strokes, he opened a video file which displayed a still-frame close-up of a woman's face. She was in her mid-forties and Asian. Elias guessed that she was Vietnamese. With another tap on the keyboard, the speakers came to life and the woman's face animated. To Elias' eyes, the region below her nose was a blur, almost as if he were watching a news commentator recorded earlier and now being played back at thirty times the normal speed. The sound coming from the speakers could only be described as a tonal torrent. On the right side of the monitor, a column of text scrolled past at a rate too fast for Elias to read.

"Am I seeing this at normal speed?"

Boehn cleared his throat. "Yes, Doctor Brightman, you are. The playback you are observing has not been accelerated in the least."

"But, other than the frequent pauses for a breath, it doesn't resemble speech. I can't seem to distinguish any variations in inflection or enunciation."

"*We* can't. Without the benefit of immersion, our brains are not prepared to process what we hear from this subject or the others who have attained her level of skill."

"Patrick, it is very much like the two discreet segments of the brain which are assigned the distinct tasks of object recognition and motion detection," Kreitzmann explained. "These two segments are competing for the attention of the conscious mind. This is an observable phenomenon in our everyday lives. If you lie on your back and watch a ceiling fan which is not yet moving, you can see the individual blades. As the rotation of the ceiling fan blades begins and is slowly increased, you are still able to discern the individual blades. But at some point, and this varies greatly from person to person, depending on experience and orientation, the segment of the brain which observes motion takes over and the blades become a blur. The individual blades are still visible to you, but the skill to separate them from their motion is not developed."

Elias thought about the blur he had witnessed during his altercation in ZooCity, but decided against broaching the subject.

"Watch what happens as Doctor Boehn digitally slows the tempo. Let us know as soon as you can understand what the subject is saying."

Boehn typed a command on the keyboard as Elias watched the monitor. The change was, at first, subtle. But within seconds he was able to tell that she was speaking words, even though he was not yet able to distinguish them. After a few more seconds passed, the words became understandable to him.

"Now."

With a nod from Kreitzmann, Boehn typed a command which stopped the deceleration of the speech.

"Doctor Boehn, please tell Patrick the level we've reached."

With another few taps on the keys, a small white box, filled with numbers, appeared at the lower right-hand corner of the monitor.

"Seventeen percent."

Instead of explaining, Kreitzmann smiled at Elias, waiting for the fellow scientist to figure it out on his own.

"Seventeen percent? The point where I was able to understand her speech was at seventeen percent of her recorded rate?"

Kreitzmann only nodded to indicate that Elias was correct.

"That means that she was speaking at more than five times the normal rate?"

"It depends on how you define normal. Remember, all of these things are truly relative. We have had other subjects who have not been immersed in the speech enhancement protocol but who were able to understand her at twenty-three percent. Some required slowing to as low as eleven percent. But, yes, she speaks at approximately five times the average human rate."

"Rudy, I hate to ask this, but what's the point of having individuals speak that quickly if they can't be understood?"

"But they can. Their speech is perfectly understandable to others who have gone through the immersion protocol. They are able to converse with each other easily at that rate. You see, Patrick, not only can we enhance the ability to speak at a rapid rate, but merely by exposure from, essentially, birth, the brains of the subjects are also able to hear, distinguish, and understand at that rate, as well."

Elias stared at the face of the unnamed woman on the monitor. The video had been paused and she was locked in mid-word, frozen. He tried to read her eyes in an effort to imagine what her life had been like as a subject for Rudy Kreitzmann, but they were flat, blank.

His thoughts were interrupted by Kreitzmann. "To answer your question, there are numerous applications for this skill, some immediate, some requiring a wider-scale societal immersion before the true benefits can be gained. There are many fields in which technology has progressed so rapidly that the slowness of human speech has become a true impeding factor to further advancement.

"Take air traffic controllers, for example. At the current velocities, if a plane veers off course and there is suddenly an impending midair collision, the controller is capable of viewing the data and mentally formulating the appropriate instructions to both pilots so that the disaster can be avoided; yet, the physical time it takes to verbally convey those instructions, when the closure rate is mere seconds, can last far too long to be effective. With the volume of airline traffic at major airports and the speed at which the planes travel, the benefit of the controllers and the pilots being able to convey information at a more rapid pace would, most assuredly, prevent accidents and allow for a more efficient utilization of the physical facilities. I have no doubt we could accommodate a higher volume of landings and takeoffs if the communication were radically accelerated. And imagine the effectiveness that could be attained if fighter pilots, in the midst of a rapidly evolving air combat situation, were able to communicate with each other and their base at five times the normal pace of verbal communication."

"I can see how that would be beneficial."

"Another obvious application would be the battlefield. The current limits of technology to deploy RPGs, missiles, tank-mounted weaponry, and the like far exceed the on-the-ground soldier's ability to convey or modify targeting and tactical information or to request support quickly enough. The moment-by-moment coordination possible with a group of soldiers proficient in this skill would be dramatically improved."

"I was wondering about that, Rudy. Is the military funding your research?"

Kreitzmann chuckled. "They would seem to be the likely source, wouldn't they? The mad scientist working secretly with limitless funding from the Pentagon – it's almost a cliché. The truth is, although I did receive a few grants from DARPA early in my career, I have not had a relationship with that particular group for well over a decade."

"Why is that? You're right. It does seem to be a natural for them to support someone who could be creating an entire army of super-soldiers."

"It was mutual. Accepting funding from the military is surrendering control of the direction of your research to them. I did not care to do that. Additionally, with our history of imperialism and heavy-handed, corporate-driven adventurism, I'm not certain that I want the military of the United States to be the sole possessor of these abilities.

"And from their perspective, the military is seen, first and foremost, as a political organization, subject to the emotional whims and vagaries of public sentiment to maintain their funding. They were as uncomfortable with my methods and techniques as was the general public. Sorry, but there is no exciting black-ops funding going on here. Besides, from my early days directly out of Johns Hopkins, funding has never been a problem for me."

"If you don't mind my asking, where does it come from?"

The smile returning, Kreitzmann answered, "At the risk of shattering another cliché, I can tell you that there are no huge, multinational corporations shoveling dollars, yen, or euros at us so that they may reap the benefits of a faster, more efficient work force. No, our funding comes from like-minded individuals who believe that the human race needs a little assistance to realize its true potential. The names are guarded, as you can well imagine, due to the social stigma which has attached itself to our work."

"Speaking of which, before I came to Aegis, I heard all of the comments about you and your work."

"I've been called a monster, Hitler, a demon…an almost never-ending list of epithets."

"Yes, you have. Although some of my colleagues, in private of course…."

"Of course," Kreitzmann interjected with a smile.

"Some of my colleagues have called you a visionary and a genius."

"How do you feel? About my work, that is. I am not fishing for a stroke to my ego."

Elias knew that in order to continue receiving the free flow of information, stroking Kreitzmann's ego was exactly what he needed to do. "You can count me as one of those who believe you are a visionary."

The comment triggered the desired reaction on the scientist's face. His reaction, Elias thought, was not dissimilar to that of a young girl being told she was beautiful.

"However, I must admit that I did struggle somewhat with your methods."

The appreciative expression dimmed, but did not disappear.

"And by that I don't mean your methods in the lab. I guess that I would be referring to your…."

"Acquisition of subjects?"

"Yes. If I have any unsettled questions in my mind, they would be related to that issue, and if you would prefer that we discuss this at another time…."

Kreitzmann glanced at Boehn, who was standing silently with them, and said, "No need. All of the members of my team have been a party to this conversation at some point. Many, prior to joining me, raised the same question."

Boehn nodded his agreement and commented, "I was one of those in the latter category. I had a tough time of it, at first."

Elias asked, "You changed your mind? You are comfortable with turning newborn babies into subjects of experiments?"

Boehn shrugged while releasing a heavy sigh. "Comfortable? No, I wouldn't say that. I don't believe that I can ever be what you would call comfortable with the idea."

"I don't understand then. You're here."

"Yes, I am. And I am glad to be a part of this team. You asked if I was comfortable. My sister is a research chemist with a major pharmaceutical company in Europe, one of the largest in the world. Whether she is working with laboratory animals or humans, she never reaches the point where she could say she is comfortable with the pain, disease, injury, or even death that is inflicted in the name of coming out with a new drug. But she believes that the benefits to mankind outweigh the costs."

"And what we are doing here," Kreitzmann broke in, "is a little different. Some of our projects will have a much farther-reaching effect than curing restless leg syndrome."

"Our subjects," Boehn continued, ignoring the brashness of his boss's comment, "have a very good life. Other than the fact that they are, or will be, different from the ostensibly normal people of our current society – different in the sense that they possess a skill others do not – they have all of the benefits of a human life. This includes human interaction, intellectual stimulation, recreation, and of course procreation, when they become of age, with others who also possess the skills."

"They are educated," Kreitzmann took over, "perhaps better than they would have been in the world on the other side of these walls. What they don't have are the daily trials and tribulations of life on the outside. They do not ever have to seek a job and tolerate the difficulties and frustrations of that endeavor. No taxes. No recessions. No military service."

"They're happy?" Elias asked.

"I would say *yes*," answered Boehn. "Obviously, this is all they know. They don't have a point of reference, a method for comparison to be able to tell us that they would prefer another lifestyle. But I believe they are."

Kreitzmann snorted to indicate contempt. "Happy? Patrick, do you believe that the vast majority of people born into this world are happy? Whatever that means. There are certainly isolated pockets of privileged children, individuals who are destined to grow up in the best of homes, go to the best of schools, drive a Lexus, and marry another from the same subset to go on producing more self-indulgent children.

"But even within the United States, the norm is anything but what I've just described. The society is in a downward spiral. Have you so isolated yourself that you haven't noticed? Did you know that in the past few decades, the percentage of children who graduate high school...*high school*, for God's sake, has declined. In the years following World War II, the graduation rates improved dramatically; the percentage of children who went on to college skyrocketed. A multitude of other indicators were also on the rise, some moderately and some substantially. Almost all of those trends have reversed.

"Statistically, a female born in America fifteen years ago has a better chance of being a high school drop-out, unmarried and raising children on her own, than she does of eventually finishing school, obtaining a college degree, and finding a professional career. The males fare no better. And leave it to the current culture to create a new anomaly: the malnourished obese teenager.

"The examples and statistics I've cited thus far are for our own supposedly wealthy country. Once you leave these borders, as I have in my career, with the exception of a few truly enlightened countries, the prognosis for the children is far worse.

"*That*," Kreitzmann emphasized dramatically, "is the life we have stolen from our subjects. Instead, they are fed perfectly balanced meals prepared by nutritionists. They receive the finest health care available. They are educated, in some cases, due to the uniqueness of their acquired skills, to a level far exceeding that which is available or even possible out there. They all participate in a daily regimen of exercise and physical activity, developed and monitored by experts in the field of physical education. They have never seen a moment of television, with the incumbent messages contained in both the entertainment and the advertising. They've never once in their lives seen a cigarette or cigar. Not one breath that they take is ever polluted with first- or second-hand smoke.

"Their diet is that of a vegetarian, with all of the fruits and vegetables locally grown and organic, so they have been spared the growth hormones, pesticides, and chemical fertilizers which you and I were raised ingesting."

"Whoa!" Elias exclaimed, holding up his hands in mock surrender. "I see your point. I really do."

Kreitzmann took a deep breath, calming down from the frenzy he had worked himself into. With a wry grin, he began to speak softly. "I'm sorry. As you can well imagine, the topic is a tender one for me as it has been the source of so many attacks over the recent years."

"I understand. My only concern, when I broached the issue, was the treatment of the subjects. Obviously, they are well cared for, and their overall development is a high priority."

"It is. Very much so. Does that address your concern?"

Hesitating first, Elias gently asked, "What is your...source for the newborns?"

Kreitzmann, rather than becoming tense or defensive, chuckled. "If you envision unmarked vans backed up to the maternity wards of hospitals where paid-off staff are secretly carrying babies out the back door to waiting men in dark sunglasses, I am sorry to disappoint you. There has been no baby stealing, no kidnapping. There have been no erroneous reports of infant mortality, while the newborns are transferred to us. We have multiple sources, Patrick. All of them are voluntary, with the full knowledge and consent of the parents or, in many cases, the mother, who is the only available parent."

"I'm sorry to belabor this point, but I'm having a difficult time imagining the establishment of the supply chain, so to speak. Are you running advertising?"

"We have, in the past, done exactly that in other countries. It was that practice which brought the unwelcome attention to our work. We have since discovered that there is no necessity for such an overt practice. But there honestly isn't any reason to expand upon the specifics because our need for maintaining the supply chain, as you so bluntly put it, has diminished to the point where it is almost not an issue."

"Why is that?"

Kreitzmann waved his arm to encompass his surroundings. "This facility, Aegis, has reached a point of self-sustainment. We have so many subjects within the program who have been with us for so long that they are now, as Doctor Boehn mentioned a moment ago, procreating. Their children are now part of the program. Additionally, the misfits, losers, and terminally depressed who come through that front turnstile have no compunction about engaging in the act with anyone who consents and, in many cases, those who do not. And, for the most part, these people have no interest in parenting. If they did...if they had any sense of responsibility for their families...would they have abandoned them to enter Aegis? No, Patrick, our days of securing subjects from the outside are essentially over.

"And the day will soon come where one hundred percent of our subjects are second, or later, generation. When that day arrives, the accusation of working with infants who have been torn from the loving bosoms of their mothers will no longer be valid, as the mothers and fathers will be right here with them, participating and helping them to develop."

While they had been speaking, Elias noticed that Doctor Bonillas had entered the lab and was standing patiently, waiting.

After Kreitzmann finished, he turned to her. "Yes, Doctor Bonillas?"

Nervously, she said, "Doctor Kreitzmann...if I could have a minute."

As she said this, Elias noticed her eyes dart to him for a brief moment before returning to Kreitzmann.

"Of course. If you would both excuse me."

He walked away from them, and Elias could hear him ask what she needed. Her response was nearly a whisper; he was not able to make out her words. But upon hearing her reply, Kreitzmann glanced over his shoulder at Elias, and then the two of them moved out into the hallway.

Assuming that somehow his cover had been blown, Elias began planning his next move while refining the mental map of the hallways that he and Kreitzmann had covered, and deciding upon his escape route.

If there had been any doubts in Elias' mind about the purpose for Bonillas' visit, those doubts were dashed when Kreitzmann returned alone. Gone was the friendly, collegial expression on his face. It was replaced with a look of anger and distrust. His eyes bored into Elias' eyes, as he rejoined him and Boehn.

"Doctor Boehn," he said, his voice taut, "if you would excuse us, please."

Boehn, catching the inflection, became suddenly nervous. "Of course," he replied as he turned to Elias and extended his hand. "Doctor Brightman, I hope that you decide...."

"That won't be necessary," Kreitzmann interrupted harshly. "Please...."

Boehn's arm dropped quickly back to his side and he nodded, saying nothing else. Kreitzmann turned to Elias. "Come with me."

With perfectly manufactured inflections of curiosity and confusion, Elias asked, "Is something wrong?"

The scientist did not reply. He merely restated, "Come," and turned toward the hallway, clearly expecting Elias to follow, which he did.

They retraced their steps in the direction of Bonillas' lab in silence. Elias made two additional attempts to engage him verbally, as the real Patrick Brightman would in this situation. His comments were ignored as they continued to walk. Rounding a corner, he saw Bonillas standing outside her lab, accompanied by another person Elias did not know. He noted that Bonillas was repetitively bunching and releasing the pocket on her lab coat with her right hand, turning that small part of the fabric into a crumpled mess. They walked directly to the two of them, and Kreitzmann, saying nothing, looked at the stranger, waiting.

The stranger took one quick look at Elias and turned to Kreitzmann. It was obvious this was a person who knew the real Brightman, as he curtly shook his head to indicate that Elias had failed the test.

Kreitzmann spoke, his voice stern and somber. "Thank you, Doctor Pannectuck. Thank you, Doctor Bonillas."

They both nodded and retreated to the lab, leaving Elias alone in the hallway with Kreitzmann.

"Who are you?"

Giving it a final try, Elias sputtered, "I'm Patrick Brightman. You already know...."

"Sir, that gentleman who just left knows Patrick Brightman. He worked with him for two years. Now, I'll ask one more time. Who are you?"

Without hesitating, Elias answered, "Elias Charon."

Kreitzmann's reaction was instantaneous. "Charon! They sent you?"

Elias said nothing, waiting. He watched the scientist's face and saw that the anger was gone. But it was not replaced with fear; rather, confusion momentarily flickered across his countenance.

Elias took advantage of this by asking, "How did Bonillas figure it out?"

In a matter-of-fact voice, Kreitzmann answered, "You either didn't know about or underestimated the psychic children."

Not all that surprised, Elias said, "The girl behind the glass read my mind."

He nodded. "And she is one of our *speakers*. After we left, she told one of Doctor Bonillas' assistants what you were thinking and that you were pretending to be someone you were not. The assistant told Doctor Bonillas who took the initiative to contact our HR people. At first, she believed she was simply documenting another lab result from the children for the case file. But after HR told her we had someone on staff who had worked with Brightman, and that person, upon hearing your physical description, was fairly certain you were not the man you pretended to be, she summoned me.

"It was only a matter of time until you encountered someone who knew the real Brightman. You must have assumed that. Therefore, Mr. Charon, the only conclusion I can draw is that whatever you had planned to do, you were going to act quickly, and that your masquerade, after it served its initial purpose of gaining entry, was only to gain some insights into our work first."

Elias said nothing.

"My question is the obvious one. What is it you were planning to do?"

Shrugging, Elias answered, "I came into Aegis for the same reason everyone else does. Well, almost everyone, apparently. I'd had enough out there."

Kreitzmann was closely studying Elias' face as he spoke. "I had heard that you lost your wife."

Elias nodded.

"I don't believe you, Mr. Charon. But, for the sake of conversation, if this is true, why the Patrick Brightman charade? Why infiltrate my labs?"

"When I was active…when I was engaged in, well, things…you and your activities were always near the top of my pile. I didn't know you were in here until after I arrived. It seems there aren't too many secrets in this facility. I heard that you had set up shop inside the very place I had chosen for my self-imposed exile, and the coincidence was too great to ignore. I was curious."

"But the Patrick Brightman ruse? That must have been planned."

"Not at all. Brightman had come to my attention as one of my last issues before I retired. I knew the details of his life and thought I could wing it long enough to get a look around. It was hasty and it was ad-libbed. As you said, I knew it was a short-time cover. But I only wanted a peek, anyway."

One side of Kreitzmann's mouth curled up in a half smile. "You are quite persuasive, Mr. Charon. Really! As I stand here and talk with you, I find myself wanting to believe what you say."

"It's true."

"So you say. And perhaps it is. In the days prior to my work, I would have been forced to make a value judgment, a gut decision, as it were. Fortunately, that is no longer the case."

He turned and opened the door to Bonillas' lab and Elias saw the doctor, as well as the young girl from behind the glass. They had been standing just inside the door. Kreitzmann glanced questioningly at Bonillas, who bent down and put her ear close to the girl's lips. Elias watched while the girl whispered something. As Bonillas heard the girl's words, Elias saw her face knit into an expression of fear. He did not need to see anything else.

Before she could communicate the girl's comment to Kreitzmann, Elias swung, clipping Kreitzmann on the jaw and sending him to the floor with one punch. Bonillas, seeing what had happened, immediately pulled the young girl back and slammed the door to the lab in the same motion.

Pivoting, Elias turned and ran in the direction of the reception area, hoping his weapons were still there and not stored away. There was no attempt by the workers he dashed past to restrain him, his actions only causing curious stares and the hasty withdrawal of a few of the technicians into the nearest doorway.

The final hallway, which would lead him to the receptionist, was coming up next. Elias made a snap decision to maintain his pace, rather than stop before the intersection to peer around the corner, counting on the fact that only a minute or two had passed since he had made his move. He hoped that the time it would take Bonillas to sound any sort of an alarm and the security staff to respond would be more than long enough to allow his escape.

Rounding the last corner, he noticed nothing but the forty yards of empty hallway between him and his goal. Putting on an extra burst of speed, Elias sprinted to the finish line, running into the room where he saw the same young woman still seated at the desk. Her eyes swung in his direction as he abruptly entered.

Skittering to a stop, nearly losing his balance as the rug under his feet slid, Elias looked at the side table where she had placed his Beretta and AK-47 earlier. It was bare.

"Where's my...?"

Before he could finish, something slammed into him from behind, knocking him to the ground. Elias tried to push himself over, while twisting his head around to see who his assailant was, when he suddenly felt a flash of pain at the back of his head, followed by an instant blurring of his vision, which dissolved into blackness.

CHAPTER
TEN

Despite the pain, the experience of years of working in the field caused Elias to keep his eyes closed as he returned to consciousness. A person's first impulse if hurt and rendered unconscious would be to stir, groan, or make any number of other forms of attention-gaining gestures upon awakening. He remained still and silent, listening.

As he waited patiently, the throbbing in his head subsided a bit as he forced his racing metabolism, a normal bodily reaction after emerging from the darkness of being knocked out, to calm.

He began taking inventory of all that his senses observed. From his position, which was horizontal, and the feeling that he was lying on a mattress, he could not determine whether he was restrained in any way, without either looking or moving, neither of which was advisable at the moment. His nose detected a panoply of scents. There was a faint hint of ozone, accompanied by a stronger level of machine oil. His ears heard a steady thrumming/whooshing sound, mechanical in nature. They also perceived the faint rustling of movement that seemed to be approximately a dozen feet away. It sounded as if there was a single person walking about, handling or rearranging some items unseen by Elias. With the absence of input from his eyes, his mind automatically conjured an image that matched the sounds. It was an image from his past: a peaceful, pleasant moment when he had awakened from a nap on the couch to find Leah hard at work dusting her knick-knack shelf in the den.

The rap to his skull had not diminished his recollection of where he was and what he had been doing. Elias knew that if he opened his eyes, he would not find his wife carefully lifting and dusting the beautiful items she had collected from their travels, and placing them back on the display shelf. He knew that he was in a hostile environment, occupied by uncongenial people, and that these moments, while his captors waited for him to regain consciousness, were more than likely his last moments of peace.

He had deduced that since he felt no physical restraints on his wrists or ankles and was on what seemed to be a mattress or padded cot, he was probably in some sort of cell, and that the sounds he heard were coming from his jailer.

Satisfied that he had gathered all of the information he could about his surroundings from the available input, he slightly opened his eyes, immediately directing his gaze toward the sounds of movement. He saw...a woman, standing with her back to him, holding what appeared to be a carved wooden bookend with her right hand and dusting it with her left.

Elias was momentarily shaken. He involuntarily opened his eyes wider. She was about ten feet away and was wearing dark green cargo pants, a camouflage T-shirt, and white athletic shoes. Her red hair was cut short, very short. As he silently watched her clean, he noticed that she was in excellent shape. The musculature on her arms was defined without being bulky, the T-shirt snug enough to show the ripples of toned muscle beneath.

Tearing his eyes away from her, Elias saw that they were in a mechanical room, filled with sheet metal ductwork and an array of process piping. They were not the type in the electrical raceways where his base camp was established, but color-coded pipes of larger diameters, obviously designed to carry water, steam, and high-pressure coolant loads. Mixed in with the jumble of ducts and pipes were an assortment of chairs and tables, a bookcase, and a sofa. He determined that he was indeed occupying a small bed. The area appeared to be the woman's living quarters.

The juxtaposition of mechanical gear and an apartment's worth of furniture was unusual enough, but the effect was hyperbolized by the abundance of decorative objects carefully arranged on nearly all of the available horizontal and vertical surfaces. There were ornate vases on the floor with peacock feathers arcing upward, lacy and jeweled fans mounted to the walls, small brass castings of wild animals such as lions and panthers, a shadow box mounted on the side of a support column and filled with miniature wedding accessories, including a tiny wedding gown pinned to the back panel. The most unusual area was a large section of sheet metal, clearly a main trunk line for the air conditioning system. It was essentially covered with hundreds of small refrigerator magnets: candy bars, kitchen appliances, all kinds of fake food like cheeseburgers and slices of pie, and a large assortment of other colorful and delicate items.

Elias saw his Beretta and AK-47 perched on the edge of a coffee table, the rest of which was filled with decorative objects. Quietly lifting his head slightly, he found that he was not restrained in any way. The back of his head ached from the blow that had knocked him out earlier, but otherwise he was fine, as far as he could discern.

"You're awake," she said, the tone of her voice friendly and casual.

Elias noticed that she had finished dusting the bookend and was holding a mirror set into a gold-leaf frame. She had obviously seen him in the mirror when he raised his head.

"I am. Where am I?"

She carefully placed the mirror onto its resting place in the filigreed plate-holder on the shelf and turned to Elias. "You're in my place."

Attempting to sit up, Elias paused as a wave of dizziness coursed through him, and he fell back onto a supporting elbow. "Your place? This looks like a mechanical room."

She walked gracefully across to him and reached out, offering a hand of support. "It is. I like it here. It's a much better spot than the area you picked out for your camp."

Startled by her knowledge, Elias said, "You've seen my digs?"

A sudden smile wrinkled the corners of her mouth. "Digs? I like that. Nineteen-fifties beatnik jargon. Cool, man!"

He took her hand and slowly sat up, triggering a new flash of pain from his head. She must have seen the effect of that pain, because the smile left her face, replaced by an expression of concern. "Aspirin or ibuprofen?"

"Got anything stronger?"

"No, I don't."

"I do. There's some Percocet with my things, but they're back at *my* place."

"You're in no shape to go there now, so you'll just have to make do with what's in my medicine cabinet."

"Ibuprofen. Four of them. And thanks."

She was still holding his arm to steady him. Reluctantly, she released her grip and walked across the area to a small cabinet, which was trimmed with an elaborate silver design around the face, opened it and removed a small bottle. Compressing the cap to defeat the childproofing, she shook out four tablets and returned to Elias, grabbing a bottled water from the refrigerator on her way back.

Gratefully, Elias took the pills and washed them down, wishing them Godspeed on their circuitous journey to his skull.

"Thank you very much. If I may ask, who are you and how did I get here?"

She was still standing in front of him. Sitting gently on the bed beside him, she extended her hand and introduced herself. "I'm Tillie."

They shook hands.

"I'm Elias."

"I know."

"You know?"

She nodded. "Uh-huh. Wilson told me."

"You know Wilson?"

"Everybody knows everyone here. But, yes, Wilson is probably my best friend in this place."

"So, he told you about me?"

"Actually, Mr. Death," she replied with an impish grin, "I was inside his shack during your visit with him."

"Another one with the 'Mr. Death' thing," Elias said with mock exasperation. "How did I get here? The last thing I remember was that I was escaping Kreitzmann's lab and someone knocked me out."

Her smile turned into a good-natured laugh. "You were anything but escaping. If I hadn't gotten you out of there, you'd be one of his lab rats right now."

Elias' mind flashed back to the scene. He remembered making it all the way to the receptionist, when he was suddenly hit from behind.

"What happened? I didn't see what hit me."

"You were taken out by one of the Zippers."

"Zippers?"

"That's what Wilson and I call them. I think you call them the *blurs*."

"Why Zippers?"

"You're kidding, right? Because they zip around."

He looked closely at her for a moment. She was in her early thirties, had bright green eyes and a full crop of freckles, all accentuated by the shaggy, close-cropped red hair. But her most prominent feature was the, for lack of a better term, aliveness of her face, which displayed each passing emotion with clarity. Her eyes shined with an intelligence and wit rarely seen, and they fixed upon Elias' eyes with a directness and firmness which was almost disconcerting. At that moment she was watching his face, her innate curiosity seeming to pull his thoughts from him before he was ready to let them out. She leaned toward him slightly, in anticipation.

"Tillie, what are they? The Zippers, I mean."

With a dismissive shrug she responded, "I wasn't able to track you completely inside Kreitzmannstein's lab, but I'm assuming you got the tour."

"I did, until I ran into someone who blew my cover." Elias was not sure why he was being so forthcoming in his information, other than the disarming nature of the woman, not to mention the fact that she had more than likely saved his life.

"Then you already know what he does."

"Yes. He takes people from birth and immerses them, as he calls it, in a different reality to enhance their skills."

"Right. Did he show you the Auctioneers?"

Elias chuckled. "I'm guessing you mean the fast-talking subjects. Yes, he did."

"That was his first experiment, right?"

"So he said."

"His second experiment, motivated by his early success on the first, was with the Zippers. He's been doing this one for years, way before he came to Aegis. He took babies...little tiny infants...and put them in a special room, basically from the day they were born. The room had screens for walls and even the ceiling."

"He told me that Phase One was a virtual reality."

"Virtual unreality is more like it."

"What did he do with them?"

"These infants, every waking minute of every day, saw normal life on the screens all around them – people talking, people performing tasks, everything – except it was...."

"Speeded up!"

"Exactly. All those little babies knew was life at a pace way faster than our regular pace."

"How were they cared for? Certainly the people who came into the room to do that moved at a normal pace."

"They did. I didn't get the benefit of the full tour, like you almost did, but I talked to a man who used to work with Kreitzmannstein. He told me that they would change the babies' clothes, bathe them, and do everything else while the babies slept so that they never saw people moving at a slower pace. And they would blindfold the babies during this, in case they woke up while someone was still in the room."

"But what about feeding? You can't feed a baby while it sleeps."

Her face took on a more serious expression. "You can't? Ever heard of a feeding tube?"

"You're kidding!"

"No, I'm not. That's what the man told me."

"So that's what they are doing over there?"

"Not anymore."

Elias started to speak; then he figured the rest of it out. "Phase Two."

Tillie nodded. "They don't need the virtual reality now. They have their first crop of graduates who do everything a lot faster than we do. They still have newborns there. And they are still *enhancing* them, but now they have a staff of Zippers who take care of the new ones. Many of the Zippers are old enough to be getting together and creating little Zippers."

Tillie giggled and added, "Sorry. It's not funny. But every time I think about them making little Zippers, you know, I visualize them.... Never mind."

Elias shook his head. "It is a funny image. But back to your rescue. I've seen what the Zippers did to the thugs who tried to grab me when I first got here. How were you able to get me out of there?"

"Thanks a lot. What are you, a chauvinist? You don't think I just jumped in and overpowered them?"

Before Elias could protest, she stopped him. "I'm kidding. Actually, it's pretty simple if you think about it. They zip around real fast, right?"

"Yes."

"So, therefore, they have accelerated metabolisms, like hummingbirds."

"Makes sense."

"That's what I thought. I call it the Hummingbird Effect because every hypothesis should have a name. So I did a little research in my library." With a swing of her arm, Tillie indicated a row of three mismatched bookcases off to the side, which he had not seen before. They were all overfilled with literature and textbooks.

"What I thought was that if they were running so fast internally, they would be susceptible to drugs at a level which wouldn't bother us."

"Very clever."

"Gee, thanks," she said sarcastically, before continuing. "I have a few medical books here. One has a great section on anesthesiology. I basically put together the same gases they use to put us under in the infirmary for surgery, Desflurane and Sevoflurane, and loaded them in an aerosol dispersal device. I use the Desflurane for the up-close work because it is less irritating to my mucous membranes."

Elias was amazed. "An aerosol dispersal device?"

With a broad grin, Tillie stood up and crossed the room, opening a door on a tall metal cabinet. She reached in and removed a balloon partially filled with a liquid.

"It's a water balloon," she explained proudly.

Elias laughed. "Ingenious."

"I fill up the balloon part of the way with water. I have the pressurized tanks with the anesthesia and use them instead of air to inflate the balloon. I need the water in the balloon so it will burst when I throw it. I still have to throw it real hard, and it's more reliable if I hit something sharp, but it works."

"Tillie, I'm impressed."

She reacted to his heartfelt compliment immediately, beaming. "They work fairly well. One or two balloons in the area where there is a Zipper, and he drops within seconds."

"Won't Kreitzmann figure it out soon and give them gas masks?"

She shrugged. "Probably. I've only used them a couple of times. Well, three, counting my first test. And I've always made a point of picking up the broken rubber from the balloon so all they find afterward is a wet spot and unconscious Zippers. Rescuing you was the first time I did it in front of a non-Zipper witness."

"The receptionist."

"Right. So I'm not sure how many more times they'll be useful."

Elias thought of something. "Did you drop your little gas bombs from above?"

"What do you mean?"

"I'm guessing, since we are in the air system of Aegis, that you utilize the plenum to move from area to area."

"I do. It also allows me to watch and listen through the return air grilles."

"I understand. But if you opened a grille in front of the receptionist to drop your balloons, she would have seen that and told her boss. They'll be checking this system right now and will find us soon."

Tillie rolled her eyes. "I was kidding before, but either you really are a male chauvinist or maybe I just look that stupid."

"I am not a male chauvinist!"

"Okay. Then I guess I have a stupid face."

"You don't have…."

She interrupted, "I didn't use the plenum. I was standing near the entrance door, waiting for you. You know there is no lock or security there. Kreitzmannstein has such a massive ego he doesn't think he needs it. When I heard you go thundering into the room, I knew they wouldn't let you leave. I chucked the balloon into the room from the doorway. They had only sent one Zipper, and he fell like a dead tree. I ran in, made the woman at the desk tell me where your guns were, grabbed them, grabbed you, and skedaddled."

"You did all of that by yourself?"

Seeing the look on her face return, he held up his hands defensively and added, "Not that you couldn't have. I'm sure you could lift me over your head with only one arm. I was merely wondering. I mean, dragging me up to the plenum to get me here would be a little tough, even for Wonder Woman."

With a smirk, she said, "You're right. I had some help."

"Help? Who? Was it Wilson?"

Reaching out, Tillie patted him on the arm. "All in good time, Mr. Death. Just because I rescued you doesn't mean that we know you well enough to share the whole membership roster with you."

"I understand. I wouldn't either in your shoes. And please stop calling me that."

"How about some apple juice?"

"Sure, that would be great," Elias answered, shaking his head in frustration.

He watched her as she walked to the refrigerator and pulled out the bottle. "If you don't mind my asking, how did you get all of this stuff?"

Over her shoulder, she asked, "Do you like it?"

"I do. It's all beautiful. But I didn't think they would have the type of stores in Aegis where you could pick up decorating items."

"They don't." She returned with two full glasses and set them on the coffee table in front of the sofa. "Would you like to move over here? Sitting up would probably be good. Think you can make it?"

Elias stood slowly, wobbling for a moment. Tillie, seeing this, started to come over but he waved her off. "I can do it. Give me a second."

In a moment, his head cleared and he was able to walk the five paces to the sofa, dropping heavily into the overstuffed cushion.

With a deep sigh, he said, "There! Made it."

"Congratulations. To answer your question, I've accumulated all of it over the years from newbies."

"People bring in this kind of stuff?"

"This kind of stuff? What kind of a comment is that?"

"I didn't mean it that way. Really. I'm only surprised that people checking in at Aegis would bring their refrigerator magnets with them."

"People have their favorite items buried with them when they die. Why wouldn't they bring them here? At least here they know they can look at them again."

"That's true. But how did you get them?"

"Well, I didn't steal them if that's what you mean."

"I didn't...."

"Don't give me that. I saw it in your eyes. You were visualizing me dropping out of the ceiling grille while people slept and stealing their favorite peacock feather fans."

Elias laughed. "I admit I did briefly entertain that image. Are you sure you aren't a graduate of Kreitzmann's psychic class?"

She held up both hands, palms facing Elias. "No way! I would never submit to any of his experiments."

"I'm curious because if people went to the trouble of bringing their prized possessions, their lovely objects...."

"That's better."

"...into Aegis with them, why would they give them up?"

With a subtle upward jerk of her shoulders, Tillie answered, "I guess they just liked me."

"They just liked you? People spontaneously gave you these things?"

"Sometimes. Sometimes I'd barter with them."

"What do you mean?"

"I've been here a long time. I was one of the first-day group."

"You were?"

"Yes. So, that and, well, another reason – I know my way around. A lot of times the newbies wanted something and I knew where and how to get it. I'd trade for something they had that I liked. I'm kind of like that genial character in the old World War II movies who could always procure whatever his sergeant needed, and nobody ever asked him how he got it.

"People would arrive here with a whole bunch of stuff. They never seemed to mind giving up one or two of their pieces. The only exception was all the refrigerator magnets. That whole collection was given to me at once."

"Who would do that?"

"You aren't my only rescue. A very nice lady arrived who had them all packed in one of her suitcases. I watched her come in and was tracking her when the Zooks...."

"Zooks?"

"That's my name for the ZooCity hooligans. Anyway, they jumped her. God knows what they were going to do to her. But they never got the chance."

"You are the Wonder Woman of Aegis, aren't you?"

The huge smile again filled her face. "I do what I can. Now it's my turn to ask some questions, if you feel up to it."

"Fire away."

"Who do you work for?"

"No one. I'm retired."

Her mouth scrunched up in an expression of displeasure. "Okay. So you're going to lie to me. And after I saved your butt back there."

"I'm not lying," Elias protested emphatically. "I am retired."

"From where?"

Elias looked up at the cast-in-place concrete ceiling, in an unconscious attempt to reduce her ability to read his mind by looking into his eyes. "A department within Homeland Security."

"Which department?"

He laughed. "One you've never heard of."

"Try me."

"It is called the OCI."

"Office for the Coordination of Intelligence."

"How do you...?"

"Just do," she interrupted. "What did you do there? Before you *retired*, that is."

Giving up any pretense, he answered, "I ran it."

Her eyes widened. "Really?"

Elias nodded.

Without another word, Tillie quickly rose from the sofa and walked to the same cabinet where she kept her knock-out bombs. From it she withdrew an object which was blocked by her body. With a flourish, she turned and held it up for Elias to see. It was a square of cardboard with two words printed on it with a Sharpie. Elias made an involuntary sound as he recognized it as the sign from the video in Faulk's office. On it were the words – *Help us!*

"That was you."

She nodded, carefully placing the sign back into the cabinet and closing the metal door. As she returned to the sofa, Elias asked, "How did you know about the camera there?"

Dropping down, she answered, "As I said before, all in good time. I'm still not one hundred percent sure I can trust you."

Elias was not certain what direction to take next. She took advantage of his silence by asking, "Why was it so long before you got here?"

"So long? You only put up the sign a few days ago. I think that's pretty damn quick."

"Not like a 9-1-1 call. Should've been hours, not days."

He shook his head in frustration. "Well, I'm here now."

"Whoopee! The cavalry has arrived, and the first thing that happens is I have to rescue *him*."

"Thanks."

"Actually, since you've been here, you've been rescued twice. The first time you had to be saved from the Zooks."

"You were watching?"

"Yes. I've been watching the entrance since I put up the message."

"Why didn't you help me then? Not that I needed it."

"Of course not," she said, rolling her eyes. "I was going to jump in, but the Zippers beat me to it. I would have if *they* were going to mess with you, but they didn't."

"Okay! So I haven't gotten off to a great start."

"You could say that again."

"I do have a question for you, though. Since you seem to know everything going on in here, have you met a man named Eric who would have arrived about two and a half months ago?"

Her brow knitted in thought for a moment. "No. At least not by that name. What does he look like?"

"About six feet tall, brown hair, brown eyes, dark complexion, average build but in good shape."

"That sounds like about a fourth of the population. Do you have a picture?"

"Not on me, but I do have one back on my laptop."

"We'll have to look at it. When I see his face, I can tell you if he arrived and maybe where he is now. Who is he?"

"They sent someone else in first."

"They did? You said about two or three months ago?"

Elias felt his back muscles tighten as he sensed the direction of the conversation. "Yes. That's about right."

"But that was before my sign."

Elias only nodded.

Her eyes flashing, Tillie raised her voice in agitation. "You didn't come here because of my sign. You came to look for this Eric!"

Trying to defuse her anger, Elias explained, "Both, actually. In fact, there were three reasons why I decided to come out of retirement. The first was that we found out Kreitzmann was in Aegis. The second was losing Eric. And the clincher was your sign."

"I don't believe you. And, besides, Kreitzmann's been in and out of here for years. Why would your people suddenly worry about it now?"

"Honestly, I'm confused about that myself. I was told, hell, I was shown a video with Kreitzmann entering three months ago. It wasn't until I talked with Wilson that I found out he's been here longer. And no one knew, or at least no one told me, that he basically has keys to the door. If you were at Wilson's, you heard me say the same thing when I was talking to him."

She paused for a moment, replaying the conversation upon which she had eavesdropped. "Okay, that might be true. But I still think you came here just to get your friend out."

"I would have," Elias told her honestly. "Your message was the clincher, though."

She flopped back into the cushion behind her, blowing out a loud breath.

Sensing the tide was turning a bit in his favor, Elias pressed on. "I know that you don't believe me, but I would have come here after I saw your sign, even if we hadn't lost Eric in Aegis."

Her eyes turned to look at his. He could almost feel them probing his thoughts, seeking the level of sincerity she wanted or needed. He could feel some of the tension drain from her as she apparently made up her mind. "You're right. You're here, whatever the original directive or motive might have been."

Elias remained quiet, allowing her to make the rest of the journey on her own.

Standing suddenly, she suggested, "Let's go look at that picture of your friend. Maybe I do know him."

He stood and snatched up his pistol and rifle. As they headed toward the door, they passed an alcove, equipped with several decorative hooks on the walls, many of them holding jackets and colorful scarves, her shoes lined up carefully against the back wall. Even that area sported some small shelves, adorned with porcelain statuettes and feather roses. He looked at her quizzically, and she replied, as if he should know, "Every home needs a mudroom." He chuckled at his quirky new acquaintance, and followed her out into the maze of concrete passageways.

They communicated in whispers, as the grilles installed in the floor of the walkways were open to the space below. After the ninth turn, she told him that there was no direct connection between her mechanical maze and his electrical raceways, so they would need to briefly descend to the public corridors until they reached an access point. Before taking one of the ladders down, she lay on the floor and shimmied to a return air grille until her head was hovering directly above it. Turning her head to the side, Tillie listened for the sounds of any residents below.

Quietly, she rose and whispered, "Sounds all clear. Let's go."

They proceeded to an access ladder and climbed down to a mechanical closet. Again, with great care, Tillie cracked the door open and peered out. Seeing no one, she opened the door the rest of the way and stepped into the corridor, immediately followed by Elias. The closest electrical room with access to the raceway was only fifty feet away, and they reached it without incident, quietly closing that door and swiftly climbing the ladder, a longer climb since the electrical raceways were positioned above the mechanical plenum. As Elias was following Tillie through the trip, he had an opportunity to admire her grace and fluidity as she moved, climbing and descending ladders as effortlessly as a gymnast.

Once within the raceway, Elias moved into the lead position, even though he was aware that she knew the location of his base. Within less than ten minutes they arrived, and he did a quick inventory and checked his discreet security measures. Everything appeared to be undisturbed.

Leaning over the laptop, he brought up the appropriate file and clicked on the jpeg of Stone. The face of his old friend filled the screen.

"There he is."

Tillie leaned closer for a better look and almost instantly recognized him. "Yes. I did see him come in. It was about that time, too."

"What happened?"

She turned to face Elias, her expression blank. "Not good."

"What, Tillie?"

"The Zippers got him. Right off the bat. Not too far from where the Zooks accosted you."

Elias felt an anger building inside and, with more of an accusatory tone in his voice than he intended, asked, "You didn't help him?"

Tillie flinched back, hurt by his inflection. "I would have. Really. But I didn't have any of the balloons with me. Normally, the only thing to worry about in that area would be the Zooks. Those guys I can handle without a problem."

Her unhappiness at not assisting Elias' friend was blatantly obvious, and he immediately felt like a bully for his comment. "It's okay, Tillie. I didn't mean it that way."

His attempt to reassure her did not have much of an effect. "Do you know where they took him? Or...," he paused, not wanting to know if the alternative was the case. "Did they take him alive?"

Relieved at the prospect of delivering a positive bit of news, she blurted, "He's alive. At least he was when they took him away. They took him to the lab."

"Do you have any idea where in Kreitzmann's lab they are keeping him?"

"I haven't seen him in there, but that doesn't mean much. There are several areas of that lab where I haven't gone, in the overhead area. What I have seen bothers me too much, so it's a real approach–avoidance deal."

With a hopeful tone in her voice, she added, "But I can start looking for him."

"That would be great," Elias said, smiling at her.

He closed the image file and began clicking through the video menu, checking first on his available views of Walden. Seeing nothing unusual, he switched to the Madison views.

"What are you looking for?"

"Nothing, specifically. I've been away from here for a little while, so I thought I would do a quick check to see if anything was happening."

He finished checking the video feeds from Madison and clicked on ZooCity. The first two views were of empty rooms. As he was about to change to the next feed, Tillie pointed at the screen. "What's that?"

"What?"

"I don't know. I think it looks like a foot and leg."

Elias blinked and stared harder at the screen in the spot where Tillie pointed, before remembering that he had the capacity to zoom in on a region of the view. Doing so, the vague blob at the corner of the screen resolved clearly into precisely what she had described.

"You're right. That's exactly what it is."

"It doesn't look like he's moving. Do you think he's asleep?"

Elias turned and looked at Tillie. "Do you?"

She did not answer.

Satisfied that there was nothing more to see in this view, Elias clicked on the next, and all of his questions were graphically answered.

"Oh, my God," Tillie gasped. "Are they all dead?"

"I can't tell for certain, but it surely looks like it," Elias answered softly, his eyes taking in the apparent mayhem in the room he now viewed. Strewn about the floor, arms, legs, and torsos were twisted at all impossible angles; he could not imagine they were still alive. His finger moved on the touchpad, and he clicked on the stored-video menu, leaving the live mode and beginning a slow rewind. Other than the screen flicker, the fact that he was watching the past in reverse at 3X speed was not apparent, as nothing moved. With another click, Elias increased the speed to 16X, intensifying the flicker. As the clock counter in the corner of the monitor passed the previous hour, all of the inert bodies suddenly flew into motion, almost comically.

He quickly paused the reverse mode and clicked on PLAY. There were at least nine men and women visible in the frame. They were eating a meal, talking, and laughing. Elias and Tillie stared at the video silently, waiting in dread for the outcome that they knew was coming at any moment. Within a minute, one of the men stopped in mid-stride as he was returning to the table with a glass in his hand. His right arm suddenly jerked upward, the glass flying across the room, and a moment later his head twisted violently. He fell limply to the floor. Before the others could even react, Elias saw that, one by one, each of them met a similar fate. The attack, in total, took less than a minute, according to the clock counter.

At no point was Elias able to distinguish the attackers on the high-resolution monitor.

"My God!" Tillie echoed her sentiment from earlier. "The Zippers!"

"Let's try this," Elias said as he backed up the video to the moment the first man was walking across the room, then clicked on the playback menu, and selected the mode which allowed playback at a frame-by-frame speed. The man's gait instantly froze until Elias, clicking with the pointer, began to advance the motion one frame per click. After approximately twenty frames, a figure suddenly appeared in the picture, sheathed entirely in a beige body suit which extended to cover his head, except for the eyes, nose, and mouth, his arms reaching toward the walking man. In the next frame, the figure's hands were gripping the walker's head on both sides. The following frame showed the walker's head twisted at an angle normally impossible. In the next, the beige figure had already released the walker and was moving toward the next nearest victim.

"I can't watch any more of this," Tillie whispered, her voice raspy, and turned away.

Elias spent a few more minutes scanning rapidly through the remaining frames. He wanted a clear understanding of their techniques. He found that there had been only two of the Zippers, as Tillie called them. That was all it took to kill, by hand, an entire roomful of nine people.

Finishing his study of their actions, Elias quickly checked the live feeds from the balance of the cameras he had placed around the ZooCity area. Everywhere else he looked, he found more bodies and, apparently, no survivors.

"Elias, are you ready to go yet?"

"Thank you."

"Thank you? For what?"

"For calling me Elias and dropping that whole 'Mr. Death' thing."

He was rewarded with a sardonic half smile. "That doesn't mean you get to learn the club handshake yet, mister."

"I am just about ready. I need to do one thing."

Changing programs on the laptop, he typed a report to Faulk, filling him in on what he had learned about Kreitzmann and the Zippers, the apparent status of Stone, and the demise of the Zooks. Without consciously knowing why, he left out any reference to Tillie or Wilson.

"What are you doing, a paper on how you spent your summer vacation?"

"I'm preparing my daily report."

"How can you report? There's no way."

"Ah," he began, glad to be giving her a revelation, "but there is." He explained the comm system to Tillie while he finished the report and instructed the program to encrypt and compress it for transmission. That done, he transferred the compressed report to the phone with a USB cable, making certain the phone had a full charge and was still set to automatically upload and download the day's transmissions.

As he placed the phone back in its location, Tillie asked, "Aren't you bringing it with you? We might need it."

"No reason to. It's no good as a regular cell phone since it only works for about one second a day. It's only good with the laptop."

"Bring them both."

Elias turned around to face her, a slight grin playing across his face. "Both? Tillie, are you asking me to move in with you?"

She punched him on the arm. It stung. "Creep. No, I'm not and you know it. But we might need to get a message out, and why should we have to come back here to do it?"

"True, but if I bring the laptop to your place, I won't have my surveillance anymore. The video feeds are through these conduits," he explained, pointing at the groups of pipes mounted to the walls, "and they don't enter your mechanical area."

She stared at him, her gaze drifting to the pipes and the wires dangling from the pipes down to the connections at the side of the laptop. "Okay. We'll leave it here. Can we go now? I want to get back to my place."

"I'm ready to go, but I'd like to check out ZooCity."

"Why? They're all dead."

"Maybe not. One of them might need some help. Besides, there might be something we can learn. Come on, it won't take long."

Without waiting for an answer, he started walking down the raceway that led to the sector with ZooCity.

"Oh, all right."

When they arrived at the access ladder into the ZooCity area, Elias went down first, followed quickly by Tillie. Duplicating her actions at the previous entrance to the public area, he cracked the door open slightly and listened first, then peeked out before exiting.

The silence was disconcerting as they entered the formerly occupied enclave.

He paused and said, "Wait here," wanting to spare her the ghastly scene which would begin around the next corner.

"Nope," she answered in a matter-of-fact tone.

Elias saw no point in arguing and continued forward. As he threaded his way through the first of the bodies, there was only one soft gasp from behind. After that, no sound or comments came from his companion.

He proceeded methodically, room by room, checking every closet and every cabinet which might be large enough to contain a person. Most of the way through the enclave, Elias was beginning to admit to himself that Tillie might have been right. Not only had they encountered no survivors, he had seen nothing which could be considered helpful in his search.

They came to the end of a long hallway and Tillie, who had passed him as he checked the previous room, reached for the doorknob – when Elias heard a distinctive *click-clack* from the other side of the door. In an instant, he wrapped his arm around her, pulling her forcefully to the side. They slammed into the side wall of the hallway at the same moment that a large chunk of the door Tillie had been about to open exploded outward.

Handing the rifle to her, Elias pulled the 9mm from his pocket and shouted, "Who's in there?"

He heard the person inside pump the shotgun, loading another round in the chamber.

"We're not here to hurt you. We're here to help."

A nervous voice shouted through the hole in the door, "Go 'way. I don't need no help."

Tillie spoke up. "Look, we saw what happened to your friends. We're checking for survivors. Are you hurt?"

"No!" The voice from beyond the door sounded young and terrified.

Trying to make his voice sound gentle, Elias reassured the stranger, "We're not with the ones who did this. They're gone."

"You sure?"

"We just checked the whole area," Tillie answered. "This room is the last one. They're not here."

"They might be. You can't even see them."

"If they were here, we would be dead, not talking to you."

There was a minute of silence from the stranger as he tried to figure out his next move. To help him decide, Elias said, "Look. We're going to lay down our guns and step in front of the door. You can see both of us."

"Are you crazy?" Tillie whispered.

Elias, instead of replying, tucked the 9mm into his waistband behind his back, making certain it was covered by his windbreaker, and stepped back from the door, walking to the center of the hallway so the stranger could partially see him through the hole in the door.

"You are crazy," she muttered and carefully leaned the AK-47 against the side wall, moving to follow Elias.

Both of them stood about twenty feet from the splintered opening, both making their hands visible to the man behind the door.

Elias spoke slowly. "Okay, see, we're unarmed and there is no one else out here."

The barrel of the shotgun slowly protruded unsteadily from the hole, centered on the area between the two of them. Elias could feel his muscles tighten while he waited for the second blast from the shotgun. Moments later, the stranger's face appeared next to the side of the gun, his eyes darting around as he checked the hallway for anyone who might be hidden.

"I told you, we're alone."

The barrel withdrew and the door opened. A young male, no more than seventeen or eighteen, stepped out into the hallway, still clutching the shotgun and keeping it aimed in their general direction, as he quickly glanced from side to side to make sure no one was crouched on either side of the doorway. Seeing that the hallway was empty except for Elias and Tillie, the teenager lowered his weapon.

Elias heard Tillie release a large exhale. She had obviously been holding her breath. Talking a cautious step forward, he asked, "Is anyone else in there?"

The boy shook his head. "No. Only me."

"Are you sure you're all right?" Tillie asked, following Elias' lead and slowly moving forward. The boy no longer cared whether they kept their distance, and did not react. Elias covered the remaining distance and gingerly took the shotgun, now held limply, from the young man, leaning it against the wall next to the AK-47.

As soon as he was relieved of the weapon, the teen seemed to crumble, as if every muscle in his body had simply given up. Elias and Tillie both grabbed him by the arms and supported him.

"They're all gone, all dead," the teen said in a voice which was closer to a whimper.

The two of them walked him to the side wall and slowly lowered him to the floor. Tillie sat down next to him and held his hand.

"What's your name?" she asked softly.

The teen, who was staring down blankly, as if he were examining his sprawled legs, murmured, "Zack."

"Zack, I'm Tillie. This is Elias. Tell us what happened."

The young man seemed to be slipping deeper into a daze. Elias leaned over and snapped his fingers in front of Zack's face. "Zack! We need you to tell us what happened. We will get you someplace safe in a minute, but we need to know what happened and why."

He rallied slightly. "I don't know what happened. I was back here. I heard the sounds, the yells. I peeked out my door and saw one of those things grab BQ. One minute he was runnin' and the next he was just dead. Dude, I hid! I didn't help. I didn't do nothing."

"There wasn't a thing you could have done, Zack." Tillie's voice was gentle.

"Why did they do this?" Elias asked.

The young man's eyes drifted up to look at him. "It's because of Frank D. We had made a deal with the Man. It was a pretty good deal, considering. Frank D broke the deal."

"What deal?"

"I know it wasn't right, but we didn't have no choice. The Man told us to deliver all the newbies to him, untouched, or he would kill us. All of us."

Elias said nothing, waiting.

"Frank D took one of the newbies 'cause he liked her. After he and his partner were done with her, he delivered her to the Man. I guess she told."

They decided it was past time to move on. Since Tillie's knowledge of the available routes was the most detailed, she assumed the lead. The other two followed. She and Elias had agreed in a whispered conversation that Zack should not be taken to either her living quarters or Elias' base. Wilson's atrium seemed the only logical option. Kreitzmann undoubtedly had men out looking for Elias, and Zack was certainly a target as well, so they took a circuitous route through mechanical chases, raceways and, when necessary, public corridors.

Finally entering the man-made jungle of Wilson's domain, Tillie shouted, "Wilson! It's me."

The foliage parted to their left, and Wilson stepped out into the open, carrying his shotgun. He eyed Zack but said nothing as he led them to the shack. Within minutes the teen was asleep on the bed inside, and the three of them were assembled on the porch.

Tillie did most of the talking as she brought her friend up to speed on all of the latest developments, including her rescue of Elias and the death of all of the residents of ZooCity. She had saved one fact for last.

"I hate to admit it, Wilson, but you were right."

The older man squinted at her. "About what, dear?"

Tillie glanced at Elias and explained, "He didn't come because of my message."

Wilson's mouth pursed in an expression of concern. "No?"

"No. They sent someone in here two or three months ago. When he disappeared, they sent Elias."

"Oh." Wilson looked at Elias, a hint of sadness showing on his face.

"As much fun as both of you are having, talking about me as if I weren't present, would you mind telling me what it is that Wilson was supposedly *right* about?"

Wilson's eyes shifted from Elias to Tillie, who gave a subtle shrug to indicate her answer to his unspoken question. Turning back, Wilson said, "Tillie, although having passed the ripe age of thirty-two a brief while ago, is still quite naive. Although she prefers to act as if she is jaded and cynical, she continues to believe that there is a Santa Claus, an Easter Bunny, a Tooth Fairy, and a government in Washington with noble motives. In my mind the jury is still out on the Tooth Fairy, but I am certain about the latter not being the case."

"I'm with you on that."

"I am sure that you are, Mr. Death."

"Please...."

"He calls you that for a reason," Tillie broke in.

Elias looked at both of them and said, "Okay. I would appreciate it if you could dispense with the oblique and tell me what you think."

"Tillie believed if she sent a message that we needed help, the conscientious guardians of the public would mobilize a team of Navy Seals to charge into Aegis, guns blazing, to save us all. I, on the other hand, have become convinced that our leaders have a quite different fate in mind for all of us."

Elias leaned forward impatiently. "And that is?"

A lopsided smile of chagrin on his seasoned face, Wilson replied, "I believe that you have been sent to clean up a mess."

"Of course I...."

Holding up his hand to stop Elias, Wilson continued, "I believe that you have been sent to shut Aegis down and eliminate all of its residents."

C HAPTER
ELEVEN

Wilson was inside the shack, preparing lunch. Tillie had departed to search for Eric Stone, utilizing her knowledge of the hidden passageways. Zack was still sleeping, and Elias sat alone on the porch, watching and listening vigilantly for any indication that the Zippers had arrived.

Moments after he heard a soft clatter of dishes and silverware, Elias saw Wilson emerge from inside with two plates of food.

"I hope that you like ham and cheese omelets."

"Sounds great."

Elias moved to the small table and joined Wilson. He had not realized how hungry he was until the aroma of the meal reached his nose. Wasting no time, Elias began to eat. After several bites, he asked, "If you really think I'm here to kill you, why are you feeding me?"

With a chuckle, Wilson answered, "Why not? Perhaps you will find my omelets so tasty that you'll reconsider."

Elias gently placed his fork on the table next to his plate. "That's not why I'm here, Wilson."

The mathematician did not bother to look up, tucking another bite into his mouth before responding. "Either you are here to do precisely that or you are not, and in each case, that is exactly what you would say. I do not endorse the skill of mind reading, as it is being cultivated by Rudy – too much can go wrong, as you noticed – so I am left with my own ability to deduce and decide."

"And your decision?"

"Insufficient data at this time."

Staring at Wilson for a moment, Elias sighed and picked up his fork to resume eating, when Wilson spoke. "For the purpose of conviviality, let's assume for the moment that you are not our executioner."

"Fair enough."

"What is your explanation for your boss not knowing that Kreitzmann has been coming and going from Aegis for years?"

Elias shrugged. "I don't have one. But I'll tell you that I used to sit in his chair and, from what you and Tillie have told me, Kreitzmann has had open access to Aegis for long enough that part of the time was on my watch. And I didn't know about it."

"Since you've broached the subject, may I ask why you left the job?"

Suddenly, the omelet tasted sour in his mouth. Elias lowered his fork and sat back in the chair.

Seeing Elias' reaction, Wilson hurriedly added, "I'm sorry. My question is clearly painful to you, and I have no right to ask."

"No, you have every right, considering the situation we're all in together."

Looking away from his meal companion, Elias stared at the dense greenery surrounding them and allowed his eyes to go unfocused.

"My wife and I were field agents together in the CIA. That's how we met."

"You did not mention you were married."

Elias did not respond directly to Wilson's comment. "It was in the days before 9/11, the days before Homeland Security existed. After 9/11, there was a massive push to coordinate the intelligence gathered by the various agencies. Too many things were falling through the cracks because the different agencies each knew a part of the puzzle but they never talked, never compared notes. Homeland Security came into being, and the OCI was established. I was the first director. My wife…Leah was her name…stayed in the field."

"Those are not the makings for an easy marriage."

Elias smiled. "We were used to it. The times apart were hard. The times together were so intense, so good. I guess it balanced out. But we were planning on Leah coming in from the field and taking a desk job at OCI."

His voice dropping to barely above a whisper, Elias said, "We just didn't make the move quickly enough."

"Oh!"

"I lost Leah while she was on an assignment in Afghanistan."

"Elias, I am so sorry."

Elias kept his eyes on the greenery, allowing his mind to conjure pleasant images of his prior life. "Richard Faulk, the man who took my place, was her immediate supervisor. He's the one who ordered her to infiltrate a Taliban training camp."

"A woman to infiltrate a Taliban camp?"

"Actually, it works better than you think it would. As long as the woman follows Sharia law, including keeping herself covered in public, she is nearly invisible. The mentality of the Muslims is that women are less than nothing. They don't take them seriously as a possible threat. And burqas are a great way to conceal weapons and communication gear."

"Makes sense."

"And she had a backup. Eric Stone."

"Eric Stone sounds like an Anglo name. How was he able to fit in with the Taliban?"

"Eric's father was English, his mother Lebanese. He got the lion's share of his genes from his mother. He looked the part, and he also spoke the language fluently."

Frustration welling up, Elias stopped himself. "I don't know why I'm referring to Eric in the past tense. I don't know that he's gone."

"If he's in Kreitzmann's camp, Tillie will find him."

"I hope so. Leah was also amazing with languages and sounded like an Afghani. She had free rein – could come and go from the training areas, serve food to the Taliban leaders as they met, clean their quarters, everything. All she had to do was listen to their conversations and record them. While cleaning their quarters, she photographed documents, maps, plans, you name it."

"Impressive."

Elias smiled ruefully. "Leah was good. Very good."

"Do you want to tell me what happened?"

"We ordered a missile strike on the base. Leah and Eric were notified and knew to be out of the area before the strike. Eric made it out. Leah didn't."

"Why didn't she get out?"

Wilson watched as Elias' face went through a gradual transformation into an unrestrained mask of rage. Through gritted teeth, Elias explained, "They, the Taliban, knew the strike was coming. Somehow. From what I've been able to put together since it happened, the Taliban leader, Khalid, ordered the evacuation of the camp. But only the key men were told to leave. The women, the children, the elderly, and all of the others he considered to be nonessential were made to stay."

"Why would he do that?"

"He knew that we maintained high-altitude aerial surveillance right up to the strike time. He didn't want us to call it off. He wanted us to think, at least initially, that we were successful. Remember, it's as much a war of PR as it is a war of bullets and bombs. He wanted to embarrass us. We would announce the successful bombing of a Taliban camp and then, through Al-Jazeera, he would release videos showing that we had only killed women, children, and old people, news that would inflame the anti-war side in America and the rest of the world."

"What happened to your wife?"

"That was icing on the cake for Khalid. Apparently, he not only knew about the impending strike, but her cover was also blown. When the missiles hit their lased targets, Leah was staked spread-eagled on ground zero."

Wilson was speechless. The horror of the description burned everything else out of his consciousness. All he could see with his mind's eye was the image of Elias' wife staked to the ground, knowing the exact moment the missile would be arriving. He could not even begin to comprehend how she must have felt in those last minutes and seconds.

Recovering enough to speak, Wilson asked, "Did you ever find out where the leak came from?"

"No." Elias' mood transformed from furor to despair. His voice became muted. "I left the agency right after it happened. I had to. I couldn't think about any of the other aspects of the job. All I could think about was Leah, Khalid, and the traitor. I've spent every waking minute since that day trying to find the sonofabitch who was responsible for her death."

"Elias, I cannot begin to express my sympathy. Going through what you've been through is unimaginable to me."

Elias did not speak. He had long ago run out of appropriate responses to the condolences he received.

"I don't understand something, though."

Elias looked back at Wilson. "What's that?"

"If Eric Stone was able to get out in time, why didn't he call off the strike?"

"He did."

Wilson could see the anger returning to Elias' face.

"Then why did it still happen?"

"He contacted his immediate superior. It was the supervisor's job to convey the news to the military. Let's simply say that they didn't receive the 'abort' message in time."

"His immediate...wouldn't that have been Faulk? The man you said took your place?"

His voice drenched with bitterness, Elias answered, "One and the same."

"And he is the man who sent you into Aegis?"

Elias nodded.

"Wilson, it's a shame I didn't know you earlier."

"Why's that?"

"It occurred to me that your knack for pattern recognition could apply to intelligence work, particularly the process of finding a mole...a traitor...within an organization."

Wilson leaned forward, resting his elbows to the sides of his half-eaten plate of food. "That would be an avenue I've never traveled, but I believe that you could be right. If we get through our current dilemma intact, I would be happy to take a look at your notes."

"Oh, we will get out of this. I promise you that."

"How can you be so sure? You're locked inside a fortress designed to keep everyone in, and you have an army of superhuman beings searching for you."

"I'm sure because I know beyond a shadow of a doubt I am going to live long enough to hunt down the bastards who killed my wife."

Wilson fell into silence. He picked up his fork and took a bite of the now cold omelet. Then he set the fork back down and listened to the howling of the wind.

"When I first saw your atrium, Wilson, I thought you were just a kook who liked jungles."

"You may be right about the nominative 'kook,' Elias."

Elias ignored the comment and continued, "When we spoke and you told me you wanted to surround yourself with complexity, I didn't quite buy it."

Wilson made no comment as he waited for Elias to finish his point.

"You filled this place with dense foliage to create an environment where the Zippers can't function effectively."

It was not a question, but a statement.

"Very perceptive, Elias. The Zippers, like any other high-speed mechanism, require a relatively clear playing field to function as they were designed. The obstructions force them to either move in short-distance spurts or thunder through the leaves and branches, making as much noise as an elephant charging through the brush. At least that is the theory. It hasn't been tested as a defense against them...yet."

"The shotgun should prove to be a fairly effective weapon against them, as opposed to a pistol or rifle."

"That probably is the case."

"Does Kreitzmann have any other super-soldiers in his bag of tricks?"

"Not that I'm aware of. Unless of course he's going to send one of his motor-mouths to talk us to death."

"Motor-mouths?" Elias repeated, cracking a smile. "That sounds like yet another Tillie-ism."

"She is quite gifted in that regard."

"That isn't the only area. Taking on the Zippers and rescuing me was no mean feat."

Wilson nodded. "Mathilda is quite a unique and resourceful individual. I can truthfully say I've never known anyone quite like her."

"I'm surprised that she is in Aegis."

"She's been here since it opened, day one."

"So I've heard. But she didn't mention her reasons for coming in."

"I would be surprised if she had."

"She doesn't talk about it?"

Wilson shook his head. "She has never broached the subject with me, and I've never asked."

They both heard the loud cowbell, followed a moment later by Tillie shouting, "Wilson, it's me."

He turned to look at Elias. "It appears that our able friend has returned."

They could hear Tillie as she quickly pushed through the branches which hung over the pathway, breaking into the clearing, flushed and nearly breathless.

"I found him!"

⊙

Elias and Tillie were crouched next to a large-sized return air grille. On their way, they had stopped at Tillie's apartment, as she referred to it, to gather up some items they might need. Elias had made a perfunctory attempt to talk her into staying with Wilson, but she would not hear of it. She insisted that he would never find Stone through the maze of passageways without her.

Now that they were above the room where Stone was being held, Elias tried again. Huddled close to her ear, he whispered, "I'll take it from here."

Instead of saying anything, she shook her head violently, without ever taking her eyes off the room below. Elias looked down and saw that Stone was sitting on the edge of a bunk, cradling his head in his hands. From their vantage point, and the fact that Stone was not interacting with anyone else, they surmised that he was alone. At least they hoped he was.

Elias knew that their next move could not be accomplished without making some noise, and he hoped not only that the room was empty, but that there was no audio or video monitoring equipment installed in what seemed to be Stone's holding cell.

"Well, here goes," Elias muttered to Tillie, gripping the edge of the grille. It lifted out of the track with less of a clatter than he expected. Stone did not even hear it in the quiet room. Lying down on his stomach, Elias lowered his head through the opening, and in a soft voice called, "Eric!"

The man on the bunk jerked up his head in surprise. Elias saw that it was definitely Stone. At first confused, Stone swiveled his head back and forth, searching around the room for the source of the voice without looking upward.

Elias repeated, "Eric!"

This time Stone looked up, stunned to see his friend's head dangling upside down from the ceiling grille, eighteen feet above him.

"Elias?" Stone's face was a mixture of confusion, fatigue, and despair.

"We're gonna get you out of here," Elias promised, keeping his voice subdued.

Stone stood and moved closer to the grille, tilting his head back to look up. "I can't."

"Of course you can, Eric. We brought a rope and we'll pull you up if we have to."

"That's not what I mean," Stone said, lifting his right trouser leg and showing an ankle bracelet with a blinking green light. "This thing sounds an alarm if I leave this room."

Tillie, who was watching the exchange from over Elias' shoulder, assured him, "No worries. I brought something."

Elias pulled his head back from the opening and looked at her as she opened the duffel bag that she had lugged with them through the mechanical chases. Within moments, she extracted a pair of bolt cutters, held them up for Elias to see, grinned, and said, "Lower me down to him. I'll get that sucker off."

Shaking his head in amazement, he told her, "Tie the rope around your waist."

She did and, clutching the long-handled cutters under her left arm, grabbed the rope with her right hand and eased herself through the opening as Elias slowly payed out the rope. Within moments she was on the floor.

"Who are you?" Stone asked.

"My friends call me Wonder Woman." She immediately bent over and applied the cutting teeth to the curved steel rod which surrounded his ankle, careful to not pinch any skin in its grip. With a smooth motion, Tillie closed the hinged handles, and the teeth cut through with a soft *snick*. There was enough play in the attachment points to allow the bracelet to fall away. Both watched the blinking green light, hoping they did not see it change to red.

When it was obvious that it was not going to change, and they heard no alarm sounding, Tillie tucked the bolt cutters back under her armpit, telling Elias, "Hoist me up so I can help you pull."

Elias obeyed, and in less than a minute she was, again, beside him. Wasting no time, she untied the rope from her waist and dropped it down to Stone, who was waiting quietly.

Before tying himself, Stone glanced up and mouthed a quick "One sec." He grabbed the ankle bracelet and tucked it under the mattress before returning to the rope. With both of them pulling, it took less than a minute before he was in the mechanical chase with Elias and Tillie and the grille was back in place.

To Elias, Stone softly said, "What took you so long?"

"I had to wait for a UPS delivery from Amazon, a boxed set of Jethro Tull."

Stone nodded. "That makes sense." He tilted his head toward Tillie. "New partner?"

Elias grinned. "I'll explain later. Let's go."

They began silently moving away from the room that had been Stone's cell. No more conversation occurred between them as they stealthily made their escape.

$\odot$

The four were seated around the porch table. Wilson had made a pot of tea and some sandwiches. Introductions completed, they ate as Elias filled Stone in on his call from Faulk, their meeting, his trip to Aegis, and what he had encountered upon his arrival, including the fate of the ZooCity populace.

"I'm locked up in this place waiting for my rescue and you took the *train*!"

Elias just grinned.

"Still, I should be grateful that you didn't hitchhike across the country."

Turning serious, Elias responded, "Eric, you're assuming facts not entered into evidence."

"What do you m…oh!" Stone stopped, his eyes boring into Elias'. "You've got to be kidding?"

"What is it? What am I missing?" Tillie asked, leaning closer.

Stone was staring at Elias for confirmation. The expression on his colleague's face was enough.

"He wasn't sent to rescue me." His voice was flat.

Tillie's head swung back and forth between the two men; she was clearly confused. "I don't understand. You said you wanted to find him. You asked me."

Elias nodded, still not speaking.

With a shake of his head, Stone explained, "Elias was never very good at following orders."

Wilson decided to join in the discussion. "If you weren't ordered to rescue Mr. Stone, am I to assume that I was correct in my assumption?"

Tillie froze, fear and anger clouding her face. "You are here to kill us all, aren't you?"

"I was sent to carry out the mission that Eric failed to complete."

"Oh, this is just great. I helped you find your friend, so now there are two of you. You can buddy up, divvy Aegis between the two of you, and wipe us out in half the time!"

$\odot$

"What are you still doing there?"

The voice on the phone was agitated and obviously furious.

"I was clearing up a few loose ends. The visit from Charon didn't help," the man said defensively.

"I told you to gather up everything that we needed and clear out! You should have been gone before that even happened."

"Bonillas has made some real breakthroughs in her lab in the past few weeks. I was waiting for her monthly summary."

This bit of news caused the voice to pause. When he resumed, he was more calm. "Breakthroughs?"

"Yes. Even she is surprised at what some of her subjects are doing now. It's almost as if the immersion group has reached this critical mass. Now that there are so many of them, so many who are developed in the skill and are interacting with the younger subjects, the abilities are amplifying exponentially. Did I tell you that it was one of her subjects who was responsible for identifying Charon?"

"No. You're kidding?"

"I'm not. Right through the observation glass. Charon was meeting Bonillas, and the subject read his mind."

The line was silent as the man at the other end mulled over this development. Finally, he asked, "Do you have her notes?"

"Not yet. At least not all of them. That's why I was waiting for the monthly. When she puts that together, it should all be tied up in a neat package."

"When can you get that?"

"Today, tomorrow...I'm not sure, but soon. She's already late, so it should be anytime now."

"All right. Wait for it. But if you can't get it within twenty-four hours, take what you have and clear out."

"I understand."

They broke the connection, and the man unplugged the line from the jack, disconnecting from the special hard-wire line that had been run into his suite. He packed the phone away, slipped on his white lab coat, and left.

CHAPTER
TWELVE

"As Eric mentioned, I'm not very good at following orders."

Tillie stared at Elias, her expressive face displaying a blend of worry, anger, and something else...something resembling hope.

"Are you saying that you're not going to blow us all away?"

He shrugged. "I guess that depends on the mood I'm in at the time."

Tillie kicked him hard under the table.

"Oww!" Elias barked, reaching down and rubbing his shin.

"If we are to accept what you say at face value," Wilson began, his voice calm and reasonable, "that still begs the questions...why *are* you here? And, now that we've assisted you in the release of Mr. Stone, isn't *he* going to carry out his orders?"

Elias looked at Stone inquisitively. "Eric?"

Stone gave him a hard look. "Thanks. Nothing like putting me on the spot."

"You're the heartless mass murderer," Elias chided with mock innocence. "You mean to tell me you can't handle having some tea and sandwiches with your future victims?"

Before Stone could react, he continued, "I think I know Eric fairly well. I have a feeling that he has already decided to put his initial assignment on hold until he gets a few of his questions answered."

"Questions?" Wilson leaned forward in his chair, interested.

"The same questions I have."

"Are we going to keep playing 'twenty questions'?" Tillie shouted. "Or should I grab a sketch pad and Sharpie so we can switch to a game of Pictionary?"

Elias could not resist laughing at Tillie's impatience. "I'm sorry. You're right. Before I set foot inside Aegis, I knew there was more going on than Faulk said. That's one of the reasons I never intended to carry out the orders he gave me. I'd be surprised if Eric didn't come up with the same concerns as he was cooling his heels in that room."

Stone was still staring at Elias and, his voice low and intense, asked, "Elias, how well do you know these people?"

Focusing on his old friend, all traces of mirth gone from his voice, Elias replied, "Eric, Wilson is John Wilson Chapman, a Nobel laureate. He is the person who told me that Kreitzmann has been in here for years, not weeks as Faulk wanted us to believe. He is also the one who told me that Kreitzmann has his own private back door to the place. Tillie...she is the one who found you and led me to you."

"I'm also the one who thought to bring the bolt cutters."

"She's also the one who thought to bring bolt cutters. She also saved my life. And she also has shown me her secret lair."

Elias made the last part of the comment with his right eyebrow arched for dramatic effect. "So, have I done a background check on them? No. Have I had a chance to strap them down and interrogate them? No."

"Go ahead and try, mister."

Ignoring Tillie, he continued addressing Stone. "But my instincts are telling me that if there is a team that we should be joining in here, this is the one. If you are uncomfortable with my choice, you're, of course, free to split off and go your own way."

"Yeah," Tillie again jumped in. "Now that we've saved your butt, you're free to head off and complete your assignment...without even a 'thank you.'"

Stone looked at Tillie as she made her last comment with all of the bravado she could muster. He saw that buried directly below the surface was a very real concern that he would do precisely that. His eyes moved to Wilson, who sat comfortably in his incongruous office chair, leaning back, sipping his tea, and analyzing Stone as an entomologist might observe some new bug he discovered under a rock.

Then Stone returned his gaze to Elias and reacted to the expression on his friend's face. "You know, it would almost be worth it to stand up and walk out of here just to wipe that smug 'I know what you're going to decide' look off your face."

Tillie was perched on the front edge of her seat, waiting. Wilson was now casually gazing off into the greenery, chewing a bite from his sandwich. Elias watched and waited.

Stone, reaching up and brushing some of his long, dark brown hair off his forehead, finally broke the silence. "It doesn't make any sense."

"No, it doesn't," Elias agreed.

Tillie snarled testily, "What doesn't?"

"As I was sitting in that room, cooling my heels, as Elias put it earlier, I couldn't figure out why Faulk sent me for this job."

"You're not exactly a killing machine," Elias offered.

"You're right. I'm not. Over the years I've done my share. But it's always been single targets, enemy garrisons, terrorist cells, not a huge gathering of American citizens."

He paused and looked pointedly at Elias. "And if I wasn't curious before, I sure as hell would be now."

"Why?" Tillie asked.

Stone turned to look at her. "Because he sent Elias in with the same assignment."

"I don't understand."

"Eric's trying to say that I couldn't kill a fly."

Stone laughed. "Right! You're the next Gandhi."

"Come on! Would someone please explain?"

"Faulk knows Elias and I have a history, a long one. He knows we're friends. He also knows how Elias feels about him. Keeping all of that in mind, do you think Faulk would send Elias in here with the same assignment I had, tell him that I was in here, but not to rescue me? That he was to only carry out the mission?"

"I do believe that Mister Faulk has other plans for the two of you."

All eyes turned toward Wilson, who had turned back to face them as he spoke.

"Plans?" Tillie repeated.

As if he were engaged in an abstract discussion at some old-fashioned gentleman's club, Wilson casually took another sip from his tea mug, his hand shielding the top from the incessant wind in an effort keep out airborne detritus. "It would appear that your Mister Faulk wants to be rid of both of you."

"I was wondering if you would come to the same conclusion," Elias commented sourly.

"Wilson, why would that man want to get rid of Elias and Eric? They work for him."

"Correction...I never worked for him."

"Until now," Wilson corrected.

"Right, until now," Elias admitted.

"Now that we have that cleared up," Tillie retorted sarcastically, "why would he want to get rid of them?"

"Tillie, you were absent at the time Elias and I had a chat about his past. It seems that there was an operation which had gone horribly wrong, resulting in the death of Elias' wife. Eric was involved in that operation, and Faulk was in command."

Her voice abruptly shifting to one of sympathy, Tillie remembered, "I heard you and Kreitzmann talking before you punched him. He mentioned that you had lost your wife."

Elias nodded and repeated the story he had told Wilson. When he was finished, Tillie said quietly, "Oh, my God. I am so sorry."

Before Elias could say anything else, Stone spoke. "There's one thing that doesn't add up."

"Just one?"

"Well, quite a bit, Elias. But why was I captured by the speed demons almost the minute I arrived, but you weren't? If this is all a setup orchestrated by Faulk, it makes sense that they would know I was coming, but they would have known about you, too."

"That's true, Eric. In fact, I was jumped by the ZooCity Zooks right after I got here. It was one of Kreitzmann's Zippers who got me out of it."

"That's very strange. Kreitzmann's freaks stopped them but left you alone?"

"Yes."

"It's quite simple, actually," Wilson stated in the condescending voice of a college professor talking to a freshman.

"At least he didn't say 'elementary, my dear boy,' huh?" Tillie muttered to Elias.

Ignoring her aside and Elias' snicker, Wilson continued, "Elias was effectively captured the moment he walked through the turnstile. Eric, you were merely the bait. You had to be held in abeyance. Otherwise, Faulk couldn't be certain that Elias would accept the assignment."

"Makes sense," Stone stated flatly.

"Once Elias was inside Aegis, it didn't matter to Faulk if he was nabbed by Kreitzmann or not. He was inside and that was the point."

Several of the pieces fell into place in Elias' mind. "There was obviously never going to be an extraction, for Eric or for me."

"It would appear not."

As Elias mulled over the implications of Wilson's hypothesis, the mathematician continued, "I am curious about one thing."

"What's that?"

"How were you to dispose of all of us in Aegis? By what mechanism?"

"Thermal explosions," Elias answered, wondering what path the old man's mind was following now.

"Makes perfect sense. To the outside world it could be explained as an unfortunate, accidental fire, a tragic accident. After all, who knows what those people inside Aegis have been doing? And fire would have the added benefit of obliterating so much physical evidence, as well as the DNA of the victims. All in all, it would be an excellent way to clean up after an operation. You obviously didn't carry that ordnance in with you when you arrived."

"No, I received a drop last night. It came with that."

"I doubt it."

"Of course it did. I unpacked it myself."

"Oh, they may have sent something resembling the devices, but I suspect that what they sent to you is quite harmless."

"If that is true," Stone posited as he joined the conversation, "that would clinch it. There couldn't be any doubt that Faulk is behind all of this."

"True," Elias agreed.

"I'll go check it out," Stone ventured. "All I need to do is open up one of them and I'll be able to tell."

"I'll go with you," Tillie added quickly.

"No, you should stay here."

"Huh-uh. I know the way to his stash."

"So do I. I assume that you used the same spot I was supposed to use?" he asked Elias.

"As far as I know." Elias went on to describe the location.

"Yep, that was going to be my drop location."

"It doesn't matter!" Tillie maintained, raising her voice insistently. "I'm going, too."

"Look…," Stone started to argue, but was cut off by Elias.

"She isn't quite sure about all of this, Eric. And in her shoes, I wouldn't be, either."

"What do you mean?"

"Okay, hotshot," snapped Tillie. "I'll spell it out for you. You were sent here to kill all of us. You were captured the minute you arrived, so you never got your supply of firebombs or whatever they are. Elias tells you that they arrived last night, and all of a sudden you are eagerly offering to go check them out. You haven't even asked us if you could use the bathroom yet! I don't think so, pal. Not without me."

Stone grinned at Elias and commented, "She's quite a piece of work!"

Elias nodded his agreement. "You don't know the half of it."

⊙

With Stone and Tillie gone, Elias settled into the comfortable silence which seemed to surround Wilson. The two men listened to the whipping wind and watched the trees and plants in their frenzied dance.

After some time, Elias finally spoke. "I never knew it was normal for the wind to have such intensity in this part of the desert."

"It isn't. Or, at least, it wasn't always."

"You lost me."

Wilson tilted his head back and looked up at the sky, partially revealed above. "When I first arrived here, it was gusty, to be sure. And it seemed to be constant. I'm not a native of this land, but when I met Tillie, she informed me that at the time she came to Aegis…on its opening day, mind you…it was still. According to Tillie, whom I trust implicitly – not only her integrity but her observational skills, as well – the wind has gathered steadily since that day."

"How can that be?"

"Alas, I am no meteorologist. However, my meager knowledge of the field tells me that there is no viable explanation. What I do know of desert winds is that the rule is a general calmness during the late night through mid-morning, followed, as the day heats, with an escalating wind. What you have, perhaps, not noticed in your short time here is that this wind is unceasing…unabating twenty-four hours a day. Of course, there is always Tillie's explanation."

"Which is?"

"That God is mad at Aegis."

This was not the answer Elias expected from Wilson. "Is she serious?"

"She is. And she has assembled a fairly impressive list of reasons why He should be incensed. First reason, many of the people who have checked in here, by all rights, ought to be dead. Without Aegis, they would have committed suicide. She believes that their continued existence is upsetting some sort of balance."

"The second reason?"

"The fact that Kreitzmann has set up his main, or perhaps even total, operations inside Aegis, that all of his experiments are an offense against nature or God's plan or something like that."

"Is there a third?"

"There is. She maintains that the continued existence of Aegis is like a lighthouse on a stormy night, beckoning to this ostensibly safe port those who might have lost their way – except that this is not the safe port it was, presumably, intended to be. Instead, all of these lost folks are entering a lion's den. She compares it to a lighthouse that might be maliciously built to lure ships onto the rocks."

"She may have some good points."

"She may, indeed."

Elias stared at Wilson, attempting to determine the depth of his sincerity.

Wilson continued, "There is biblical precedent, in which it is said that Sodom and Gomorrah were destroyed due to their wickedness. I dare say that what is happening within these walls rivals the nefariousness of those two cities."

"There could be another explanation for the increased winds. Global warming?"

"Global warming? Puh! Besides, even the Intergovernmental Panel on Climate Change couldn't stretch their findings enough to explain one simple fact about what is happening here."

"What's that?"

Wilson carefully placed his cup on the table and stared directly into Elias' eyes.

"The direction. Rather than coming out of the north, south, east, or west, the wind is blowing straight down from the heavens."

⊙

"Are you sure you know what you're doing?"

Stone was slowing unscrewing the stainless-steel lid on one of the incendiary devices Elias had stowed away.

"Yep. These are standard Incendergel bombs."

Removing the lid, he pointed at the thick, still liquid inside. "About forty-six percent polystyrene, thirty-three percent gasoline with boosted octane, and the other twenty-one percent benzene. Pretty nasty concoction but fairly difficult to ignite. That's why we use white phosphorous as the pyrotechnic initiator, because that stuff is hotter than hell."

"So it is napalm, like they used in Vietnam?"

Stone gave Tillie a crooked grin over the top of the bomb, which he had placed on the end of one of the crates. "You like to read, don't you?"

Tillie nodded, not taking her eyes off the device between his hands.

"Incendergel is a later-generation napalm developed after the Korean War, but quite a bit different from the original, which was naphthenic and palmitic acids. Napalm is really the thickening agent to be mixed with flammable liquids like gasoline. They used it long before Vietnam. It was the juice in the flamethrowers during World War II and the firebombing in Germany. It needs a fuse, or pyrotechnic initiator, to ignite. We also have bombs made with trimethylaluminum. Those don't need a fuse. Exposure to the air is all it takes for one of those babies to go off with a bang."

"So how did you know this wasn't a trimethylaluminum bomb? It could have gone off when you unscrewed the lid and the air hit it."

Stone tapped the side of the bomb with his index finger. "The label. It says right there what kind of device it is."

"And you trust everything on labels?"

He shrugged. "Good point. I am doing this since Elias and I don't trust the guy who sent these. I guess they could've been booby-trapped. One other reason though, a trimethylaluminum device wouldn't have a lid you could just unscrew. The explosive material is sealed in."

Stone dipped the tip of a pencil into the gel, only enough to extract a drop, which he placed onto the top of a piece of sheet metal they had picked up along the way. Setting down the sheet metal, he replaced the lid on the bomb and picked up the metal. After he had put a few feet of distance between himself and the device, he pulled a butane lighter out of his pocket. With one click, the lighter ignited, making a soft whooshing sound. Stone tilted the lighter until the flame licked the droplet on the metal.

There was no instant bright flash; the mixture did not ignite. Instead, the liquid bubbled ferociously until it steamed away, leaving a brownish spot on the hot metal.

"Not the real thing?"

"I don't know what's in these, but it isn't Incendergel or any other form of napalm."

She wrinkled her nose as the smell from the burnt gel reached her nostrils. "Smells like molasses."

$$\odot$$

"Duds, huh?" Elias stated flatly. "I guess that answers that question."

Stone glanced into the front doorway of the shack, where Tillie and Wilson made a show of busying themselves. He was certain they were having a hushed conference about their two new visitors.

"What I don't understand, Elias, is why even send the bogus bombs to you. If the goal was to get you trapped inside Aegis, then once you were here, there wouldn't be any reason to maintain the ruse."

"I've been thinking about that and might have a theory, but it isn't really far enough along in my mind to share."

"Same old Elias," Stone said, shaking his head. "Sometimes I think that you play your cards so close to the vest that even you can't see them."

Elias chuckled.

"At least tell me your theory as to why Faulk wants to get rid of both of us – or, if I was only the bait, you. Is there anything you were working on before he sent you in here that he might have been worried about?"

"I can't imagine. You know what I've been doing ever since the day...."

"Trying to track down Leah's killer."

"Right."

"That's all? No other projects?"

"No. Nothing else. Not for a single minute."

"Then there is only one possible explanation."

"What's that?"

"You were getting close to an answer. And that answer was one Faulk didn't like."

Elias stared at Stone. "Are you saying that Faulk wasn't responsible for her death solely because of his supreme incompetence?"

Stone paused, realizing that planting this thought in Elias' mind was tantamount to lighting the fuse on a guided missile. "Maybe," he answered, hedging.

Many times in the recent past, Stone had seen a certain look cloud the face of his friend, a faraway, unfocused stare…an intense clenching of his jaw…accompanied by an infusion of redness in his complexion. All were telltale signs that Elias was, once again, living through a fantasy which included the meting out of justice against those who were responsible for his wife's death.

"Don't tell me you hadn't considered it in the past."

Elias mentally returned from the movie in his mind and looked at Stone. "I have, but never really had anything I could hang my hat on. All of the clues led me back to colossal stupidity on his part, a conclusion I never had a problem accepting, knowing him as I do."

"Specifically, tell me what new pieces to the puzzle you had found recently. Maybe there's something that will help."

Elias thought for a moment, sifting through the details in his head. "Just one, really. And I'm not even sure if this fits in. I only bring it up due to the timing. You remember Benjamin?"

Stone's eyes widened. "Code name Benjamin? Mossad?"

"One and the same. I heard from him, out of the blue."

"What did he want?"

"I don't know. There was a call from him on my voice mail. He didn't leave any details, but said that it was urgent we speak."

"Did you call him back?"

"I did, but I got his voice mail. We haven't talked yet."

"When did he call?"

Elias stared intently at his old friend and said, "The day before I heard from Faulk."

Stone shook his head. "I don't see the connection, not if Faulk sent me in here two and a half months ago as bait to trap you."

"True. I only brought it up because it was so close to my hearing from him."

The screen door swung open and Tillie came out of the shack, followed by Wilson.

"Tillie, Wilson tells me that you think we are about to receive the wrath of God here."

She dropped her lanky frame into the chair nearest Elias. "Would you blame Him?"

"What's this about?" Stone asked.

Elias pointed up toward the sky and answered, "This wind. When I got here, I thought it was probably normal for this part of the desert. According to our hosts, it isn't."

Stone glanced to the side, focusing on the mad gyrations of the foliage. "So?"

"I was one of the original group to enter Aegis, a first-dayer," Tillie began. "I still remember that day clearly. It was hotter than hell, and they were keeping us under a tent to give us shelter from the sun. We were all hoping for at least a breeze – but nothing, not even a breath of wind."

"I still don't get it. Isn't this a different time of year right now? Couldn't that first day have a been a freak day? I remember years ago, when I was stationed at Edwards, it was windy all of the time, even the trees grew leaning in the same direction. But every once in a while there would be a still, calm day."

Tillie let a lopsided smile curl the right side of her lips. "I *wish* that was all it was. When I first came inside this tomb, I couldn't hear the wind. I picked out one of the empty apartments they had built for us and moved in. But I got stir-crazy pretty quickly and went up to the roof. That was within a couple of weeks of my arrival. By then it was already breezy.

"Going up to the roof became a once- or twice-a-day trip for me. Sometimes I'd spend hours up there. Wilson says that I was regretting my choice to come into Aegis, and that my urge to go on the roof was a symptom of my desire for freedom."

"Was he right?" Elias asked.

She shrugged. "I think Wilson can't help but analyze things. At times he gets a little carried away with himself."

A soft snort came from the mathematician as she continued, "I noticed at the time that it was always breezy. Day, night...didn't matter. It was steady. I know you've all heard the lesson about the frog in the pot of water. Like the frog, I didn't notice that the wind was imperceptibly intensifying. It was so gradual I didn't figure it out for the longest time – a year, maybe two. I happened to tune in one day and realized that it was quite a bit stronger than it had been the first few months I was here."

"Weather patterns are changing," Stone offered.

"Wouldn't know. Remember, I haven't had access to cable TV or the Internet since I got here. The news I did get was from newbies. They told me all about global warming, or I guess they call it 'climate change' now, since it isn't really warming. I don't know. But nobody had any explanation for this wind, especially the way it's been the last year or two."

"What do you mean?"

Tillie looked thoughtfully at Stone. "As fierce as it is right now is the way it is every day. It *never* lets up. Not for a minute. Not for a second. But that still isn't the real kicker. I'm surprised it took me as long as it did to spot this. One night I was up on the roof and I was hanging out in my usual spot. I usually spent all of my time above the entrance so I could see newbies coming. I would drop messages to them, telling them not to come in. At first the gusts were so strong that the second I let the notes go, they would blow about a mile away, out into the desert. So I put them in bottles for a while. That helped at first. But pretty soon the winds got so powerful that, even if I carefully dropped the bottles close to the perimeter wall, the wind would catch them and toss them far out from the building, shattering them. All that did was scare the newbies.

Then I tried wrapping the notes around chunks of concrete block, but the newbies thought I was trying to hit them. I eventually gave up on the whole idea of notes. They never did any good with the few people who read them, anyway.

"It was real late and I thought no one would be coming at that time of night, so I just started walking across the roof, making a beeline across the center of the complex, the wind in my face. You know that big open area in the middle of the complex?"

"Yes," Elias answered, "the center courtyard."

"After I got there, I circled halfway around it to the opposite side and kept walking. That's when I noticed that the wind was now at my back even though I was still going in the same direction."

Stone started to say something. Tillie held up her hand to silence him. "I know that winds shift all the time. I'm not basing all of this on my one experience. Since that night, I have made weekly checks. I've cut across the complex, as I did that night. I've walked the perimeter. You name it, I've walked it. The wind is blowing outward from Aegis toward every point on the compass, seven days a week, twenty-four hours a day. There aren't any anemometers in the supply drops we get here, so I started rigging up crude wind-measuring devices, using ropes and weights. It is getting stronger every day."

"That's impossible," Stone blurted. "The wind can't just blow out in all directions without having come from somewhere."

"Oh, it's coming from somewhere, all right. It's coming from...." She stopped and pointed her finger straight up.

Stone stared at her with open derision. "That's crazy!"

Tillie lifted her shoulders, conveying with the uncomplicated gesture that she did not care if he believed her or not.

The door to the shack swung open and Zack slowly walked out, rubbing his eyes.

"Zack! You're awake," Tillie exclaimed loudly.

The young man muttered something incomprehensible and walked unsteadily to the table.

"You need a place to sit," Wilson noticed, and quickly stood, going inside and returning a moment later with a straight-back chair.

Zack dropped heavily into it the moment Wilson placed it in the circle around the small table.

"How are you feeling?" Tillie asked.

"Would you like a sandwich?" Wilson offered at the same time.

Still vigorously rubbing his eyes and spreading his fingers to encompass his entire face, Zack's answer was nearly muted. "Fine. Yes, please."

Wilson re-entered the shack.

The others waited, giving Zack a chance to orient himself to consciousness and his surroundings. After a moment, his eyes fixed upon Stone. "Who're you?"

"Eric Stone. I'm...."

"He's a friend of mine," Elias finished.

The exact moment that Zack remembered the events prior to his rescue became obvious to the three others around the table, as his face transformed from the normal fogginess of having recently awakened, to a taut, anxious manifestation of fear and apprehension. His eyes instantly began to dart around the perimeter, resting upon one location for only a moment before quickly moving to another.

Seeing the incipient panic, Tillie reached forward and placed her hand on his. "Zack...."

The former Zook jerked his hand back, startled by the contact.

He jumped up, the back of his knees ramming the chair backward; it slammed into the wall of the shack with a crash.

"I gotta go!"

"Where? Why are you leaving? You're safe here," Tillie sputtered, wanting to calm him down.

Zack took several side steps toward the front of the porch, his head now swiveling wildly as he tried to see into the dense curtain created by Wilson's plantings. "My mother. She's in W...Walden. I gotta go find her."

Tillie and Elias both stood and moved toward him. This caused him to bolt, almost jumping down the steps.

"Zack, you shouldn't leave yet," Elias cautioned in a steady voice. "They're out there, and we don't know where they are. You're better off here."

With a violent shake of his head, Zack nearly shouted, "No! My mother is out there. I gotta go."

Before either Tillie or Elias could move closer to him, the young man bolted again, running down the path with his arms flailing, batting the encroaching branches away from himself.

"Zack!" Tillie yelled, and started to follow him.

Elias grabbed her shoulder and stopped her. "We can't keep him here if he doesn't want to stay."

She whirled to face him. "But he doesn't understand. The Zippers are going to kill him, too!"

"He understands."

They both heard the clanging of the cowbell as Zack found his way to the end of the path and exited from the atrium.

Wilson emerged from the shack, carrying a plate with two sandwiches. Seeing the knocked-over chair, he sighed and placed the plate in the center of the table, picked up the chair, set it upright, and sat down.

"I take it that our guest did not want my sandwiches."

As Elias and Tillie walked back slowly, Stone explained, "His mother lives in Walden. He wanted to get to her."

"I see."

Tillie, still obviously upset, rejoined them at the table, followed by Elias. "He doesn't stand a chance."

"And we do?" Elias asked.

"We have a better chance than he does."

"I'm glad you think so."

"Dammit, Elias...."

"Please," Wilson interrupted the two of them before they could escalate. "Don't you think we should stop squabbling and come up with some sort of a plan of action?"

"I agree," Elias said, turning in his chair so that his back was to the angry Tillie.

Balling up her fists on the table in front of her, she forced herself to calm down. Through clenched teeth she asked, "What kind of plan? What's the goal?"

"We need to figure a way out of here," Elias responded.

"What would that accomplish?" Tillie grabbed one of the sandwiches made for Zack and took a bite.

Stone spoke firmly. "What do you mean? Both Elias and I have been tricked into coming inside Aegis. Obviously, this is supposed to be our prison. Of course we need to get out of here."

They all waited while Tillie chewed the large wad of sandwich and swallowed enough to be able to talk. "Wilson, what the heck is in this sandwich?"

"Hummus."

"Hummus! No wonder Zack left. Where am I? Suddenly in Walden? Whoever heard of a hummus sandwich?"

She peeled back the bread and looked inside. "And cucumbers! A hummus and cucumber sandwich! Next thing I know you'll be wearing tie-dyed T-shirts."

She leaned to the side and looked under the table at his running shoes. "Oh, thank God. At least you haven't switched to Doc Martens."

Slapping the two slices of bread back together on the partially eaten sandwich, she tossed it into the foliage.

"That will attract ants," Wilson protested.

"No self-respecting ants are going to eat a hummus and cucumber sandwich. If Zack hadn't run away before, he would have after one bite of that garbage."

She looked innocently around the table and resumed, "Anyway, where were we? Oh, that's right, a plan. Eric, you think that you and Elias should clear out of Aegis, and you probably don't care if you take Wilson and me with you."

"I didn't say...."

She cut him off. "Save it. Whether you do or you don't is irrelevant. The point is, I don't think the two of you were suckered into Aegis only to get rid of you. I mean, isn't a normal part of your everyday job killing people? You know, do a little filing, make some copies, kill Joe Blow, have lunch. If Faulk wanted either or both of you gone, he would just rub you out."

"Rub us out?" Elias barked. "I haven't heard that phrase since I watched an old James Cagney movie."

She waved a hand in his direction dismissively. "Kill, eliminate, take you out, terminate with extreme prejudice, bump you off, send you to sleep with the fishes, snuff, wipe you out, blow you away, extirpate...."

"Extirpate?"

"Exterminate," she continued, ignoring Elias' interruption, "deracinate, *whatever*! All I'm saying is, why wouldn't he just do *that*? Wouldn't that be a lot easier than this whole elaborate ruse?"

Still grinning from Tillie's rapid-fire tirade, Elias looked at Stone and said, "She has a point."

Stone looked at Tillie and back at Elias. "And a hell of a vocabulary, too."

"She's right, you know," Wilson interjected.

"Well, then what *is* the point?" asked Stone. "Why did Faulk want us both here?"

"That's the $64,000 question," Tillie asserted.

All three of the men turned to look at her. Elias was the first to speak. "Did you spend all of your time watching TV Land as you were growing up?"

Grinning mischievously, Tillie answered, "Not important. What is important is why you two were sent here."

Elias started to say something, when Wilson suddenly jumped up, grabbing the ever-present shotgun that was leaning against the wall of the shack. "They're here!" he shouted as he whirled the barrel around to aim it at the wall of fronds and branches.

Elias turned to look and caught a glimpse of beige through the boughs.

KA-BOOM!

He saw a wide area of leaves and branches turned into mulch as Wilson's first shot blasted into the spot where the beige had been.

Cursing the wind for masking the sounds the Zippers would make as they dashed through the bushes, Elias ran through the door of the shack, grabbed the AK-47, and was nearly knocked aside by Tillie, who was also dashing inside. On his way out, he saw the shotgun they had taken from Zack, and grabbed it. Once on the porch, he tossed the shotgun to Stone, who was attempting to spot for Wilson. Before the springs could fully close the door, Tillie burst out with her backpack.

"Keep them in the bushes!" Wilson shouted. "Once they get into the clear, we don't have a chance. Tillie, the net!"

Dropping her pack, Tillie ran to the corner of the porch and yanked down hard on a large wooden lever mounted to the wall near the point where the overhang attached to the shack. Hearing a loud *THUNK*, Elias saw netting tumble down all the way around the perimeter of the porch roof. The netting completely surrounded them, leaving no openings.

"Close the door!" Tillie barked, and Stone ran to the shack door and slammed it shut.

"We don't want them breaking through into the shack and coming out here from behind us. Bar it!"

For the first time, Stone noticed a drop-down bar clipped into the door frame, and swung it down. It fell neatly into the u-shaped catch on the door.

Through all of this, Elias had not taken his eyes off the perimeter. Since the first quick look at the Zipper, he had not seen any other indication of him or any others. In his peripheral vision, he could tell that Tillie was pulling things out of her pack and, by the sounds he heard, assembling something. He appreciated the fact that the railing around the porch was not a typical open frame, but was solid from approximately thirty-eight inches high down to the porch floor. As he crouched behind it, he was able to determine that it was built using stacked 2x6s, with no gaps. There was enough density to stop bullets fired from most guns.

Tapping the railing, Elias noted to Wilson, "You obviously planned for this."

Wilson, who was about ten feet away from him and also crouched behind the barrier, glanced over and huffed, "It would take a fool not to plan for an attack. With a clear picture emerging as to what Kreitzmann and company were up to, I assumed that at some point we might be under siege."

"Incoming! Three o'clock!" shouted Tillie, simultaneously triggering the launcher she had assembled from her pack.

Elias' eyes snapped to the area to the right of the path, in the direction Tillie had indicated, as he heard the *WHOOMP* of her launcher. He saw another beige figure, or perhaps the same one as before, at a standstill, struggling to untangle himself from a jumble of ferns. Whatever it was that Tillie had shot slammed into the trunk of a tree right next to the frenzied figure, releasing a white cloud of gas. Elias was not sure how effective the gas would be in this wind, but his question was soon answered as the rapid movements of the beige attacker suddenly slowed.

The moment her first shot had been released, Tillie madly reloaded and, as she saw the effect from her first hit, launched another, which this time slammed directly into the chest of the assailant, briefly enveloping his head and upper torso in white gas. Elias drew a bead on him and was ready to pull the trigger, but Tillie stopped him. "Save your rounds. He's going down."

Sure enough, the beige figure abruptly dropped to the ground.

"Good shooting!" Stone shouted. "How many more do you think there are?"

"When I watched the video of the attack on ZooCity, I only saw a pair of them," Elias answered.

"I think," began Wilson, his voice ominous, "that the frontal attack was merely a diversion."

Elias looked at Wilson, who had turned around to face the shack.

"What is it?"

Wilson held up one hand, indicating that Elias should listen. Within moments, over the din of the constant gale, Elias heard the distinct crackling coming from within the shack.

"They're burning us out," Wilson sighed.

"Oh, no!" gasped Tillie.

"Clearly, while Zipper number one kept us occupied out front, the other made his way to the rear and torched my home."

"They don't need to come at us," Elias warned. "With the shack burning, we'll be running out to them in a couple of minutes."

Wilson looked crestfallen. "I can't believe I didn't anticipate this possibility."

The man looked so sad that Elias, even in the midst of their predicament, wanted to say something to make him feel better, when Tillie, from the far side of the porch, shouted, "What do you expect, Wilson? You *are* an old fool!"

Elias, startled by her harsh comment, turned and saw that she was grinning at Wilson. Looking back, he noticed that Wilson had snapped out of his remorse and had begun to chuckle.

"You're right, my dear. I am an old fool. But at least I did think of plan B."

"Plan B?" Stone asked, his eyes flitting back and forth between looking at Wilson and watching the bushes and trees around them.

Instead of explaining, Wilson nodded at Tillie, who set her improvised launcher on the deck and scrambled to the corner of the porch. The crackling of the fire on the other side of the wall had escalated to a loud rumbling, and smoke was already streaming from under the door.

Tillie grabbed a long pole with a hook on the end, which was held to the wall with a spring clip. Keeping herself low and out of the line of sight of the Zippers, she twisted around and, using the hook, unlatched a hinged plywood panel mounted to the ceiling of the porch.

Released, the panel swung down and butted perfectly to the top of the railing, enclosing the side of the porch. She slammed down a bolt latch, fastening the two, and rolled the pole to Elias, motioning for him to do the same with the next panel. He looked up and saw that there were panels for each open section, lined up between the support posts. He unhooked the next one and it dropped loudly. Within a moment, it was latched, and he moved on to the third, doing the same.

As he did, he saw that Wilson had begun the same procedure at the other end of the porch and had two panels down, handing off his pole to Stone to drop the third and fourth, the last one longer, as it had to cover the opening in the railing at the steps going down to the grounds. Within less than a minute, they were completely shut in, and Elias could smell the smoke from the fire which was certain to burn through the front wall at any time now.

"Okay," Elias asked, "now that we're trapped, what do we do?"

Standing, Wilson quickly moved to the center of the porch, where the table was, and pushed it roughly to the side as he explained to Elias, "This is an atrium. It is surrounded on all four sides by the structure of Aegis."

"Right."

"Although it doesn't rain with great frequency in this part of the country, when it does, it tends to be a deluge."

As he spoke, Wilson had reached down to the wooden deck and gripped a handle which was flush with the planks. "Where do you think all of the rain that falls into the atrium goes?"

"Soaks in?"

Shaking his head, Wilson replied, "Hardly. There is too much volume of water in too brief a period for a builder to be able to count on that. And you must remember, this entire complex is built on concrete. These atria are nothing but huge planters filled with soil. Below the dirt there is an impervious surface. Therefore, the water would have nowhere to go." With a grunt, he pulled up a section of the deck and indicated, "A storm drain. Every atrium in the place has one."

Elias looked down into the opening and saw a manhole-sized steel collar set into a concrete pad. The collar had at some point held a grate but was now unobstructed.

"I built over the manhole and made the trapdoor my secret back door."

With an ugly crunching sound, the flames burst through a small section of wall.

"We'd better get moving," Stone cautioned, eyeing the flames.

"Yes," agreed Wilson. "Tillie, grab our kit, please."

"You got it."

Tillie kicked a panel in the wall at the opposite end from where the flames were breaking through. The face of the wall, where she had kicked, swung open, and she pulled out a duffel bag and dropped it down the storm drain. She returned for her backpack and launcher while Elias, Wilson, and Stone gathered up their weapons. They all heard a loud crash when something heavy hit one of the latched panels at the perimeter.

"They're trying to get to us. I guess they don't want to wait until we come running out." With that, Tillie dropped down into the opening, catching the top rung of a steel ladder affixed to the side of the riser.

Another crash followed the first, and Elias aimed his rifle at the spot and triggered a short burst from the automatic. Even over the thundering sounds of the wind and the crackling and roaring of the fire as it broke through more of the wall, they all heard the scream come from outside.

"Guess I hit someone."

Tillie was already down into the darkness, and Wilson was just beginning his descent. After Elias' shots, there were no more attempts to batter the panels around them, but the fire was rapidly making the porch an untenable location. As soon as Wilson's head disappeared into the darkness below, Elias slung his rifle over his shoulder and stepped down onto the first rung, following quickly.

As Elias descended, Wilson shouted up to him, "Tell Eric to pull the lid closed behind himself!"

He started to relay the message but was cut off. "I heard."

Far enough down to allow Stone to join him on the ladder, Elias took a second to look down and saw that Tillie was standing on the sandy bottom of the storm drain system and had unpacked an LED lantern from the bag. They all finished their descent, and Wilson turned to Tillie. "You're the one who explored this labyrinth, so lead the way."

Loaded up with her backpack, duffel bag, and the launcher swung over her shoulder, Tillie raised the lantern above her head. "This way."

They all followed. After the melee on the porch, the silence of the storm system was unnerving. Elias noticed that his ears were still ringing, and he assumed that all of the others suffered from the same discomfort. The channel they were traveling was constructed of cast-in-place concrete walls and ceiling. The whorls and textured patterns from the plywood form boards decorated the surfaces, and every eight feet, where the panels had butted together, was a slightly bulging linear ridge of cement. Their path was covered with sand, a result of years of surface erosion carried into the system by torrential rains; Elias did not know if it was obscuring a concrete surface or if the channel had been built with only walls and a lid, left open to the soil beneath.

They had covered several hundred yards, and Elias sensed that they were traveling slightly downhill in what would be the direction of the water flow. Because of the preternatural quiet of the system, Tillie did not need to shout as she warned over her shoulder, "We need to be careful up ahead. No one get ahead of me."

"No problem," Stone replied, breathing heavier from the pace.

"Am I going too fast for you, Eric?" There was a definite tease to her voice.

"No," Stone panted. "I'm fine. More than two months of sitting on my butt got me a little out of shape, that's all. But thanks for asking."

Tillie giggled as they reached what appeared to be the end of the channel. "Here's the deal. This is the retention basin. All of the storm drains from all over Aegis dump into this."

She had stopped and Elias moved up to the front. Their channel had abruptly ended, and he and Tillie were standing on a concrete ledge, which extended approximately eighteen inches from the side walls. Beyond was darkness.

Elias kicked a small rock off the edge and listened as it disappeared into the abyss. Several seconds passed with no sound of impact before Tillie explained, "It's sand down there. You're not going to hear anything hit."

"You've been down there?"

"No. Too far down. Sheer concrete walls all the way to the bottom. No access ladders all the way around."

"How far down is it?"

"About thirty feet or so. Enough to hurt a lot if you fell."

"How do you know what's at the bottom?"

"I was curious and threw a flare down."

"I don't understand," Stone said as he joined them at the opening. "I would have thought that the storm drains would dump all of the water outside Aegis somewhere."

Tillie shook her head. "Remember, this place was built with the idea that no one was supposed to be able to leave. How long would it take the residents to figure out that all they had to do was follow the dry storm drain system to the outside? No, like I said, this is what they call a retention basin. They calculate the maximum amount of runoff that can end up in the system from a one-hundred-year storm, probably add a fifty-percent fudge factor, to be safe, and then basically build a big swimming pool that will hold all of it. The only difference is that this swimming pool has only dirt on the bottom. No concrete. No plaster. Just the soil."

"So when it rains," Wilson chimed in, "all of the drains carry the water to this pit, which is designed to hold it all until it can percolate into the ground."

"Huh!" Stone grunted.

Tillie rolled her eyes and muttered to Elias, "Real bright buddy you've got there."

Elias laughed. "He's a man of few words. So where do we go from here?"

Tillie leaned outward, holding the lantern over the edge. "See. We've got this ledge. It's about a foot and a half wide, and it goes all the way around to all of the other inlets. We need to get to the channel that's two openings this way."

Elias eyed the ledge. "Why that one?"

"That channel takes us to an atrium which is right next to a service closet which…."

"Gets us to your place."

"Right."

"Do you think your little den is safe? If they made a move on Wilson's jungle, they might have gotten wise to you, also."

"Little den? Hey, that's my 'batcave.' Besides, we won't know if we don't go."

Stone was still staring into the darkness of the retention basin. "How do you know about all of these routes?"

Tillie gave him one of her trademark shrugs and said, "I like to explore and I've had twelve years to do it."

"But don't any of the others know about all of these tunnels and channels?"

"People really don't," she answered in a matter-of-fact tone. "They take things on face value. They are told 'here's a room,' 'here's a hallway,' 'there's the bathroom.' That's all they need. I guess I've always wondered what's behind things and underneath things and above things."

"Given a choice," Wilson joined in the conversation, "Tillie will travel three times the required distance from point A to point B as long as she can use some secret passageway."

"I think I would have been happy living in one of those old castles in Europe – you know, one of the places with all of the hidden doors and passages behind the walls."

Elias was beginning to get spooked listening to the echoes from all of their voices. "We'd better get going. If Kreitzmann is getting more aggressive, I don't think dawdling is a good idea."

"10-4!" Tillie snapped back at him, saluting.

Stifling a laugh at her antics, he simply said, "Lead the way."

Still carrying her homemade sleeping-gas launcher, the duffel bag, and wearing her pack, Tillie casually stepped out onto the ledge and began walking, as if she were strolling on a sidewalk.

"I can carry that bag," Stone offered.

She did not even bother to look back as a single snort came from her. With a sigh of resignation, Elias followed her, carrying his rifle. Despite her example, he crab-walked along the ledge, keeping his back against the concrete wall. Wilson came out next, mimicking Elias' method. Stone came out last, doing the same.

"My dear Tillie," Wilson called in a raised voice after some minutes had passed, "I know that you so enjoy showing off, but you are the one with the light."

Tillie stopped and looked back, swinging the lantern around behind herself and seeing the three men about twenty yards back. "You're kidding me, right? Would you like me to install a handrail first before you all come this way?"

Taking a deep breath and forcing himself to ignore the absolute blackness to his right, Elias turned, faced her, and began walking.

"See, I knew you could do it," she teased with the inflection of a mother cheering on her five-year-old who had just made it ten feet on his new bicycle with training wheels.

"Give me the damn duffel bag," he ordered as he caught up to where she was standing.

Without waiting for a reply, he grabbed the rope loop at the top of the bag and swung it off her shoulder and onto his own.

She actually wavered on the ledge for a moment as the counterbalance was abruptly removed. Elias started to reach out to steady her, when she slapped his hand away. "I'm good." Her voice was less even than she had intended it to be.

With his free hand, Elias gripped her arm and softly said, "Tillie, you don't have to prove anything."

He felt her muscles tense and was certain she was going to shake off the contact. Then there was a sudden change. She relaxed and, in the pale white light from the lantern, he saw her smile at him.

"You're right. I don't. That isn't the deal, anyway."

Elias could hear Wilson and Stone catching up, but asked, "What is?"

The smile frozen on her freckled face, Tillie answered, "The deal is…I came here to die, remember? That was the point."

She glanced past him and saw that the two men were right behind Elias. "Can we keep moving now? I promise to keep it slow."

She unceremoniously turned her back to Elias and began walking. He followed, and within a minute or two they arrived at the first of the inlets.

"Anyone want a break?"

"Tillie, don't be a smart aleck," Wilson snorted testily.

"Just trying to be nice."

"You have to try?" Stone commented.

Tillie whirled around to face him and stuck out her tongue, blowing a raspberry in his direction.

"Children, please!" Elias exhorted.

Tillie turned back around and continued her pace on the ledge. The others followed quietly until reaching the next inlet. Entering it, she announced, "The riser isn't far from here."

Within minutes they were standing beneath the round concrete drainpipe. At the top, the steel grate was visible. Tillie grabbed for one of the access rungs; Elias beat her to it and, still toting the duffel bag and rifle, climbed to the top, with her following right behind. There was no rust, but the grit from the sand had packed into the tight space between the grate and the collar. It took three grunting shoves before the lid broke loose, a shower of fine dust and dirt cascading down upon them. He slid it to the side and climbed up another rung, poking his head above the collar.

"This doesn't look good," he barked, once again shouting to be heard over the din of the winds.

"What's wrong?"

Elias did not answer. Instead, he climbed the rest of the way out of the drainpipe, clearing the way for Tillie to follow. When her head cleared the top, she quickly looked around and, seeing what had occurred, muttered to herself, "Good God!"

Wilson, who was the next to come up, heard the exchange but did not inquire. Rather, he hurried the final distance. Pulling himself out of the manhole and flopping onto the powdery soil, he took in the scene with his own eyes.

As Stone crawled out right behind him, Wilson remarked, "It seems that the wind has picked up a bit."

"What do you m…?" Stone stopped in mid-sentence as he also took in what had happened. "This looks like the bottom of a dumpster on a construction site."

The atrium, without the benefit of Wilson's horticultural obsession, coupled with the absence of any caretaking by the other residents, had been nothing but a desiccated sandbox. But now, instead of four walls and a dirt floor, the area was filled with a jumbled pile of broken steel struts, millions of shards of shiny black glass, twisted and mangled aluminum framing, and hundreds of yards of copper wiring.

"What the hell happened?" Tillie gasped, barely audible above the whistling, rampaging wind.

"Those are the solar panels from the roof," Elias answered.

"It looks like some giant just swept them into the atrium with a swipe of his arm."

Wilson twisted around and sat upright, dangling his feet into the storm drain from which the group had emerged. "I'm certain the entire solar collector system up there is…was tied together. The panels would all be interconnected. One weak link, one vulnerable bolt not completely torqued down, would be enough to start a chain reaction. It would violently lift, catching and tearing the adjacent panels as it went. In effect, there would be an avalanche driven by the wind instead of gravity, crashing and ripping more sections as it gathered momentum until it found this atrium, into which it all tumbled."

Elias stood up and slowly turned around, taking in the details of the disaster. As the others rose, Wilson, his voice for the first time conveying something more than his steady academic tone, said, "I believe we might be running out of time."

CHAPTER THIRTEEN

"We've lost two Accelerants! How is that even possible, Mr. Killeen?"

The young man, still in his twenties, and for the first time in his brief life feeling that he was in over his head, answered, "I'm still not sure, sir. It's a little difficult to piece together exactly what happened."

"A little difficult? Maybe you could provide me with your best guess."

Stinging from the overt sarcasm, the subordinate began talking quickly. "They might have been prepared for the visit. We found unburned remnants of netting on the perimeter of the area where the shack had been."

"We already knew the old man was anticipating us, you fool. That's why he filled his little courtyard with all the vegetation, to slow down our Accelerants!"

"Yes, yes. I know. But it looks as though there were other measures – the netting…defensive barriers…and this."

Killeen stepped carefully over the heaps of debris and still-smoldering wood until he reached the spot where the porch had once stood. Pointing downward, he explained, "They had an escape route."

The other man looked down at the opening to the storm drain and said nothing.

"We didn't discover this until after the fire was out, and even then, not immediately. We had assumed they died in the blaze. The fire caused the roof to collapse, and we were digging through the rubble looking for their bodies when we found it."

The man stared down into the manhole, feeling his blood pressure rise. "You still haven't told me how we lost *two* Accelerants? Are you telling me Charon is that good?"

"No sir," the younger man replied hastily. "From what we can tell, I think it was a fluke."

"A FLUKE! We lost two subjects, who were both the result of years of the most advanced immersion and training, to a *fluke*?"

Sucking in a deep breath, Killeen plunged ahead. "I guess that was an unfortunate choice of words, but apparently one of the Accelerants was wounded from gunfire. The doctor said that the wounds wouldn't have been fatal. The other had been knocked unconscious before *this* happened."

At the end of his sentence, the man had swept his arm around to indicate the overall area surrounding them.

"Evidently, while both Accelerants were down, all of these solar panels crashed into the atrium. With their speed and agility, they probably would have been able to outrun or outmaneuver the metal and glass. But they were both incapacitated before it happened – one from the gunshots, the second from some other cause. They were both crushed to death."

Before the older man could respond, they were joined by a third. "I may have your answer on why the second Accelerant was unconscious at the time."

"That would be appreciated, Doctor."

"After we pulled the heavy steel frame off him…which was the cause of death, by the way…my assistant and I put him on a field stretcher. This area was far too cluttered for us to use our gurney, so we left it outside the atrium, in the corridor. I helped him carry the stretcher to the corridor, and it's a good thing I did."

"Why, Doctor?" the older man inquired, trying to hide the edge in his voice.

Oblivious to his superior's testiness, the doctor resumed, "Out here it was far too windy for me to notice it; however, as soon as we reached the corridor, the smell of Sevoflurane was unmistakable. The front of his tunic reeked of it."

"Sevoflurane?"

"Anesthesia. One of the two compounds we use frequently."

"Anesth…! How could one of our Accelerants be anesthetized out here, in the middle of a mission?"

"Really quite clever, actually. And this would explain a couple of other incidents which had us befuddled in the past."

"Doctor, please…!"

Raising his hands in a gesture intended to calm his superior but having the opposite effect, the doctor began, "The Accelerants have a hyper-metabolism. Their consumption of all things we normally need – water, food, air – is dramatically pumped up, as it were. And when they are in motion, so to speak, their hearts and all of their other muscles demand oxygen at a radically heightened rate."

"I know all of this. They pant like dogs, so what?"

"That same demand for oxygen would make them vulnerable to an anesthetic at levels which would be essentially harmless to us."

"Do you expect me to believe that Elias, or one of his group, managed to sneak up on an *Accelerant* and held a rag over his mouth until he passed out?"

The doctor shook his head. "That wouldn't be at all necessary. Sevoflurane or Desflurane, either one of them loaded in a dispersal device, such as a tear-gas canister, would knock out an Accelerant, and the people around probably wouldn't even need gas masks."

Killeen looked off into the distance, thinking. "That would also explain how Charon escaped from our lab."

The doctor nodded.

⊙

Crossing the short distance from the storm drain to the nearest exit from the atrium proved to be tedious and time-consuming, as the four had to climb over or occasionally move the twisted and shattered solar panels. As they entered the corridor, Elias looked at the ceiling and noted, "I'm surprised the lighting still works. I would have thought that what happened on the roof would have shut down the electrical systems."

"We don't know yet if it has," Wilson cautioned. "Almost all of the daytime lighting in the complex is from solar tubes, rather than electric fixtures. But I doubt that the rooftop calamity shorted out our power. The systems would be isolated and protected by breakers. Anyway, the sun is setting. We'll know soon enough."

"Won't the batteries die without the solar panels feeding them anymore?"

"Yes, eventually. You must remember, Aegis is still not even approaching its design capacity, insofar as population and, therefore, electrical demand. The batteries should last for many days, perhaps even weeks."

"Besides," Tillie added as she walked over to them, "I've got two generators stashed."

"You know, Tillie," Elias remarked, "you are rapidly losing the ability to surprise me."

"Oh, yeah? Well...hey, what's that?"

As Elias jerked around to look in the direction she was staring, she suddenly punched him in the stomach.

"Ooww! What was that for?"

"Just wanted to show you that I could still surprise you. Come on, we'd better clear out of this open corridor and get to my place."

Rubbing his abdomen with both hands, he watched as she grabbed the duffel bag he had taken from her down in the storm system, and tossed it over her shoulder. Carrying only his rifle, he followed her as he heard Wilson softly laughing.

The balance of the journey was uneventful, and they were all soon entering her den. In deference to Tillie's mudroom, they all paused and leaned their weapons and packs against the walls. Elias hung up his windbreaker on one of the decorative hooks, leaving his 9mm in the pocket. Exhausted, they rounded the corner and proceeded to get settled in her main room.

Almost immediately, Stone excused himself, and was gone for several minutes. As he walked back in, Tillie glanced up at him. "Where were you all this time?"

He reached up and shook the back of his shirt collar. "On our trip through the storm sewer, I got sand everywhere – inside my shirt, pants, socks, my...."

"I don't need to know the details," she interrupted. "You didn't shake out your clothes in my environment, did you? If I find sand scattered all over my pretty stuff, I'll make you pick it off one grain at a time."

"No, I didn't," he answered quickly. "I went down the passageway. That's why I was gone so long."

Tillie eyed him suspiciously, but said nothing.

"Now, I'm really confused." Stone's brow furrowed.

"About what, Eric?" Elias asked.

"Before we were attacked at Wilson's, I thought we had concluded that Faulk wants you alive. It didn't look as if that really was the case when they torched Wilson's place with us trapped on the porch."

"Not necessarily," Wilson surmised. "It could have been their plan to smoke us out. It is a rare individual who will remain in a burning building, no matter what might be outside. People have even leapt from twenty-story windows to avoid the experience."

"I think Wilson's right. If he, or whoever we're working against, wanted me dead, I would have died during that first run-in with the Zooks."

Tillie, who was lying on the sofa, with her feet dangling over the back and her arms crossed and covering her face, blurted, "Duh! That's a no-brainer. What I don't get is, if they knew you were coming, why did Kreitzmann buy your act and give you a tour?"

Elias paused and did not answer. Neither Wilson nor Stone offered an explanation, either. Tillie, waiting for a response and getting none, uncovered her face and twisted her head around to look at them. "You mean I'm the only one who has been wondering about that? It's what I'd expect from these two, but Wilson, I'm surprised at you."

"Tillie, there is no reason to be insufferable. I am certain that all of us have wondered the same thing."

"It hadn't occurred to me," Stone said.

"See!"

"Tillie!"

"Okay, okay."

Elias cleared his throat before speaking. "I've been wondering the same thing. Every explanation leads me in a circle. I feel like a dog chasing his tail."

"I have no doubt that we are missing an essential piece to the puzzle," Wilson agreed. "Once we find it, that particular question will be answerable."

Elias looked at him thoughtfully. "You're right. But I'm not sure we have enough time to find that piece. By the way, we've been through quite a bit over the last few hours. How are you holding up?"

Wilson, who had sunk so deeply into an overstuffed chair that his arms, perched on the armrests, were level with his ears, smiled at Elias. "I appreciate your asking. I really do. I've managed to keep myself in fairly good condition over the years...."

"Because I've worked his butt off," Tillie interjected.

"She's right. There are very few things better for an old man than to struggle to keep up with a young friend. To answer your query, Elias, I am fine and looking forward to what may come next."

"Wish I could say the same," he responded.

Stone, who had taken to the bed Elias had awakened in earlier, joined in, "Speaking of what may come next, Elias, do you have any idea what we are going to do?"

"I do. I think we have two issues. We need to find that missing piece to the puzzle Wilson mentioned, and I think that we need to figure a way to get out of here. And, considering that God, nature, or who-knows-what seems to be intent on tearing this place apart, I don't think we have much time to do both."

"Which means we should probably split up," Stone offered.

"That might be a good idea."

"It's a dumb idea," Tillie huffed.

"Why?"

"If we are going to make it, we need to stick together. In all the movies I ever watched before I came in here, it was always the same. Somebody in the group said, 'We need to split up,' and as soon as they did, they all died."

"Tillie, this isn't a movie."

"Don't you think I know that, Elias?" As she answered him, she swung her legs around, placing her feet on the floor, and sat up, facing him. "But it doesn't matter. Each one of us has something to offer. You split us up, we all lose. Besides, I can solve one of your two issues."

"Which one?"

"How to get us out of here!"

Elias stared at Tillie, trying to read her eyes. She stared back defiantly.

"Tillie, my dear, you know a way out?" Wilson inquired softly.

She nodded. "I always have, basically since I came into this place."

"Why didn't you ever tell me?"

She turned to look at Wilson. "Why? Did you ever once say you wanted to leave?"

"No. You know that I didn't."

"Then why would I tell you?"

"How did you find it?" Elias asked.

"Not important. I just did. Remember me? I like to explore. I like to crawl through every nook and cranny to see where it goes."

Elias took a deep breath, aware that he was rolling the dice. "I don't believe you."

"*WHAT?*" She nearly swung up off the sofa as she shouted.

"I don't believe you. I've been in the business my whole life. The reason I'm still alive is that I can tell if someone is feeding me a line of baloney."

She laughed once, derisively. "I don't know about the rest of your life, but the reason you are still alive at this moment is *me*. If your ability to survive is what you're hanging your hat on, from the little bit I've seen, I'm not impressed."

Wilson began to chastise Tillie, but Elias held up his hand to stop him. "Tillie, this is easy to resolve. If you know a way out, why don't you show me?"

"Why don't you go to hell?"

The three men fell into silence, all staring at her. She was perched on the edge of the cushion, leaning forward, her eyes wide, her breathing ragged, her fists clenched, her entire body so tight it might have been a coiled spring.

In a soft and gentle voice, Wilson spoke to her. "Tillie...I have known you almost since the day I arrived. I have counted you as my friend. In that time not a day has passed in which we did not spend time together. Throughout much of it, you have been my lifeline, my thread of optimism, a stabilizing force when I might have wandered too far from the realm of hope."

His words had an effect on her, as the tension gradually seeped out of her body. Her fists slowly unclenched.

"You have been the only friend I have had in this unnatural habitat. And you have been the only friend I have needed."

She turned her eyes to look at him. A hint of a smile curled her mouth.

"I must say that the Tillie sitting before me is not the same person who wielded the shovel as we planted my trees and bushes. It is not the same person who sat with me for hours as we laughed, cried, and shared our thoughts; not the same person who gave me my only reason to look forward to each day in this self-imposed prison."

A single tear welled in the corner of her eye and spilled down her cheek.

"Mathilda, please tell me what is wrong."

As Wilson spoke, more tears had joined the first in a trek down the sides of her face. In the course of less than a minute, the hard, angry countenance of the woman evaporated, replaced by the fragile, vulnerable face of a younger girl.

Speaking to Wilson as if they were the only two in the room, Tillie, her voice muted and breaking, said, "This isn't what I wanted, what I hoped for when I put up the sign."

Wilson smiled at her reassuringly. "I know. It is not what I hoped for, either."

"It's almost like I made things worse."

"No, no, Tillie. What is happening around us now was all in motion long before you put pen to cardboard."

She tilted her head slightly to the side, a move which seemed to accentuate her sudden vulnerability. Elias and Stone watched silently.

"I know that, Wilson. But I thought the cavalry would come charging in, or at least Bruce Willis and Arnold Schwartzenegger, not Andy Griffith and Don Knotts."

Elias took a breath to speak but was stopped by Wilson who lifted a single finger, never moving his eyes away from Tillie. "I believe that sometimes people might actually pleasantly surprise you."

She shook her head. "I don't think so, Wilson. I mean, look! Everything that's happened since Elias has arrived *I've* done, not him. And when we were on your front porch, it was you who had planned for an attack and prepared the things that saved us. If we were relying on them, we'd both be dead or in one of Kreitzmann's cages by now."

"You need to trust, Tillie...trust in your judgment. You need to be willing to give people a chance."

"*I can't!*"

Wilson hesitated, sensing that he was entering some forbidden territory, one that over the years he had verbally stumbled close to and always quickly backed away. He knew that this time, now, he must plunge ahead. "Why, Tillie? Why can't you?"

She was biting her bottom lip, no longer looking at Wilson. Her gaze and her mind had traveled to another place and another time. Almost a minute passed before she spoke, her voice even more subdued than before, her tone flat and emotionless. "It has to be me. I can't count on anyone else."

"You still haven't told me why."

Wilson could see the muscles in her jaw flex repetitively. Her eyes now darted, unable to fix upon one location. "Because if I do, someone dies."

"Tillie?" Wilson spoke her name and waited for her eyes to connect with his. His patience was soon rewarded, and he continued, "This is why you are in Aegis, isn't it?"

Staring at him, she unsteadily jerked her head up and down to indicate that he was correct.

As soothingly as he could muster, Wilson asked, "What happened?"

Her voice suddenly sounded as if it came from someone years younger. "I don't...I don't want to say."

"I've never asked you before, Tillie. I've always known not to. But I think perhaps it is time."

Her head began swaying side to side, a nonverbal denial of the cascading thoughts within her mind. The motion intensified, almost as if she were trying to shake out the images or memories. Wilson waited.

The swaying reluctantly ceased. She said nothing for such a long time that Wilson was about to coax her, when suddenly she began.

"I was sixteen. Almost sixteen. My mother had told me that I couldn't date until my birthday. I thought I knew better. I always did. I was secretly seeing a boy named Jason from the school I used to go to.

"My dad was dead. He had been for about three years. Right after he died. . .I mean *right* after, my mother started dating. A lot of guys. A regular parade through our house. I hated her for what she was doing. I thought that she was glad he was gone, that now she felt free. And probably since I hated her for dating so soon after Dad died, she started hating me, too.

"It wasn't long before one of the guys...she wasn't even sure which one...got her pregnant. It didn't matter, since all she did was pick the one she wanted to believe it was and told him he was going to be a father. She might as well have said that a meteor was coming and was going to hit our town; he split so fast it was nuts!"

The men listened to her story, transfixed. Although her voice, to this point, had been flat, inflections and emotions began to creep in.

"She had the kid. I don't know if it was the whole Catholic thing or what it was, but she didn't have an abortion. So there I was, almost sixteen years old, with an eleven-month-old baby brother named Maxwell."

She made a nervous, stuttering sound intended to be a giggle.

"Goofy name, huh? I refused to call him Max. I thought that sounded like a dog's name. Anyway, I loved Maxwell from the moment I saw that wrinkly little guy come out of her. Yep, that's right. I was at the delivery, standing right where the father was supposed to be.

"It's a good thing I did love him, because she sure as hell didn't. Well, at least I thought I did."

There was a momentary pause in her monologue before she went on. "The second she was over the birth deal, she was back out on the town. I think she lost the extra weight in about a month. Oh, she would breeze in and out making a big show of fawning over Maxwell, saying 'Mommy this' and 'Mommy that,' but *I* was the mother. There were only two times that she would really hold him and spend any time with him – when her girlfriends were over and they were carrying on about how cute her baby was, and when she breast-fed. And I think the only reason she kept breast-feeding was that it made her boobs bigger for the guys.

"The rest of the time it was all me. I got up at all hours of the night, every time he cried or was sick. I loaded him in the stroller and we went for walks. I dropped out of school so I could take care of him. I don't think she even noticed I was out of school. I took him to the doctor. I did everything."

Tillie paused, her eyes closed as if she were trying to block out an image. As she began speaking again, her voice was so soft that the three men had to strain to hear her words. "I wanted to take a real shower. That was it. That was all it was. Just a shower.

I always kept Maxwell with me. Every minute of every day. He was *never* out of my sight. I even took him in the bathroom with me every time I went to the toilet. One evening, as usual, my mother was out on a date, and Jason had come over to hang out with me. We were going to watch a movie and eat some popcorn while we stayed home with Maxwell. Fun date for an almost sixteen-year-old, huh? Anyway, before we started the movie, I picked up my brother and asked Jason to carry the little playpen into the bathroom. I was going to take a shower, and that was what I always did. Maxwell would be in the playpen right outside the shower stall.

"I couldn't ever take a long shower. As soon as I closed the glass door and the little guy couldn't see me, he would start to fuss. So I would always rush. Jason knew this and suggested that I leave Maxwell with him so that I could take my time. The thought of a long, leisurely shower, the first one I would have had in almost a year, sounded wonderful. But I wasn't sure. I argued, but Jason promised me over and over again that he would watch Maxwell."

Elias, sensing the direction her story was going, began to tense.

"He convinced me that it would be fine. I started to put my brother in the playpen in the living room, but Jason said he wanted to play with him, so I handed Maxwell to Jason and went to take my self-indulgent shower. My God, it felt great. There was a little voice in my head telling me that I should hurry up and get out, but it felt wonderful. I stayed in there for almost half an hour. Then I toweled off, blow-dried my hair, got dressed, and even put on a little makeup for my *date* with Jason.

"I came out, and Jason was sitting on the couch, talking on his cell phone to some friend of his! Maxwell wasn't on the couch with him. He wasn't in the playpen. I freaked. Jason dropped the phone, and we both started running around looking for Maxwell. But we couldn't find him anywhere. I was going totally crazy. Screaming at Jason. Calling him every name in the book. He just kept apologizing and giving me some crap about how he was only on the phone for a minute before I came out. Later on, afterward…I checked his call history. He lied to me. He had been on that damn call for almost the entire time I was out of the room.

"Maxwell was quite the crawler and could have gone anywhere. We checked the whole house twice. All the outside doors were closed and locked. It was one of my habits. I locked them after Jason arrived. We looked under the beds. We called my brother's name a hundred times. Nothing. I was totally panicked and didn't know what to do. I went into the kitchen to call 9-1-1. As I was dialing, I looked down at the bottom of the back door and saw the doggie door. I had never given it a thought while we were looking for Maxwell. We hadn't put it in. We never had a dog. It was there when Mom and Dad bought the house, and I had forgotten about it completely.

"I dropped the phone, screamed for Jason, and ran out back."

Tillie's eyes were squeezed tightly shut, her mouth twisted into a grimace. "Did I mention before that we had a swimming pool?"

"Oh, Tillie," Wilson murmured.

Talking slowly, almost trance-like, Tillie continued, "I must have finished dialing 9-1-1 before I dropped the phone, because the police showed up within a couple of minutes. One of them had EMT training and took Maxwell away from me and tried to revive him while the paramedics were on their way. But it...it was too late."

She fell into silence, vividly reliving the scene she had spent the last sixteen years running away from. Her shoulders began to heave, and a series of racking sobs burst from her. Elias was the first to move and sat on the sofa next to her. As soon as she felt his arm on her shoulder, she twisted toward him and threw her arms around his neck, the sobbing intensifying.

They sat holding each other for minutes, neither speaking. The crying gradually ebbed off to a gentle weeping, which diminished to a muted series of sniffles. Lifting her head from his shoulder, Tillie looked up at Elias, her eyes bright red. "Well, now you know the answer to both of your questions – why I'm here and why I don't trust anyone else."

Elias struggled to find something to say. He wanted to tell her that he was not Jason, that she could count on him. He wanted to promise her that he would make sure everything turned out all right. It was a combination of her very rawness and her abject vulnerability, as well as his own lack of certainty that he would be able to keep such a promise, which stopped him. All he could think of to say, he said. "Tillie, I'm so sorry."

From across the room, as if reading Elias' mind, Wilson again spoke soothingly. "Jason is not in this room. So much time has passed since then, Tillie; you are older now and you must learn to trust your insights. You have already had some time to get to know Elias, haven't you? I'm not saying that any of us are the heroes from some blockbuster movie. In fact, as of this moment, I have no idea who will prevail. I don't believe that we could hazard a guess in that regard. But, Tillie, the effort will be made, and you must trust in that. And if I am wrong, if I have so grossly misjudged the situation, then I am a bigger fool than I thought."

Tillie swayed back, away from Elias, dragged the sleeve of her shirt across her face, and sniffed. She looked at Wilson, lingering on his face for a moment, before she glanced briefly at Stone, who had moved to the front edge of the bed, and finally returned her eyes to Elias, quietly asking him, "Promise something?"

"I will. What is it?"

"Promise me that you'll at least try to be Bruce Willis. Just till this thing is over."

He smiled at her and nodded. "I promise, as long as I don't have to shave my head or sing."

"He's bald?"

A subdued laugh came from Elias. "You have been out of touch for a while, haven't you?"

She smiled back. "Deal."

⊙

They had agreed that this might be their last opportunity to get some rest before facing the ordeal ahead. The sun had gone down long ago and the florescent lights had come on, so the battery and electrical system seemed to be functioning. Since Stone had been resting in his quarters before they rescued him, he offered to stand watch as the others slept.

Tillie, exhausted from the day, as well as from her emotional outpouring, crawled into her bed and fell asleep almost immediately. Wilson, maintaining his unruffled composure, propped his feet on the coffee table and tilted his head back, commencing a sonorous symphony of snores within minutes.

Elias was having trouble clearing his mind enough to take the much-needed nap. Stone walked quietly to where Elias stood and cautioned him, "If you don't catch at least some sleep, you're gonna be worthless later."

Elias, answering softly to not disturb Tillie or Wilson, replied, "I know. But there are a couple of things that don't fit. They're driving me crazy."

"Only a couple? You're doing better than I am, then."

"I'm serious, Eric. Why did they, whoever *they* are, want me in here alive? Tillie's right. Normally, I would just disappear. It doesn't make any sense."

"Insufficient data at this time."

Elias spun his head and looked at Stone. "What?"

"I'm saying that we don't know enough to answer that question. That's part of what we need to sort out after we get some rest."

Elias stared at him for a minute before he reached up and rubbed his eyes. "I guess you're right. A little unconsciousness would be a good idea."

"Yeah, it would."

"Keep *your* eyes open."

"Not to worry."

Since Wilson was supine in the wing-back chair and Tillie had crashed on the bed, Elias moved to the sofa and lay down. He saw Stone position himself off to the side of the main area so that he could watch both entrances. Satisfied, Elias lowered his eyelids. Within five minutes Stone heard the steady, rhythmic pattern of snores coming from Elias.

He sat patiently and waited an additional five minutes before silently easing off the stool where he was perched, and carefully walking away. It took him the better part of twenty minutes to reach Elias' cache. Wasting no time, he picked up the large backpack loaded with the firebombs and started to leave.

"Put them down, Eric."

The voice came from the darkened passageway ahead, and Stone froze, recognizing Elias' voice.

In slow motion, ensuring that both of his hands were visible throughout the procedure, Stone unslung the bulky pack from around his arms and shoulders, and eased it to the floor.

Elias stepped forward, and Stone could see that he was pointing the AK-47 directly at his chest.

"Talk."

"How'd you figure it out, Elias?"

Elias shrugged, the barrel of the rifle did not waver. "When you and Tillie returned, I asked her to describe the procedure you used to test the Incendergel. Pretty clever, actually. A rookie wouldn't know that the gel needs pressure, fuel, and ignition to go off. The fuel was present. You only introduced ignition."

"You wouldn't have asked her if you weren't already suspicious."

"You're right. I was. To tell you the truth, *old friend*, I was a lot more than just suspicious."

As he detected the tone in Elias' voice, understanding dawned on Stone. "I see. They told me you were getting close. I assume you found out."

Elias was staring at him dispassionately, and did not answer.

"So I guess you didn't come in here to rescue me."

"I came in here to kill you."

CHAPTER FOURTEEN

Entering not his administrator password, but the password assigned to Dr. Bonillas, which one of the Accelerants had obtained for him, his hand quickly manipulated the track ball, moving the cursor around the modules on the interface where all of the department heads uploaded their summaries of notes and reports. It took less than a minute to find Bonillas' designated subdirectory.

"She must have just filed it," he muttered aloud, smiling. With a few more clicks he was done; his only delay was as he decided whether to copy the files or move them, opting for the latter.

"Got it!" he said to himself as he slipped the flash drive into his pocket. The lab was deserted at this time of night, for which he was grateful. Shutting down the computer, he crossed the large room to the exit, switching off the lights before he opened the door and stepped out into the hallway.

"Doctor Boehn! What are you doing here so late?"

Boehn whirled around to see Rudy Kreitzmann standing five feet from him, a quizzical look on his face.

⊙

"Manager Pierce?"

Mildred Pierce, who was sitting at her desk in near darkness, the only illumination coming from a candle flickering beside her elbow, turned to see that Will Rogan was standing at the door to her office.

"Come in, Will, please. Have a seat. Would you care for a glass of this dreadful wine?"

"We have wine? I thought the supply drops didn't include any recently."

"One of our people tried to make some."

She took a sip and crinkled her nose in disgust. "It is vile."

"No, thanks."

As Rogan walked in, Pierce noticed an air of depression enveloping him like a cloud. Dropping into a chair near her, he sighed, "We've lost eight more."

Pierce reacted to the news in much the same way that an overloaded mule might react to one more sack of goods being dropped onto its back. "That puts us down to less than forty."

Rogan only nodded.

Her voice flat, she asked, "Not that it matters, but do you have any idea why?"

Rogan drew in a deep breath, letting it out slowly before he replied, "I guess it was because of the electricity going out."

"The electricity? That's all? We have candles, and it isn't too hot or too cold right now. I don't...."

"Manager Pierce, you know it doesn't take much with our people. By the way, it's almost ironic, but Johnson just got back from a little patrol, and I guess that Walden is about the only part of Aegis without power."

Her eyes widened slightly. "How is that possible?"

"I don't know. I'm not an electrician. But I assume that when the solar panels on the roof were destroyed, breakers would have tripped, protecting the batteries and circuits. It seems that our breakers didn't trip quickly enough."

$$\odot$$

"Ms. Stephenson?"

Erin tilted her head so that she could see around Liz, the makeup artist preparing her for the late broadcast. "What is it, Amber?"

"It's Rusty, from the National Weather Service. He wants to talk to you."

"I can't right now. I go on the air in ten minutes."

"I know. I told him that. But he said it was important."

It only took Erin a moment to decide. "Bring a cordless to me."

"Already did." The intern stepped closer, squeezing between the makeup tray and the chair, handing the cordless phone to her boss.

Reaching up and brushing her blond hair behind her ear, eliciting a loud sigh from Liz, Erin lifted the phone and said, "Hello, Rusty."

"Erin! Glad I caught you."

"Is there something wrong?" she asked, as Liz continued to dab at the pancake makeup on her face.

"You could say that. I'm sure your news department is probably aware of this. If they aren't, they will be soon."

"Rusty, I've only got a minute or two...."

Speaking more quickly, he continued, "We lost a plane."

"What? What do you mean?"

"I reported the anemometer readings to D.C., and they had the 53rd Weather Recon Squadron send a WC-130J to check out the situation. What they discovered was that the anomaly was centered on Aegis."

"Aegis? The suicide tank?"

"One and the same. All of the winds are radiating outward from that point."

"How...? I don't understand, Rusty. How can winds blow outward in all directions from one point?"

"I don't know, Erin. I wish I did. But it is definitely happening. And as they got close to the complex, the winds were approaching ninety miles an hour."

Erin went blank. She had no idea what to ask next. Then she remembered his initial comment. "You said you lost a plane?"

Before he could answer, the assistant director, ignoring the protests from Liz, pushed his way in next to the makeup chair and urged, "Erin, we need you on the set."

The tension of the moment caused Erin's emotions to flare. "I'll be there when I can!" she barked uncharacteristically.

Unaccustomed to this sort of an outburst from her, the assistant director backed off, mumbling something to the effect that she should hurry, and then he scooted away, talking excitedly into the mouthpiece arced around his cheek.

Returning her attention to the phone, she began again. "Rusty, sorry about that. Tell me about the plane. What happened?"

"We don't have all the details yet. Those things are built to fly inside hurricanes, so I can't even imagine what happened. In our last communication with them, they were about to enter the center zone."

She could hear him cover the mouthpiece of the phone and begin speaking to someone else. A few seconds later he spoke into the phone. "Erin, I've got to go. I'm heading out there now."

Once more, she only took an instant to make her decision. "Rusty, pick me up. I'm going with you."

⊙

The technician pulled back on the manipulator gloves and slipped her hands out of them, picking up a cotton towel and vigorously rubbing her face.

"Yolanda, why is it the minute I put the gloves on, my face starts to itch?" she asked the technician at the station beside her.

The other woman laughed. "Psychological, Syndi. You know you can't scratch it, so it itches. Remember, this is much better than the full suits."

Standing, Syndi agreed, "That's true. Well, I'm done. Thirteen hours is long enough."

"I hear you. I'm about ready myself. I still can't believe they're having us retest."

"Guess they figure after two years of storage, they'd better make sure it still works."

Syndi left, and Yolanda completed the medium transfer she was working on. She pulled back on the gloves to extricate her own hands, and noticed an unusual tug as she freed her right hand. Looking down, she muttered, "Damn!" On her right wrist was a gold-plated charm bracelet, a gift from her sister and strictly forbidden in the lab.

Nervously, she unclasped the bracelet and dropped it into her pocket, angling her body to obscure what she had done from the ceiling-mounted camera, which was behind her and to the left. Glad that she was the last person in the lab, she pulled out the right glove a bit farther and examined the portion of it that had been adjacent to the bracelet.

She did not want to lean down and stare at it closely, as that would be too obvious on the security camera. With the inspection Yolanda was able to do, the material looked intact. She did not notice any tear or snag in the laminated and reinforced fabric.

The tension of the near catastrophe was causing her to sweat profusely. She picked up the cotton towel from the neighboring station and mopped her face and neck, before getting up and hurriedly departing the lab.

$$\odot$$

"I'm guessing you did connect with our colleague from Mossad."

"I did," Elias answered tersely.

Wistfully, Stone continued, "That's the weakness with intel – never the full picture. We thought he had tried to set up a meeting but it hadn't happened yet."

"You and Faulk have too much faith in your technology and your own competence. I knew I was being watched. I knew my emails were read and my phones were all monitored. When I heard from Benjamin, I used an intermediary, made a blind drop."

"Ah, yes," Stone said, shaking his head, "the old-fashioned way."

"Everyone has become far too dependent on electronics. You've got whole rooms full of people staring at computer monitors, waiting for the other guy to make a call, text a message, use a chat room, or send an email. There's nothing like pen and paper, transported by a person you can rely upon."

"How did you meet him? After he left you that voice mail, we were watching him, too…every minute of the day."

"I didn't say that I did, only that we connected. I sent him a message, using the drop, telling him that he was also being watched. As you said, the old-fashioned way. Benjamin sat down, handwrote everything he had learned, and the courier, someone I *knew* I could trust, brought it back."

Stone chuffed, a sound of disgust. "So I suppose you think you know it all."

"I have no idea if I know it all, and I don't care. I know about the lab. I know why you killed Leah. And I know Faulk is behind all of it."

The one reaction Elias did not expect from his erstwhile friend was the one he got. Stone laughed, the sound echoing off the concrete walls of the raceway. "It would be generous to say that you only know the tip of the iceberg. But even what you think you've figured out is wrong."

"Why don't you enlighten me?"

"Why don't you go to hell?"

"The only person going to hell in the next few minutes will be you. I'm just giving you a chance to clear things up for me before you go."

Stone stared at Elias for a moment. "Sure. Why not? You already know that Mossad raided a Taliban nest in the West Bank. There was only one survivor, Bassam. You also know that Bassam was Khalid's number-two man. Our Israeli friends don't have the weak stomach that we have as far as using effective interrogation methods, so Bassam talked his head off. He told Benjamin about the lab. He told him that Leah had found out about it and she had to die. How am I doing, so far?"

"He also told Benjamin that it was you who came up with the idea for the missile strike."

"He's right. It was. It was perfect. It got rid of Leah and gave Khalid a perfect PR story for the whole world."

Elias felt his finger tighten on the trigger. With monumental effort, he relaxed the pressure.

Acting as if he were oblivious to the fury building in Elias, Stone inquired, "Tell me, Elias, what did Bassam disclose to Benjamin about the lab?"

Even through the self-induced fog of his rage, Elias was unsettled by something in Stone's demeanor, something he could not quite identify.

"That Faulk and others were operating a bio-weapon lab, in violation of our laws and international treaties."

Elias saw a slight smile play across Stone's face. "That's it?"

"That and the fact that the lab was on the verge of perfecting a new aerosol agent."

Although he had the muzzle of an automatic rifle aimed at his chest, Stone relaxed. Elias, noticing this, sensed that he was running out of time. "Eric, where's the lab?"

This last question from Elias caused Stone to break out in a broad grin. "Elias, thank you. Your question was the last answer I needed from you. Now you only have one remaining function to fulfill."

Sensing the muscles in his back and neck tighten, Elias suddenly felt at a disadvantage but still was not sure why. All at once, his thoughts crystallized. He shifted the barrel of the AK-47 downward so that it pointed at Stone's leg, and pulled the trigger. He heard only a single *click*. At that moment, Stone stuck his fingers into his pants pocket and pulled something out, tossing it on the floor between them. It fell with a metallic clatter, coming to rest inches from Elias' feet. It only took him a moment to recognize it.

"If you're going to shoot one of those things, Elias, it helps to have the firing pin installed."

As Elias was about to charge at him, Stone slid his hand behind his back and pulled out the 9mm.

"Stop!" Stone snapped.

Elias froze in mid-stride.

Taking in a deep breath, Elias asked, "Eric, why? What turned you?"

With a vicious snarl, Stone answered, "We don't have that kind of time. And I doubt that you would understand, anyway. Leah sure didn't."

The final threshold had been reached. Stone had made one too many references to Elias' wife for him to be able to keep a lid on his emotions. Despite the fact that Stone was holding him at gunpoint, Elias threw the useless AK-47 at him, charging directly behind it, not caring at that moment whether he lived or died. His mind registered the slight elevating of the pistol…the slow tightening of the finger on the trigger. Stone was too well trained to panic and snap off a hasty shot. More than half the distance between them was closed, when Elias heard the thunderous crack and roar of the discharge. Pure adrenaline kept his legs moving forward as he waited for the effects of the bullet ripping through his chest to register.

Inexplicably, he saw Stone's head explode into a cloud of pink mist, the already dead body toppling, the 9mm tumbling to the floor, unfired. Unable to counter his emotion-charged momentum, he slammed into the halfway-fallen body of Stone, with both himself and the body crashing down.

Pushing the inert form away, Elias scrambled to his feet and swung around, trying to figure out who had intervened.

From the darkness of the raceway from which he had arrived, he heard a familiar voice. "This saving your life thing is getting a little old."

Tillie stepped into the dim light, a bolt-action rifle resting casually on her shoulder. She walked to where Elias was standing and looked down at the body. "Elias, I'm sorry."

With his ragged breathing, the hammering of his heartbeat in his head, and the ringing in his ears from the rifle shot in the confined area, Elias was barely able to hear her soft apology. "You're sorry? For what? You saved my life…again."

She looked up at him. "I know you wanted to be the one to do it."

He could not help but chuckle at her perceptiveness. "This'll do just fine."

"I tried. I was standing back there listening, waiting for you to get your shot. I only pulled the trigger once it was obvious that you didn't have a chance."

"I appreciate it. But you probably didn't have to cut it quite so close."

"Hey! I saved your butt again and you're complaining?"

"No, no, I take it back," Elias backpedaled, holding up his hands defensively. "How did you know?"

She glanced down at the dead Eric Stone one more time. "I'd really be happy to tell you, but I'm not as inured to this kind of stuff as you are. Could we head back?"

"Sure. Let me grab a couple of things."

He began to walk to the shoulder pack that held the firebombs, when Tillie volunteered, "I'll get that."

"Still don't trust me, huh?"

"Let's say, you've got enough to carry."

With a shake of his head, Elias returned to the laptop and disconnected all of the feed wires for the surveillance equipment, packed it in its carrying case, and hooked it over his shoulder. He pocketed the smartphone and snatched up the canvas pouch filled with rations and a bladder full of water. He returned to Tillie as she finished wrestling the heavy pack onto her back. Elias bent over and picked up the 9mm and the AK-47, remembering to grab the firing pin.

"Ready?" she asked.

"Let's go."

As they walked away, she began to explain, "I never trusted him."

"I could tell."

"I don't know why. Maybe I'm psychic or whatever. But I never felt right about him. And then you asked me how he tested the bomb gel, and I could tell in your eyes that something wasn't right. Besides, he was way too dumb."

Laughing, Elias replied, "What do you mean?"

"You know, his questions. Always asking all of us questions. He didn't seem to have anything figured out, and that didn't make sense for someone who is supposedly a hotshot secret agent and who had more than two months to sit and think."

"Good point. When did he have the time to break down that AK-47 and remove the pin?"

"That's easy. Remember, as soon as we got back from our tour of the storm system, he...."

"That's right," he interrupted. "Eric excused himself and was gone quite a while."

"Too long, considering that he didn't shake off any sand. Later, I got into the bed after he'd been on it, and it was full of the stuff."

They were almost back to Tillie's den, before Elias remarked, "There was one more thing."

"What's that?"

"After you were lying down and, I guess, pretending to fall asleep, Eric and I talked for a minute or two. I asked him a question, and his answer has been bothering me ever since."

"What was his answer?"

"Well, that's just it. It wasn't the answer itself; it was the phrase he used. He said, 'Insufficient data at this time.'"

"I don't get it."

"That's not a typical phrase. And I've it heard twice since I've come to Aegis."

"Twice?"

"Yes. The last time from Eric. The time before from Wilson."

"I still don't see the big deal. Eric probably heard Wilson say it, and liked it. That is the way the old man talks, you know."

"I know. And I think you're right. I think Eric did hear Wilson say it, and either he liked it or it simply stuck unconsciously."

"So...?"

"Wilson used the phrase when he and I were talking alone. It was while you were out looking for Eric."

Tillie stopped walking and turned to face Elias. "You think they've been listening in on us?"

Elias shrugged. "I don't know. It may be nothing. And now Wilson's shack is only cinders. But I think we should check out your place."

Tillie turned and took the remaining few steps into her makeshift home, looking around at all of the ductwork, piping, and junction boxes which filled the walls and ceiling. "Between all of this stuff and all of my pretties that I've hung everywhere, it would be like finding a needle in a haystack."

Elias stood next to her, surveying the space. "You're right. We'd never find it unless we were unbelievably lucky."

Hearing them talk, Wilson shook his head to clear it from the slumber and asked, "Look for what? Where's Eric?"

Tillie held up one finger in front of her lips to silence Wilson as they both took him by the arms and walked him several yards out into one of the passageways, where they, in whispered tones, filled him in on the last several minutes. After they finished, Wilson softly said, "That makes much more sense than the puzzle pieces I was struggling to assemble before."

"We've got a lot to talk about before we make out next move. But my base is out of the question. Eric and Faulk both knew about it. And now that Eric's been at Tillie's, we can't stay here. Your shack is gone, Wilson. We need a new place."

"I agree," Wilson concurred. "Tillie, you know Aegis better than anyone. Can you think of a logical base camp?"

"It needs to be easy to defend," Elias added, "and close to the electrical raceways, mechanical passageways, and plenums, as well as the main corridors. We may need a variety of options."

The two men watched as her mind reviewed the layout. With a quiet huff of exasperation, she uttered, "Hell, we're going to need them, anyway."

"Need what?"

Rather than answering Elias' question, she abruptly turned and trotted back into her living area. He hurried behind her, followed by Wilson. Her first stop was a drawer in the kitchen area, from which she removed a screwdriver. Closing the drawer, she hurried to the far corner of the space where a green steel box was bolted to the concrete floor. In red letters, a warning was stenciled – *DANGER ~ HIGH VOLTAGE* – immediately adjacent to a yellow sticker of a lightning bolt inside a circle with a diagonal line through it.

Tillie jammed the screwdriver into the first screw head and began turning. Moving close to her, Elias whispered, "Do you know what…?"

She paused and held the screwdriver in front of her lips to shush him, before returning to her work. Soon, all of the screws were neatly lined up on the floor. Placing the screwdriver next to them, she gripped the sides of the front panel and lifted and pulled. With a *THUNK* the panel came away. Inside the box was a transformer of some sort, Elias knew. By the size and the steady hum coming from it, he guessed that it was fairly high voltage.

Ignoring the gear inside, Tillie turned the front panel around and leaned it against the wall. Fastened to the inside of the panel was a vertical metal tray, open at the top. She reached inside and pulled out a several-inch-thick sheaf of large papers, bound on one end by a blue wrapper. Elias recognized the papers as a set of plans.

Cautiously, she laid the plans out on the floor and rolled them up, whispering to Elias to reattach the transformer panel. As he did, she found three rubber bands and gently slid all of them onto the roll, careful not to catch the edge of the top sheet and tear it. This task completed, Tillie hefted the bulky roll, grabbed some supplies and, with a final glance around, exited the area which she had made her home for the past several years.

⊙

Boehn, hoping his face did not betray the fact that he felt like a kid caught with his hand in the cookie jar, attempted a casual grin. "Good evening, Doctor Kreitzmann. I must be developing a case of OCD. I was certain that I had neglected to file my report. I couldn't sleep until I checked."

Kreitzmann's smile was wary as he responded, "I see. Everything's in order, I trust."

"Quite so. Now I can get some sleep."

"Excellent. I'll see you in the morning, then."

"Yes! Bright and early."

Boehn walked off in the direction of his quarters. Kreitzmann stood at the door to the lab, staring at his associate's retreating back. After the man had turned the corner, Kreitzmann opened the lab door and entered, walking directly to the terminal Boehn had used minutes before, placing his hand on the back of the flat-screen monitor, and feeling the residual warmth from it.

To himself, he muttered, "He did tell me that he was using it."

Switching the system on, Kreitzmann waited for the login sequence to complete before he entered his personal password. Triggered by his top-level access, the monitor displayed a much different interface from what Boehn had seen minutes earlier. He selected the icon labeled "security admin" and waited a moment for the new screen. He then clicked on "tracking." Defining the parameters, he chose "search." In the blink of an eye, the monitor was displaying, in raw form, all of the activity which had occurred on this station beginning at 6:00 p.m. this evening and ending a minute ago.

The last entry showed that the terminal had been used to access Doctor Bonillas' most recent reports and lab notes, and that they had been moved to the USB port, an action which would normally delete them from the system. He was glad that the system was configured to delete nothing. Doctor Bonillas' work was safely archived onto a separate file system simultaneous to her upload.

While he stared at the screen, Kreitzmann's eyes narrowed and the muscles in his jaw clenched, as anger began to slowly build within him. The task had been executed under Dr. Bonillas' password, not Boehn's, and the timestamp on the activity showed that the file transfer had taken place minutes ago, obviously at the time Boehn was in the lab and Bonillas was not.

He keyed the internal phone system, and a voice answered instantly.

"This is Doctor Kreitzmann. Please meet me in Lab 1C immediately."

CHAPTER
FIFTEEN

Kenneth Mortenson parked as close as he possibly could to the entrance. The intensity of the wind was beyond anything he had ever seen in his entire life, despite having grown up in El Paso. Now that he had parked, his Camry bounced and shook as if it were positioned atop a fun house platform instead of solid pavement. Making a point of parking his car so that the driver's door was on the leeward side, he grabbed his backpack from the passenger seat, slid one arm through the canvas loops, and opened the door.

Despite the car's orientation, the door was instantly jerked from his grip and pivoted violently, disintegrating the steel stops on the hinges. Mentally preparing himself, Kenneth climbed out and was almost knocked to the ground. Using the side of the gyrating car for support, he circled around it, turning directly into the face of the wind.

As he trudged on, leaning far forward, he was barely able to see the turnstile due to the dust stinging his eyes, his route cluttered with the shattered and twisted remnants of the solar panels which had ripped from the roof of Aegis. He had to dodge chunks of debris from this wreckage as the incessant winds caught pieces and rocketed them through the air. Taking fifteen minutes to traverse a distance which, in normal conditions, would have taken one or two, he discovered that as he reached the final twenty yards before the entrance, the wind lessened and he was able to walk in a somewhat more upright position. As this was his first trip to Aegis, he had no idea that he was standing where the plywood tunnel had been constructed, an earlier casualty of the gale. He stopped at the turnstile and looked back in the direction of the parking lot and the surrounding desert, surprised to see several more vehicles, headlights on, braving the tempest.

⊙

Marilyn stared out the window, looking at the tailings from the open-pit mining operations south of Tucson. Her plane was minutes away from landing, and her mind wandered back to the lie she had told to Faulk this morning. Knowing that her boss controlled the communications to Elias, she could think of no other way to get a message to him other than personally. Knowing Faulk's propensity for checking out what people told him, as it had been a task assigned to her many times since he had taken over the position formerly held by Elias, she kept her story vague about needing to visit an old friend who was ill.

Uncharacteristically, he had not inquired as to the name of the fictitious old friend, and she neglected to supply it. In fact, he seemed vaguely distracted as she talked to him, almost as if he did not care whether she left or not.

$$\odot$$

Elias, Wilson, and Tillie were huddled around a scarred dining room table in one of the apartments in ZooCity. They had agreed that this was not to be their new base, but should give them some privacy for a time while they figured out their next move. The blueprints were spread out on the table before them.

"When I was preparing to come in, I had a few pages showing the overall layout and the raceways, but nowhere near what you've got here. How did you get these?" Elias asked.

Tillie told them about her first day at Aegis and the chance meeting and chat with the contractor who had built it.

"Just as he was leaving, and after the main door had been set, he remembered that he had left his inspection set of plans inside. At that point the door had been closed, and it was impossible for him to go back in and retrieve them; it was too late. So, he told me where they were and that I could have them if I wanted."

"You knew how to read plans?"

"I learned," she told Elias, a hint of pride in her voice. "I must have spent about a thousand hours staring at them, flipping between the pages, walking the areas they corresponded to. Eventually, they started to make sense. I never did decipher the gobbledygook on the electrical pages, or the mechanical stuff. Most of the plumbing was fairly obvious. But the real gold mine was on the 'A' pages and the civil engineering pages. That's where I found the layouts and accesses for all of the secret passageways and the storm system. It's all there."

She sat back in the dinette chair with a look of pride and satisfaction. "There was one thing I never could figure out, though."

"What's that?" Wilson inquired, amused.

"He told me where his *blueprints* were. These aren't blue."

Chuckling, Wilson explained, "It's a throwback to the old method for reproducing plans. A French chemist discovered that ferro-gallate in gum is light sensitive. Light turns it blue. Basically, if you drew a sketch on a translucent material, then overlaid the sketch onto a sheet coated with the ferro-gallate and exposed it to light, the paper would turn blue, except for where the lines had been drawn. Later on, they began to use ammonium ferric citrate and potassium ferricyanide, but the process was essentially the same. The next generation were actually called whiteprints or bluelines because the paper was white and the lines were blue. In recent years, the industry switched to very large photocopy machines, which can print a copy on regular bond paper. That is what you are looking at now. But the original name remains."

Tillie had stared at Wilson throughout the lecture, wide-eyed. "Cool, thanks!" she exclaimed at the end.

"Back to our issue," Elias broke in. "We need to find a good hiding spot. Tillie set up housekeeping in the mechanical system. I used the electrical raceways and junctions. We took Eric through the storm system. So they are all compromised."

"Do you think so?" Wilson pondered out loud. "Looking at these plans, it is clear that all three of those systems are elaborate. Couldn't we just pick another spot in one of them? A place well removed from our previous locations?"

Elias responded thoughtfully, "Although we only occupied or traveled a small portion of each, if Eric communicated with his handler, they will all be checked. That's what I would do. And with the Zippers doing the looking, they should be able to cover quite a bit of territory."

"Why don't we break up the 'A' pages and the 'Civil' pages and divvy them up instead of all three of us staring at the same sheet?"

"Excellent idea, Tillie," Wilson agreed. "As proprietary as you are about them, I was afraid to suggest it."

She made a rude sound with her lips. "C'mon guys, I'm not *that* bad. Am I?"

"Oh, no!"

"No! Not at all."

She looked at them both and grinned. "Okay, maybe I've been a little testy. But we do have to work together, so let's split them up."

She carefully peeled back the blue binding paper on the stapled edge, and pried up the staples, one by one, with a fingernail. Removing all of them without tearing a sheet or cutting herself, she created three stacks. Elias took his pages and moved to a coffee table. Tillie, being the youngest and most limber of the three, sat cross-legged on the floor with her set, and Wilson stayed at the dinette.

The three worked quietly, the silence only broken with the occasional sound of a sheet being set aside. Nearly twenty minutes passed before Elias thumped the blueprint with his finger. "This may work."

The two came to the coffee table and looked at the portion of the page where he pointed.

"There appears to be a primary water reservoir which is filled by the pumps. That one, I'm sure, is full right now. But, look, there are four reserve tanks. They only take on water if the primary is filled, and they take on the water sequentially."

"In other words," Wilson interjected, "the first reserve tank only has water in it if the primary tank is full. Then the second reserve only gets water if the first reserve fills to capacity."

"And so on," Elias completed the thought for him. "I think it might be worth a try to check out the last tank in the series. It is probably dry as a bone."

"How do we get in the tank?" Tillie stopped herself. "Oh, never mind, I see it. There's an access door."

"Exactly. It's actually called a hatch."

"I think it's worth a shot," she decided.

The journey from ZooCity to the water tank took three-quarters of an hour, due to the loads all three carried, compounded by the circuitous route taken to avoid others.

"This thing looks like a vault," Tillie observed, breathing as easily as if she had just finished a leisurely stroll.

Elias and Wilson, panting heavily, dropped their packs, duffel bags, and weapons, approaching her side as she examined the oval steel hatch set into a retaining ring.

"This is the clean-out access at the bottom of the tank. There is also another access hatch at the top that can be used when the reservoir is holding water. You'll notice that this hatch swings inward. That wheel on it releases the dogs gripping the retaining ring, but if water is present on the other side, the pressure from the water pushes against the door, keeping it closed."

Listening to Elias' explanation, Tillie concluded, "So if we spin the wheel and try to open it, nothing will happen if the tank is full?"

"Right."

"You're sure?"

He grinned. "I am."

"Then let's do it."

She stepped forward, gripped the wheel with both hands, and turned it. It moved easily, quickly accelerating to a blurred spin. When it slammed noisily to a stop and they could see that the hinged dogs were retracted from the retaining ring, she glanced once at Elias, said, "Here goes," and put her shoulder to the hatch, which almost flew open, pulling her inside where she tumbled to the concrete floor.

"Ouch!" she shouted, her voice followed by a multitude of overlaid echoes from the inside walls of the dry tank.

"I think it's dry," Wilson proclaimed with a smirk, and high-stepped through the hatchway behind her. Elias followed, chuckling.

Within a few minutes they had quickly checked out the interior of the tank with their flashlights. Determining that it was clear, they brought in their packs and supplies, and closed the hatch behind themselves. The hatch had a matching wheel on the interior, and as the others toted the gear to the middle of the tank, Elias spun the wheel shut, putting his weight behind it to make it tight.

Returning to Wilson and Tillie, he told them, "After I catch my breath, I'll go back out and find a long bar or something we can use to jam the wheel. That might cut down on unwanted visitors."

"Just a sec." Tillie motioned at him and pulled open her duffel bag, extracting a short pole with what appeared to be a wide bicycle seat at one end. She pressed a button and the seat came off. Then, pressing another, the pole extended and locked into position with a *click*. She tossed it to Elias.

"Will this work?"

Elias examined the device. "I think it will. It looks fairly sturdy. What is it?"

She grinned. "Something goofy one of the newbies brought in. It's a pole seat that you can carry with you on camping trips. It's uncomfortable as all get-out. I don't even know why I brought it."

Elias took the pole and walked back to the hatch. He jammed it through an opening between the spokes on the wheel at an angle so that if someone tried to open it from the outside, it would stop. Satisfied, he returned to the group to see that Tillie had unpacked collapsible chairs, which converted into sleeping cots, and had set them up next to the steel ladder that ascended to the hatch at the top of the storage tank. She had also unpacked a lantern, creating an island of light in the center of the cavernous tank. She was now assembling a small portable stove.

"Did you bring the s'mores?" Elias teased.

With a sly grin, Tillie pulled out packages of marshmallows and graham crackers. "Need to find the chocolate. I know it's in here."

"Mathilda, you amaze me," Wilson said sincerely.

"That's my goal in life. To amaze people wherever I may go."

Within twenty minutes they were sitting in a circle around the stove, sipping hot tea and munching on the drippy, chocolate concoctions.

Tillie, between bites, asked, "Were you able to make any sense out of what Eric said to you at the end?"

Elias swallowed the last bite of his snack and took a long sip before answering. "Not as much as I would have liked."

Tillie wiped her mouth with her sleeve. "How long have you known Eric?"

"A long time. About twenty years."

"Were you friends?"

"I used to think so. Eric and I had worked in the field at the same time. Went through quite a bit together. Saved each other's butts more than once. I was even his son's godfather. And Leah was the godmother."

"What happened?"

"There are basically three kinds of spooks in the business. The first group would be the patriots. For them, it's all about what's best for the country. The second group would be the mercenaries. They do it because they crave the adrenaline rush. They have no allegiance to any country. The third group would be what I call the pragmatists and some of the think-tank experts refer to as survivalists. They pick the side which is in their best self-interest. They are, by far, the easiest to turn since they have no loyalty at all. If they are busted, if their cover is blown, then they talk, and they cooperate.

"The pragmatists will switch sides in a minute if they perceive that the other side is winning. As for the mercenaries, a lot of people think that they will always work for the highest bidder. In my experience, that isn't the case. They tend to gravitate toward the entity offering the most cutting-edge hardware and the highest risks. The patriots are the toughest to go against; you can't turn them, and they will charge the machine gun nest, if that's what it takes."

Leaning forward on his canvas chair, Wilson asked, "Which one was Eric?"

"I used to think that Eric was a patriot, years ago. Maybe he was at one time. He never exhibited the adrenaline-junkie tendencies to tell me he was a mercenary."

"So that leaves survivalist."

"That's right. Something happened in Eric's world. Something changed, which caused him to come to the conclusion that the side I was on was no longer the winning side."

"But you have no idea what that might be?"

"No, Wilson, I don't. And I didn't have a chance to find out from him."

"Sorry about that," Tillie apologized. "I should have waited longer before I pulled the trigger."

Chuckling, Elias assured her, "Tillie, that's not what I meant. If I had confronted him with a weapon that functioned, I might have learned something."

"Before you blew him away."

"Before I blew him away."

Wilson continued his questioning. "From what you and Tillie told me, I believe there is little doubt but that you and your wife were getting too close for their comfort. Did she communicate anything to you before she...while she still had a chance? Anything which might give you a clue as to what they are planning?"

"No. Nothing. We had no contact for days prior to the end, which was normal for that type of an assignment."

"So all we've really learned, thus far, is why you were brought here instead of simply being executed. They needed to know how much you knew and, of course, whether you had told anyone."

"Exactly. And once Eric found out that I didn't know the location of the lab or specifically what they were making, he knew there was no reason to keep me around."

Tillie frowned. "But he said something about one more function you needed to fulfill. What was that all about?"

Elias thought back for a moment. "That's right. He did say that. I have no idea what he meant, though."

"And what do you know about the lab?" Tillie asked, taking another sip of tea.

"Not much. All Benjamin told me was that it was a bio-weapon lab and that they were working on a new aerosol material."

Wiping the melted chocolate off his fingers, Elias began to break down the AK-47. Wilson and Tillie watched the practiced, swift movements.

After a few moments, Wilson pressed on. "Is your colleague in Israel continuing his efforts to gain additional information from this Bassam?"

Elias shook his head as he inserted the firing pin in place. "No, Benjamin has squeezed all of the juice he could out of that particular lemon. What he told me was all there was to glean from Bassam."

"Why was Eric specifically in Aegis?" Wilson asked. "And what does Kreitzmann have to do with this puzzle?"

"I thought we decided that Eric was here as bait to attract Elias," Tillie stated.

"He was. That's not what Wilson is asking. I think his question is why Aegis and not someplace else. And the answer is that they wanted to put me in an environment where there is nothing I can do with the knowledge I might have. They have effectively cut me off from any allies or any other agencies or even governments who might have a concern about Faulk's actions."

"I'm a little confused about that," she said. "Don't the agencies and governments talk to each other? Wouldn't Faulk have been told about Bassam? Oh, wait! That was a dumb question. Bassam told the Israelis that Faulk and Eric were bad guys. Benjamin, or his bosses, wouldn't have told our government anything."

"You're right, Tillie. Well, almost right. Benjamin told me that they did inform Faulk when they first caught Bassam. I guess it caused quite a ruckus, with Faulk demanding they turn him over to us for questioning. The Mossad refused. After they interrogated Bassam, and heard what he had to say about Stone and Faulk, the Israelis realized they couldn't pass on any more information. They decided to tell Faulk that Bassam was a dry well."

"I assume he didn't buy that."

"Obviously not, but getting information out of Mossad if they don't want to share is almost impossible."

"Faulk must have been beside himself," Wilson commented. "In his desperation to find out what the Israelis knew, he must have remembered that you and Benjamin had a relationship."

Elias nodded his agreement. "We did. And it was well known in the intelligence community that there was no love lost between Faulk and me."

"Looking at it from Benjamin's perspective, it made perfect sense," Wilson thought out loud. "He knew you hated Faulk. He knew you had lost your wife in the attack. He knew the information he possessed was of the highest order of magnitude, and yet, since it implicated a highly placed individual in our government, it couldn't be shared through normal channels."

"Absolutely. He would have no idea who he could trust over here."

"Except for you."

"Except for me. I was really his only option."

Elias had finished assembling the now functional AK-47, and leaned it against the ladder beside his chair.

Tillie drank the last of her tea and set down the cup. "We have some of the pieces, but we're still missing a bunch. Why was Eric here for so long? What does Kreitzmann have to do with Faulk's plans?

Wilson spoke up, "If I may ask a question, perhaps I can clarify one point. How long ago did the Israelis capture Bassam?"

Elias thought back for a moment, suddenly making the connection. "Of course!"

"What?" Tillie asked excitedly.

"The Mossad first picked up Bassam almost three months ago."

"That's when the Israelis first notified Faulk that they had him?"

"Exactly."

"And that's close to when I saw Eric enter Aegis."

"Right."

"So at that point," Wilson interjected, "they knew that it was only a matter of time until Benjamin contacted you. So they baited the hook, placing Eric inside Aegis."

"Either as bait or as a safe place for him to hide."

"And when they learned that Benjamin had contacted you, Faulk offered you an assignment he knew you couldn't turn down."

"That's right. Either way I'd go into Aegis. If I hadn't heard anything from Benjamin about Eric, I would take the job to rescue him. And if I had been told the truth, I would come in to get him."

"That makes sense," Tillie said. "But how does Faulk tie into Kreitzmann?"

"That we don't know. But there is no way that Kreitzmann could have his own way in and out of here without Faulk's knowledge, not just because the door would be noticed, but there are also the guards. As Kreitzmann, maybe Eric, and God knows who else have come and gone, they would be waltzing right past them. So there must be some connection. I'm guessing that Faulk is using the research for some purpose."

"And what was Eric planning to do with the firebombs?" Tillie asked.

"Faulk sent enough ordnance to take out all of Aegis," Elias replied.

Wilson leaned back in his camping chair, making it creak, the sound echoing back at them. He stared into the darkness above. "The key is still Aegis. For some reason Faulk wants it destroyed."

"Let's talk about that. There is something about this place Faulk wants gone. I haven't been here long enough to get a feel for what that might be. Maybe if both of you verbalized your observations, opinions, conclusions, hunches, anything about Aegis, something will make sense."

Elias could tell that Wilson was organizing the disparate tidbits in his mind before speaking. Tillie, impatient for him to begin, blurted out at Elias, "You know what Biosphere 2 is, right?"

"Sure. It's the huge glass environment north of Tucson."

"Do you know what the original intent was for building it?"

"Science experiments of some type, but not really."

"John P. Allen conceived of it as a way to study Earth. The Earth is Biosphere 1. He wanted to create what was to be basically a lab where the impact of life, techniques, chemicals, everything...could be studied in a closed system."

"I didn't know that."

"For several reasons, it didn't work. Now it is basically a tourist attraction. But my point is, I think that's what Aegis was really designed to be. Except, instead of studying the physical impact of mankind on nature, I think this place was an experiment to see what people would do with no government, no rules, no structure, no outside influence. I think Aegis was intended to be a controlled psychological experiment. Or maybe even a political experiment."

Elias was intrigued by the concept.

"I mean, think about it," she continued excitedly. "The government can't build an outhouse at a campground without posting a metal sign listing all of the do's and don'ts for its use by the public. Yet our government built this gigantic complex where citizens were supposed to be able to come and live out the rest of their lives, and there's nothing! Not any signs posted. Not even a handbook. I was blown away the first day I walked in here. We're so used to being handled, directed, controlled, and ordered around that I went through kind of a shock when I discovered I had the whole place basically to myself and there wasn't anyone or anything telling me what I could or couldn't do."

"You don't think President Walker built Aegis for the reasons he gave?"

Tillie moved to the front edge of the canvas seat and leaned forward, resting her elbows on her knees. "Look, I'm sure he was devastated that his daughter killed herself. But I just think that somewhere along the line between the day the idea was first proposed and the day Aegis was opened to the public, someone saw an opportunity to use it for another purpose entirely. I wouldn't be surprised if the idea of Aegis was actually suggested to Walker during his darkest moments by someone with a whole different plan."

"Wilson, Tillie raises some fascinating points. What do you think?"

"As you can well imagine, she and I have had countless discussions on this very topic over the past few years. Purely from a logical standpoint, Aegis, insofar as its stated purpose, makes no sense. It never has. We spoke of this briefly when we met."

Elias nodded, thinking back to that first conversation on the porch.

"But if you impute more devious or sinister motives to its construction, it makes much more sense."

"Such as?"

"You oughta know," interjected Tillie. "It's a great place to dump inconvenient people where they are never heard from again."

"It is also an excellent source for subjects if you happen to be a scientist in need of human beings for your work," Wilson added. "No one can ever come looking for them. There is no oversight of any sort whatsoever."

"True."

"And, to return to Mathilda's point, it does afford one an opportunity to watch and see exactly how the supposedly educated, civilized people of this country would structure their new environment without the benefit of rules, regulations, and a constitution."

"From what I heard, the result was chaos."

"The uprising, yes. It was quite horrible. However, the reaction to the riot was the organization of Madison and Walden, and to a lesser degree ZooCity. That development created a certain level of stability."

"But, Wilson, you told me when I arrived that there was a disturbing trend now."

"There has been. Most assuredly. The extinction of the ZooCity element ameliorates things somewhat. But we are still left with the Kreitzmann segment of the equation, as well as the tenuous coexistence of Madison and Walden."

"Are they enemies?"

Wilson chuckled. "Hardly enemies. They are merely at the opposite ends of the ideological spectrum. Walden is weak, ineffectual. Madison is organized, strong, and well equipped. If an overt conflict were to occur between those two enclaves, the battle would be brief and the outcome certain. You must remember, throughout our history, anytime there has been a dramatic imbalance between two competing societies, the status quo never maintains."

"One swallows the other."

"Either swallows or destroys."

"Besides," Tillie added, "there aren't that many left at Walden."

"No? Why is that?"

Wilson took a long, deep breath before answering Elias' question. "Perhaps some historical reference would be of some help. From my own observations over the years I've been here, and the insightful input I've received from Mathilda, there has been a rather clear and linear evolution occurring within these walls. At first, when my friend arrived, there was pure anarchy."

"That's not necessarily a bad thing," Elias ventured.

"No, it is not. Anarchy, for the enlightened, is the only way to live a life of self-actualization. A truly good person needs no rules, no governance, no courts, no prisons...none of the rigid and confining aspects of society at large which stifle us and cause us to reside at the level of the lowest common denominator. Sadly, only those who fail to acknowledge the realities and frailties of the vast majority of mankind believe that anarchy is a viable alternative.

"I am quite certain that the three of us could coexist in an environment of anarchy, without a problem. It would only be after a fourth or a fifth or a sixth person might be added that we would suddenly recognize the need for a leader, rules, and methods for enforcement. These are precisely the stages of evolution that transpired at Aegis. At the time our young friend here first arrived, there was ample space with abundant resources. Despite the substantial initial influx of residents, the enormity of Aegis absorbed them easily."

"That's true," Tillie agreed. "At first, we all scattered. It was possible to go days or even weeks without coming across another resident. If you wanted human interaction, you could find others, and some did. They banded together in little groups. Some of us made a point of avoiding everyone else completely. And it was no problem back then."

Wilson resumed his narrative. "More and more people arrived, followed, inevitably, by conflicts."

"It reminds me of the description of the first settlers arriving on this continent."

"There is more to that comparison than you know, Elias. But I am getting ahead of myself. The first conflicts were resolved on an *ad hoc* basis. Alliances rapidly formed and were quickly broken. Populations shifted around the complex. Segregation was rampant as many of the clusters identified themselves by the color of their skin or their religious beliefs or...well, it just burgeoned. Each of those groups believed that this superficial commonality would somehow provide a cohesiveness that never fruited.

"For some, the constant migration was to avoid conflict; for others, it was to find it. All the while, the ability to find a piece of Aegis that you could call your own and where you could be left alone became harder and harder to manage.

"People need a leader, someone who can impose order upon them and enforce it. In the absence of such a man or woman, the uprising, the riot, was an inevitability. But it served its purpose. It demonstrated to the survivors the undeniable need for structure, for governance. Walden and Madison were formed. ZooCity came into existence as a result of many feeling disenfranchised. They could not relate to either entity, nor did they feel that either enclave accepted them."

"Aegis really is a microcosm of society, isn't it?" Elias asked him.

"In many ways it was."

"Was?"

"Yes. In the time after the formation of the enclaves, there was a shift in the paradigm. Subtle, at first, but discernible."

"What happened?"

"Less and less of the newbies were deferred suicides," Tillie answered for Wilson.

"Deferred...?"

Wilson ignored the interruptions and continued his explanation. "In the early years of Aegis, the vast majority of entrants, or newbies, as Tillie refers to them, came to this place for the purpose stated in its initial proposal to the American public. They checked in to Aegis rather than committing suicide. There were some, such as the young girl from Racine we discussed before, who came here for other, more spurious reasons. But most fit into the first category.

"That has changed. Tillie and I have both noticed that in the last year or two the largest percentage of arrivals, by far, are not coming to Aegis as an alternative to killing themselves."

"Is there a common reason they have come?"

"To get away from *out there*," answered Tillie.

Wilson nodded. "That would appear to be the case. As you mentioned a moment ago, just as the Pilgrims voyaged to America to escape England and the King, most of our recent arrivals have been men and women who have given up on society. They no longer feel as though they belong to what the culture has become. They can no longer relate to the music, the movies, the politics... even their immediate surroundings when they venture forth into the public arena. Yet they are at a disadvantage because there is not a culture anywhere in the world which attracts them, nor is there an available plot of land, ungoverned and unspoiled, to which they may flee as did the Pilgrims. So they have come to Aegis. And their numbers are growing exponentially."

"That's amazing! I've heard nothing about this on the outside."

"Of course you wouldn't. I would doubt that those leaving would announce their reasons."

"And I'm guessing from what you said earlier, most of them have gone to Madison."

"Indeed. In fact, their arrival, the growth in their numbers, has focused and crystallized the foundational beliefs of Madison considerably."

"I am surprised that so few of them go to Walden. My visit was brief, and I admit it wasn't my cup of tea, but it did seem pleasant there."

Wilson permitted a slight smile to curl his lips. "Many did try Walden first. It seemed to them that it was closer to an idyllic structure than Madison with its more visible rigidity. They quickly changed their minds."

"Why is that?"

"They recognized it as what they were running away from," answered Tillie.

"Really?"

"Yes," she snapped. "It usually took them about a week to figure out that all of that politically correct pseudo-tolerance, finding one's inner child, celebration of victimhood, building your self-esteem, narcissistic garbage is what was causing all of the problems *out there*."

"How do you really feel?" Elias asked with a smirk.

"It's true! The only newbies who went to Walden and wanted to stay there were the deferred suicides, not the societal refugees Wilson described."

"And now we are finally answering your original question, Elias," Wilson said.

"I've forgotten what it was."

"You inquired as to why there were so few remaining at Walden. The answer lies within what Mathilda so eloquently described. That particular enclave found itself to be the last refuge of the desperate."

"That should still be a sizable number."

"It should, but for one small issue. It seems that for those unfortunate souls, the decision to enter Aegis only briefly delayed the inevitable."

"They killed themselves anyway?"

"Nearly all of them have."

"I don't understand. If they escaped whatever it was out there that was driving them to the brink, why would they do it in Aegis?"

"I think," Tillie replied, "it was because they couldn't get the right wine to go with their organic veggie burgers."

Wilson glanced over at Tillie, a subtle, chiding expression on his face, as he continued, "In a sense, I believe that Mathilda was correct in her assertion that Aegis is a psychological or political Petri dish. The jury is still out in my mind as to whether that was the deliberate intent of its creators. However, it has become a *de facto* social experiment. The very nature of Aegis had an accelerating influence on the Darwinian process of selection of the fittest."

Risking another look of disapproval from her old friend, Tillie added, "And the Petri dish on the left, the one labeled 'Walden,' is full of nothing but an almost dead crust."

Wilson pursed his lips. "Crudely put, but that is essentially the case."

"What about ZooCity? That colony is now wiped out by Kreitzmann. But prior to that happening, how was it faring?" Elias addressed Wilson.

"It, too, was on the decline."

"From suicides?"

"Not at all. Again, you must remember that Aegis hastens the progress of the social experiment. ZooCity attracted the bored, the hedonistic, the disenfranchised, and the nihilistic. The appeal of gangs *out there* is the perceived, fallacious concept that the underprivileged in society exist as a result of a deliberate and calculated oppression. One of the inescapable realities of human nature is that when you oppress people, they will band together. That coalition has taken many forms throughout our history. In some cases the result has been the overthrow of the government which has been oppressing them, as was the case with the French Revolution. In America's past, workers were grossly abused. They banded together and formed labor unions. The ensuing shift of power between the worker and the employer caused all of the most egregious offenses against the workers to be corrected or eliminated. There have obviously been moments in history when the natural urge to self-organize has been beneficial to the oppressed, when oppression has been ameliorated somewhat.

"Sadly, as is the case with most things, natural human tendencies are quickly identified by the less than scrupulous, and exploited for less than noble causes. There are those who relish the power they accrue from the formation of a group. In the case of the labor unions, there is no longer any oppression of the workers. Society has evolved and the abhorrent labor practices of the past do not exist, nor would they re-emerge should the unions cease to exist.

"If we were to compare the creation of labor unions to the public revolt in France, the revolution was accomplished and the oppressors were removed and killed. The people who joined forces for a cause succeeded in their goal, and there was no longer a need for the extemporaneous coalition. Yet, in the case of the labor unions, the construct has become self-perpetuating and institutionalized. They must now manufacture straw-man oppressors from whole cloth to justify their continued existence and indeed, in some cases, have become the oppressor themselves in their relentless quest for power and wealth.

"In the case of inner-city gangs, there are influential neighborhood figures, community organizers, local and national politicians, popular entertainment figures, and a variety of others who benefit from the existence of gangs. Whether they are the senators seeking funds for their states or the corner drug dealers interested in growing their customer bases and distribution networks, there are legions of parasites who live off the strife and tragedy which accompanies the gang structure in the urban community. They must, on a daily basis, sustain the lie that these youths are being oppressed, for the purpose of maintaining *their* power base.

"That is the underlying reason for the tremendous peer pressure felt by an urban youth to dress in a certain way, walk with an affected style, talk in a manner which is unintelligible to others, and at all times exhibit an air of hostility. If the lie is that the larger community hates you, will not employ you, and will never embrace you as a peer, it is crucial to create a persona which makes these messages a self-fulfilling prophecy. As the young man in the neighborhood emulates his peers and is greeted with unfriendly glares, harassing police, and rejections from potential employers, that message is reinforced. The young man's commitment to the group is cemented.

"Why else would these same fraternities turn so viciously on a member who dares to trim his hair, dons the garb of a suburban businessman, speaks the King's English, and adopts a positive attitude, all so that he may obtain a job? Because they don't want their members to discover the truth.

"It was the very uniqueness of Aegis, this surreal facsimile of a culture, that made it impossible to maintain the illusion of oppression. How can you claim to be oppressed when all of the lodging within these walls is identical and, other than those already occupied, available for all, when the food and clothing dropped from the sky are more than the residents require and are freely shared?"

"That would be difficult."

"It was. All of it was compounded by the absence of currency. There could be no, even fabricated, claim of oppression since none existed."

"Also, in Aegis, there was no power structure that benefited from the illusion."

"Essentially true, Elias. There were a few entrants who had been leaders in their old gangs and missed the power that went with that position. They became the core of ZooCity. Internecine rivalries were the rule during that period, with minor skirmishes until the end, as they vied with each other for the position of top dog. But there was no manipulation from above…from the aforementioned community organizers, politicians, and celebrities.

"However, they soon discovered that the underlying impetus which provided a steady stream of recruits was absent. Instead of claiming to fight what they could portray as a noble and just crusade against the oppressive establishment, they were unable to disguise the fact that they were organized, indeed existed, for the sole purpose of robbing, beating, raping, and killing the newcomers to Aegis.

"They found that these goals attracted a significantly smaller following than the former, appealing only to the sociopaths among them. A great many entrants, having come from a similar environment out there, enthusiastically joined the habitants of ZooCity, only to quickly migrate to either Walden or Madison, once they saw the true *raison d'état*."

"So other than the occasional gangster newbie," Tillie stated, "they dwindled down to a hard-core collection of thugs. And the ones who still had souls when they arrived here split so fast your head would spin. And like Wilson said, a lot of them went to Walden to get away from the punks. You have to admit that Walden would look pretty good after that – enlightened, peace-loving, tolerant, all that stuff. It didn't take them long to hightail it out of Walden and zoom over to Madison. That's where they are now, for the most part."

"We've been dancing around the issue regarding Madison and Walden," Elias broached the subject. "Would you describe the two enclaves as microcosms of the political right and left, or Republican and Democrat...conservative and liberal?"

"Yes!"

"No!"

Tillie and Wilson had answered simultaneously. Tillie was the first to expound. "Walden *is* a collection of liberal pukes. Their whole thing is 'if it feels good, do it.' They see Walden, and Aegis as a whole, as a commune. All they preach is tolerance, but they are the most intolerant bunch I've ever seen, when it comes to someone or something they disagree with. They are smug, self-righteous, proscriptive, and sanctimonious, and they believe that they know what is best for everyone. They have actually tried, more than once, to intercept the food drops and remove any item they find offensive because it isn't organic or it might cause obesity or whatever, before it is distributed to the rest of the residents.

"And they can't stand anyone who might rise above the others. Conservatives believe that if you fertilize and water the garden, things will grow – things of all shapes, heights, sizes, and colors, things that will look pretty, things that will bear fruit, things that will produce vegetables, things that are destined to be eaten by the farm animals so they can grow. And you can't always predict what might sprout next.

"Liberals are like the lawn mower that comes along and lops off any plant that excels and tries to grow higher than the others. They are like the spray that kills anything other than the designated and acceptable form of life.

"No wonder the newbies who came to Aegis to avoid killing themselves went ahead and did it anyway after a dose of that stuff!"

By the end of her diatribe, she had worked herself into a frenzy, her voice bouncing off the surrounding concrete walls, reinforcing her passion.

"Tillie, I never cease to be entertained by your tirades," Wilson remarked, chuckling.

"Well, it's all true!"

"I take it that you don't agree with her," Elias commented to Wilson.

"It isn't that I don't agree with our exuberant friend; in many ways I do. When I responded in the negative to your question, I was being more literal."

"How so?"

"You asked if Madison and Walden were microcosms of the political right and left, or perhaps the Republicans and Democrats."

"Yes."

"Since Mathilda launched us, emphatically, in this direction, let's begin with Walden. I believe that if you took a poll of the residents, present and past, you would indeed find that almost all of them would describe themselves as Democrats; however, I have never perceived that political party to be as ideologically monolithic as others might. Their current socioeconomic bent is certainly not consistent with the firmly held beliefs of prominent Democrats from the not too distant past."

"Ask not what your country can do for you. Ask what you can do for your country."

"Precisely."

"But that speech was from half a century ago."

"It was. And it has taken that half century for the now dominant voices to wrest control of the party from the others. But that does not mean that those who believe in that concept, or in a strong military or a thriving business community, do not still consider themselves to be Democrats. It is only that their voices have been drowned out by the others. And I believe that they are waiting for their party to return to them.

"With regard to the residents of Madison, I would venture a guess that they, too, would admit they were registered as Republicans prior to entering this facility. But the very same uniqueness and purity of this environment, which precipitated the other changes we discussed earlier, have caused an awakening or realization of some fundamental truths within them. If they were to leave Aegis tomorrow, they would be as offended by the dominant voices within that party as, I believe, Thomas Jefferson or James Madison would be if they were to return to America today."

"So you're saying that they most reflect the beliefs of the Tea Party?"

"That entity is a phenomenon which arose subsequent to my departure from society. I have discussed the Tea Party with some of the new entrants but don't know nearly enough about it to say. I get the impression that it is still in its embryonic stages and only time will tell what it may become. And labels, although convenient, are generally misleading more than helpful."

"Yeah," Tillie interrupted. "They don't allow you to drone on for hours."

Wilson smiled at her and continued, "I do have a tendency to do that. Unfortunately, most of the things I ponder are not easily distilled into bullet statements."

"It's a good thing we have all the time in the world," Tillie huffed.

Shaking his head in amusement, Wilson continued once again, "I believe that the folks at Madison have benefited from the mental clarity afforded by the absence of media, currency, and all of the myriad distractions which are an integral part of the society out there. And as a result, they have formulated a philosophical foundation that rewards excellence, effectively discourages disruptive behavior, holds each person accountable for his or her actions, offers opportunity to all who sincerely seek it, and, most important, recognizes the realities of human nature.

"And the last is the fatal shortcoming of Walden. For Walden, in all of its practices, policies, and procedures, conducts itself on the basis of how we should be, rather than how we truly are."

"I have a question for you, Elias."

"What is it, Tillie?"

"What kind of spook are you?"

Hesitating for a moment, Elias asked, "What do you mean?"

"Patriot, pragmatist, or mercenary?"

Elias swung his eyes between Wilson and Tillie. Both of them were waiting for his answer. "For almost all of my life I was a patriot. Hard core. Down to the bottom of my soul. But lately" – Elias stopped and shifted his gaze to the darkness beyond his two companions – "something has changed. Now, I'm not so sure."

"That's reasonable enough, considering someone within your own government ordered the killing of your wife."

"I'm sure that's a part of it, Wilson. But I've had a lot of time to think about things since then, and since I left the agency. I still love my country. I truly do. I would give my life defending its principles and ideals. Yet now...it is as if America isn't America anymore. It has changed. And not for the better."

"A very good friend of mine, during the time I was on the outside," Wilson began, in an effort to help Elias explain his thoughts, "spent his entire life in the same town. When he was born, it had a population of slightly more than one hundred thousand people. The day he passed away, the number had grown to almost two million. In the latter years of his life, he confessed to me many times that his attachment to this community had become irrational, that it was no longer the city he knew or remembered. The newcomers from all over the country had changed it drastically. The old businesses had gone away. The old neighborhoods were no longer recognizable. The politics of the city had transmogrified from a just right-of-center, moderate mentality to what he forlornly characterized as 'a knee-jerk, left-wing lunacy.' In one of our final conversations, he told me that what he now loved was the memory of the town, not the reality."

CHAPTER SIXTEEN

Donovan Killeen sat at the computer terminal, reading the log as Kreitzmann looked over his shoulder.

"As you can see, Mr. Killeen, the files belonging to Doctor Bonillas have been taken."

"And you think they were taken by Doctor Boehn?"

"What other explanation is possible?"

"According to the log file, it was Doctor Bonillas' password that was used. She could have changed her mind about something in her report and decided to remove the files while she rewrote it."

Kreitzmann's lips compressed into a tight grin. "I have no doubt that the perpetrator intended for us to come to that conclusion. And we would have, if I hadn't arrived when I did. According to the tracking logs, the files were tampered with just one or two minutes before I walked in the door. The only person here at that time was Doctor Boehn. If Bonillas had been here, I could not have missed her."

Killeen swiveled the chair around and looked at Kreitzmann. "What would you like me to do?"

Kreitzmann, still angry from his accidental discovery, snapped, "I would *like* you to confine Doctor Boehn to the security offices. I would *like* you to question him. I would *like* you to commence a full audit of all of our research to determine what else, if anything, has been taken or copied. And I would *like* you to seize Doctor Boehn's computer and search his quarters. Aegis being isolated as it is, whatever he may have gathered is probably still there."

The young man stood up from the chair and faced Kreitzmann. "You want me to do all of that based upon this one circumstantial issue? That seems a bit harsh."

Kreitzmann's eyes widened at Killeen's comments. "One circumstantial issue? Mr. Killeen, you were selected to oversee our security. There is no doubt in my mind that we have been breached and that the culprit is within our midst. Your performance relating to Elias Charon's visit was less than stellar. You need to decide how to best handle this latest development, or I will choose a replacement for you from our staff.

Is that clear?"

Rather than becoming cowed, as Kreitzmann expected from the young security chief, Killeen smiled at him. "Oh, quite clear, Doctor," he responded, his eyes drifting to somewhere over the scientist's shoulder. Kreitzmann was not certain but thought that he detected a slight nod from Killeen.

"Then I insist that you get on with…."

One moment Rudy Kreitzmann was speaking; the next he lay unconscious on the floor.

⊙

Syndi pulled her car into her assigned parking space and got out, glancing at the empty stall beside her car, and wondered why Yolanda was not at work yet.

"Where's Yolanda this morning?" she asked the uniformed guard at the entrance as she signed in, checking the sheet for her friend's signature.

The guard shrugged. "Haven't seen her yet."

There was no point in asking him any other questions, so she continued on to the lab area, where she found Bonnie Schwartz sitting at a desk and staring intently at her monitor.

"Have you heard from Yolanda?" she asked Schwartz, who looked up and smiled in greeting.

"No, she hasn't called in." She typed a few keystrokes and added, "No email from her either."

"That's strange. She always beats me to work, especially now, as close to finishing as we are."

Bonnie shook her head. "You both pulled a long shift yesterday. Maybe she's still sleeping."

The explanation did not ring true for Syndi. With a sigh, she proceeded through the two-stage air-lock entrance to the lab, donning her sterile gown at the final room before entering. She was the first of the team to arrive this morning and immediately took a seat at her station. The white cotton towel she had left in her work area the night before was partially hanging down the front lip of the counter.

Syndi pursed her lips for only a moment, as she recalled placing it neatly beside her work space last night.

"I guess I was more tired than I thought," she said aloud and picked up the towel, folding it twice, and setting it off to the side.

Next she turned on her work station and, while waiting for it to boot up, lifted up the sterile gown so she could reach her pocket. Syndi pulled out her cell phone before she remembered that there was no service inside the lab. Tucking the phone back into her pocket, she hit the speaker button on the desk phone, dialed for an outside line, and called Yolanda. After five rings, it went to voice mail. Syndi hung up without leaving a message, assuming that Yolanda must be on her way.

Taking a moment to rub her temples in an attempt to sidetrack the advance of an incipient headache, she tucked her hands into the manipulator gloves and opened the capped vial she had been working with the night before.

⊙

Marilyn sat on the front seat of the rental Ford Explorer, staring at the front of Aegis in the morning light. Despite the fact that the marshals guarding the perimeter regularly had tow trucks haul away the vehicles of new entrants to Aegis, to either turn over to family members or to auction off, the parking area was surprisingly full. During the thirty minutes since she had arrived, at least fifteen other vehicles had pulled into the lot, the occupants abandoning their cars, bundling the possessions they wanted to take in with them, and braving the hellacious winds.

She knew that once she walked through the front turnstile, there could be no turning back.

"Marilyn, you're a fool!" she chided aloud, her words barely audible, even inside the enclosed SUV, over the clamor of the incessant gale.

Slipping on the hooded windbreaker, zipping it up to her chin, and pulling the hood over the top of her head, she yanked on the drawstrings and cinched it tightly around her face. With a final deep breath, as if she were about to duck her head underwater for a long dive, Marilyn opened the door.

⊙

Jerry Clowrey knocked one time on Faulk's door before he turned the handle and swung it open, wondering why Marilyn was not at her usual station. Faulk glanced up from some papers and did not greet Clowrey, only looking at him expectantly.

"There was no transmission last night from Charon."

Faulk did not seem to be surprised by the news. "And Stone?"

"Nothing from Stone either, sir."

"Have we received a report from Boehn? Is he out of Aegis yet?"

"Yes and no, sir. He has the notes from Bonillas, but in the process was detected by Kreitzmann. It was necessary to subdue and detain Kreitzmann."

Faulk turned over the new input in his mind for a moment. "At this point, it doesn't really matter what Kreitzmann knows. Why hasn't Boehn left Aegis?"

"I can't say, sir. We were communicating through the hard line, when it went dead.

I've tried contacting him repeatedly with no luck. I've even tried to reach him through the dedicated point-to-point T1. I was unable to connect with his computer."

Faulk's mood visibly worsened. Tersely, he asked, "Did he, at the very least, upload Bonillas' files to us?"

"No, sir."

Slamming his fist down hard on the desk, Faulk took a full minute to compose himself before he could trust his voice. "Very well. Let me know if anything changes." He snatched up the telephone handset and punched in a four-digit extension.

Anxious to leave the room, Clowrey simply answered, "Yes, sir," and backed out, closing the door. As he walked back to his office, Clowrey's phone vibrated in his pocket. Pulling it out, he saw in the display that the call was coming from the lab.

"Now what?" he muttered aloud.

$$\odot$$

Elias awakened on the cot to the gentle sounds of percolating coffee. Turning his head, he saw that it was Wilson who had lit the camp stove and put the pot on. A few feet farther away Tillie was sleeping on her side, her back turned to Elias. Wilson noticed the movement from Elias, and they made eye contact in the dim light.

Not wanting to disturb Tillie, Elias carefully twisted around on the narrow camping cot until he was in a seated position, the tops of his knees almost level with his chest. Neither he nor Wilson spoke for the few minutes it took for the coffee to finish. When two metal cups were filled with the black brew, the men walked away together, putting some distance between themselves and their sleeping friend.

Elias spoke in a muted voice. "I assume you had a quiet shift."

"Quiet as a tomb. Did you get enough rest?"

"It'll have to do."

"Have you thought of a direction for our efforts this morning?"

"I think so. With the killing of the ZooCity residents, the destruction of the solar panels, and their loss of Eric, I have the feeling that the rats are going to abandon this ship."

"I would agree. It seems that whatever benefit they may have had from operating in Aegis is deteriorating rapidly for them."

"When Kreitzmann told you about his back door to Aegis, did he give you a clue as to its whereabouts?"

"He did not. I am not aware of the location of that point of ingress and egress."

"I think we need to find it."

"What good will that do? You aren't planning on leaving Aegis, are you?"

"No. But if we want answers, Kreitzmann is probably the only one in this place who has any. And if we're right and they are getting ready to leave, then covering the exit makes the most sense."

Wilson nodded his understanding. "How do you propose we do that?"

Elias shrugged. "I'm not sure. We all went over the plans for this place yesterday, but we were looking for a hiding place, not the logical spot for Kreitzmann's private entrance."

"Perhaps a second review, with that in mind, might be helpful."

"As much as I hate to do this, I guess it's time to wake up Tillie."

⊙

"Has anyone seen Sweezea and Crabill?" Milton Pierce shouted over the heads of the rapidly assembling crowd.

He singled out three of his regular Madison security team; each in turn shook his head to indicate he had not.

Without giving the two men another thought, Pierce continued in a loud voice, "We are all aware of what has happened at ZooCity. That enclave is no more. We also know that there has been a catastrophic occurrence which destroyed the solar collector system atop Aegis. This has caused partial outages throughout the complex. But the long-term...actually, not so long-term...effect of this is that we are now running on reserve battery power, which will run out in a matter of days, or perhaps weeks."

The gathering had quieted to listen. He went on, "We are fortunate in that we have two men in our community with training and experience in this area: one, an electrical engineer; the other, a journeyman electrician. But without help, they cannot begin to address what is required. So I need volunteers to assist them in their work."

"What can we do?" asked one of the group standing closest to Pierce.

"They have prioritized our efforts. One of the tasks at the top of the list is to redo the circuiting and redirect the available battery power so that it is only being used by the occupied portions of Aegis. This should substantially lengthen the reserve life of the batteries. Anyone who has worked as an electrician or an electrician's helper would be our first choice, followed by auto mechanics, then tradespeople of all sorts who might be comfortable working with tools, and lastly, those who are capable of doing the heavy lifting, the grunt work, as it were."

Pierce was gratified to see that several hands were raised in the group.

"Those who are volunteering, thank you. Please move into the anteroom where our two men are waiting. We must get started immediately on that phase of the work. The second item on the list is the tedious and dangerous task of picking through the devastation on the roof of Aegis. If there are any solar panels which are still serviceable, they must be salvaged, and this must be done quickly before they fall victim to the continuing winds. This is inherently dangerous work because of those constant gale-force winds, as well as the presence of glass and even steel with a deadly potential."

Again, several hands rose, and Pierce segregated the volunteers from the balance of the gathering, dispatching them to the foreman who would oversee the work. When they were gone, he looked at the remaining crowd and, with a more somber tone, resumed, "Finally, I believe it is critical that we deal with ZooCity."

A few of the men and women around him had quizzical looks which quickly changed to disgust as he elaborated, "That enclave is littered with corpses. The process of decay has already commenced. If we do not gather these bodies and bury them, all of Aegis will suffer from a myriad of problems…disease, infestation by insects and rats, and so on. It is for our own health and safety that we do this.

"I know that after the riot, we addressed this same issue by unceremoniously dumping the bodies of the dead into the compactor. I have been sickened by that action ever since and cannot abide repeating it. I understand the repugnance of this task. I sincerely do. But I believe that, in addition to the obvious health and safety issues, it is also the civil and the moral thing to do. If you are curious as to who will be at the front of this detail, the answer is that it is I."

With that final comment, Pierce stopped and turned his gaze from one of his citizens to the next, shifting his glance through the assemblage, and waiting. Slowly, at first, then gaining in pace, hands went up until every man and woman in the group had volunteered.

With a smile, he made his final comment. "I can't tell you how gratified I am by your response. I would like all of you to gather masks, gloves, and any other protective clothing you may have, and meet here in an hour."

The gathering broke up and the meeting room quickly emptied. It was not until most had gone that Pierce noticed his sister standing in a corner of the room, waiting.

Their eyes connecting, she took a timid step forward, unsure how she would be received by her brother. Milton quickly covered the several yards to Mildred and embraced her.

"Mildred, how are you?"

Stepping back, she answered, her voice muted, "I've been better, Milton."

He gestured toward a table and chairs with his arm. "Let's sit down."

She nodded and moved toward the chairs. As they walked, Milton realized that he had never seen his sister like this. If he had ever been tasked with creating a list of descriptive words for Mildred Pierce, it would have been populated with *bold*, *assertive*, *strong*, *fearless*…and many similar adjectives indicating the level of her confidence and commitment.

Seating himself beside her as she slowly lowered herself down, he asked, "What's wrong?"

Her eyes fluttered uncertainly for a moment before she spoke. "We lost eight more residents."

"Oh, my God!" He instantly regretted his choice in words. Mildred had long ago divorced herself from the religion of their upbringing and, in fact, any and all belief in God. Even this casual comment normally would elicit a ten-minute tirade. But this time there was none.

He decided to quickly move the conversation forward. "How? What happened?"

With a dull stare, she replied, "Suicide."

"Suicide? Eight more in how long a period? In the past few weeks?"

"Last night." The two words fell flatly from her.

Milton had no idea what to say.

"With these latest losses, Walden is down to less than forty people."

So immersed in the day-to-day challenges of managing Madison, he had not followed the progress of Walden. "I had no idea."

His words caused her eyes to pivot, connecting with his, and he saw a brief flash of the former fire which had been her hallmark. "That's garbage, Milton, and you know it."

"What do you mean, Mildred?"

"You have always competed with me. You've always wanted to prove that you were right and I was wrong."

"Mildred, that's not true."

"*Yes, it is!*" she snapped back at him.

Tentatively, he reached out and gently placed his hand on hers. "We've always had our differences; that's true. And, as you know, those differences have been quite extreme…even to the point of alienating us from each other. But, in all of our discussions, arguments, and verbal battles, there's one thing I've never shared with you."

Suspiciously, she asked, "What is that?"

"There has always been a part of me that hoped you were right."

A breath caught in her throat as she absorbed his words. "What…what are you…do you mean that?"

Attempting a weak smile, he answered, "I do."

"But you have always fought so hard. You've been so *certain* in your convictions."

"I still am. But that isn't the point. My world view is missing one element your philosophy has."

She was analyzing his every word, looking for a trace of insincerity. "What do you mean? What *one element*?"

"Beauty."

"Beauty?"

He nodded. "Your view, your image of the world...and, specifically, people...is gilded with a loveliness, a hopefulness. It is an essence my vision sorely lacks."

She stared deeply into her brother's eyes, searching for duplicity and finding only candor. "If that's true, then why...?"

He interrupted, "We have fought over this issue because I am convinced that your belief, your philosophy, is grounded in wishful thinking instead of reality. The fundamental cornerstone upon which your paradigm is built is an illusion. But that, also, is not the point. Out there" – he gestured vaguely with his arm to indicate the world outside Aegis – "the most hawkish, militaristic politician, as he works incessantly to strengthen our defenses, even at the expense of social programs, wishes, deep within his soul, that the flower-child mantra of 'give peace a chance' would work. He really, truly desires a world where no one wants to conquer us or kill us.

"The store owner, who spends huge sums installing surveillance cameras and staffing his business with loss-prevention people, intensely yearns for a world where his employees wouldn't dream of stealing from him. The owner of the manufacturing plant would be ecstatic if he could run his plant without needing foremen to make certain that every employee does his or her job and does it well. And every parent or every competent teacher longs for the day when students want to learn, need to learn, and testing and grading would not be necessary.

"Sadly, Mildred, the reality is that if we were to disband our military tomorrow, our country would be overrun within days. The pathetic truth about the retail industry is that more than seventy percent of the theft of merchandise and cash is caused, not by the customers and shoplifting, but by the very employees who are already provided a job. If workers are left unsupervised in a manufacturing plant, production drops to less than half and the quality of the output falls to an abysmal level. And students who are not tested...who are not evaluated in their progress...leave the institution illiterate."

Mildred took in his words without comment.

Milton's voice lowered and softened. "All of this is not an indictment against men and women or our children. It is simply the way it is. It is human nature. It is who we are. The reality of the human animal is that if we are not watched, policed, graded, tested, and evaluated, we will not do well."

"That isn't true of everyone."

"No. You're right. It isn't. There are exceptions in each of the situations I described above and countless others. There are some people who are not aggressive, who will not take advantage of an undefended nation. There are honest employees, men and women who won't steal from their bosses whether they are watched or not. There are workers who push themselves far harder than any foreman would ever dream of pushing. And there are students who do come to learn and will do so voraciously, taking advantage of every opportunity provided. The mistake is when you attribute the traits of these individuals to all others."

Her tone neutral, rather than accusatory, Mildred stated, "Then you're a cynic."

Milton allowed himself a wan smile. "Someone who is a 'Pollyanna' sees things more positively than they are. A cynic is at the other end of the spectrum. Neither bias produces an accurate read on what is seen. I try…I hope that I am a realist. I recognize everything that I've described to you as being a fact of human nature. But I also see the good within humanity, the potential to rise above, to be heroic, noble, honest, fair, decent, and kind. In other words, to be exceptional."

"So do I."

"That is where we differ. You believe that all people are born that way and will inherently live their lives that way, unless they are thwarted by some outside force. For you, Mildred, all people are exceptional until they encounter an oppressive leader or a greedy boss. At that point, you believe they become victims. And because they started out as exceptional and only became bad children, bad parents, bad employees, or bad citizens as a result of their victimization and oppression, they cannot be blamed. You believe that if we could only remove the malignant influences on people from the moment they are born, they would all be exceptional."

"There *are* nasty and ugly people out there! They do victimize. Don't try to tell me that the wealthy businessman isn't trying to hold on to his wealth and keep the others down."

"He *is* trying to hold on to his wealth. In fact, he is trying to increase it."

"Because a billion dollars isn't enough for those people. They need two billion…three…ten billion." As she spoke, her former feistiness crept back into her voice, and Milton became concerned that this was going to degenerate into another in a long line of screaming conflicts between them.

Trying to shift the direction of the conversation slightly to mollify her, he asked, "What's the alternative?"

He watched as she calmed somewhat. "We need to remove the incentive to make egregious profits."

"You know I disagree, but tell me, how would this be done?"

"A graduated tax, increasing to a higher rate the more they make."

"Since people always work in their own self-interest, what happens under a graduated tax is that their need, as they perceive it, to make even more money increases as they are taxed at the higher rates. They must redouble their profits just to compensate for what is being taken from them. So that would not solve the problem, as you perceive it; it would exacerbate it."

"Not if once they passed a threshold, a certain income level, the tax rate became one hundred percent. Then there would be nothing they could do, no amount they could make which would compensate for that."

"That's true. If the government decided the maximum that people should be allowed to make, and took everything above that amount from them, you are absolutely right; they would no longer have any self-interested motive to cross that line. By the way, what would that number be?"

Mildred began to answer and then stopped herself.

"Come on, Mildred, what's the number? Is it a billion dollars a year?"

"No, that's much too high."

"One hundred million?"

"Too high."

"A million?"

"No...yes. I'm not sure."

"Aren't there several people on your side of the ideological fence who believe that a million dollars is much more than a person needs to make?"

"That's true. There are."

"So even if you felt that a million was a good threshold, there would be others who fought against you, maintaining that such an amount was extravagant?"

"Yes."

"For the purpose of our little chat here, let's say that you got your way – that the threshold was set at a million dollars, and every dollar in excess of that amount had to be turned over to the government. What do you think would happen next?"

"Well, I think that the wealthy would have no choice but to share it, pass it down to the employees."

"So, back to your 'wealthy businessman'...you think that he would simply share it? Put it in a pension plan or a profit-sharing plan?"

"Or give higher wages and benefits."

"He wouldn't."

"What do you think *he* would do?"

"He would leave. He would leave the United States and find a country which allowed him to make more money, gain more recognition, earn more prestige."

She began to rebut him, when he interrupted her. "Mildred, just as your residents left to come to Madison."

She stopped. As Mildred had plunged, over the past several minutes, into the familiar and somehow comfortable debate with her brother, she had briefly forgotten about Walden. The reality of the failure of the community – her failure – came flooding back to her.

His voice once again becoming gentle, Milton continued, "Aegis has been an experiment, an experiment to determine human nature, whether we are born with exceptionalism or we are not. I believe that it has to be earned, to be striven for. I believe that the flaws and frailties which produce the other behaviors, the nasty and unpleasant ones, are the natural condition and that it takes hard work and consistent effort to overcome them, to drive them out of oneself. It is that basic difference between us which prompts those of your philosophy to eschew the concept of an exceptional person. Because if all people are born with it, by definition they cannot be exceptional; they would merely be normal."

She started to speak, but he cut her off. "But watching, enforcing, disciplining, grading, and the rest are only half of the equation. The other half is to reward, since people will only operate, with rare exceptions, in their own self-interest. That was what intrigued me when we came to Aegis and when Walden and Madison came into existence."

"What's that?"

"The normal, traditional ways to reward were eliminated. We have no currency. No one here can attain or exceed that million-dollar cap you propose. The housing, clothing, and food are all provided. There is no access for the purchasing of status items. To be honest, Mildred, I was initially convinced that Aegis was a ready-made environment, a perfect medium, for you and your belief structure."

"I remember," she said, a slight trace of a smile coming to her face. "Not too long after we arrived, you shouted at me that Aegis was nothing but a commune."

He smiled in return. "It definitely looked that way. I was certain that your philosophy would be the one which prevailed in here, rather than mine."

Her smile quickly left, replaced by an expression of forlorn dejection. "It didn't work out that way, did it? Walden is essentially dead. Less than forty people left. How many do you have in Madison?"

"Well over six thousand. You still haven't really told me what happened."

She paused for a moment to formulate her words before surprising him. "I was hoping you could tell me what happened."

"What do you mean?"

"Milton, don't be disingenuous. It was hard enough for me to say it. I don't want to repeat it."

Pierce took a deep breath, using the moment to organize his thoughts. "All right. You obviously didn't lose many to ZooCity."

She nodded to indicate her concurrence.

"That leaves Madison or death as the only other main choices. From the time we initially formed our enclaves, Madison has picked up many of your people. From the beginning it has been a fairly steady stream. The number we've lost to you has been negligible, especially if you consider how many of those changed their minds within a month or so and returned."

"Why do you think that was, Milton?"

"I don't have to guess. With our residents who told us they were leaving, we did an exit interview whenever they agreed. We also did a formal interview when they returned. Of the few who left, their reason was generally an emotional reaction to what they felt had been harsh treatment on our part."

"And why did they come back to you?"

"Overwhelmingly, the reason they gave was that, although in Madison they became occasionally irritated by the standards and expectations imposed upon them, they found that they could not tolerate the complete absence of any standards or expectations they encountered at Walden."

"That's not...." Mildred halted in mid-sentence. "Go on."

"We also interviewed those who started out at Walden and relocated to us. There was, again, a consistent message. The recurring theme in their answers was a feeling of frustration, of pointlessness over there."

"Pointlessness?"

"Do you remember a behavioral study performed many years ago where they took a group of college students who badly needed money, and paid them quite well? I think it was three times the current minimum wage. All they had to do was spend every morning out in a field digging holes. They would break for lunch and, after they had eaten, their afternoon was spent filling up the same holes."

"Vaguely."

"Within ten days they had all quit, despite the fact that they needed the income. When asked why, the reason given by almost all of the students was the same. They couldn't stand doing something meaningless...pointless."

"How does that translate to Madison and Walden?"

"That was my struggle at the beginning. As I said earlier, everything was provided for us. All of the normal yardsticks for success, for achievement, for distinguishing oneself were not viable here. For you, it was perfect. You created an environment of harmony and equality, an egalitarian Shangri-La. After some thrashing about and some false starts, we created the Madison you see now."

"You created boot camp." Her tone was gentle, without a hint of ire.

With a grin, he acknowledged her comment, "In a sense, yes. We had to find a way to give people something to work toward, a way to be recognized and acknowledged. We began small. Creating a basic education curriculum, we opened our first school. Attendance was mandatory. Achievement was tracked and published. Degrees, and their accompanying status, were earned and granted. We also created work for people to do. Frankly, much of it was busy work, although we made sure not to fall into the trap of digging and refilling holes. We instituted a political structure with elected representatives for each block of residential units, as well as a security team with ranks.

"In short, hierarchies began to form and crystallize. The community had leaders, second- and third-tier leaders, work supervisors, scholars...the list goes on. And with each of the distinctions came privileges, some of them amorphous, some quite obvious. We randomly selected secondary corridors within Madison and made them accessible only to the higher-tier citizens. They got preferential seating at the common-area dining rooms and at any meetings or events. Things like that."

"You created *haves* and *have-nots*."

"We did, essentially out of thin air. But what we actually created were goals. Individuals on a lower tier of the hierarchy, who wanted to be a part of the group receiving the best seats, worked harder until they reached their goal. We provided challenges. Almost all of our residents accepted the challenges."

"And those who did not?"

"We found, within the concept, a method for taking things a step further, a way to utilize our structure to create a gentle form of punishment. If we have a citizen who does not participate, does not buy into our social structure...who is, essentially, a slacker...then he or she is assigned to do the laundry for one or more of the others, or, perhaps, clean their quarters."

"You make the person a servant?"

"We do. And before you say anything else, in almost all cases, it works. The people soon become functional, participating members of the group, and those tasks are eliminated. We actually have a ceremony for them as they come out of subservience. The entire population shows up to honor, welcome, and applaud them for making the transition. It is always quite an emotional moment for them to be accepted and embraced enthusiastically by the others."

"But why make them servants? Isn't that humiliating for them?"

"Of course it is. It's supposed to be humiliating. In addition to the unpleasant duties, they must also wear a bright red shirt at all times, denoting their status."

"Supposed to be humiliating? Why? It seems as if it would be damaging to them."

"It is the humiliation that shocks them out of their lethargy. It is the impetus which drives them to make the changes in their lives needed to escape from it. Without it, there is no motivation. Mildred, we are back to the issue of human nature. It is normal to be ashamed in a situation such as I've described. But it is also normal to want to end the shame, to escape from it, to rise above it. Remember when our father left our mother and she went on welfare and food stamps?"

"Of course, I do. I'll never *forget* that time. It was horrible!"

"You're right. It was. Our mother came back from the store completely humiliated by the looks and even the occasional comments from the others in the cashier's line when she paid with food stamps. The same was true when she cashed the welfare check."

"It wasn't right! She was in that position through no fault of her own."

"I know. I agree. I think much of the way we both are today is a result of watching her come home and cry during those times. But you and I learned very different lessons from that experience. You were mortified and vowed that society should never put any citizen through that again. I realized that it was the shame which caused her to buckle down and work very hard to make certain that she never had to ask for public assistance again."

Mildred listened to his words, saying nothing.

"The culture moved in your direction. Now that times have changed, now that the stigma is removed and the outward evidence of public assistance is hidden, how many people, who are standing in that cashier's line and are allowed to pay with a debit card instead of the conspicuous food stamps, are still on assistance because they don't feel the shame our mother felt?

"The shame, the social ostracism, is necessary. Without it, you not only lose the motivation to escape from the assistance, you begin to feel that you are entitled to receive it. I'll be honest, the concept did not have a one-hundred-percent success rate. There were a few on whom it failed."

"What did you do to them?"

Milton permitted a slight smile to cross his face. "They left and joined Walden. Within a month, maybe two, they returned. And when they came back, they were ready to join in our society.

"I took a very long time to answer your question as to why I thought Walden failed. But Madison is only accountable for a portion of the population loss from there. I said at the beginning, the only other way you could lose people was through death. I would know nothing about that. Please tell me, has it been an issue?"

"Almost from the beginning, suicide has been, if you'll excuse the expression, a way of life at Walden. A week would never pass that didn't include the loss of some of our residents, sometimes several."

"You must have developed a feel for their motives."

"We tried to get a handle on the motivations. We had group sessions, counseling, interventions, hundreds of one-on-one meetings before the fact. Nothing ever emerged as an underlying reason."

"What reasons *did* they give?"

"Most of the time, none. But if they did, the reasons were best described as superficial, more akin to a convenient excuse, rather than anything substantive. As an example, we had a young, healthy man commit suicide because he had torn his favorite shirt."

"I have a theory, Mildred, about the so-called utopian mind-set, which I believe is far too exclusionary, unrealistic, and eventually damaging. Over time, the never-ending progression of actions, words, and even thoughts which must be forced into that tight mold of utopia gradually create such an intolerance to even the slightest deviation that an almost allergic reaction, a full-body and full-mind reaction, occurs, taking the person directly to furor or desperation. A house of cards has been constructed, so high and so tenuous that literally anything can knock it down. There is no resilience.

"Altogether, how many have you lost to suicide?"

Mildred sat back in her chair and looked up at the ceiling for a moment before answering. "Over the life of our community, approximately two thousand."

CHAPTER SEVENTEEN

Bonnie Schwartz refilled her coffee mug and laughed. "I can't believe he said that!"

"He did! Right in front of his wife and my husband," Jennifer exclaimed emphatically.

"What did you say?"

"I told him to dream on!"

They both broke into high-pitched squeals, causing the others in the break room to twist around in their chairs and glance at them. Bonnie looked at the clock on the wall. "I'd better get back. I was only supposed to be gone a minute."

"Yeah, me too."

Schwartz turned and walked hurriedly back to her station outside the lab. Thankfully, no one was around to see her return. She placed the full mug on the desk, accidentally setting it on top of a pen, which shot out from underneath, causing the coffee to slosh out of the cup.

"Dammit!"

She scurried to the restroom and grabbed several paper towels from the dispenser, returning to her desk. After the spill was mopped up, Bonnie sat down and checked her work phone for any messages she might have missed. Then she picked up her cell phone from the desk and checked for text messages. There was one from Jennifer, which had arrived only moments ago: "By the way, I gave him your email, lol."

Laughing again, she moved her thumbs madly as she typed back a threat to send the man Jennifer's cell number. After having dispatched the text message, she checked her phone for any others and, finding none, replaced the cell phone on her desk. As she did, she noticed something strange on one of the video screens set up as an array in front of her.

"What the...?" Pulling out her keyboard, Bonnie typed in a few commands, and the video camera she was watching zoomed in for a tighter view. She was instantly mortified by what she saw. Recovering, she dialed the extension for her supervisor.

Sheldon Kennerley arrived within two minutes, winded from the jog to Bonnie's station. When he stopped and his eyes fixed on the screen, he gasped. It was a close-up view of Syndi sprawled on the floor in front of her work area. From the angle of the camera, he could see that a copious amount of blood had gushed from apparently every orifice in her body, pooling around her and saturating the white lab coat.

"We have a breach!" he shouted. "Sound the alarm. Thank God, no one has opened the air lock. Bonnie, get Director Faulk on the phone."

⊙

Faulk opened the door of the Hummer before the driver had come to a complete stop, the wind forcing the door shut again, almost slamming his leg against the frame. Putting his shoulder to it, he pushed it open again and climbed out, holding on to the side grip-bars to prevent the gale from knocking him to the ground. The roar made it impossible to speak to his team, but they knew their orders and followed him out of the transport.

The group, leaning forward at an impossible angle, made their way to the entrance.

⊙

Boehn glanced over at Killeen. "Gather all your men. It's time we departed Aegis."

"What about him?" the young security chief asked, motioning toward the still-unconscious Kreitzmann.

"Bring him and the others. Since the land line and the T1 are both down, I'll gather all of the files on flash drives."

"It's going to be difficult to assemble everyone without the others noticing. What should I do with them if they ask questions?"

Boehn's first impulse was to issue a harsh order. He quickly realized that extreme measures were no longer required. "Bluff, bully...I don't care if you simply ignore them. I doubt that any of them will physically attempt to stop you, especially since we have their boss."

"Done."

⊙

Elias and Tillie were crouched in the air plenum, both peering down into the corridor below. Wilson was stationed back at the last junction, watching for any search teams.

"I hope you're right," Tillie whispered.

"So do I. It was the only spot on the perimeter that made any sense."

He referred to a note on the plan that indicated there had been a block-out, a temporary opening in the continuous concrete wall which made up the envelope surrounding Aegis. Once they stood the wall, there would not have been any access to the interior for the workers to use, other than the single opening which was to become the permanent entrance. Having only one way in and out of a project of this magnitude would have been impractical and unsafe. The temporary opening was actually a gap formed in the tilt-up wall, a hole created when the panel was cast. After it was no longer needed, it would have been filled in and covered.

"It is much easier to remove the in-fill of a former opening than to try penetrating an engineered panel. Besides, I don't think it's a coincidence that Kreitzmann picked the section of Aegis where the old opening is located to call home."

Tillie, still staring intently down, murmured, "Like I said, I hope you're right. It looks quiet down there now."

Elias slipped the knotted rope off his shoulder. "Might as well take a look."

Gripping the edge of the lay-in grille, Tillie quietly pulled it up and out of the opening, while Elias took one final look at the page from the plans, memorizing this section of the layout. He had already tied one end of the rope to a nearby pipe and dropped the free end down to the floor below. "I'll go first."

With the now functional AK-47 slung over his back, Elias gripped the rope and lowered himself through the opening, taking only a few seconds to climb down to the floor. Tillie was already following him down before he finished his descent.

"Should be only about forty yards that way," Elias whispered.

As they moved forward, Wilson had come to the opening and pulled up the rope, quietly sliding the grille back in place, before returning to his post. The corridor was unnervingly quiet, almost as if this part of Aegis had already been deserted. Elias began to worry that he was too late.

Ahead, at the end of the hallway, he could see that a door had been installed, a door which, according to the plans, should not even exist since the hallway ended at the perimeter wall of the complex. There was a keypad attached just above the door handle. On either side of the hallway were closed doors, exactly as shown on the plan; on the right, the door entered into restrooms, and on the left, into a larger than normal utility room.

It was irrelevant that they did not know the code to the door; it was not their intent to escape. Carefully, Elias opened the utility-room door and peered inside. The room was connected to the network of solar tubing, and it was not necessary to turn a light on. Looking back at Tillie, he nodded and entered; she followed at once.

The room was filled with an assortment of what appeared to be spare parts for the plumbing, electrical, and mechanical systems of Aegis. Rows of freestanding shelving were filled with items segregated by category, including copper and galvanized pipes in various lengths, unions, couplers, and a variety of fixtures. In another section were junction boxes, rolls of wiring, and replacement switches and outlets, and in another were spare grilles and registers, thermostats, and barometric dampers. Standing in one corner of the room was a job-site gang box with the lid open. The box was filled with hammers, pry bars, and an assortment of power tools.

"So far, so good," Tillie muttered, once the door was safely closed behind them, and immediately began to shed the various bags, packs, and other items she carried, arranging them neatly near the door for easy and quick access.

"This is perfect," Elias noted, pointing at the closed door. "A peephole."

"That should be fun – the two of us taking turns with one eye plastered to that thing for hours at a time."

He permitted himself a soft chuckle.

⊙

After patiently waiting for nearly two hours, Wilson, having stationed himself in the three-way junction, was the first to hear them coming. Carefully, to ensure that he did not make a sound, he shifted slightly to one side in an effort to see who they were.

Leading the pack were two armed men, followed by a sizable group of people he identified as civilians from Kreitzmann's lab. The assemblage seemed to be evenly split between lab-coated scientists or technicians and regular people who, Wilson assumed, must have been the subjects of many of the experiments. From his vantage point, he was unable to distinguish most of the faces of the group.

Next came a much larger contingent of armed guards. Wilson counted seven more. And finally, there were two men he did not recognize; but, based upon their position in the procession, they seemed to be directing this movement.

Having seen enough and wishing that the three of them had devised some sort of communication system, Wilson eased back from his viewport and made his way to the grille used earlier by Tillie and Elias. As he looked down at the passing heads below, he realized that his two friends had insisted on this position for him not because of any strategic or tactical reason, but merely to place the old man out of harm's way.

⊙

"Someone's coming!" Tillie hissed in a loud whisper.

Elias, who had been exploring the array of parts and supplies for something useful while Tillie took her turn as lookout, trotted over next to her. He noticed that he was still holding the five-foot length of galvanized pipe he had been examining. "What do you see?"

"Two guards carrying assault rifles. But this is weird."

"Let me take a look."

She moved aside to allow him to peer through the peephole. Despite the distortion caused by the fish-eye lens, Elias could see that there were several people milling around outside the door. They were not a part of the security team, but appeared to be test subjects and scientists.

As he watched, someone came into view from his right, someone he did recognize. In a voice so hushed that it was almost inaudible, he said, "It's Boehn."

"What is he doing?" Tillie whispered back at him, directly into his ear.

He did not answer her as he watched Boehn move past the crowd and approach the door. Clearly, he was the one who knew the code. At the fringe of his left field of vision, Elias could see Boehn punch numbers on the keypad. At the same time, he saw that at least four more men carrying assault rifles had moved into his view from the right.

"This doesn't look good."

"What's wrong?"

"It isn't Kreitzmann opening the door; it's Boehn."

This was bad news for them; their plan had been to grab Kreitzmann as he passed in front of their door, assuming that holding the leader would be sufficient leverage to direct any others, who might be with him, to back off.

"Crud!"

Since the exit was at the edge of his view, Elias could barely see that Boehn had opened it. However, instead of exiting from his view, Boehn backed away from the door and began shouting.

"Tillie, press your ear against the crack around the door. Maybe you can make out what they are shouting."

She instantly did so and, with pauses to listen, relayed what she heard as Elias continued to watch the hallway through the peephole.

"I think he said the exit is blocked....I guess the panels from the roof tumbled off and are piled up in front of the exit....He's telling some of the men to get some tools."

"Tools?" Just as what Tillie had told him sank in, Elias saw two of the armed men hand their rifles to their colleague and begin walking straight at the utility room.

"They're coming in here."

Elias jumped back from the door, seeing that Tillie had jerked back to the side. Looking around, he saw that his rifle was several feet away. His first impulse was to draw the 9mm tucked behind, when he realized that he was still gripping the length of pipe from earlier.

There was no more time to think. The door to the utility room opened and the two men walked in. They did not have a moment to react before Elias swung the pipe, solidly connecting with the first man on the side of his head. An instant later, he thrust the pipe forward with all of his weight behind it, aiming for the row of cartilage between the second guard's ribs. The man grabbed his chest, his eyes wide, and staggered to the side, allowing Elias to slam him with another blow, this one directed at his neck. The man dropped.

There was instant commotion outside in the hallway, as several of the civilians and more than one of the security team had witnessed the attack through the open door. One of the guards was already shouting for the people to clear a path as he brought his automatic weapon to bear on the opening into the utility room. Elias did not hesitate. He was stepping forward to slam the door, but Tillie beat him to it. The metal door crashed closed.

Elias, sweeping his eyes around the area, found a hard-plastic, collapsing sawhorse. He dropped the pipe and grabbed the sawhorse, sliding it under the door handle.

"That should slow them a bit. We need to move back."

They both snatched up their weapons and retreated to the freestanding shelving. Fortunately, the first row was filled with steel plumbing parts and was parallel to the doorway, providing fairly good cover.

They had only turned in to the aisle a moment earlier, when the door was suddenly perforated with bullet holes as the security man outside emptied his clip into it, some of the rounds hitting one of the two unconscious guards on the floor, others shattering the sawhorse. Elias, choosing Wilson's shotgun, had poked the barrel through the jumble of parts on the shelf and was able to get off a shot just as one of the men outside kicked the door open. The double-0 shot caught him squarely, and violently tossed him backward. He fell to the floor, motionless. None of the others in the hallway ventured in front of the open doorway.

Tillie, armed with the AK-47, positioned herself five or six feet away from Elias along the shelving, and cleared enough of the stored plumbing parts to provide a gun slot. "I wish we knew how many we were up against."

"That makes two of us. I saw at least five or six. Doesn't mean that was all of them."

"I'm worried about the Zippers."

"Roger that."

⊙

Boehn was isolated. At his back was the opened exit door, which was completely blocked by the tangled mess of solar panels and twisted steel. In front of him was the open door to the utility room. The civilians had all been herded back to the far end of the hallway, and one of the security team was stationed with them. The rest of the team and the one remaining Accelerant were on the other side of the opening, waiting for instructions.

Boehn did not want to lose his last asset by sending the Accelerant into the room. Chances were, he would prevail, but there was always the possibility that some sort of trap had been set. After all, these three had foiled the Accelerants in the past. The beige-suited freak, as Boehn still thought of all of them, was in constant motion, twitching, shifting, and pivoting, even though he was standing still for instruction. They simply could not help it, he decided; it had been hard-wired into their being.

Making eye contact with Killeen, Boehn pulled a black marker out of his pocket. On the wall adjacent to the exit, he wrote *TEAR GAS?* The security chief nodded and turned to his men, sending one of them back to the armory.

⊙

"I wish there was a damn grille in here. Wilson could drop the rope to us and we'd be out and could get behind them." Tillie's voice was quiet.

Elias nodded. "That would be nice."

"What do you think they are going to do?"

"If it were up to me, I'd send in gas, along with some flash bangs."

"Flash bangs?"

"An armament you haven't heard of? I'm surprised."

"What are they?"

"Concussion grenades. Super loud, super bright. They stun you, blind you, temporarily disable you."

"Shouldn't we find something to protect ourselves against them?"

"Already thought of it. Here!" Elias turned and tossed a couple of small plastic packets to her.

She caught them and ripped one open. "Earplugs!"

"Yep. Pretty common on job sites. They use them to protect the hearing of workers during the loud stuff."

"What about the flash part?"

Elias rested his shotgun on the shelf. "Keep an eye on the door." She nodded, and he checked the adjacent shelves until he found what he wanted. Returning, he handed her a pair of dark goggles.

"I suppose construction workers need these in case someone throws a bright hand grenade."

"No. These are for the workers who are around welding. Protects their eyes. And, here, take one of these."

He handed her a painter's respiration mask.

"Will this keep out tear gas?"

"No. Not really built for that purpose. It's designed to keep out the fumes from enamel paint, but it should slow it down quite a bit."

She grinned and slipped the mask over her face, its two filtered inlets causing her to look like a large insect.

"No reason to put it over your mouth until they send something in."

She pulled it down so that it dangled around her neck by the straps.

"What about the goggles?"

"I'd put them on now. There wouldn't be any warning with that."

She shoved the bright orange earplugs in, donned the goggles, and picked up her rifle. "I feel silly." She spoke too loudly, compensating for the earplugs.

"You shouldn't. You should feel like a member of a SWAT team. These are basically all of the items they wear during an assault."

"Cool!"

Elias put on his own gear and took a deep breath, shouting, "KREITZMANN! I WANT TO TALK!"

⊙

Out in the hall, Boehn heard Elias and grinned. Again catching Killeen's eye, he motioned back toward the group, pointing at Kreitzmann, who was leaning against a wall, his head bandaged. Killeen indicated his understanding and trotted back to get the scientist.

⊙

Elias was surprised to see someone stumble into the opening, framed by the doorway. It was Kreitzmann. The man looked much different from the last time Elias had seen him. He appeared to be dazed, disoriented. There was a thick bandage wrapped around the top part of his head, and he stood unsteadily.

"Don't shoot, Tillie."

Elias side-stepped to the end of the shelves, continuing to point his shotgun forward.

"Kreitzmann?"

The scientist's eyes seemed to have trouble focusing. After a moment, he looked at Elias and quietly asked, "Charon? Is that you?"

Trying to figure out the situation, Elias only said, "Step inside the room."

Kreitzmann began to move forward, when a voice boomed from the hallway behind him, "That wouldn't be advisable."

Kreitzmann stopped, his confusion now clouded with fear.

"Why are you doing this, Kreitzmann?"

The man in the doorway shook his head, trying to clear it. "Doing this? I'm...I'm not doing this. I don't know what's happening." His speech was slurred and difficult to understand.

Trying to make sense of what he was seeing and hearing, Elias pressed, "Who is?"

With a monumental effort, Kreitzmann, fighting the effects of a severe concussion, answered, "Boehn."

"Doctor Boehn?"

"Yes," he confirmed weakly.

Elias' mind whirled as he readjusted all of the variables, painting a new picture inside his head. "You didn't kill the people at ZooCity?"

The words slammed into Kreitzmann with a physical force, his mind beginning to clear. "Kill people? ZooCity? What are you talking about?"

From the hallway came the same voice Elias had heard earlier. "Mister Charon, I'm afraid you've been chasing the wrong dragon in your crusade. Rudy Kreitzmann is and has been nothing but a convenient front man for us, although I do admit that some of his findings have proved to be quite useful."

Tillie quietly switched her weapon out of fully automatic mode and slowed her breathing.

"Boehn, why are you doing this?"

"Why am I doing what? Letting you discover the truth, or parading the pathetic Rudy Kreitzmann in front of you? I'll tell you. You are learning the truth because, very shortly, it won't matter what you know. And telling you a little gives me some satisfaction. But, mainly, the reason we are talking and the reason you have Kreitzmann standing before you is to buy a little time. And judging by the return of my man, I believe that we have purchased quite enough."

Boehn must have signaled the member of the security team who had pushed Kreitzmann in front of the door; the instant he finished his sentence, an arm came into view, the hand reaching for Kreitzmann's shoulder. Before the fingers could close on the fabric of his coat, a shot rang out and the man's forearm exploded into a pink cloud. In the next moment, Tillie shouted, "GRAB KREITZMANN!"

Elias was already in motion, plunging forward. He seized him by the front of his shirt and pulled him in, violently. Kreitzmann stumbled and almost fell, but Elias' grasp of the shirt held, and the scientist swung wildly, trying to get his feet back beneath him as he was dragged back behind the shelving. Two rows back and out of the line of fire, Elias let go and Kreitzmann fell to the floor. Without taking any more time, Elias grabbed the shotgun he had hastily leaned against the wall, and rejoined Tillie behind their barrier. He saw that she had pulled the respirator over her mouth and he did the same, right as he heard the clunk-and-roll sound of something being tossed into the utility room with them.

There was no thunderous crash, just the muted popping sound of a tear-gas canister. A second followed the first, and Elias could see that this one rolled against the side of the guard he had decked earlier. Tillie shelved the AK-47 and dashed around their barrier, picking up the second canister and tossing it back out the doorway. She then snatched up the first one and did the same.

Elias saw a third grenade fly into their room and could tell that this one was not tear gas. "TILLIE, TAKE COVER!"

She only had a few seconds to turn back toward her end of the barrier before the grenade exploded. Even through the earplugs, the sound was a horrendous assault. The simultaneous bright flash was easily neutralized by the heavily coated lens of the welder's goggles. She returned to her position, rubbing her ears, and raised her weapon just as the first man came in, laying down suppression fire as he entered. None of his bullets came near the mark, striking the side wall of the room rather than hitting the barricade of metal in front of them. Elias was sure Tillie was about to fire, but stopped her with an abrupt hand gesture.

With a glance he could tell she understood. Within no more than three seconds, two more armed men followed the first one in, guns at the ready. When they were all the way inside, Elias triggered the shotgun at the closest one, blowing him against the door frame. Tillie immediately opened fire with her AK-47, dropping the other two, who had no benefit of cover and had obviously expected the two of them to be disabled by the blast.

No more attackers followed, and the ensuing silence, ruined only by the ringing in their ears, was eerie. After a moment, Elias shouted, "HOW MANY YOU GOT LEFT, BOEHN?"

Understanding the minds of the people outside the room was a very special skill Elias possessed. A static situation had been created. He and Tillie were in the room. The others were in the hall. There was a narrow kill-zone in front of the door. He was certain that this was the picture they all held in their minds as a reality, something they could count on.

With a gesture, he indicated that Tillie should swap weapons with him. She did, and he slapped in a fresh magazine, left the aisle, and ran out the door into the hall. He knew Boehn was to the left and was fairly sure that he was alone. All of the others, whatever security team he had remaining, would be to the right. As he cleared the doorway, he dropped to the floor and rolled once, coming to rest on his stomach, the AK-47 in firing position in front of him. There were three men in uniform conferring with one in a suit. None of them were pointing a weapon at the doorway, so certain had they been that no one would come out.

As one of the men saw Elias suddenly burst into the hallway, he attempted to bring his rifle to bear on him, but was cut down before he could complete the move. The others attempted to open fire but never had a chance, as Elias was less than ten yards from them and in a perfect firing position. The man in the suit, seeing nowhere to go and not carrying a gun, raised his hands in a gesture of surrender.

Tillie had followed to the doorway and was aiming the shotgun at Boehn while sneaking quick peeks in Elias' direction to make sure that he did not need her assistance.

Elias saw, standing dead-center and farther back in the hallway, one of those he knew was a Zipper. The man had obviously withdrawn to escape the effects of the tear-gas clouds still swirling around in the proximity of the utility room. Elias had no idea why the beige-suited character was holding his position, and he was torn as to whether to simply put a bullet into the man. Watching the Zipper, Elias could see that the speed demon's eyes were looking past him, riveted on something or someone else, and determined that he was waiting for a signal from his boss.

Elias was about to twist around to tell Tillie to take Boehn into the utility room, when several things happened at once. The grille, which was directly over the Zipper, lifted, and something dropped. Before he completely took his eyes off the beige figure, he saw the change of expression on the Accelerant's face and realized that Boehn had turned him loose. At the same moment, Elias pulled the trigger on his rifle, knowing that the stranger was too fast and would no longer be standing where he aimed.

Despite the behaviorally enhanced performance of the Zipper, the rules of physics still applied. The coefficient of friction between the stranger's shoes and the tile floor required his initial acceleration to be relatively gradual. This fact, in the case of the Accelerant, caused two things to occur. The net, dropped by Wilson from above, ensnared him just long enough for Elias' bullets to hit home. The last of Boehn's rapid assassins dropped to the floor. And like everything else that he had done in his adult life, he died quickly.

Elias stood and walked to one of the dead security team, unhooking a pair of handcuffs from his belt and tossing them to Tillie, who was still guarding Boehn. She caught them one-handed and slapped one of the cuffs on Boehn's wrist, then attached the other to a long steel strut which was part of the tangled mess outside the exit. Finishing this, she walked to where Elias was busy steadying the bottom of the rope so that Wilson could climb down from the plenum.

Elias looked up at their descending ally and remarked, "Quick thinking, my friend."

Panting slightly, Wilson answered as he reached the floor, "You two exiled me to old-man heaven up there. I was glad to be able to contribute."

As the three of them walked back to the group which had been left unattended by Boehn's men, Tillie punched Elias on the arm and told him, "Between taking out two men with only a pipe, and then diving into the hallway and blasting the rest of them away, I'd say you've earned it."

He stopped and looked at her. "Earned what?"

With a broad smile crinkling her freckled face, she answered, "Your new name. From now on, you are Bruce!"

"I think I'd prefer the...."

He stopped in mid-sentence, quickening his stride.

"Elias, what is it?"

He ignored Wilson's question and plunged into the middle of the civilians. He recognized the mind-reading girl who had caused his close call during his meeting with Kreitzmann. He saw the Asian woman with the amazing verbal abilities. Apparently, Boehn had skimmed the crop of the behaviorally-modified, planning on taking the cream with him as he left. But it was none of Kreitzmann's subjects who had his attention. A figure standing in the middle of the crowd, head bowed, blindfolded, and handcuffed, was his focus.

Breaking through to her, he grabbed her shoulders and, his voice breaking, gasped, "Leah!"

CHAPTER
EIGHTEEN

With the rest of the group released to return to their quarters, and Boehn's two wounded men stabilized and handcuffed next to Killeen, Elias was sitting on the hallway floor with his back against the wall, next to his wife. Tillie had found the keys to the handcuffs in the pockets of one of the dead men and unshackled her. Elias had removed her blindfold. She sat nestled against him, with his arm draped over her shoulder.

Since finding her, he had not let her out of his reach or sight for a moment. He could not stop staring at her face as she slowly sipped from the canteen provided by Wilson, who hovered over them like a mother hen. She had been beaten badly, her face covered with old bruises and poorly healed cuts that should have been stitched. Her hair was matted to her head from the clotted blood.

"You look beautiful."

She made a soft snorting sound that might have been an attempt at a laugh, but Elias could not be certain.

Capping the canteen, she placed it on the floor between her sprawled legs and turned to look at him. Her voice barely audible, she whimpered, "I missed you, Elias."

He put his other arm around her and pulled her closer. "I missed you, baby."

Wilson also had pulled a protein bar from one of their packs and had given it to Leah as she first sat down. She removed it from her pocket and unwrapped it, biting off more than half.

As she chewed, Elias asked, "How did you manage to stay alive all this time?"

Between chews, she answered, "By not giving them what they wanted."

"What was that?"

"Exactly how much I knew and the names of people I told."

"You hadn't told anyone, had you?"

"No. But they didn't know that."

"Not that I'm not glad you're here, but it seems as though they would have given up on that after a while."

She responded in short bursts. "Not that simple. Khalid had me first. He was obsessed with the possibility that I told the Mossad. Refused to accept that I hadn't. I have no idea how long he had me. Days, weeks, months, kind of blurred. He finally lost interest."

Elias' mind involuntarily conjured up images of what her ordeal had been like at the hands of that monster. He consciously pushed them out. "Then what?"

Leah stopped chewing and forced a lopsided grin onto her face. "You haven't seen me all this time and you're debriefing me?"

"You're right! I'm sorry. I was...."

She kissed Elias to stop him from talking. "I'm kidding. We're obviously still in the middle of something, so you should know. Besides, if no one else has found out about what I know, it's critical that we get the word out. By the way, what happened to Eric?"

"Dead."

"Good. *You* killed him."

"I didn't...she did." He pointed at Tillie, who was trying very hard to maintain a respectful distance across the hallway.

"She did it?"

He nodded.

"I like her!"

"I thought you would. You'd better tell me what you know. What was the big secret?"

Elias watched his wife's face as she struggled to answer. He could tell by her tortured expressions that she was wrestling with a phenomenon well known in the intelligence community: If you hold a piece of knowledge and the other side wants it, if you are truly going to succeed at never giving it up, you have to build an impenetrable wall around it. The bad guys will initially dispense pain – mind-numbing, unimaginable pain. If that does not work, they resort to drugs, trickery, humiliation, and deceit, coupled with a regimen that keeps you barely alive, constantly exhausted, confused, disoriented, continuously starving, and thirsty. They attempt every possible ploy to get you to slip up, let down your guard, believe that you are talking to a trusted friend. Whatever it takes. If you are able to conceal your knowledge through all of that, it is only because you have locked it away in a place that even you cannot access anymore, at least not without a tremendous effort. Leah was going through that effort now.

She had forgotten about the last bite of the protein bar, dropping it down to the dusty floor. Her hands came up and she rubbed her temples, hard. Elias even thought he heard a shallow groan coming from her as she leaned forward. He knew there was nothing he could do to help her, so he waited.

More minutes passed before she suddenly leaned back, resting her head against the wall, and stared intently at his face, studying the smallest details. Not satisfied with what her eyes were telling her, she reached up and less than gently probed the skin around his eyes, his ears, and the base of his neck. He knew that she had to convince herself that all of this was not merely another trick and that she really was sitting beside her husband. Next, she leaned forward, putting her nose under his chin and inhaled deeply, pulling in his scent.

After a moment, she sat back against the wall.

"Satisfied?"

She shook her head briefly, then nodded. "I guess so. Either that or I'm just too damn worn out to care anymore."

She looked around at her surroundings, studying Wilson, who had backed away from them and was talking to Tillie as she guarded Boehn across the hall. "Who are they?"

"Friends."

Leah crinkled her mouth and rolled her eyes. "*Friends?* Come on, Elias."

"I don't think we have enough time for me to tell you the whole story. Let's just say that they've saved my butt more than once, and if they are leading me down a path, they're better at it than anyone I've ever met before."

She expanded the range of her visual examination. "By the way, where are we?"

"We're in Aegis."

"Aegis!"

"As I said, it's a long story. You need to decide whether you are going to tell me or not, because we should probably get moving. Once we get out of here, I'll take you wherever you choose so you can pass it on — the White House, the Pentagon, the Capitol. You pick."

"The problem, Elias, is that none of those will work."

Her comment stopped him dead in his tracks. "What are you saying?"

"What I'm saying is that it's big. It's ugly. And I have no idea where it stops."

He stared at her. "Leah, what is it?"

She took a long, deep breath, letting it out slowly. "A lab, Elias. They were working on a biological weapon."

"I already know that."

His comment surprised her. "You do?"

He filled her in on the information obtained by Benjamin.

She nodded. "He obviously only knows a small part of it."

"This wouldn't be the first time that a government, even our government, was working on a bio-weapon."

"Those were all different." Her tone was dismissive.

Before Elias could comment, she hurriedly continued. "Elias, honey, they were working on a doomsday bug. Something fast-acting, deadly, and unbelievably contagious."

"It's been tried before. It always kills the hosts too quickly to be widely contagious, like Ebola, or it mutates into some ineffective strain."

She shook her head. "No. They've done it. They've got it already. It works. They've had it since before I was picked up."

"How did you find out about it? Your assignment was a Taliban training camp."

"Khalid was providing some of the funding for the research. He was in the loop and he was sloppy. I found the reports he was getting. This stuff is terrifying."

"I don't get it. Countries develop bio-weapons for tactical reasons. They use them to take out populations, like Saddam, or to kill opposing armies, as the Germans did in World War I. But a doomsday bug, by definition, kills everybody, including the side who uses it. What's the point?"

"The point is to clean house."

The voice came from the "T" intersection with the adjacent corridor. Elias whirled around to see Faulk, standing at the corner, and started to spring up when he heard the unmistakable sound of the bolt being pulled back on an automatic weapon. He had so focused on Faulk that he had not initially noticed the four other men, all carrying assault rifles, flanking the object of his hatred.

Tillie jumped for the shotgun, which she had leaned against a nearby wall. One of the men brought his rifle to bear on her, clearly intending to open fire. Faulk shouted, "DON'T MOVE!"

At the same moment Elias barked, "TILLIE, DON'T!"

She froze, her hand inches from the weapon, and slowly dropped her arm back to her side, an expression of restrained fury on her face.

Elias slowly stood and faced the man for whom he had nurtured a burning hatred for more than two years. He took two steps, placing himself between the gunmen and his wife. Wilson, who had been near Tillie at the time Faulk arrived, raised his hands slowly over his head and moved away to a point halfway between her and Elias.

There was a rapid triple-beep tone, and Faulk pulled out his cell phone, answering it in the walkie-talkie mode. "Faulk."

"Communications blanket is deactivated, sir."

"Good. You've placed the charges?"

"Yes, sir. Two are missing. One of them is the primary."

"I believe we've solved that problem. Bring your men and join us at the exit corridor. On the double."

"Yes, sir."

Faulk put the phone back in his pocket, and turned to one of his agents, instructing him to release Boehn. To Elias, he said, "I presume you have a key for the handcuffs."

Elias glanced at Tillie and gave her a slight nod. With a loud chuff of disgust, she reached into her pocket and threw the key on the floor in front of Faulk. The agent picked it up and trotted to the end of the hall, where Boehn was still shackled to the steel framing piled outside the exit door. The two moved back to join their boss.

"Quite a touching scene," Faulk snarled with undisguised venom, "seeing the two of you reunited."

Elias bit his lip and said nothing.

"I must admit, Leah, you surprised me. All of the time and effort we expended to break you and you never gave us a thing. Even Khalid, with his barbaric bent, failed."

"What's the point of all this, Faulk? You faked her death and grabbed her two years ago. That's a long time to work anyone over. Whatever she had learned...whatever she might have known...would have resulted in someone taking action against you at some point during that time. Holding her that long doesn't make any sense."

Faulk gave Elias a withering stare. "I suppose you are right, old friend. Oh, wait, as you have corrected me at every possible opportunity, I am not your friend and never have been."

Elias let the comment slide.

"If all we were worried about was whether Leah revealed our plans, we would have disposed of her almost two years ago. But it was much more complicated than that."

"I'll try my best to understand."

"As she played the part of cabin maid for Khalid, she found two things, the report we sent him on the completion of the pathogen, and something else. Something much more important."

"Do I have to guess?"

"No. And I doubt that you would be right if you did."

"The vaccine." The two words came from Wilson.

Elias spun around to stare at his friend as he explained. "That is the only logical explanation which fits all of the facts. It appears that the goals of Mr. Faulk, and whomever he has associated himself with, have taken a turn for the eschatological. You and your people have created a doomsday bug, something that will exterminate all human life on the planet. No complex delivery system needed. No infiltration into enemy territories required. One infected person anywhere in the world will do the job for you."

Faulk glared at him. "Not bad, old man. Please go on."

"As Elias mentioned, a weapon like that is worthless, insane...unless you have a vaccine to protect yourself. With my admittedly shallow knowledge of you and this brief interaction, it appears that you are indeed insane, but of a type very different from that of a suicidal madman. My diagnosis, as a layman and not a trained psychiatrist, is that you are a classic narcissist. You vaccinate every person whom you have chosen to be a part of the new world and turn the bug loose on the rest of us. Leah must have found that vaccine. I am guessing that by the time Eric Stone captured her, she no longer had it with her. Only that single fact had the potential to completely ruin your plans. You needed to make absolutely certain that she hadn't passed it into the hands of anyone who wasn't on your list. You also needed to know that she hadn't delivered it to a place where it could be replicated and widely distributed."

"I'm impressed. You are quite perceptive, Doctor Chapman. I guess that the cat is out of the bag."

"You couldn't cancel the ongoing operation to infiltrate Khalid's camp," Elias interjected. "It would have been too difficult to explain. That's why you sent Eric. He wasn't there to provide cover and support for Leah; he was there to watch her, to make sure she didn't stumble upon your secret."

"Obviously true and obviously required, as, unfortunately, she did."

"You weren't certain that you wouldn't need me at some point, to help you break her. But you didn't want me spending every waking minute searching for her, so you had to stage her death."

"Also true. And killing her off had the additional advantage of allowing me to take over your position. Sadly, as entertaining as this game of Jeopardy might be, I do need to finish my business here and move on. And now, thanks to the good professor, we all know what it is I want from her. I also assume that you have the missing bombs, Elias – which I need."

"If you think, after all of this time, that Leah will talk now, you're crazy," Elias uttered coldly.

A nasty grin spread across Faulk's face. "I think you are wrong, Elias. Because, for the first time, we have at our disposal a tool previously not utilized by us…you."

Faulk motioned to one of his men, who stepped forward and pointed his gun directly at Elias.

Despite her weakened state, Leah jumped up. "No! Don't."

Faulk shrugged and, in an almost conversational tone, explained, "But, Leah, we've tried everything else: beatings and torture, drugs, sleep deprivation, starvation. Nothing has worked. Starting to shoot holes in your beloved husband is really the last trick in the bag."

"Leah, don't."

She had stepped next to Elias, and he could see that she was biting on her bottom lip so hard that she was drawing blood. No one moved. No one spoke for several seconds as Faulk allowed his intentions to sink in. Blinking back tears, she turned to Elias. "Baby, I'm sorry. I can't tell him."

Elias felt no anger at hearing his own death sentence coming from the mouth of the woman he loved more than anything in the world. "Don't be. I would have made the same choice."

Their intense connection was shattered by a harsh laugh from Faulk. "Heartbreaking. No, it truly is. We will test the firmness of her admirable resolve when you are on the floor, screaming in a pool of your own blood."

He turned to the armed man. "Let's start with a leg."

The agent switched his rifle out of automatic mode and lowed the barrel so that it was pointing at Elias' right thigh. As he was about to pull the trigger, Leah stepped in front of Elias, blocking the shot. The gunman, momentarily flummoxed, moved closer, raising the rifle with the clear intent of bashing the stock into her face.

The proximity of the man was what Leah was waiting for. As he swung the rifle to strike her, Faulk, recognizing her intent, shouted, "GET BACK, YOU FOOL!" but it was too late. She ducked under his arms and pivoted, burying her elbow in his groin. As he doubled over, Elias, who had reacted instantly, pulled the rifle from him and, using the same butt of the stock the man was going to use on his wife, battered the top of his head, sending him to the floor.

The other three men were already bringing their weapons to bear, when Tillie, taking advantage of the distraction, snatched up the shotgun and quickly fired a booming shot in the their direction. Given the distance, the shotgun blast did little damage, but served to send Faulk and the other three diving around the two opposite corners for cover.

Elias, still holding the rifle seized from the now unconscious agent, went to take Leah's arm, but she was retrieving the AK-47. After she grabbed it, she and Elias dashed for the utility room, following Wilson, who was already running in that direction. Tillie kept the shotgun pointed in the general direction of the intersection, ready to fire off another round if a head suddenly appeared, as she also backed toward their former hideout.

Kreitzmann was still sprawled on the floor in a stupor when they entered, with Tillie arriving last.

"Who is that?" Leah asked.

"You aren't going to believe this," Elias explained as he took position next to the door jamb. "Rudy Kreitzmann."

"Kreitzmann! Man, after we get out of this, you've really got to fill me in."

Tillie left her spot by the doorway and walked over to Leah, sticking out her hand. "I'm Tillie."

Leah gave her a broad smile and shook her hand. "Leah. Pleasure to meet you. I understand you're the one who popped Eric for me."

Tillie shook her head. "Wow! You and your husband are going to give me a complex about that. Look, I'm sorry I didn't figure out a way to save him for both of you."

Leah glanced over at Elias. "Sensitive type?"

"No, not at all. Leah, the gentleman to your left is John Wilson Chapman."

She turned and looked at Wilson with surprise on her face. "Chapman. You're the...."

He held up his hands. "I'm just a friend of Tillie's."

Exasperated, Leah turned back to her husband. "Yep. We're going to have a lot to talk about."

Elias nodded. "Maybe later. Right now, we need to get ready for those guys. Tillie, break out more of the fume masks, goggles, and earplugs."

Tillie gave him a mock salute and hurried to the storage shelves. Elias, keeping his head close to the frame, peeked out and saw that two of the agents were beginning to round the corner, moving toward them. Flipping his rifle back to full automatic, he loosed a quick spray toward the agents, brushing them back.

"What's the plan?" Leah asked, checking the AK-47.

"Plan? I don't have a plan. You're the field agent. I'm just the desk guy."

Making a rude sound to show her disgust, she pressed him, "Okay, Mr. Desk Guy, can you at least fill me in on our situation?"

Elias, keeping his head tilted slightly outside the door to watch the hallway, answered, "Happy to. We are currently inside Aegis, which is basically a huge prison. We are trapped in a utility room. This door is the only way out of it. There are at least three trained agents plus Faulk blocking the end of the corridor. That open door out there and to the left, the one packed with several tons of twisted steel and shattered solar panels, was the only exit from Aegis. They probably have tear gas and concussion grenades. We have welder's goggles, painter's respirators, and foam earplugs. Tillie has a shotgun. You have an AK-47. I have my Beretta and this."

Leah shrugged. "Not as bad as I thought. You forgot to mention that Faulk has a second team on-site and they are on their way."

Tillie returned and handed Leah the protective gear, which she quickly donned, as did the rest of them, with Wilson putting the items on the semi-conscious Kreitzmann.

"What about the bombs?" Tillie inquired hopefully.

"Bombs?" Leah's voice was almost flat.

Elias glanced at his wife, fighting back his amusement at how she was receiving what must seem like an endless stream of outrageous facts, and explained, "The two that Faulk is looking for. After he sent me in here, he stocked me with Incendergel devices, enough to take out all of Aegis."

"Why?"

"Not now. But I did bring a couple of them with me, including the primary. I really don't see how we can use them in this situation."

Immediately, Tillie snapped, "Why not?"

"Well, they have timers on them, not fuses. The timers don't even have the option for seconds, just minutes with a minimum duration programmed to give the person setting the charge enough time to get away. Besides, with the size of the charge, even if I could roll one down the hall at them, like a bowling ball, and it detonated at the exact moment it reached them, we'd have another problem. The fireball would probably take out this end of the hall at the same time, and us with it, or it would consume all of the available oxygen and we would suffocate."

"All right, so that won't work."

$$\odot$$

Faulk had positioned himself several feet back from the corner and was planning the next move with his team, when his cell phone rang. He pulled it out and looked at the display, seeing that the call was from Sheldon Kennerley at the lab.

Punching the button, he barked into the phone, "What is it?"

"Director Faulk, we've had a breach at the lab."

Faulk hesitated for a moment before deciding that a breach at this point was not a serious issue. "How bad?"

"We're not sure yet. We're putting together a team to go in. They're suiting up now, sir."

Feeling the muscles in his neck suddenly tighten, Faulk asked, "Why do they need suits?"

Kennerley's nervousness was apparent in his voice. "Well, sir, one of the lab techs is dead."

"Dead? How is that possible? Was it a heart attack? A coincidence?"

There was a long pause on the connection before Kennerley explained, "That's why we're sending in the team, to make sure. But from the video feed, it looks as though she died from massive hemorrhaging."

He could not believe what he was hearing; there must have been another explanation. "But she was vaccinated. All of you were."

"I know, sir. It could be some anomaly. She might have received a defective vaccine. Perhaps it doesn't work on a small percentage of the population. We simply don't know until we can check her out."

"That doesn't make any sense! The vaccine worked on one hundred percent of the test groups." Taking a minute to digest the information and forcing himself to calm down, Faulk continued, "You said she was in the lab, right?"

"Yes, sir."

"And the air lock hasn't been opened yet?"

"That's correct, sir." Kennerley, hearing the direction of Faulk's questions, began to gain a little confidence.

"So even if there is a problem with the vaccine, the bug is contained, right?"

"Yes, sir. We haven't broken the seal yet."

"Then don't."

"But we need to examine her. We need to identify why she was vulnerable."

"Not yet, you don't. First I want you to retest the vaccine in the exposure chamber. You still have some subjects, correct?"

"Yes, sir."

"If there is a problem with it, I don't want that lab opened. Do you understand?"

"Yes, sir. I do."

"Handle it."

Faulk ended the connection as the second team arrived. He noticed that Boehn had been listening and wore a concerned expression. Looking at the men around him, Faulk declared, "We need to end this – now."

$$\odot$$

"What form do you think their attack will take?" asked Wilson, who was standing right behind Leah and Elias near the doorway.

"They've got us trapped," Leah answered. "We're boxed in with no way out. We're outnumbered. They can't just come around their corners in a frontal assault without taking some losses, and we can't move on them without being cut to pieces. I guess it depends on how badly Faulk still wants me alive. But I would guess they are going to go the tear-gas route."

"They tried that before," Tillie chimed in. "Between our painter's masks and lobbing the canisters back out the door, it wasn't all that effective."

Leah shrugged. "Wish I knew what they had at their disposal."

A sudden blast of automatic fire came from the end of the hall, peppering the door jamb with bullets. Elias dropped to the floor, in a prone position directly inside the frame. He did not dare extend himself farther out for fear of making his head a target. The string of shots had come from the corner along the same wall as their doorway, which was now a blind spot for Elias.

"All of you fall back. Take cover behind the first row!"

Leah and Wilson roughly helped Kreitzmann up and moved him to the back of the room, then joined Tillie in the first aisle. She had already taken her old position behind the makeshift gun slot.

Seeing they were all behind cover, Elias, after firing off a short burst, more for effect than anything else, moved back and joined them. Within moments, the left side of the door frame was marked with a red dot, a sighting laser, yet no fusillade came.

Seconds passed before he saw a flash of light just outside and slightly past the doorway, followed an instant later by an explosion. The jamb was shredded by shrapnel.

"They have an OICW!" Leah shouted. "EVERYONE DOWN!"

As they all dropped to the floor, Tillie yelled, "What's that?"

"Basically, a mini grenade-launcher," Elias answered, "with a range finder. It shoots a 20mm or 25mm projectile that travels to a preset distance, then explodes."

"So they can kill people around corners?"

Before Elias could respond, there was a second flash and the room was filled with the sound of a thousand pieces of shrapnel striking the walls, floor, ceiling, and the pile of steel parts on the shelving in front of them, ricocheting wildly.

"I guess they fine-tuned the range," he said matter-of-factly.

A third round arrived with the same result. Tillie yelped in pain as one of the tiny metal shards tore into her upper arm.

"Next will come the tear gas," Leah yelled loudly enough to be heard through the muffling earplugs, as she turned to check Tillie's wound. "The OICW will keep us back. We won't be able to toss them out."

Before she could even finish her warning, the first canister flew into the utility room, careening off the side wall and popping. The confined space quickly began to fill with the white gas. A second arrived moments later. In less than a minute, they could no longer see the doorway through the gas.

Elias' eyes were already watering heavily, as the welder's goggles were not designed for this type of eye protection. His nose and throat started burning. He could hear hacking coughs coming from the others. He knew that it would be only a matter of a minute or so before rational thought became difficult, if not impossible. Twisting around in the dense white cloud, by memory and feel, he crawled to the end of the aisle and around it, moving toward the doorway.

As he crawled, he reached up and lifted the painter's respirator and called out, "FAULK, I'M COMING OUT!" Lifting the mask to be heard caused a strong dose of the gas to flood his throat and lungs. He pushed his rifle through the doorway, sending it skittering out to the center of the corridor.

Behind him, Leah yelled, "Elias, I'll go. It's me he wants!"

"It doesn't matter," was all Elias was able to get out before his throat closed in spasms.

Using his elbows, hands, knees, and feet, he scrambled forward, hoping that he was not greeted with a bullet to the head the moment he emerged from the doorway. As soon as he cleared the threshold, the intensity of the gas diminished and he could see five agents, wearing full-face gas masks, and body suits to protect their skin from irritation. They were all pointing their assault rifles directly at him.

Several yards back stood Faulk, looking foolish in his face mask and business suit.

Pulling the mask away from his face, he ordered brusquely, "Get up, Elias. You two, keep him covered. The rest of you, cover the doorway. We should have the other members of this gang in about a minute."

Behind him, Elias could hear harsh, racking coughs coming out of the utility room. Wilson and Tillie emerged, their arms raised. The last to come out was Leah, supporting the semi-limp form of Rudy Kreitzmann, who leaned against her heavily.

As Faulk was about to speak, Leah let Kreitzmann drop, revealing that she was holding the AK-47 behind his back. Firing before she had it fully elevated, she directed the first spray of slugs toward the two closest men, wounding one in the leg and hitting the other in the elbow as her rifle swung around. The backup agents were afraid to begin shooting, as their boss was standing in the line of fire.

Leah's magazine was empty, and as she hurried to slam a full one in, Elias dove for the closest agent, the one she had hit in the leg, and wrestled his weapon from him. Turning and hoping to take out Faulk, he saw that his target had hastily run behind the other men, freeing them to open fire, which they did, their first shots going wild. Tillie and Wilson, seeing the pandemonium, hurried back to the utility room, as Leah and Elias, lying flat on the floor to minimize their profile to the agents, opened fire, catching the three men who had accompanied Faulk forward and were now attempting a retreat.

Faulk and the remaining agents had all taken cover behind the corners again. Elias knew it was only a matter of moments before the OICW was brought to bear, or even basic grenades. He knew that Leah's decision to attack was a decision based on the knowledge that they were all minutes from their deaths, anyway.

The agents, flanking both sides of the "T" intersection, took turns executing their new plan. One extended his weapon around the corner and fired blindly, followed a moment later by a second man who stuck out his head and weapon, aiming his shots. The slugs ricocheted off the concrete near Elias, and he heard the sudden whimper when Leah was hit. In the chaos of the moment, he dared not look to see how badly, as he was intent on taking out the second shooter.

A part of Elias' mind, still coldly calculating their chances, determined that they had less than a minute to live. They were out in the open with no cover; they were outmanned and outgunned; and the opponents could continue their current technique until a lucky shot took both of them out. It made no sense to retreat to the utility room, as Faulk would only repeat the OICW and tear-gas attacks. Elias decided that if he jumped up and did a running, screaming charge, he would last four paces before he was cut down.

The second man popped out to fire again. Elias was able to brush him back before the man got off a shot, but still did not connect with his target. Suddenly, above the thunderous noise from the gunfire, he heard a loud rumbling coming from the utility room and managed to sneak a peek. What he saw lifted his heart. Tillie was running full-tilt through the doorway, pushing the rolling, steel gang box ahead of her. As soon as she cleared the doorway, which was only inches wider than the box, she moved up to run along the side of it, still propelling it forward, until it came to a stop in front of Leah and only a couple of feet from Elias.

He rolled to his right to move behind the cover, as Tillie punched the button lock on the lid and lifted it, pulling out the shotgun. The gang box immediately rang with multiple shots from the agents. But with the steel walls of the box and the solid pile of heavy tools inside, the bullets did not penetrate to the other side.

He took a moment to see how badly Leah was injured and was alarmed at the amount of blood coming from her shoulder. Tillie, seeing this also, reached back inside the box and pulled out a plastic bag filled with clean rags, wrapping the wound quickly and slowing the blood flow, as Elias kept up a steady succession of short bursts from his rifle to keep Faulk's men back.

Finished with her hasty bandaging job, Tillie lay flat on her stomach and extended the shotgun under the gang box in the narrow space.

Elias' momentary hopefulness crashed at what he saw next. Leah, who had moved to the opposite side of Tillie and was watching from the right side of the box, saw it too, and gasped, "Oh, shit," pulling and holding the trigger on her rifle.

Elias did the same as they watched the hand, extended out from behind the corner, draw back to throw a grenade, both hoping a freak shot could hit the moving forearm and wrist before the hand released it.

Elias could not believe his eyes when he saw the grenade abruptly drop straight down. He knew that neither his nor Leah's panicked firing had hit the target. Something else had happened because, just after the agent dropped the grenade, his body flew violently into their view. As he fell, his torso jerked repeatedly as he was struck with rounds from an automatic weapon positioned behind him. Seconds later, the grenade detonated, shredding the already dead agent and blowing the corners off the two walls.

From their vantage point, Elias, Tillie, and Leah saw more of Faulk's men, who were wounded and stunned from the grenade, run, stagger, or fall into their view. They took advantage of the shooting-gallery situation to finish them off as they appeared. It was clear that there was gunfire coming from the right of the hallway where Faulk, Boehn, and his agents were sequestered, as they attempted to react to the new direction of the fight.

The rapid and deafening battle was short-lived, as Elias heard the unmistakable voice of Faulk shouting from around the corner. "DON'T SHOOT! DON'T SHOOT!"

Elias stood quickly, followed by Tillie and Leah, and they trotted to the end of the hallway, an intersection which had become a killing ground, with Faulk's team as the victims. Elias peered carefully around the corner, not completely sure that their savior or saviors would not be equally disposed to shoot him. All of the black-garbed agents were dead or dying, including the wounded men from the earlier firefight and Killeen who had all been handcuffed in the open. Boehn lay against a wall, bloody and looking as if he had been tossed there by an angry giant. Faulk stood in the center of the corridor, raising his hands, and staring past Elias.

Elias switched his gaze to the right. It took him a minute to identify the two men walking toward him with huge grins plastered across their faces.

"Sweezea...Crabill!"

"Hello, Doc," said Sweezea casually, his assault rifle perched jauntily on his shoulder. "How's that AK-47 workin' for ya?"

Tillie, hearing the names, ran around Elias. "Tim...Jay!" She ran straight up to Sweezea and threw her arms around his neck, almost knocking him down.

Leah had moved into the intersection, pointed her rifle at Faulk, and barked harshly, "Get down, you bastard! Facedown!"

Faulk did not hesitate, dropping to the floor in a prone position, his hands immediately laced behind his neck.

She turned and looked at her husband, jerking her head in the direction of the two men who had saved their lives, as they reached the group. "More friends of yours?"

Elias laughed, realizing that only a few moments ago, he had never dreamed he would have that pleasure again. "Yes, they are. And apparently Tillie's, too."

Crabill was standing back and grinning at Tillie, when he noticed the blood from the shrapnel injury. "Mathilda, you're hurt!"

She glanced down at the blood. "No shit, Sherlock!"

He pulled his pack off his back and quickly removed the first-aid gear. "Come here. Let me take care of that."

"It's not bad. Take care of her first."

He looked at Leah and saw the hastily applied bandage on her shoulder and the still-flowing blood coming from beneath it, and trotted to her.

Elias stepped nearer and took over the job of watching Faulk. Looking down at him, he snarled, "Got a good reason I shouldn't just pop your skull with my boot right now?"

His voice muffled from being facedown on the floor, Faulk said, "I do. The vaccine. Even though you've won today, without it you die. All of you die."

"Yeah? How soon?"

"The release is scheduled for midnight tonight."

"Where? Spreading something like that takes multiple locations."

"Not this bug. One will do. But we are releasing it at one location for each continent. A total of seven spots."

"How fast, Faulk?"

"According to the computer models, three days...four tops."

Elias was stunned and sickened by what he was hearing. Forcing his voice to be calm, he asked, "What's the survivability rate? All viruses have one."

"It isn't a virus. It's an engineered mycoplasma in a cocktail. It attacks several bodily systems. Shuts them all down. Creates massive hemorrhaging. Survivability is zero."

"Transmitted?"

"It isn't only transmitted in the air, it actually lives and thrives in it. It multiplies as it spreads. That's what makes it so effective."

"What kills it?"

Faulk's tone, as he adjusted to the pattern of questions and answers from Elias, was becoming more and more conversational. "The usual. Extreme heat and cold. UV rays."

"Don't the UV rays from the sunlight scrub it out of the atmosphere?"

"It ebbs and flows. Sunlight kills it off when it is free-floating in the atmosphere. That's why we are doing a night release. But the bugs which have already moved into the available humans are safe from the UV. Once the pathogen is in a host, it starts replicating itself rapidly; a large enough percentage will be emerging during nighttime to continue the cycle."

"Your demented group is going to want to emerge from the rat holes you'll be hiding in while the rest of the world dies. And I'm sure you won't want to have all your future generations dependent on the vaccine. How are you going to get rid of it?"

"The first mechanism is that once there aren't any more hosts...."

"You mean people."

"Yes. Once all of the people are gone, the bug has nowhere to invade and multiply. We also built in a second mechanism, a fail-safe. The mycoplasma has been engineered with a preset life span and a preset number of generations it can reproduce. Then it goes sterile."

During Faulk's answers, Wilson had walked closer to listen. "Why would you do this?"

Hearing Wilson's voice, Faulk turned his head to the side to look at him. "Why do you think, Chapman? Of all people, you should understand."

"What do you mean?"

"The world has already gone to hell. You said so yourself in interviews. I believe your phrase was that the human race was 'circling the drain.' You must agree that the already bad cultures, societies, and governments in the world have gotten even more vile, despicable, and degenerate in the past one hundred years. And the best are infected and cancer-ridden, merely waiting to die. Isn't that why you came to Aegis?"

"Sir, you and I may share some concerns about the path mankind has chosen, but I cannot fathom your precipitous course. I find it repugnant."

"Do you now? And what would you propose? Oh, that's right – running to Aegis and hiding in an overgrown atrium for the rest of your days, leaving behind you a society which might still benefit from your insights. No, I'm afraid, Chapman, that the human race reached a point similar to the Donner party. Either everyone dies a horrible death, or a few survive and can start again."

"And you've appointed yourself as the selection committee for who lives and who dies?" As Wilson spoke, the rest of the group drifted over to make certain they did not miss the revelations.

"Actually, no. I was an invitee. The genesis for this plan came from within the halls of power."

Elias interrupted, "The White House?"

Faulk sighed, as if he were tired of explaining himself to such dolts. "The White House *and* the Capitol. It doesn't stop there. France is involved. Germany, Italy, China, and Japan. There are more than forty signatories on the compact."

"I can't believe this!" Sweezea groaned. "We're all gonna die, but all of the scumbag bureaucrats live to start a new world."

"Bureaucrats and leaders," responded Faulk, "as well as the top people in commerce and industry. And we are realistic enough to realize that we'll need a military, so some of those who have received the vaccine are the cream of the crop of the armed forces."

Crabill thumped Sweezea on the arm. "Cream of the crop! That's code for officers only. I'll bet there's not a 'joe' in the bunch."

"I'll be a ..."

"Enough of this!" Elias cut Sweezea off. "I think we have the picture. The elites, picked by the elites, got the shot, and the rest of us can all just die. Faulk, where's this vaccine that you're offering to us to save your own skin? I can't believe you carry around a few spare doses of the stuff."

"I do have it. It's out in the transport."

"I don't believe you."

"I do, Elias." Wilson's voice was calm. "With what he is describing as being right around the proverbial corner, I can think of no more valuable currency than several doses of the vaccine. It makes sense that someone like Faulk would make sure he had a good supply. From now until midnight, and probably in the few succeeding hours after the release, they would be worth far more than their weight in gold."

Elias paused. What Wilson said made sense. And if they had a chance of surviving, they had to take it. He looked at Leah. "What do you think?"

She had been listening quietly, as Crabill finished dressing her wound. "Worth a try."

Elias poked Faulk with the barrel of the rifle. "Get up. Let's go."

Faulk started to rise, when a voice shouted, "NO!"

Everyone whirled around to see Rudy Kreitzmann leaning against the shattered corner and holding Elias' 9mm.

Wilson faced him squarely. "Rudy, what are you doing?"

His eyes still clouded, his words slurred, Kreitzmann stammered, "You...you can't let him get...get away."

Wilson took a step closer. "We're not, Rudy. We're going to escort him outside, to his truck. We need the vaccines he has there."

The scientist was obviously not thinking clearly. All he knew was that the man getting up from the floor was the same man who had used him as a patsy, infiltrated his staff, and exploited his subjects. His hand shaking, he raised the pistol and aimed it at Faulk.

Then Wilson, surprising everyone, stepped in front of him and grabbed the pistol, looking Kreitzmann in the eyes. "Rudy, this isn't you. You are a scientist, not a killer."

Kreitzmann, still feebly gripping the butt of the Beretta, stared at his colleague, his eyes clearing somewhat. The barrel was pointing directly at Wilson's abdomen, and Elias tensed, waiting for the sound of a gunshot. With a final, regretful glance at Faulk, Kreitzmann said, "You're right," and released his grip on the weapon. Wilson, without turning away from him, reached behind himself and handed the gun to Elias.

For the first time they noticed that Kreitzmann was bleeding from his side.

"He must have caught a shot out in the hallway," Elias shouted. "He needs some help."

"Guess I'm the medic today," Crabill remarked sardonically and, with his first-aid gear tucked under his arm, walked Kreitzmann off to the side, slowly lowering him down to a lying position.

They all heard the rapid approach of footsteps, and everyone but Leah, who was focused on Faulk, and Wilson, who was unarmed, spun in the direction, guns pointed down the hallway as a man came around the corner at a full run.

"Don't shoot," Sweezea barked. "He's one of mine."

They all lowered their weapons as the man approached.

"Hutson, what'd you find?"

"You were right, Sergeant. The entrance is trash. Completely demolished."

CHAPTER NINETEEN

Sheldon Kennerley was pacing in front of the glass wall of the exposure tank, shouting into his phone, when Bonnie Schwartz hurriedly entered the room. It was clear by her expression that she wanted to talk to him and that it was urgent. Covering the mouthpiece with his hand, he asked, "What is it?"

Intimidated by his tone, she stuttered, "It's...it's the TV. You'd better come...you need to come see this."

He was tempted to ask her to simply tell him what was wrong, but something about the look on her face made him realize that he needed to follow her. "I'll call you back! Round up the subjects and get them here now!"

Without a word to Bonnie, he rushed past her to the outer lobby where there was a television. As he arrived, he could see that several of the staff were crowded around the set, watching silently. On the screen was a very still tableau. It was of the front yard of a house he did not recognize. There were numerous police cars and ambulances parked haphazardly on the street and in the yard but, other than the flashing lights, there was no movement. He began to ask what was wrong, then thought better of it and listened to the commentary coming out of the speakers.

> "At this point we have very few details. We can tell you that the police and fire departments have cordoned off the area in a ten-block radius. From one source, we learned that the Center for Disease Control has been notified, and all citizens are strongly urged to avoid this section of the city.
>
> "To recap what we know so far, at approximately 9:30 this morning, a man who lives on this same block, concerned about his neighbor, called 9-1-1. Police and an ambulance arrived within minutes and, after receiving no response at the door, the officers looked through a window and observed the resident lying, apparently unconscious, on the floor. They broke down the front door and entered.

"That is where the details become somewhat sketchy. According to a police information officer, one of the paramedics made a distress call, asking for additional medical support. The call was abruptly ended before the dispatcher could get details as to what had happened on the scene.

"It was at that point the decision was made to dispatch a bio-hazard team. Due to a variety of factors associated with mobilizing one of these specialized units, they did not arrive until more than an hour after the call. By that time, the police and paramedic personnel were seriously ill, with one having died on the scene. The stricken officers and paramedics were transported to a quarantine unit at Georgetown University Hospital. It is my understanding that all of them are now deceased. The entire neighborhood surrounding this house has been quarantined. Walter Reed Hospital has sent its own team to assist. All adjacent residents have been evacuated to a sequestered area for monitoring and possible treatment, if needed."

Kennerley stared at the screen, unable to form any words. Bonnie, standing next to him, turned and said, "That house…that's Yolanda's."

⊙

Sweezea, Hutson, Crabill, Tillie, Elias, and Wilson, working with tools from the gang box, had been toiling for an hour in an attempt to clear the tangled heap of steel that was blocking the exit door, cutting the struts into small pieces with a reciprocating saw and stacking the sections inside. Faulk was handcuffed to a riser in the corner of the hallway and had been quiet during the work. Twice, they thought they might be making progress, only to have more material crash down to fill the gap they had created.

Despite the frigid winds penetrating through the obstruction, Elias was soaked with sweat, and his hands and arms were covered with cuts from the sharp edges of the debris. He turned to Tillie. "You told me before that you knew another way out."

She was carrying an armload of twisted metal, which she dropped on the pile. "I do."

"Have you ever used it?"

"No. I've checked it out. But you can't get outside without opening a grate. It has a padlock on it. Should be able to cut the lock with bolt cutters."

Wilson was walking past them and overheard the direction of the conversation. "How do we know it hasn't been covered with more of this detritus?"

"We don't, but it's worth a try. Tillie, will you take me there?"

She nodded.

Elias whistled to stop Sweezea from operating the loud saw and explained his plan to everyone, which was to split the group in two, leaving some to keep working here in case they ran into the same barrier at the other point of egress. Tillie and Sweezea began filling a pack with a second set of tools, making sure to include a beefy set of bolt cutters, while Crabill rounded up cell phones from Faulk's men and made sure that their phone numbers were programmed into all of the speed dials.

Elias walked over to Leah. "We need to talk for a minute."

The two walked away from the rest of the group, making certain that they were well beyond the earshot of Faulk before Elias stopped and turned to his wife. "I haven't asked yet, but I think now's the time. I know that you couldn't possibly have the vaccine on you. They would have found it. But if you have it stashed somewhere, we have a way to communicate now; we can call and tell someone where it is."

Leah's expression told him the answer. "I stashed it at the camp. Eric and Khalid searched the place thoroughly and didn't find it. I put it in the one spot they never really checked all that much, inside a wall in Khalid's quarters. I never got a chance to go back and get it."

Her tone fell to a somber note. "I'm sure it was lost in the missile strike."

Elias was painfully aware that they were running out of both time and options.

"You stay here with Faulk. Hutson, Crabill, and Wilson will keep hacking away at this mess. Keep Faulk's cell phone handy. I'll take one of the other phones. If we get there and it's wide open, I'll call you. If you break through here, let us know."

"We've been reunited for less than two hours and you're leaving me?" Leah had an impish smile on her face as she spoke. Elias leaned forward and kissed her.

"Yep. I've discovered that absence makes the heart grow fonder."

"Jerk!"

He turned to Tillie and Sweezea, who were shouldering the load of implements, and said, "Let's go."

$$\odot$$

"Tillie, I thought you told us that there was no outside drainage for the storm system?" Elias commented as they reached the cavernous basin.

"I lied. It wasn't actually a lie. I was being very literal. The retention basin *does* collect all of the storm water. The water *does* percolate down into the soil at the bottom. But there's an overflow in case the amount of water coming in exceeds the capacity of the basin. It's about ten feet down from the top, and it extends past the perimeter wall of Aegis and dumps into an arroyo about four hundred yards outside the wall."

They were once again standing at the concrete lip of the basin, staring into the darkness.

"How do we get down to it?" asked Sweezea.

"It's on the face of the vertical wall, about fifty feet that way and about ten feet down. The only way to get to it is by rope."

Sweezea leaned out over the edge and looked in the direction she pointed, shining his light. "Rope's got to be tied to something. Looks like a smooth wall to me."

"Told you, I went down it before, back when I had nothing but time. Follow me. I'll show you."

Still wearing her backpack and carrying the shotgun, she casually stepped out onto the lip and walked to the right.

Sweezea muttered, "She reminds me of the captain I left on the outside," and followed her, walking as surefootedly as a mountain goat on the narrow ledge.

With a chuckle, Elias brought up the rear. Soon, Tillie stopped and began clutching at her backpack, trying to remove it. As the strap slid over her wounded arm, she involuntarily jerked from the flash of pain, causing her to lose balance. As she began to fall, Sweezea's arm snaked forward and he grabbed her, pulling her back. "Next time, ask for help," he grunted, lifting the pack from her and setting it on the ledge.

Tillie hurriedly bent over and pulled open the straps on the pack, mumbling, "Thanks," as she took out a long coil of rope.

In the reflected light from their flashlights, Sweezea looked at questioningly at Elias, who commented dryly, "She isn't much on asking for help."

The sergeant glanced at Tillie for a moment, looked back at Elias, and said, "I can relate." He picked up the coil of rope she had unpacked, as she closed the flap on her pack. "What now?"

Standing, she directed her flashlight on the concrete wall above their heads, where a shiny eyebolt was embedded. "Tie it to that." She was already slipping back into the backpack, carefully avoiding the bandage on her arm.

Elias, seeing the eyebolt, said to Tillie, "I suppose you brought a rotary hammer down here, along with some two-part epoxy, and put that in yourself."

She looked at him with a half grin. "Yes...well, no, not really. Actually, not at all. It was already there."

Elias laughed at the evolution of her answer and shook his head. "Tillie, I'm already impressed. You don't need to make things up."

"Hey, it never hurts to embellish a bit."

Sweezea, as he tied off the end of the rope, asked, "By the way, if the outlet below us is flush with the wall, how did you ever find it?"

"She had a set of plans for the place," Elias supplied.

"You did?"

"Yep. But that isn't how I found it. As I was exploring, I saw the eyebolt. I wanted to rappel down to the bottom anyway, so I thought I'd use it. I was pretty surprised when I pushed off and swung out, lowering myself. On my second rappel, instead of my feet hitting a solid wall, I flew right into the opening. I was curious, so I followed it to the end. That's how I saw the steel grate. Later, I got back to my pad and found the opening on the plans. I haven't been back to it in a long time, at least four or five years."

She took hold of the rope from Sweezea and dropped it down the side. Turning her back to the open pit, she tugged hard on the rope and arranged it around her torso.

"You don't need to check my knots."

"Yes, I do."

"Fine. Check them."

After three more hard tugs, all of which were purely gratuitous, she stepped back so that she was perched on the edge of the lip, her weight resting on her toes. "See you down there."

Flexing her knees, Tillie pushed away from the ledge as she payed out some rope, lowering herself. Elias and Sweezea leaned over, watching her descent. It took her three rappels this time, as she disappeared into the face of the sheer wall.

From below, they heard her voice. "Next!" The single word echoed around the dark reservoir.

Sweezea looked at Elias and muttered, "Don't tell her I said this, but she's kind of cool."

"THANKS." Tillie's voice came up from below.

Not responding to her, he said, "You go next. I'll come down last."

"Actually, Tim, I was thinking one of us should stay up here. I'm not one hundred percent certain that we've taken care of all the bad guys, and I would hate to be in that pipe while somebody came by and untied the rope."

"Good point, Doc."

"So you go ahead. I'll stay here."

"Huh-uh. If I'm down there alone with her, I might just strangle her."

"YEAH, TRY IT!"

"Hell, maybe I'll untie the damn thing now."

"HEY!"

The two men shared a silent laugh.

"All right, I'll go," Elias gave in. He moved to the rope, looped it around himself, and descended. Within seconds he was standing beside Tillie. In the indirect light of their flashlights, Elias thought that he saw a fleeting look of relief on her face as he joined her. He chose not to comment.

The outflow pipe was a box culvert nearly eight feet high and square. Since no storm during the life of Aegis had exceeded the capacity of the reservoir, there was no sand or silt on the bottom. Wordlessly, they began the journey.

Both flashlights had fresh batteries and were more than bright enough to illuminate the way. They walked without talking for several minutes.

The tomblike atmosphere of the tunnel caused Elias to speak in a hushed voice. "I'm guessing we are past the perimeter of Aegis."

"Probably."

"And you said the opening was about four hundred yards farther than that?"

"Yes. Give or take."

Because of the straightness of the culvert and the almost perfectly square shape, there was no reason for shadows ahead. Yet Elias saw something dark on the upper lid about fifty yards in front of them.

Stopping, he asked, "What's that?"

Tillie, who had paused with him, strained to look forward and said, "Don't know. It looks like the top of the tunnel is stained or crusted."

"That doesn't make any sense. Let's check it out."

They again moved forward, and when the two of them were nearer, they could see that the dark ceiling was not smooth and flat, as it had been. It was now heavily textured. They could also make out the floor of the culvert and saw that it, too, was no longer the light color of concrete, but was mottled with darkness.

"Looks like some kind of sludge," Tillie whispered, slowing her pace.

Apparently as a reaction to the sound of her voice, hundreds of tiny red dots appeared in the glow from their lights.

"Bats!" Elias said.

"Bats?"

"I'm guessing fruit bats, thousands of them. They like to sleep under bridges during the day. I think they've decided to call this culvert home."

"Yuck! If they all sleep hanging from the ceiling, what's that on the floor?"

"Guano. Bat dung."

"Poop! We're supposed to walk through bat poop?"

Elias moved forward several more paces, sweeping his light around. "If we're going to get out of here and can't clear the other exit, I don't see what choice we have."

"You said fruit bats, right?"

"Yes. Or maybe brown bats."

"What do they eat?"

"Bugs or plants."

"So they won't bite us?"

"Usually, no."

"Usually?"

"There are always two other possibilities. The first is that some of them are rabid. In which case, yes, they would bite us."

"And we'd get rabies?"

"Well, yes."

"Lovely! And what wonderful surprise do you have behind door number two?"

"That they aren't fruit bats. They could be vampire bats."

"Vampire bats!" she exclaimed a bit too loudly.

In reaction, they both heard a vague, leathery, rubbing, scuffling sound commence from the ceiling ahead as the disturbed bats stirred and squirmed. Elias held up a single finger in front of his lips and Tillie bit her bottom lip, not taking her eyes off the culvert ahead.

Whispering, she asked, "Is there any way to tell?"

"I'm sure there is, if I were a chiropterologist. I think that's what a bat expert is called. Either way, *I* can't tell the difference."

"Great. I vote for going back."

He looked at Tillie. This was the first time she had displayed any fear or timidity, and it surprised him. "They weren't here last time you came through?"

"Oh, God, no. If they were, I wouldn't have made it to the grate."

"They do go out and forage after dark, but I'd hate to lose any more time."

"Any other ideas?"

"One." Elias turned back the way they had come. Tillie followed very closely. After they had retraced their steps approximately a hundred yards back, he turned around to face the bats, shouldered the AK-47 he had brought with him, and fired one round. The result was instantaneous. The culvert ahead filled with a brown, tangled cloud of flying bats, startled by the thunderous crash in their normally silent lair. Panicked and slamming into each other in mid-flight, instinctively traveling in the direction away from the crash, they receded.

Their ears filled with the cacophonous sound of flapping wings, Elias and Tillie moved cautiously forward, following the retreating bats as they escaped through the passageway and out into the desert.

"OH, GROSS!" Tillie yelped as her shoes sunk into the thick, gummy substance coating the floor, trying her best to ignore the slurping, sucking noise made as she lifted each foot.

"I will never touch these shoes again."

Elias laughed and trudged on. "Make sure you don't drop anything."

"If I do, it stays. Whatever it is."

She was stepping carefully in the slime, trying to make certain that her feet did not slip out from underneath her.

Partially to satisfy his curiosity and partially to distract her, Elias asked, "I guess you knew Sweezea and Crabill before now?"

"Uh-huh. And Hutson. Tim, Jay, and Mike have been a part of our secret club for quite a while."

"I could have used all of you when I ran the agency. So, just you, Wilson, and those three, or are there any others?"

"Only the five of us. Six, if we count you."

"Thanks."

"I didn't say we were."

"Sorry."

She stopped in the muck and turned to look at him. "Elias, I'm teasing you. Okay? You can be a member anytime you want. And Leah, too. I like her."

He smiled at her. "Thanks. I think we'd better keep moving."

$$\odot$$

Leah was resting on the floor several feet from Faulk. She was still weakened by the two years of captivity and torture. Neither had said a word to the other since Elias had departed with Tillie and Sweezea. Wilson and Hutson were doing the best they could in their efforts to clear the debris from the exit. Crabill had taken Krietzmann to Madison so that his concussion could be treated.

Remembering something from earlier, Leah asked him, "Faulk, why the bombs?"

Before he could reply, Faulk's phone, which was tucked into her shirt pocket, rang and vibrated. She pulled it out and looked at the display, which showed the name "Kennerley." Jumping up, she ran to him and shoved the muzzle of her rifle against his temple. "I'm going to press the button. You're going to say 'Faulk,' and that's it. One extra word and you die."

She did not wait for him to respond. Her thumb jammed down the green button, and she held the phone near his mouth. He obediently said, "Faulk."

Pulling the phone away from him, she put it to her ear and listened, walking away.

"Director, this is Kennerley. We have a major problem." The man on the phone sounded anxious, on the verge of hysteria. "It looks as though one of the other lab technicians was infected last night. She left the lab and went home before she became symptomatic. She must have gotten an extremely small dose and it took longer to incubate."

He was speaking rapidly. It almost seemed that he was not even pausing for breath.

"She's dead. Several police and paramedics are dead. The pathogen is out in the general public. I don't know if it mutated to a form immune to the vaccine or what happened, but it seems that everybody dies, whether vaccinated or not. We had two inoculated doctors on staff at Walter Reed…they're gone. At least half the staff there is gone. It's spreading like wildfire. I don't know what to do. Director…Director…what the hell should I do?"

Leah moved the phone closer to her mouth. "Kennerley, this is Leah Charon. I'll tell you what to do."

⊙

Elias and Tillie had progressed beyond the section of the culvert called home by the bats, and could see the dim illumination of twilight as a small square beyond the limit of their lights. As they drew closer to the end of the drainage culvert, the concrete floor had become increasingly coated with a thicker and rippled layer of dust, which had been carried in and deposited by the sometimes vicious winds of the desert.

Over the reverberations of their footsteps scraping on the gritty powder, Elias' ears picked out a different sound, a sound which triggered an immediate response in the primitive portion of his brain. He froze in place, his arm lashing out and grabbing Tillie's. She could sense that this was not the moment to question him.

At the instant their steps ceased, the vague warning became distinct and unmistakable. He had become so fixated on the approaching opening at the end of the drain that he had neglected to look downward in quite some time. Shining the light down now, he saw that they were standing in the midst of a nest of diamondback rattlesnakes.

It was impossible to estimate their number, as they were interwoven and coiled together, in an attempt to retain their body heat during the impending night. But he was fairly sure that he could count at least thirty in their pathway. Tillie's only reaction, when she saw them in his light, was a sharp intake of breath. Several of the snakes, reacting to their arrival, were coiled in a strike position, tails elevated and vibrating, shaking the brittle keratin rattles so quickly that they were nothing but a blur.

Slowly, Tillie brought the shotgun around, aiming it in the general direction in front of them. Elias, still gripping her arm, took one step back, pulling her with him. Then another step. Followed by a third. He shined his light on the floor behind to make certain that they had not passed any snakes on their way to this point. Seeing none, he turned and began retracing his steps, with Tillie only a pace behind.

After they had moved a safe distance, she said, "Those were definitely not there either, the last time I was here."

"I assumed that."

"How can we get past them?"

"Short of systematically shooting all of them, burning them out, or waiting until tomorrow morning in the hope that it might get warm enough for them to leave, I can't think of a thing."

⊙

As Elias neared the corner of the heavily damaged corridor where the grenade had exploded earlier, he expected to hear the reciprocating saw and the sounds of people tearing away the obstruction at the exit. Instead he heard silence. Concerned, he held up a hand to stop Tillie and Sweezea, who were following behind him. His rifle ready, he cautiously approached the intersection and peered around. His first sight was Leah, Wilson, Crabill, and Hutson huddled across the hallway from the shrapnel-ridden door to the utility room. Faulk was not in sight, and there did not appear to be any sort of threat.

Elias stepped out into the open. "What's going on?"

Leah, hearing his voice, whirled around and ran to him. "Elias!"

He met her halfway and she threw her arms around him, holding him tightly. The change in her demeanor since he had seen her last was dramatic.

His face buried against her neck, he murmured, "Leah, what's wrong?"

She lingered pressed to him for a few more seconds before stepping back. Now that she was closer, he could see that she had been crying. This aspect of her personality had always been a fascinating dichotomy to Elias. He had witnessed tears from her many times in their relationship, but always during a sentimental movie, or as she read a particularly moving book. Occasionally, if he surprised her with an unexpected and thoughtful gift, she would struggle not to cry, usually failing miserably. But in the field, in the midst of intense pressure and horrific events, she was never one to give in to this emotion. The sight of it now worried him even more.

Clearly unsure of her own voice, Leah waited a minute before she began to speak. Tillie, Hutson, Crabill, Wilson, and Sweezea had moved closer to them. "There was a call from one of Faulk's people. The pathogen is out early."

"Oh, my God! How?"

"After I heard what this Kennerley had to say, I questioned Faulk and got a few more details. Apparently, there was a lab accident either earlier today or last night. Faulk knew that a technician was dead. But he thinks the microbe is still contained inside the sealed lab. When Kennerley called a few minutes ago and he thought he was reporting to Faulk, he said that another technician was dead. Somehow the other technician had gone all the way home before she died. Kennerley was frantic…desperate…but from what I could tell, everyone who has come close to her is either dead or dying, and it is spreading fast."

Elias took in the information, his mind spinning in an attempt to assimilate it all. "So an accident released it several hours early. I don't understand why Faulk's man was panicking. I'm sure his people would have already received the vaccine."

She delivered the final piece of news, although clearly not wanting to speak the words. "He had. Supposedly, so had the two lab technicians."

"But…." Elias stopped, his mind was suddenly hammered by the flash of comprehension. "The vaccine doesn't work."

"Right."

"How could that be? They must have tested it."

"They did, several times on several groups of subjects. The monsters tested it on every race, age group, lifestyle type, you name it. It protected the subjects with a one-hundred-percent success rate."

Elias stood frozen as his mind processed the variables, the options, the alternatives, sifting through each for a possible solution. Hitting only a blank wall, he slowly drew a deep breath. "So it's over. For all of us. Faulk and his group have killed everyone on Earth."

His eyes moved from one member of the group to another. Crabill and Hutson were despondent. Tillie and Sweezea, furious. Only Wilson seemed not to be reacting to the situation, his face calm, his eyes focused on some faraway vista. Elias decided that the mathematician had entered into the comforting realm of denial.

He turned back to Leah. "Where did it start?"

"D.C."

"And from what Faulk said earlier, one release point is enough to take care of the whole planet."

Leah nodded in agreement. "I can't imagine that Kennerley wouldn't have notified the others that there was a problem and cancelled the rest of the releases."

"I don't know what good it will do, but we do have Faulk's phone. We should tell someone."

"Again, who?" Leah asked flatly. "According to Faulk, most of the leaders are in on this. I thought we owed it to Benjamin, since he was the only one who tried to help you, but when I called him, all of the circuits were busy. I sent a text message, but I have no way of knowing if he got it. There hasn't been a reply."

"I'm sure. With an epidemic spreading, the land lines and cells would be flooded with calls."

"What happened in the tunnel?"

Elias explained what he and Tillie had encountered. Then he handed his rifle to Leah. "Where's Faulk?"

"In the utility room. After the call, we handcuffed him to a standpipe in there. I wanted us to be able to talk where he wouldn't overhear anything."

"So he doesn't know yet?"

"No."

Elias began walking to the utility room. "I'll be happy to break the news to him. Just before I kill the bastard for his part in this."

Wilson suddenly spoke up. "Elias, wait!"

He paused in mid-step and began to turn toward Wilson, when they all heard a screeching, tearing cacophony from the still-obstructed exit. Elias snatched his rifle back from Leah, and they all took positions around the open door, watching the tangled jumble of steel and aluminum shudder and shake. The almost earsplitting sounds of buckling metal and shattering glass ceased momentarily, and they could hear the rumble and roar of an engine revving. After the brief pause, a new tumult commenced, and a portion of the obstruction visible to them was suddenly ripped away, revealing the dark sky outside Aegis.

Elias saw the yellow-painted bucket of a backhoe, dragging the debris away from the door and piling it several feet away. At the moment the obstruction was removed, the unceasing wind whipped through the opening, substantially colder now than the last time Elias had been exposed to it. The bucket returned for another pass, this time clearing the area outside the door completely. A corner of his mind was amazed by the serendipitous timing of the exit being cleared.

Stepping to the doorway, the AK-47 poised, Elias stared at the cab of the backhoe as the operator switched off the engine. Halogen work lights, mounted on either side of the cab, made it impossible to see who was working the levers.

As the rumble of the diesel died, Elias shouted, "Turn off those lights or I'll shoot them out."

The operator took only a second to comply. Although the lights were now extinguished, Elias' eyes had to adjust to the darkness. He could vaguely see a figure jump down from the cab and he heard a voice say, "Don't shoot. Please."

Elias looked over his shoulder and saw that Sweezea was the closest to the door, his rifle poised. "Cover me."

Sweezea nodded and stepped through the doorway and off to the side.

Elias trod carefully through the field of smaller, sharp pieces of the former barrier, as he shivered from the almost arctic blast, and moved around the front of the backhoe over to the side where the man waited. He remembered that he still carried his flashlight and pulled it out, shining it on the man's face.

"Who are you and what are you doing?"

The man from the backhoe was middle-aged and appeared fit. He raised his hands above his head and answered, "My name's Clements...Matt Clements. I'm the guy who...."

"MATTHIAS!"

The shout came from Tillie, who had been standing in the doorway. The flashlight in his eyes, Clements could not see her as she ran around Elias and up to him, skidding to a stop inches away. Only a moment passed before recognition dawned. "Mathilda! My God, how are you?"

Elias lowered his rifle.

"Do you know him?"

She was still staring at the face of her old friend. "Yes! I do. Matt is the guy I told you about. He's the one who built Aegis. He's the one who told me where the plans were."

She reached out and grabbed both of his arms. "God, it's good to see you. Why are you here?"

"Why don't we go inside," Elias suggested, eyeing the surrounding desert warily and eager to return to the warmth of the building.

"Sure. Let me get my wife and daughter."

"You brought your family? Cool!" Tillie exclaimed.

Clements pulled a flashlight out of his back pocket. Stepping away from the side of the backhoe, he flashed the light three times. A moment later a pair of headlights, from a vehicle parked in the desert, returned the signal, and they all heard an engine rev.

Feeling a light tap on his shoulder as he watched the truck drive toward them, Elias turned and saw Leah standing next to him. "This far to the west," she spoke softly, close to his ear, "they couldn't be infected yet, could they?"

The thought had already occurred to Elias. "I doubt it. I don't see how, unless one of Faulk's people heard about the outbreak in D.C., panicked, and released a supply. But we don't even know where that would be. I don't know what difference it makes, anyway. It's only a matter of time."

"That's true."

The truck had pulled up next to the backhoe, and a woman in her late forties climbed out from the driver's side. The passenger door opened and a younger woman, approximately Tillie's age, got out. The two of them were staring warily at Elias and Sweezea, who were both still holding their automatic rifles.

"Come on, let's get inside," Tillie shouted. Caught up in the moment, she sounded happy, as if she were inviting everyone in for a party.

The group moved through the door, and Elias paused to pull it closed. He noticed that the light on the keypad changed from green to red, and realized that the door was now locked.

As Leah shepherded them to the far end of the hall, away from the hearing range of Faulk, Matt Clements introduced his wife, Lisa, and his daughter, Samantha, who wanted everyone to call her Sam. Tillie performed the introductions for her group. "All right, Matthias, I'll ask again. Why are you here? Not that I'm not glad to see you."

"It's kind of weird, actually. I've been the contractor working on the staging area in front of Aegis."

"You've been right outside and I didn't know it?"

Clements smiled. "I've wondered about you more than once, Mathilda. Anyway, this wind has played havoc on the project. At first it blew the safety tunnel over, at the entrance. But lately it's been snapping the struts which are...were holding up the tilt-up panels we had already erected. I've had to send home most of the crews working out here, because it simply wasn't safe. Been coming out by myself, using the heavy equipment to push aside the panels and other debris, just to keep the entrance clear and safe.

"Sam happened to come to visit us this morning. A surprise visit, really. And I told her that I had to make a trip out here today to check things out. She insisted she wanted to see Aegis, and talked her mother into coming along. I guess she got a little more than she bargained for. When we arrived after lunch, I noticed that all of the marshals were gone and that the tilt-up panels around the entrance had fallen like dominoes. Up until today I hadn't been worried about the panels because they were so close to Aegis I thought they were out of the direct wind. But they collapsed right against the front of the building. The entrance is completely blocked, and I think that the turnstile is crushed."

"It is," Hutson supplied.

"So there is no way in," Wilson commented.

"Right."

"Fascinating."

Clements gave an odd look to Wilson. "I tried to clear the entrance with the equipment I have out here, but it was useless. I need something a lot bigger, like a track hoe, to even make a dent in it. While I was working on it, Lisa and Sam were in the truck, running the heater, listening to the radio, and waiting for me."

"They were getting a radio signal?" Leah asked.

"My truck has satellite radio, and if you stay back from Aegis a quarter mile or so, it works. I was just getting ready to call it quits, when they heard about the outbreak in Washington, D.C. They drove closer to get me and we listened to it together. At first we were thinking that we should hightail it home. Almost did."

Clements paused, his tone becoming somber. "But there was something about what was happening...the way it was happening...reading between the lines of the coverage...that changed our minds. People were dying too fast. First, it was the paramedics and cops at the scene of that house. Next, they started dying at Walter Reed. My God, at one point the news station had a reporter at the hospital and he was making live reports, and then they announced that they had lost touch with him."

Tillie gasped.

"We sat in the truck and listened all afternoon. The news stations weren't able to get a statement from the government. It couldn't have been scarier if it had been some staged Hollywood production. Within only a few hours, the network announced that it had lost touch with its Washington, D.C. bureau."

"Only a few *hours?*" Sweezea asked, incredulous.

Clements slowly nodded, his words choked off.

His wife, Lisa, her voice flat and subdued, continued, "It has started to hit more cities – Boston, New York, others. People in D.C. heard about it and started running away, getting on flights and trains, taking off in their cars. But they were unknowingly helping to spread it. The shorter flights made it somewhere. The longer flights, from what we heard, crashed. I guess the flight crews got too sick to fly the planes."

Swallowing loudly, Clements took up the narrative. "That's when we decided that we needed to get into Aegis. We thought…it's an outpost…it's isolated…maybe we'd be okay. With the entrance closed, I didn't know how else to get inside. Then I remembered the blocked-out opening on this side of the complex that we had in-filled at the end of the project. I knew where it was and I knew that I could break it open with the backhoe. We came around to the back, and I saw all of the solar panels piled up where it was, so I started to clear them out of the way. I never knew that a door had been installed."

Tillie, visibly shaken by the description of events around the country, put her hand on Clements' shoulder. "I'm sorry, Matthias, for all of the trouble you went through. But it looks like you wasted your time. Aegis won't be safe, either."

His face showing his fear, Clements asked, "Why not? I thought…I mean, we figured that with the entrance destroyed, no one who is infected can get inside. It would be as though the whole world is quarantined and we would be protected."

"The pathogen is airborne. That's how it spreads."

He absorbed her words. As they registered, Clements seemed to shrink, to collapse into himself. Shuffling, he moved to Lisa and Sam, putting his arms around both of them. Over the shoulder of his wife, he murmured, "So it's just a matter of time?"

Before Tillie or the any of the others could respond, Wilson spoke. "Actually, I don't believe so."

All of them turned to face him. Leah was the first to ask, "Wilson, what do you mean?"

In their previous conversations, Elias had opportunities to witness the outward manifestations of Wilson's mind at work. He saw them now, as Wilson explained.

"After all of this time, all of our pondering and discussions, it finally makes sense. The pieces to the puzzle fit perfectly – the creation of Aegis, the evolution of the society within these walls, the pathogen itself, the failed vaccine, today's destruction of the entrance, even the bats and snakes Elias and Tillie encountered in the tunnel. And the most critical element, the incessant, anomalous wind."

Elias felt an electrifying tingle in his spine as the beginnings of an understanding crystallized in his mind. The thought was almost too extreme to voice. "You can't mean...?"

"I do, indeed. It is the only possible explanation."

"What?" Tillie practically shouted. "What's the explanation?"

Wilson turned his eyes to his oldest friend in Aegis. "Tillie, do you recall our many discussions on the naming of this place?"

She nodded. "It never made any sense."

"Quite right. It was a topic which fascinated us and occupied many hours of our time. Why would this edifice, which was built to house those who had declared themselves and their lives a failure, be called Aegis? Aegis, in Greek, Egyptian, and other mythologies, means protector or shield. How does that apply to a compound for the suicidal? We never did find a satisfying answer to that question, did we?"

"No, we didn't."

"After all, was the intent to protect the suicidal from society, or society from the suicidal?"

"You're right. It never really fit."

"No. It did not. However, it most certainly fits now."

Tillie, who had spent hundreds, perhaps thousands of hours in conversation with Wilson, and knew his approach to solving a problem and explaining its solution, remained silent. Waiting.

"Is there anyone else here who knows the etymology of the original Greek word for Aegis?"

Wilson, falling into his professorial role, paused for an answer. When none came, he continued, "The Greek word Αιγíς, literally translated, means *violent wind*."

CHAPTER TWENTY

"Wilson," Elias uttered in partial disbelief, "do you realize what you are saying?"

"I can't believe it," Hutson murmured under his breath.

Sam, spoke for the first time since the introductions. "What is it? What is he saying?"

Tillie was staring at Wilson, wide-eyed, her expression lost midway between excitement and fear. "You can't mean...?"

His eyes still upon her, Wilson stated, "It must be so."

Lisa began to speak, when Wilson held up his hand, stopping her. "We *are* under the aegis of something or, dare I say, someone. But this facility is not merely a convenient refuge, a bunker within which to hide. Far from it. At the moment Neve Walker's finger, almost a decade and a half ago, pulled the trigger and ended her life, a unique series of events was put into motion, events which included her violent death and the ensuing emotional outcry from the President and First Lady, as well as from the people of the entire world. For it was that outcry, and the discussions following, which caused Aegis to be built."

All of them were listening, spellbound.

"The creation of this structure...this fortress...was only the first element. At some point in time, I am presuming after Neve Walker's fateful day, the doomsday microbe and its vaccine were first conceived as a perverted solution to the world's woes. No doubt a lone man or woman, distressed and overwhelmed with the currents and tides of human events, with what that person saw as the inevitable destination for all of us, came to the conclusion that something drastic, something momentous must be done.

"We will probably never know who that person was. Not that it matters. Whoever it was, it was a well-placed individual – educated, very intelligent, highly respected by the top people in governments and major institutions all over the planet. He or she saw the same things happening all around that we have seen, that we have discussed *ad nauseam* in a futile attempt to understand and change the course of mankind."

"That person could be you," Elias remarked, a hint of irony in voice.

Wilson hesitated for a moment, and a brief chuckle came forth. "I must admit, I can understand the thought processes of this person. I had come to the same conclusion wholly on my own, with regard to the direful terminus of our path. I failed to find a viable solution to our problems – a method, technique, or proposal which might nudge the hand on the tiller and cause mankind's ship to change course away from the rocks lying dead-ahead. Mister Faulk was correct; it was my own failure to conjure an accomplishable solution which caused me to forsake humanity and sequester myself within this place."

Tillie opened her mouth to say something, but paused as Wilson continued. "I have realized, during the time I have had to ponder these things, that I failed because of who I am. Be it the randomness of genetics, the vagaries of upbringing, or the serendipitous influences of my environment, I could never have allowed myself to bring out into the light of conscious contemplation the option which has been thrust upon us by this amorphous group who have plotted our demise.

"How frustrating it must be. . . or will be. . . if an opportunity to know all of the facts presents itself to the progenitor of this solution before he or she dies. For, as he – and let me use the male pronoun for the sake of convenience – first conceived of and developed the plan in his own mind, met and persuaded, cajoled, and convinced those persons necessary to carry out the plot and join the group of designated survivors to begin the new world, he must have believed that *he* was the invisible hand, guiding and determining the fate of all of mankind. Little did he know that he was nothing but a pawn. He must have held firmly to the belief that he was, with his own mind and his own will, drafting the pages of future history. It never would have occurred to him that he was merely an actor playing his role in a script."

Leah, mesmerized by his narrative, asked, "Then who actually was calling the shots?"

Wilson shifted his gaze to her. "Ah, that is the question, as it has always been. And just as it has always been the case throughout the history of man, we are forced to examine the facts at hand and draw our own conclusions. What we know, when viewed in this light, can lead us down a startling path. It is only when all of the facts are laid out on the table, side by side, that two inescapable patterns emerge. The first is the age-old relentless destruction of man by man.

"Let's begin, shall we, with the foundation of Aegis? It is a fact that poor, troubled Neve Walker took her own life. Thousands do every year. But none share the happenstance of being the only child of the most powerful man on Earth, a man who, due to his religious upbringing, believed that she had committed a cardinal sin and was irrevocably destined to spend an eternity in hell. And none of the nearly countless others, who die by their own hand, have a father with the wherewithal to build Aegis as a way to save others from the same fate.

"It is also a fact that somewhere on Earth a man, as I described a moment ago, no doubt weary and disturbed by the daily, inexorable signs that our species was disintegrating, and following a pernicious path, was presented with the possible solution: a microbe, a pathogen so deadly that no one on Earth could survive it. Coupled with the presentation of this pathogen was the antidote, the vaccine – an inoculation, or perhaps a pill – which could be administered to those of his choosing. To that man, this must have seemed like providence. It would have been as if he, and those he believed should survive, were on a sinking ship and there, before him, was offered a lifeboat, a lifeboat known only to him, a salvation which was exclusively his to dispense. The prospect would have been intoxicating.

"His plan was set in motion. Men and women of his choosing would be invited to participate. If you think about it, who could possibly refuse the offer to survive after the destruction of the species? I am certain the minutiae of generating the list of survivors would have been taken substantial time to complete and would have been fraught with drama and betrayal. Any such action, which by its very nature bestows power, would be. Men or women, offered the vaccine, would have it left to them to determine whether their spouses, their children, their children's spouses would be added to the list, or whether they would take advantage of the impending cataclysm to resolve their own petty disputes. It is indeed a rare individual who would not be corrupted by this opportunity to decide who lives and who dies."

The picture, painted by Wilson to his small audience, held them in thrall. No one dared speak.

"The two facts we have thus far discussed, the creation of Aegis and the development of the microbe and vaccine, would appear to be unrelated and proceeding on independent courses. Most likely, those involved in the doomsday plot never gave this institution a thought.

"To return to Aegis now, we have observed and pondered the evolution of the societal microcosm within these walls for some time. At its inception, Aegis appeared to be utilized primarily for its stated purpose. The vast majority of the entrants were those who chose coming to this place rather than consummating the act of suicide. It was at said time, when nearly all of the residents were of this inclination, that the so-called riot occurred, an ugly and base visceral manifestation of the mental state of the group.

"However, over the past few years, we have noticed a change. Fewer and fewer of the new arrivals were of this nihilistic nature. More and more of them were, as I was, refugees from a society gone awry, either eager to hide from the outside world or inclined to create a better society in Aegis. Many of us, including some who stand here with me now" – he glanced meaningfully at Sweezea, Crabill, and Hutson – "shared the vision of mankind held by the perpetrators of the doomsday plot, without sharing a desire for the horrendous solution."

The three men nodded slightly, indicating their agreement with Wilson's assessment.

"As the newer arrivals became the predominant population of Aegis, something strange began to take shape. The suicidal segment seemed to require a progressively more subtle trigger. Their number rapidly diminished by their own hand, leaving the newer occupants free to construct a more viable system.

"Yet, this natural course of events was not sufficient in and of itself. The anti-social and the sociopaths in ZooCity showed no inclination to move out of the way on their own. Intervention was needed, and intervention was provided in the form of one of Mister Faulk's lieutenants, Doctor Boehn, a petty and shallow man, someone ripe to fall victim to the power granted to him by the impending calamity. His initial and transitory urge was to utilize the habitants of ZooCity as foot soldiers and procurers. I suspect, however, that this utilitarian exploitation was a convenient mechanism to justify the act of eradicating them. His action in doing so was either part of the script of man's seemingly idiopathic destruction of man, or an incredible, and I use that term literally, coincidence. I am certain that he would have seen it as ironic that he inadvertently increased the safety inside Aegis."

"Wilson," Elias interrupted, "are you saying that Boehn was manipulated into killing off all of the ZooCity residents? And, if so, by whom?"

Wilson smiled at Elias. "Manipulated? That implies the presence of a person. I would opt to say *guided* by the inevitable script I mentioned; however, the answer to that question, once the facts are all presented, is for you to decide."

"Present away!" Tillie urged.

"And so I shall. We believed that Mister Faulk possessed a viable vaccine. Our ignorance of the truth would have propelled us outward, beyond the walls of Aegis. Had we obtained the vaccine from his vehicle and administered it to ourselves, we would have traveled away from Aegis and met our deaths. Yet, as we tried to leave, we found that the exit at the end of this hallway was made to be unusable by the falling debris from the roof. I ask you, Mr. Clements, as you circled the perimeter of Aegis, were the shattered remnants of the solar panels heaped everywhere along the wall, or only in the proximity of the exit door?"

His voice hushed, Clements answered, "Just the exit."

"Another coincidence? Then there is the secret subterranean exit, of which only Tillie was aware. It was, by coincidence, rendered useless by bats and snakes, even though it had been easily accessible on her last exploratory venture."

Wilson stopped for a moment and surveyed the faces of his friends. Their minds, in various stages, were absorbing his message, as he could see expressions both awed and confounded.

"Mister Faulk's presence itself is peculiar. Why, in this eleventh hour of the plan in which he was immersed, did he feel a need to visit Aegis? And yet, if he had not, we would not have discovered the reality of what is transpiring outside these walls. We would have overpowered Boehn and his men, and we would have left to meet our certain fates.

"The arrival of Mister Faulk also necessitated the switching off of the communications blanket, which has enshrouded this facility, as he did not want to be out of touch with his superiors and underlings on this final day of their plan. The end result of *this* coincidence is that we now have access to the news of what is happening out there.

"And at the time when the microbe is multiplying and spreading around the globe, as is the news of this unspeakable event, there are those already infected, or soon to be, who will decide that Aegis might be a suitable place to run, as did Mister Clements and his family. It must be yet another coincidence that the entrance to Aegis, only in the past few hours, has been destroyed, preventing anyone, who might carry the disease, from entering and infecting those of us on the inside. And even that fact, that event, has yet another coincidence wrapped within. The ostensibly chaotic wind, the downdraft centered on Aegis, is not quite powerful enough to bring down Aegis itself. But, on the day of the infectious release, after years of steadily gaining momentum, it happens to reach the force needed to bring down the new concrete walls Mr. Clements had erected at the entrance."

Clements leaned forward. "Yes. If you think about it that way, it was incredible that the government decided to add the new entrance structure when it did. Otherwise, there wouldn't have been a convenient arrangement of tilt-up panels close to the entrance, only temporarily braced and not tied in and finished, providing the weaker link for the wind to knock down."

Wilson nodded to indicate his concurrence. "And your decision to erect those specific panels first."

"That's spooky," responded Clements. "I could have started anywhere. There was no real reason to begin adjacent to the entrance. And we were able to erect just a few before the wind intensified, preventing us from standing the perpendicular panels which would have tied them together, making the new structure almost as strong as Aegis."

Tillie spoke. "Wilson, this is all amazing. But you still haven't explained why you think we are safe from the pathogen."

"Let us review the facts at hand about that. According to Mister Faulk, the microbe is susceptible to extreme heat and cold. Not only can it survive in our atmosphere, it thrives, as long as the temperature range is moderate. This precludes the possibility that the airborne malignancy will be truly one hundred percent effective across the globe. It would be my guess that the occupants of the outposts and scientific stations on Antarctica and the Arctic will survive the spreading terror. I am certain that there are other pockets, the beneficiaries of climatic flukes or extremes, which will also provide a survivable habitat for man in the coming days, weeks, or months. There is one other place, other than the poles, where the temperature of the air is always frigid, a place where the microbe cannot multiply, cannot even survive…and that is our upper atmosphere."

"The wind!" Elias almost shouted, the final piece of the puzzle falling in place for him.

Wilson awarded Elias with a smile and continued, "Precisely. For a very long time now, we have been witnesses to an unexplainable phenomenon. Beginning as a gentle breeze, steadily building and intensifying, the wind has buffeted Aegis – but not a conventional wind, not a predictable by-product of some mundane regional weather pattern. Aegis has been the epicenter of an impossible vertical draft, coming down to us from directly above and then blowing outward in all directions. There is only one place where this downdraft could originate and that is the upper atmosphere, an environment which, because of the coldness of the layer, is deadly to the microbe. And that *fact*, this impossible wind from above blowing outward upon its arrival at Aegis, pushing away and holding at bay the airborne pathogens before they can reach us, is the answer to your question. We are safe from the microbe because we are being *kept* safe from it, as we have been at every incremental step along the way; hence, the second script, the second pattern.

"As outrageous as it may seem, as contrary to what you know or believe, I cannot see an alternative explanation other than the obvious…Aegis is an Ark."

⊙

Elias and Leah sat on the floor in the hallway, both still trying to grasp the magnitude of Wilson's words. It had been decided that it was necessary to secure Aegis and, therefore, the door; but Tillie had suggested that Matt's satellite radio could come in handy, at least for a while. Sweezea, unable to obtain from Faulk the code for the keypad on the exit, shot off the lock. Crabill, a mechanic, volunteered to remove the radio, and Clements was outside helping him as Sweezea stood watch at the rear of the truck. Hutson and Tillie had gone into the utility room to clear some of the shelves for the purpose of breaking down the modular steel units. They planned to use the vertical steel angles from the units as braces for the exit door once it was closed. Lisa and Sam were helping.

Wilson was standing alone in the open doorway, staring off into the distance. Elias thought that he was probably imagining the chaos rapidly spreading throughout the world.

"Elias, do you think he's right?"

He turned to look at his wife. "I hope so. After all this time thinking you were gone and now having you back, I don't want to…."

She kissed him, the contact fanning a fire which had never gone out over the last two years, but had remained smoldering in his heart. He reached up as they kissed and buried his fingers in her hair, pulling her closer. The veil around them, created by their intense love and passion, was pierced by the sound of a crash from the utility room.

Elias jumped up and was running to the door, when Hutson, with a sheepish look on his face, poked his head out and assured him, "It's nothing. One of the storage units collapsed."

"Anyone hurt?" Elias asked, coming to a stop.

"Just Faulk. It fell right on him," he answered with a chuckle. "We're moving him to another spot."

Flashing instantly on the years of training that he and Leah had received, Elias knew that Faulk had gone through the same training. "Mike, no! Wait!"

Before Hutson could respond, they both heard a scream coming from behind him. He spun around into the utility room, with Elias arriving only seconds after. As Elias charged through the doorway, he ran into Hutson, who was frozen, his hands up. As they both tumbled to the floor, the roar of the shotgun filled the room, the buckshot slicing into the wall behind the spot where they had stood a moment before. Elias, disentangling himself from Hutson, rolled to the side and saw that Faulk was holding Lisa Clements with his left arm around her neck, while brandishing the shotgun with his right. In a smooth action following the shot, he performed a one-handed pump, filling the chamber with another round, and brought the barrel around, poking it harshly into Lisa's side.

His eyes sweeping the rest of the room, Elias saw Tillie lying facedown on the floor next to a heap of parts and shelving brackets. Sam Clements was several feet away, a look of abject terror on her face, her back pressed against the far wall of the room.

"DROP IT!" The shouted command came from the doorway. Elias saw Sweezea pointing his AK-47 directly at Faulk, using the door frame to shield as much of his body as possible. On the opposite side of the opening, Crabill had taken position, his rifle also pointing at Faulk. Clements was behind them, staring worriedly at his wife but displaying the good sense to remain quiet.

Elias stood up, making certain that his hands were visible to Faulk the entire time. Hutson rose to his feet next to Elias, moving slowly to not spook Faulk.

"Richard, it looks like a standoff," Elias stated flatly.

Faulk did not have the wild-eyed look of a madman, but was calm and steady. Shoving the barrel of the shotgun another inch into Lisa's side, he ordered, "Tell your men to drop their weapons."

"Not going to happen. They lower their weapons, you start pulling the trigger. And I'm not sure where you'd stop. Besides," Elias continued, recalling that Faulk knew nothing of what was happening in the outside world, "we're all going to die anyway, remember? We might as well take you with us."

From Faulk's perspective, Elias' words made sense. He knew better than to negotiate with someone who had nothing to lose.

"Very well. Tell them to back away from the doorway or step inside the room."

"Why?"

"Because I'm leaving, and if you try to stop me, she goes. And even though your days are numbered anyway, I doubt that you or her husband would want to see her splattered all over the walls of this place."

Leah, who was behind Sweezea and Crabill, standing off to the side and listening, said, "Elias, let him go."

Deciding to maintain the charade for believability, Elias asked her, "What about the vaccines in his truck? We need them."

Her disembodied voices answered, "Right after I cuffed him, I sent out Crabill. We've got them."

Appreciating her quick thinking, Elias turned to Sweezea and Crabill and, with a jerk of his head, said, "You two move back down the hall that way, but keep him in your sights."

He turned to Faulk. "Richard, after you."

Faulk, holding Lisa as a shield, walked her to the open door. Sweezea and Crabill both slowly back-stepped toward the interior of Aegis and away from the exit, keeping their rifles trained on Faulk. Matt Clements had backed across the hallway, never taking his eyes off his wife. Once clear of the utility room, Faulk glanced quickly at the exit door and saw that it was clear and open. Still clutching Lisa and keeping the muzzle of the shotgun tucked into her side, he backed toward the exit, pausing when his feet bumped into the threshold.

His face contorted, he snarled, "You know, Elias, I've been thinking. You have been a thorn in my side…no, a pain in my ass...for a long time. I know that even though you have the vaccines…even though you might live through the purge that's coming…we will come back for you and Leah…and the rest of your little group. We will come back and wipe all of you off the face of the Earth. But you know what? That's not good enough for me. I want to be there. I want to see it for myself. I want to be the one to make you draw your last miserable breath."

He took another step back through the exit. The doorway was not wide enough to accommodate Faulk, Lisa, and the shotgun with its stock pointed out to his right. Still holding Lisa tightly, he pulled the shotgun out from her side and swung it around, aiming it at Elias. Before Elias could react, before Faulk's finger could pull the trigger, something swung down from outside the doorway, slamming into the top of the shotgun. The impact was enough to knock the weapon, unfired, out of his hands. Instantly, Lisa stomped down hard on Faulk's instep, causing him to release her. She ran inside and into her husband's arms.

Staggering, Faulk recovered and took off at a full run. Elias was clearing the doorway when he heard Wilson shout, "ELIAS, DON'T! JUST LET HIM GO!"

He skidded to a stop and watched Faulk's rapidly retreating figure following the wall toward the parking area. Standing in the shadows beside the door was Wilson, still holding the four-foot-long metal rod he had used to disarm Faulk. As Leah and the others came out, Elias commented, "Nice work, Wilson."

"Damn," Leah exclaimed. "I wanted to shoot the bastard myself!"

Wilson, dropping the bar, said, "No, you don't. At least I would hope not."

Leah looked at him in the glow from the open door. "Why not?"

His eyes fixed on the retreating figure moving quickly out of view, Wilson explained, "Because we may be the only ones left. If I am correct, if we *have* been saved for a new beginning, I would think that killing a man, unless in self-defense, is a trait we would all prefer to leave behind."

"But...."

Before she could continue, Wilson interrupted, "I understand, believe me. I am certain that every hour of every day for the last two years of your life was a living hell. I wouldn't be surprised if your thoughts, your fantasies of escape and what you would do to the man responsible for your pain and agony, were what sustained you during the worst of those times."

He could barely make out a slight nod of her head, in agreement with his words.

"But we are now faced with an opportunity not only to survive, but to be the fundamental building blocks of a new mankind. I know that it is too soon for any of us to yet grasp the overwhelming responsibility of that, but we soon shall. Until that day arrives, we must help each other to ensure that none of us do anything for which we will be later ashamed."

Elias was staring into the distance. "Jay, did you and Matt finish removing the radio?"

"We did," answered Crabill. "We heard the shot while we were on our way in with it."

Elias was still looking off. "Then I suggest we get inside and close this door as soon as possible."

"What's the rush?"

"If Wilson is right about everything, about the script we are all playing out, then the timing of the destruction of the entrance is more than likely pivotal. With the news of the epidemic spreading, there are probably people by the front entrance already, trying to get inside Aegis. If they haven't begun looking for another way in, they will if they see Faulk coming from this side of the complex."

Even as he finished his thought, Elias could see two figures, dimly lit, running toward them from the direction where Faulk had disappeared. He silently raised his hand and pointed. The others looked in that direction and saw what he was seeing. Even more began to round the bend, running.

"Come on," Sweezea bellowed. "Let's move."

"Shouldn't we let them in?" The question came from Lisa, who was still held tightly by her husband in the doorway.

Elias was beginning to answer but Wilson spoke first, his voice urgent. "We can't."

Matt and Lisa stepped back inside to clear the entrance. Crabill, Leah, Wilson, and Sweezea swiftly followed, with Elias coming in last, taking one more quick look back. He could now see multiple figures. They were close enough that he was able to barely make out shouting from their direction. Even at this distance he could hear desperation in their voices.

As soon as Elias had cleared the metal door, Sweezea slammed it and called out to him, "We've got no lock! We need something to brace it!" He put his shoulder to the door, trying to hold it closed.

Whirling around, searching for something useful, Elias barked, "The gang box!" He and Wilson seized the heavy steel box and manhandled it toward the door. "Tip it over! We need it off its wheels!"

Wilson followed the order and lifted up on his corner while Elias did the same. Sweezea, moving out of the way, almost did not make it as the box fell against the door with a tremendous crash, followed by the clatter of tools tumbling against the lid. Crabill dashed out of the utility room with a hammer and two cold-chisels, and immediately began pounding one of the chisels between the door and the frame, wedging the door tightly shut. He was just about to drive in the second chisel when they heard the sudden banging against the outside of the door, accompanied by frantic shouts and pleas for them to open it.

Lisa, who had been off to the side, let out a single loud sob, overcome by the harshness of what they were doing. Elias caught Clements' eye and motioned with his head that he should move her back away from the door.

As Matt gently walked his wife to the far intersection, still littered with the corpses of Faulk's team, Leah joined Elias, who was leaning against the gang box, adding his weight to the barrier. She asked Crabill, "Are the keys to the truck still out there?"

He answered her as he finished hammering-in the second chisel. "Yes. We left them in the ignition. Why?"

"Because it isn't going to take those folks long to see that we aren't going to open this door voluntarily. My guess is that they'll try to ram it."

"Anyone here know how to use a welder?" Elias yelled over the banging and screaming coming through the door.

"I do," Crabill answered.

"Put your weight against this. I'll be right back."

Elias stood up from the gang box and dashed into the utility room. He realized that in the last few minutes, he had forgotten that his last sight of Tillie was of her lying facedown on the floor. He was instantly relieved to see her sitting up, with Sam and Hutson kneeling beside her, Hutson holding a rag to the side of her head.

Keeping her head still, she turned her eyes to Elias. "What's going on out there?"

He answered her as he raced past, heading for the last aisle. "Faulk's gone. A crowd has arrived. They want in."

"We can't let them in?"

"Wilson doesn't think we can take the chance. They might be infected."

"Oh, my God."

He glanced toward her and saw a tragic expression on her face.

Elias was madly tossing aside ladders, sawhorses, and other building paraphernalia, when he spotted the portable welding rig that he had remembered from his earlier scouting of the room.

"Mike, give me a hand with this."

"Yes, sir." Hutson jumped up and grabbed the opposite side of the welder, helping Elias lift it above the jumbled pile of tools on the floor. After they cleared the pile, they set the rig on the floor, and Elias rolled it out to Crabill, who immediately began the task of firing it up.

"Jay, will this work?"

"Absolutely. Self-contained rig. Everything I need is right with it."

The clamor from outside had intensified as Elias again put his back to the gang box and slid down so that he was sitting on the floor against it. Leah was next to him, as was Wilson. The people outside had ceased the disorganized pounding on the door with their fists and were now trying to break it down with coordinated slams. The three pushing against the gang box could feel the jarring vibration from the impacts. Sweezea had dug through the pile of steel they had dragged inside earlier when they were still trying to clear the opening, and found two lengths that suited him. He returned to the exit and tucked one end of a bar against the door so that it was angled against the shattered keypad. He then jammed the other end against the door frame of the utility room, providing an added brace.

"Clear!" Crabill called out.

Sweezea crouched in front of Elias and the others, placing his hands on the gang box above their shoulders, and pushing. With his back to Crabill, Elias saw the flickering light of the arc welder casting its harsh white glow down the hallway. It seemed like a constant bolt of lighting, striking behind him. He noticed Clements coming back around the corner toward them, using his hand to shield his eyes from the welding arc, and surmised that he had found a place to leave Lisa.

Reaching the four of them, Clements knelt down and shouted over the din, "That's a hollow metal frame around that door. I didn't install it, so I can't be sure, but the normal method is that you drill the concrete wall in six spots, sink bolts in the six holes with epoxy, and then fill the cavity with grout. It's pretty strong, but I'm not certain it will withstand being rammed by the truck."

Elias leaned closer to be heard and raised his voice. "What can we do?"

"There are four flange-plates exposed on the sides of the opening, two on each side. If Jay welds the frame to those plates, that'll help a lot."

The intense, flickering light ceased as Crabill was repositioning for the next weld. Elias stood up quickly and tapped him on the shoulder. Jay turned and flipped up the welder's mask he was wearing. Elias could see that he had already placed welds on both sides of the door, welding the door directly to the frame, using small steel shims as bridges to reach across the gap. He passed on Clements' suggestion, shouting over the crashing and banging coming from the outside. Crabill turned and examined the face of the opening in the concrete wall, which was substantially thicker than the door frame, and saw the two upper flange-plates.

"We'll need to push this gang box out of the way for me to get to the lower ones. We can do that after I finish up top."

Elias nodded and dropped back into his seated position against the box. One or two minutes passed, with no one attempting to speak above the din, before Crabill indicated he was ready. As a group, they all pushed the gang box to the side, and he immediately began work on the two lower flanges. The almost rhythmic crashing at the door suddenly stopped. There was no more clamor from the other side. For a moment the only sound was from the welding operation, until they heard the unmistakable growl of the truck engine revving up.

Crabill had finished welding the frame to one of the lower plates and was working on the second when the impact came. The crash was deafening and the door and frame shuddered from the force, but it all held. Unruffled by the violent distractions, he finished the bead on the second plate as they heard the truck back up for another run.

"Add this!"

Turning, Crabill saw Clements holding a three-foot-long piece of angled steel he had retrieved from the debris pile. "Weld it to the frame as a cross-brace, like this." He held it up to the door, showing Crabill what he meant. With a downward jerk of his head, Crabill flipped down the mask and touched the welding rod to the steel where it rested against the jamb. Clements and the others shielded their eyes just in time.

The truck slammed into the door a second time, bulging the metal inward. Elias and Sweezea ran to the pile and scrounged for more steel struts. They returned to the door and dropped them at Crabill's feet. He had finished with the first and selected another, positioning it lower on the door, closer to the height of the bumper on the truck. After welding the left side, he shouted for Sweezea and Elias to push the free end of the strut against the doorjamb. The bulge from the second impact was holding it away from the frame. They both put their weight into it and forced the face of the door back in, allowing the strut to touch the frame. The instant it made contact Crabill welded it, finishing the bead as the truck hit the door for the third time. The frame, the door, and the struts all held.

The tension having lessened, they worked as a team and added five more struts. The truck battered the door twice more before the driver either gave up or had damaged the truck so badly that it would no longer run.

Hutson looked at Matt. "You didn't leave the key in the backhoe, did you?"

Clements reached into his pants pocket and pulled out a single key on a small ring, and answered, "No, I've got it."

"Good."

Now that they had done all they could think of to do, Elias, Crabill, Sweezea, Wilson, and Leah moved back from the former exit, physically distancing themselves from the sporadic pounding and shouts, trying to do the same with their emotions. Tillie, walking somewhat unsteadily and pressing a rag to the side of her head, emerged from the utility room, accompanied by Sam. She made a point of averting her eyes away from the direction of the barricaded exit door and walked to the group. The two of them joined the others as they sat on the floor. No one spoke.

Soon the banging on the door gradually tapered off, until it stopped completely, as did the shouts from outside.

CHAPTER TWENTY-ONE

The group, less Hutson and Crabill, who had decided to remain behind and keep an eye on the exit, walked slowly through the corridors which had been Kreitzmann's lab. The area was quiet and deserted.

After their tumultuous episode, Elias' voice sounded unnaturally loud in the silence. "I wonder where they are."

"Perhaps we should check at Madison," Wilson offered.

Lisa Clements came to a halt and said, "Do you mind if I ask a question?"

Wilson came to a stop beside her. "Of course not."

The rest of the group stopped as well, circling around them.

"I've been thinking about what you said before, about how all of this could have happened. I know you didn't mention God in your explanation...or theory...or whatever it is, but *I* believe there is a God, and I can't imagine anyone else able to do what you've described. Do you really think that God would cause that poor girl, Neve Walker, to put a gun to her own head? And do you believe that He would hand the monsters behind this plot a disease which would kill everyone on Earth? Not to mention all of the other horrible parts of the so-called script."

Wilson looked at her intently for a moment, a gentle smile on his face, before he answered, "I only look at the facts, Lisa. I take them in, and I sort them out until, eventually, I can ascertain a pattern. My theory, as you described it, makes no value judgments. To answer your question in the same vein, and assuming that your belief is valid and there is a God, there are only two logical possibilities. Either all of the participants, including Neve Walker and her father...including the man who concocted the doomsday bug...including Boehn when he ordered the extermination of the residents of ZooCity...and including all of us, are merely actors in a script penned by the hand of God, a cold and pragmatic being who could wipe out essentially all of the people on Earth, if it served His purpose....

"Or God is a more benevolent being, someone who watched with agony as the cataclysm unfolded and knew that He could, perhaps, intervene this time; but also knew that His actions would only delay the inevitable, that the tendency of man to destroy himself had reached a point of no return. And at some point in the procession of parallel events, He saw an opportunity to salvage a small piece of His creation, an opportunity to throw a group of us a life raft in the form of Aegis."

Lisa absorbed what Wilson had said before she asked, "Which do you believe?"

With a subtle shrug, Wilson placed his hand on her shoulder and said, "If there is a God, I much prefer to see Him in the latter role."

None of the others had anything to add, and they resumed their trek.

Walking slowly, as if they had all just finished a marathon, the eight of them trudged through the reception area and out into the main Aegis corridor, which was also absent any residents. With Sweezea walking point, carrying his rifle at the ready, they traveled through three connecting hallways without encountering a soul.

"Madison is around the next corner," Sweezea muttered over his shoulder.

"I think I heard voices," Tillie remarked with a tinge of relief.

The rest of them heard the voices, too. It sounded as though a relatively large gathering had assembled ahead. Immediately upon reaching the intersection, Sweezea motioned for the rest of the group to stay back as he edged forward and carefully peeked around. Signaling an "all clear," he lowered his rifle and proceeded, the others close behind.

Ahead of them lay one of the zig-zag entrance barriers. As they came closer, the voices coming from the other side grew louder. No one was stationed at the barrier, and they passed through the series of switchbacks, still not encountering anyone.

Emerging from the final corner, Elias, following Sweezea, saw that they were entering a larger open area he had not visited before in his earlier travels. It was almost filled with people, far too many for him to be able to determine a count. They were all facing away from him, looking in the direction of a man on an elevated platform, whom Elias recognized as Milton Pierce. He was obviously in the middle of addressing the crowd when he spotted the six newcomers.

"Everyone...I see that we have a few new arrivals. If you would bear with me for a moment, I would like to speak with them. Perhaps they can shed some light on what is happening."

The members of the assemblage began looking over their shoulders and saw Wilson, Elias, and the others, as Pierce came down from the platform and worked his way to the back. Breaking through the last of the crowd, he strode up to them, a nervous smile on his face. "Wilson, it is good to see you and your friends. Rudy Kreitzmann was brought to us earlier for medical care and he has been telling us some very bizarre things. Frankly, I'm not one hundred percent sure he isn't delusional."

"I don't know for certain what he has told you," Wilson responded, "but I would venture to say that he is not."

Pierce's brow furrowed with concern. "He was talking about the end of the world."

Wilson glanced over Pierce's shoulder for a moment before turning back. "We should probably find a quiet place to talk."

Reading the seriousness of Wilson's face accurately, Pierce turned to the gathering and, in a raised voice, said, "If you could all excuse me, I will be back shortly."

The people murmured and began breaking into small groups as Pierce led Wilson and the others to a nearby room.

As soon as they all entered, he closed the door behind them. The room was filled with tables and chairs, arranged cafeteria-style. "Please, everyone, have a seat."

They did, and Wilson, augmented occasionally by Elias and Tillie, told Pierce everything, including the final standoff at the exit. Elias could not get a good read on the man, who attempted to absorb both the facts and Wilson's theory, and whose face remained impassive throughout the narrative. They finished, and Pierce sat back in his chair and stared up at the ceiling. No one spoke, giving him an opportunity to assimilate what they had said.

After minutes of silence had passed, he looked back down and leaned forward. "Well, it looks as though we have some work to do."

At that moment, Elias' respect for the man multiplied exponentially.

As calmly as if he were planning a family vacation, Pierce began, "We have already formed a salvage team to sift through the damage on the roof. We have found a surprising number of intact solar panels, and we have a team of electricians struggling to segregate them from the debris field and connect them to the grid. The winds are making their work incredibly difficult, not to mention the suddenly cold temperatures."

He paused for a moment and a slight smile crossed his face. "But now, I do not believe we will be referring to them as the *cursed* winds any longer."

"More like blessed winds," acknowledged Matt. "I'm the contractor who built Aegis, by the way. I'd be happy to help with that project."

"Excellent. We are very happy to have you. To continue, a large contingent of our citizens volunteered to clean up ZooCity. The bodies have all been moved to the nearest atrium in that part of the complex, and we have steadily been performing ceremonial burials."

"A most onerous task. I'm impressed," Wilson commented.

Pierce shrugged as if it had been a minor undertaking. "It had to be done. Medically, we are in excellent shape. Our stocks of antibiotics, asthma inhalers, and other medications are high. At Madison, we have encouraged the practice of monthly blood donations for quite some time and have built up an excellent bank. Now that Rudy Kreitzmann's staff have joined us, we have three physicians and two surgeons as a part of our community, as well as a number of researchers with skills and training in the areas of biology and psychology."

"In the coming days, I suspect that a few trained psychologists will prove to be invaluable."

"I'm sure you are correct, Wilson. On the subject of supplies…at our current level of population, even with all of today's arrivals, we have enough stored water to last for well over a month. We have turned off the pumps to preserve battery power. But when the solar panels come back on line, maintaining an adequate reserve will be a high priority."

Tillie's interest was piqued by one of his statements. "Today's arrivals? Did we get a lot of newbies today?"

"Hundreds. We don't have an accurate count yet, as many of them are still wandering about within Aegis, but we had quite an influx – that is, until the entrance was destroyed."

"We've never had that many in a day."

"I know. It's odd. But we've had too much to deal with to be able to take the time to interview them all. I have no idea."

Wilson glanced at Elias, meaningfully.

"What about food?" The question came from Sweezea.

"As it turns out, we have a higher than normal level of stored food."

"How could that be? With the wind as extreme as it's been in the past few days, I thought that our supply helicopter couldn't make a drop."

"You're right," Pierce answered. "They haven't been able to, and we were four days overdue for supplies. Apparently, the logistics people at Davis-Monthan decided to solve the problem rather than wait for the gusts to subside. Early this morning Aegis received a much larger than normal supply delivery on the roof, more than double the usual quantities. We had no idea that it was coming or that it was delivered. We found it when the salvage crew went topside to work on the solar panels. It was near the perimeter wall and had been placed directly on top of the rubble of broken metal and glass. Packed inside several of the containers was a message that they had decided to utilize a crane to make the drop. Due to the travel time and other factors, they informed us that the deliveries would be spaced farther apart. Hence, the additional supplies."

Wilson caught Elias' eye and winked, murmuring under his breath, "Another coincidence?"

"With the stored goods on hand and the addition of this morning's delivery, under normal circumstances we would have enough food for approximately two months. Assuming that we immediately sequester all of the food and begin rationing, I would guess that we can all eat for double that period of time."

"I hope that's enough," Leah said softly.

Pierce's eyes turned to her, but he did not respond to her comment. "The Air Force was aware of the damage to our solar panels, so there were also two generators placed on the roof, along with a supply of fuel. Some of the containers of food must be refrigerated after they are opened. Between the existing battery reserve and the generators, I believe that we can accomplish this until we get a part of the grid back on line. And lastly…obviously, there are more than enough living quarters for all of our residents."

There were no other questions. Pierce, his air of competence slipping slightly, looked at Wilson. "Wilson, do you think it's really happening?"

Wilson allowed a weak smile to crease his face. "We know for certain that the pathogen is happening. With the call Leah heard from Faulk's man, Kennerley, and the radio reports heard by the Clements' family earlier, there doesn't appear to be any doubt. As far as the failure of the vaccine, of that we only know what Kennerley said to Leah when he believed he was reporting to Faulk. With regard to the last, and most profound, aspect of your question, have we really been selected to be saved while the rest of the world dies? I believe so, Milton, but only time will tell."

Pierce gently nibbled on his bottom lip, his eyes avoiding contact with everyone at the table. It was clear that he was in a pitched battle between giving in to his emotions, and his need to remain calm and in control. No one spoke as he wrestled both sides. The muscles on his jaw tightening, he exhaled heavily and asked, "What else should we be doing?"

Sweezea was the first to speak. "The Air Force guys didn't leave their crane, did they? I wouldn't want the people outside using it to get on the roof."

Pierce shook his head. "No. The salvage team checked after reading the note. They must have transported it out and then departed with it."

"Getting in!" Tillie barked. "Elias, the drainage tunnel. If the people outside find it, some snakes aren't going to stop them."

"You're right. Tim, will you and Crabill round up the bombs and head down there? We need to collapse it."

"Aren't those just firebombs?" she asked. "They won't destroy it, will they?"

Sweezea grinned at Tillie. "Good question. The answer is that culverts are also called RCP, or reinforced concrete pipe. It's the 'reinforced' part that's critical. They are embedded with rebar, or reinforced bars, when they are made. Those bars are tempered with heat. If you get them hot enough, the tempering fails, the rebar violently distorts, and the concrete collapses. Those bombs will get the concrete and the embedded steel plenty hot enough."

Elias said, "Do it." Sweezea jumped up to leave.

"I'm going, too," Tillie volunteered, standing. Sweezea knew better than to object.

As the two left, Leah commented, "Speaking of perimeter defense, we should probably patrol the edge of the roof. Who knows how creative the people outside might get."

"I'll assemble a detail for that," Pierce offered. "Such a horrific tragedy, leaving those folks outside. We don't even know for sure that they are infected."

"I've been thinking about that," Elias spoke softly, attempting to crystallize what had been a vague idea. "The people on the outside are still basically within the protective blast of wind that is sheltering Aegis, or at least they might be. If they are not yet infected, maybe the pathogen won't reach them."

"What are you suggesting?" Wilson asked, clearly interested in the direction of Elias' words.

"Do you think we might be able to save them?" Lisa said hopefully.

"I'm not sure. I wanted to talk it through with all of you. Wilson, what you said before, about each of us being the kind of person who deserves to start a new society on Earth, really hit home. I'm having a problem reconciling that with locking the people out and having armed guards patrolling the perimeter with orders to shoot to kill."

Wilson began to speak; however, Elias raised his hand. "Please, let me keep talking for a minute. I'm not positive it makes any sense, but I'd like to put it on the table. If civilization is disintegrating that rapidly out there and people stop coming to Aegis soon, and I realize that's a big 'if,' then maybe that final bunch outside the wall *won't* get infected."

"Are you talking about letting them in?"

"No...I don't know. Maybe not right away. Maybe we monitor them, lower food down to them. From what we've heard, the bug is incredibly fast-acting. Maybe if they are alive in a day...two days...and no one else comes to Aegis...maybe then we let them in."

Everyone was silent.

Pierce finally broke the silence. "That seems much more humane than just locking them out and forgetting about them. They deserve a fighting chance."

"At the risk of sounding harsh," Wilson countered, "we have the continued existence of the human race on our shoulders. We have, apparently, been provided with help and protection, but at some point the decisions are ours to make. And making the wrong one could be catastrophic."

"Couldn't we take it a step at a time?" Leah suggested. "We have a more than sufficient supply of food and water. Couldn't we lower enough to sustain them for now, and decide in a few days what our next step is?"

After reflecting on her proposition for a moment, Wilson spoke. "The single most significant unknown for us is how long we must survive within Aegis. We know for a fact that additional shipments will not be forthcoming. How can we say that we have an ample supply of food when it is possible that we will need to remain within these walls for a year? It may take every morsel in our stores to keep all of us alive until it is safe to emerge from Aegis."

The image of the future, as painted by Wilson, caused all of the people around the table to visualize the upcoming weeks and months, each scenario painted with the perspective and the fears of that individual. A somber silence fell over the group.

Wilson continued, "I fear, as time marches inexorably forward, that we will be faced with some very distasteful and harsh decisions, decisions which will test the limits of our intellect and our humanity. This question today is merely a sample, the first of many. I believe it is critical that we understand two things as we wrestle with each of the impending dilemmas yet to come. The first is that we recognize the burden we carry. Our very existence, as the populations of the world succumb to extinction, may be the last hope for the continuation of mankind on Earth. We must never lose sight of this. Every choice, large or small, must be viewed through the lens of this duty."

Wilson paused and Elias asked, "And the second?"

Wilson's eyes riveted to Elias. "The second? Why, that is obvious. Mankind...our species...must be worthy of saving. Otherwise, what is the point? Therefore, despite the unknown answers to our questions, I don't see any reason we shouldn't take that first step, and feed and cloth those poor souls outside our walls."

Pierce waited for a time, giving anyone who might have an objection a chance to voice it, before he concluded, "Then it's settled. We will provide food, water, additional clothing, and blankets, since I doubt any of them expected or planned for the cold temperatures out there."

For the first time since the meeting began, Samantha spoke up. "This isn't right."

"Why, Sam?" asked Matt.

"It isn't just us we're talking about; it's all those people standing outside that door and all of the others inside Aegis. We're sitting in here deciding whether we should give away *their* food. Shouldn't we ask them? Shouldn't they get a vote?"

Wilson drew in a deep breath, clearly planning to respond, when Pierce spoke up. "Miss Clements, what you are talking about is a democracy."

"Right! Isn't a democracy the best way to govern?"

"This may come as a surprise to you but, no, it isn't."

She hesitated, startled by his response, and stammered, "I...I don't...why not? That's what America is...was!"

"Actually, it is a republic, not a democracy."

"What's the difference? We vote."

Pierce was in his element. He had, in fact, been preparing for this discussion his entire life, his position and his arguments finely honed by years of arguing with, at first, his sister, then countless others. "Numerous papers were written by our founding fathers. They referenced intense and occasionally heated debates on this very subject. The truth, Miss Clements, is that Americans do not vote on any *thing*; it is not our role to pass laws and make decisions. We have only one task to perform as citizens, and that is to vote for candidates. It is up to the elected officials to pass laws, to set priorities, in other words...to govern, the exception being the occasional proposition or referendum within the states. In fact, we do not even technically elect the President. That decision, according to the Constitution, is made by the electoral college which, originally, was intended to be a group of the wisest and most trusted members of each community, appointed at the state level, who would then travel to a meeting and, without further input from the populace, select our leader."

"But it doesn't work like that anymore. Except for a couple of close ones, the person we've elected is the one who gets the job."

"True. I'm talking about the original intent. Ever since the Seventeenth Amendment, which took effect in 1913, we also now directly elect senators. But at the time the Constitution was signed, senators were selected by the legislatures of each state."

"Really? I didn't know that. Why did they do it that way? It sounds elitist."

Pierce smiled. "The concept of checks and balances. The House of Representatives was the people's house. Congressmen were elected directly by the voters. The Senate, chosen by state leaders, was intended by the framers to be the cream of the crop in terms of intelligence, wealth, education, experience, and the like. Over our early history, the litany of bills proposed and passed in the House reflects people attempting to govern in their own self-interest. You would be amazed at the nature of some of those bills. A large number would have been, essentially, handouts to the public. Had the vast majority of the proposed legislation passed, America would have been bankrupt a century ago. Since the bills were then turned over to the Senate, they quickly died, never reaching the desk of the President for a signature.

"And the reciprocal also worked quite effectively. The Senate, in those days, frequently proposed legislation which would support, enhance, and subsidize business, industry, and the landed gentry. In other words, they, too, pursued their self-interests. When these bills stepped over the line and created a blatant handout to industry, for example, the legislation failed to survive the House. Insofar as constitutional power, the two interests were balanced. If the, as you described them, elites in the Senate wanted something, they had to modify it, temper it, and make it palatable to the House, whose only goal was to obtain the best deal it could for the people. And the reverse was true. When the House wanted something that would benefit the general population, they had to make it attractive to the Senate. The system, before it was modified, was designed to give both sides equal power so that only legislation which made sense for the job creators, wealth creators, and industry builders...as well as for the workers and the citizen population in general...could pass. And if the pendulum swung too far in either direction, the Supreme Court was standing by to swing it back."

"I still don't see how this relates to our situation here."

"I have digressed a bit, but only to provide context. As you can see, Jefferson, Madison, Franklin, and the others knew that pure democracy was as tyrannical as any dictator or monarch. That was why they placed so many layers between the voter and the final piece of legislation – to temper that despotic tendency of the population."

"Are you saying that people, when they vote as a group, would do bad things? I don't think I believe that. People are basically good."

"You are right; for the most part, they are. On a one-on-one basis, a person will help another, even to his or her own detriment. But pure democracy is nothing but mob rule. And the mob mentality is something quite different; this difference is exacerbated and compounded by the privacy of the voting booth. Let me ask you a question. Do you believe, in the late 1950s and early 1960s, that had it all been put to a popular vote, the Civil Rights Acts would have passed? Before you answer, I'll tell you that, according to the polls, according to all measurements of public opinion, they would not. Nor, in the previous century, would slaves have been freed. Women would not have received the privilege of voting. We would not have entered World War I or World War II, at least not until the enemy had reached our shores.

"There are nearly countless examples of our leaders making decisions contrary to the will of the public, occasionally destroying their own political careers in the process, to do what they perceived to be the right thing. In many cases, history has judged them as having been right. In many cases, not. But the point is, that is how our republic was intended to work."

"So you're saying that if we walk outside this room right now and present the facts to the crowd, asking them to vote on whether we share the food or not, they'll vote against it?"

"No. What I'm saying, Miss Clements, is a far worse indictment than that. The sad truth, as any student of history will tell you, is that the crowd outside this room will vote either way, depending entirely on how the so-called facts are presented."

"You lost me."

"It's quite simple. If we were to pick the most gifted orator among us to sell them on the idea of lowering food and water to the people outside, they would vote to do so with a large majority. If, on the other hand, we presented a persuasive and frightening argument against the idea, it would be soundly defeated. This was proved, conclusively, during pre-World War II Germany by Hitler. Our founders knew this. That is precisely why *we* must decide what to do and then present our position, and only our position, to them, as eloquently as possible."

"Why not pick two people, one on each side, and let the group hear both?"

"What would be the benefit of that?"

"You're kidding, right? Then they could make up their own minds."

"You refer to 'their own minds' as some monolithic thing. I'm talking about the final vote. What do you think would happen?"

"Well, one side or the other would win. Either we would feed the people outside or we wouldn't. That would be it."

"And you think everyone would be happy?"

Samantha paused for a moment. "Happy? I think they would be glad they were brought into the loop, had a chance to vote, a chance to participate in the decision, instead of being left out."

Wilson, silent to this point, said, "Sadly, Samantha, that is not the case. What would happen...what has happened *out there* in the world...is that you have winners and losers. And the losers are never appreciative of the opportunity to participate in the process. When learning that they've lost, they will claim fraud in the voting process, manipulation of the facts, and any other charge they can think to bring. Quite simply, what occurs is that prior to the vote you have a single group; after the vote, you have two. And, when the importance of the vote is significant, the two groups become enemies."

Sam was silent as she thought about what Pierce and Wilson had put forth. After a minute, she said, "That is what it's been like on the outside, isn't it? Has been for years now."

Wilson nodded. "And it festers."

"You're right," she acknowledged.

"Although it was reaching intolerable proportions in the world, that was after decades of florid prose and inciting rhetoric. Here, within the confines of Aegis, any schism or any polarization would escalate much more rapidly. For you see, Aegis is like a lifeboat upon which we are all adrift. If we are to survive and retain our civility...our humanity...dissension must be held to a minimum, order must be maintained, and we must find a way to live under a common accord."

Sheepishly, Samantha looked from Wilson to Pierce. "I don't think that just applies to us. They could've used it *out there*."

Another twenty minutes were consumed with discussions on the mundane details of logistics, before Pierce, deciding that the immediate business was adequately covered, stood up. "I believe we've already kept our citizens waiting too long. I think informing them of our situation would be the best thing to do right now."

The balance of the gathering stood as he continued, "Wilson, I would appreciate it very much if you would stand up there with me. Many of the people here know you and respect you. Your participation in this would be helpful."

"I'd be happy to."

"Thank you."

The two men led the way out into the open area. The crowd, still splintered into smaller groups, hushed noticeably, and Pierce and Wilson proceeded directly through the people toward the raised platform at the other end of the room. Elias, Leah, Matt, Lisa, and Sam walked to the rear of the assemblage, which was already turning to face the front.

"E.C.!"

Elias, startled by the familiar voice, scanned the group for the face. Within moments he saw Marilyn politely working her way back toward him. As she drew nearer, her eyes momentarily left his and moved to the side. That was when she spotted Leah, and her eyes flew wide open. Her pace abruptly increased; by the time she reached Elias and Leah, she was running.

"Leah! My God, you're alive!"

All Leah could do was hold her old friend and say nothing as they emotionally embraced, the moment eliciting tears from them both. Elias stood patiently as they held each other. Twice Marilyn leaned back and stared at Leah's face, convincing herself that this was all real. The third time, her hand came out from behind Leah's back, and she grabbed Elias' hand, gripping it tightly. The three stood this way as Matt and his family moved a respectful distance away, giving them privacy.

During their reunion, Pierce began speaking from the front of the room.

"Ladies and gentlemen, I'm afraid I have some astounding news. I have just been briefed by John Wilson Chapman and his associates on recent developments pertaining to Aegis, and the rest of the world...."

As he talked, Marilyn finally stepped back from Leah and opened her mouth to speak, when Elias suggested that they move away from the gathering. Following his advice, they walked away and rounded the same corner from which Elias and Leah had earlier arrived. Convinced they were out of earshot of any members of Madison, Marilyn, holding both of Leah's hands, stared at her and said, "Honey, what happened? We all thought you were dead. We were sure of it."

Leah grinned back at her friend and joked, "Don't know if it was Churchill or Mark Twain who said it, but reports of my death have been greatly exaggerated."

She then went on to tell of her abduction and captivity for the past two years, downplaying the torture aspects and occasionally even finding a way to make light of her travails. With all of the years Marilyn had spent working within the intelligence community, her mind filled in the details, unbeckoned. As Leah neared the end of her narrative, Elias joined the discussion, filling Marilyn in on the plot they had uncovered. Whenever Faulk's role was mentioned, Marilyn's face contorted into a mask of rage and hatred, but she kept her words to herself until they had finished and Elias asked, "Why are you here in Aegis?" and added hastily, "Not that I'm not incredibly happy to see you."

"I found out the bastard sent you here to die."

"Faulk was never sloppy," Elias said, surprised. "How did you discover that?"

"You're right. He never let anything slip through. But maybe, with this planned epidemic so close to happening, he actually became distracted."

"Or," Leah suggested, "it was so close to the event that he decided it didn't matter if you did find out. Kind of his way to torture you a little before the end."

Marilyn nodded. "That fits him to 'T.' I'll bet you're right."

"Specifically, Marilyn, what did you find out? How was he planning on killing me? And how did you discover it?"

"I was processing and routing outgoing communication for the day. As you know, the highest-level communications are encrypted by the sender personally. That's when I found this…unencrypted."

She reached into her purse and pulled out a folded sheet of paper, handing it to Elias. As he unfolded it and read it, Leah looked over his shoulder, reading it at the same time.

The message was from Faulk and was directed to someone referred to only as Dragon:

> *You are absolutely correct. With the discovery of the anomalous winds at Aegis, we cannot guarantee effective dispersion of the infectious agent into this facility. I believe that I have utilized this as a means to resolve multiple issues. I have persuaded E.C. to enter the compound. He has orders to eradicate Aegis. My personal knowledge and experience with this operative is that he cannot be relied upon to carry out this assignment; in fact, I would be surprised if he did. However, we have supplied him with Incendergel ordnance, enhanced to accomplish the objective effectively. And to compensate for the predicable actions of E.C., we have altered the detonator mechanism. Should he place the charges, the entire string of incendiary devices will detonate upon arming of the final unit in the series, regardless of the programmed time. If he fails to place and set the charges, the timing device is programmed to self-activate and detonate the entire batch of charges autonomously,*

overriding the disarm mode. In the interim, we will attempt to
utilize his captivity within Aegis for the purposes discussed
previously.

R.F.

Elias' blood turned cold. He dropped the message and whirled around, taking off at a full run, followed by Leah. As he ran, he yelled over his shoulder, "Use Faulk's phone! Call Sweezea!"

He did not bother to look back to confirm that she was doing it. Within minutes, he found what he was looking for...an atrium. Slamming the door open, he ran in, his eyes sweeping over the dirt for the telltale glint of the grate covering the storm drain, his adrenalin making him impervious to the bitter cold. He was able to spot the drain, which was almost obscured by silt, and angled his course to reach it, as Leah shouted from behind, "There's no answer!"

"They must already be in the tunnel. I bet there's no reception down there."

He reached the grate and shoved his fingers roughly through the slots, in the process abrading one of his fingers badly. Heaving the cover upward, Elias lifted the heavy round disk and tossed it aside. The grate slammed into the dirt, raising a cloud of dust which whipped around them both, stinging their eyes.

Blindly, his feet thrashed about inside the riser until finding the embedded steel rungs. He descended quickly, Leah right behind. Taking only a second to get his bearings, Elias once again pulled out his flashlight and ran through the storm drain in the direction of the retention basin. He was not certain where this particular pipe would terminate in the circumference wall of the basin, in relationship to the overflow pipe that he and Tillie had traveled earlier, the outflow tunnel which was now Sweezea's, Tillie's, and Crabill's destination.

He heard the steady treads of Leah, who had no flashlight of her own, following closely. As he ran, his mind independently calculated times: the time it would have taken Sweezea to get Crabill and the two bombs they had in the utility room; the time they would have needed to locate the devices which had been seized by Faulk's team and pick them up; the time they would take to transport the charges through the storm system and through the overflow tunnel; the time needed to place the charges and then...flip the switch on the final device. Adding up the times, and subtracting the amount of time elapsed since Tillie and Sweezea left the meeting, gave Elias a sickening feeling. There was no time left.

Elias reached the basin and nearly ran off the end of the drainage pipe into the black abyss, scrabbling to stop at the last moment. Leah skidded to an awkward halt behind him. Seeing the abrupt termination of their path, she narrowly avoided bumping Elias, who was still wavering on the edge. He cupped his mouth and shouted, "SWEEZEA...TILLIE...CRABILL!"

⊙

"One more to go," Sweezea grunted as he lifted the safety cover on the arming button and flipped the switch, illuminating the red light that indicated the bomb was armed. He stood and walked to Tillie, moving beyond Crabill, who was holding his rifle in ready mode and watching the dark tunnel for any of the outsiders who might have already found the entrance and come in past the snakes.

He was about to speak, when he paused, listening for a moment. "Did you hear something?"

Tillie cocked her head and listened. "No. What did it sound like?"

"I'm not sure, probably nothing. But I thought it was someone yelling."

He shrugged, hefted the last device, and said over his shoulder, "Jay, let's move back."

⊙

Elias' ears were only rewarded by the echoes of his own voice, but his eyes saw a dim, flickering light coming from his left at a point below the lip where he stood with Leah.

He pointed. "That's the outflow tunnel. They're in there."

"That means they've already arrived with the charges and are setting them."

"Afraid so."

He stepped out onto the narrow ledge and walked briskly toward the light, shining the beam of his flashlight straight down at his feet so Leah could follow in the glow. In very little time they reached the rope tied to the eyebolt.

"You go ahead," Leah stated firmly. "You have the only flashlight and it's stupid to send me down first to wait for you or the other way around. Just go. I'll come down in the dark and follow the light."

He knew she was right, and said nothing, tucking the flashlight into his back pocket. He grabbed the rope and rappeled down.

Hitting the concrete running, Elias retrieved the flashlight from his back pocket. Holding it as he sprinted caused the beam to bounce and jitter crazily before him. He knew that they would place the devices from the farthest point first, working their way back toward Aegis. He also knew that the last device had to be well beyond the perimeter of the complex; otherwise, there was a chance that the collapsing tunnel would compromise the perimeter wall. He remembered, from his earlier trip on this route, that the basin was located fairly close to the edge of Aegis, more than likely to minimize the necessary length of the overflow tunnel. He concluded that he had to cover at least three hundred yards before there was a chance of encountering them.

At a full run, it was difficult to gauge distance but he guessed that he had traveled close to his estimate. The light from ahead of him, created by the multiple flashlights they would be carrying, was a dim, diffuse glow with no details. Dashing forward, the vague glow gradually gained definition until he was able to discern distinct lights and three figures. He began shouting, "SWEEZEA! STOP WHAT YOU'RE DOING! DON'T ARM THE BOMBS!"

He saw one of the figures – he guessed it was Crabill – turn around to face him, holding a rifle. The other figure, whom he recognized as Tillie, was standing over the kneeling Sweezea. Crabill was now shining his light in Elias' direction. Elias knew that his assault rifle would also be pointing at him.

⊙

"Here we go," Sweezea said affectionately, as if he were putting a bottle into a baby's mouth, when he heard the unintelligible shouts.

Crabill spun, pointing his rifle.

"What the…!" Tillie exclaimed, startled, turning suddenly to face the noise. She could only see the bouncing, bright light of a flashlight, obviously carried by someone running toward them from the direction of the basin.

"Don't shoot!" Sweezea ordered. "They're coming from our side!" He turned back to the last bomb and lifted the safety cover on the arming switch.

Tillie, alternating her eyes between what Sweezea was doing and the oncoming person, asked, "Shouldn't we wait a second?"

Sweezea shrugged. "What for?"

His finger pressed the side of the switch, moving it toward the "arm" position, just as Elias got close enough to see what he was doing. "TIM, DON'T."

It was too late. The toggle, already more than halfway across, was pulled the rest of the way by the internal spring, with a quiet *click*.

⊙

Elias came to a clumsy halt. He could see the red light shining on the top of the charge. "Don't set any more!"

Sweezea stood from his crouch next to the device and said, "We're done. That was the last."

Leah arrived, panting from her sprint behind Elias.

Tillie had a wry grin on her face.

Confusion clouded Elias' mind, and for a moment he was unable to speak. Sweezea bent down and reached into his pack, which was resting on the concrete next to the last bomb. He pulled out a small, green, flat rectangle and held it up. "You were worried about this?"

Elias took a step forward and saw that he was holding a small circuit board. The adrenalin-fueled frenzy of the past minutes subsided slightly, allowing his mind to focus. "The timer."

A broad grin spreading across his face, Sweezea explained, "I'd love to take the credit for it, but actually it was Tillie's idea to open up the units and check them out."

"I figured," she added, "that since Faulk supplied them, they might be bogus."

"We just found out...," Elias muttered, his voice fading out.

"That they were booby-trapped? No kidding. Big time." Sweezea tossed the board to Elias, who bobbled it clumsily before catching it.

"As we rounded them up and were bringing the batch down here, Tillie told me the whole story. I agreed with her that we'd better check them out before we used them. Whatever they had planned for these babies to do had to be hidden in the primary, since it controls and detonates all the slaves, so I opened it up. Right on top of the detonator was that" – he pointed at the circuit board Elias was holding – "all wired in and ready to go. I disconnected the outputs and ran it through its program in diagnostic mode. That's when I saw the overrides they had set up. Man, that dude really hated you. No matter what time you entered for a delay, the second you armed the last slave, BOOM!"

"There's also a second override...," Leah said, still panting slightly from her dash through the tunnel.

"Yep," Sweezea responded smugly. "If you didn't do a thing with them, they were all set to go off at midnight tonight."

"Same time as the scheduled release of the bug," Leah noted.

Elias relaxed. "If you took out the circuit board, what are you using now to control the detonators?"

"I thought you spooks knew your ordnance better than that," Sweezea teased. "That flimsy little wafer you're holding is the weakest part of the bomb. In field conditions, about a third of 'em crack at the tiny little connections. Imagine jumping out of an airplane behind enemy lines, grabbing your ordnance, which fell alongside you in a crate hanging under a parachute and crashed to the ground, unpacking it, loading it up, toting it through heavy fire to the target, going to set it, and getting a blank LED screen. The Army specs a backup board to be packed inside the primary. Four screws, and you lift out the detonator. Underneath it, protected by bubble wrap and a waterproof, factory-sealed plastic skin, is a nice, clean, and dry backup circuit board, all ready to plug in, program, and go."

Elias shook his head in amazement. "Tim, I don't know what to say."

Sweezea shrugged, still smiling. "A simple HOO-AH will do."

Elias gratefully walked to him and put his arm on the tall sergeant's shoulder. "HOO-AH!"

⊙

The five had withdrawn back to the basin and climbed the rope, with Leah having the most difficulty, due to the injuries from her captivity and during the firefight. They had an additional fifteen minutes by the time they had reached the upper ledge and decided to position themselves within a drainage pipe at a right angle to the overflow. Although Incendergel devices did not create a massive concussive wave, as did traditional explosives, a fireball would be generated and could possibly extend to the basin, despite the distance.

They left one of the flashlights in the overflow tunnel, directed to cast its illumination toward the basin, and silhouette any person who might have entered, managed to get past the snakes, and reached the opening before the explosives detonated. Crabill and Sweezea kept watch on the lighted square, checking their watches frequently.

"We've got one minute," Sweezea announced. "Pull back."

They had removed the rope after their exit. If anyone arrived at the basin end of the overflow within the next sixty seconds, there would be no way to climb up. All of them had remained standing during the wait, keeping their packs and gear in hand. When Sweezea gave the word, they all turned their backs on the basin and began walking briskly.

CHAPTER TWENTY-TWO

Returning to the gathering in the main hall, they found the people there subdued, many with dazed expressions on their faces as they grappled with the reality of what was happening in the world outside the walls of Aegis. Elias and Leah looked for Marilyn to thank her for bringing the message; within a few minutes they saw her surrounded by a small group. She was talking earnestly to them, and it was obvious by her body language, and that of those around her, that she was attempting to help them make some sense of the news they had just recently received from Pierce and Wilson. She made eye contact with Elias and raised an eyebrow questioningly. He gave her a thumbs-up to indicate that all was well. She smiled and resumed her conversation.

Crabill saw two men working on the satellite radio he had removed from Clements' truck, and he and Sweezea joined them to assist. Wilson was standing in the middle of the crowd, flanked by both Milton and Mildred Pierce, answering questions. Elias talked briefly with Lisa and found out that Matt had gone to the roof of Aegis after the meeting, with the intention of watching the effect of the bombs on the outflow tunnel from above ground.

The door to the dining room, where they had met earlier, was open, and Elias wandered through it, determined to sit down and rest after his frenzied dash. Leah and Tillie followed him and the three dropped into chairs, exhausted.

Leah filled Tillie in on the discussions at the meeting after her sudden departure with Sweezea, and she was relieved to hear that they were going to drop food, water, clothing, and blankets to those outside the wall. Soon there was nothing more to say, and the three lapsed into silence. Through the open doorway, they could hear snatches of comments and exchanges from the residents of Aegis, and they were pleased that the tone, as well as the substance, of what they heard appeared to be serious, inquisitive, sad, helpful, and all of the other reactions which would be appropriate for the situation. No one was loud, irrational, panicked, belligerent, or confrontational, the reactions least needed at a time such as this.

Tillie had slid her chair a foot or so away and was tilting it back to the point of teetering. Her running shoes were plopped on the table. Her hands were laced behind her head as she leaned back, staring at the ceiling. Without bothering to look down, she asked, "Do you think all of us were picked?"

She had voiced the same question Elias had been pondering since the reality of their situation had become clear to him. He shared another question he had come to earlier. "If all of this *is* being guided by an intelligence greater than we are, why in the world would He pick me?"

Still staring at the acoustic tiles above her, Tillie responded, "I know! Why me, too? I don't deserve it. I'm nasty, surly, rude, judgmental. I hate most people...hell, I mean heck, I've killed people. That can't exactly be the ideal specimen for starting a new world."

"Tillie," he said softly, "what happened with your brother was an accident. You didn't kill...."

"I don't mean that. I'm talking about Eric. When he had his gun on you, Elias, and he was going to pull the trigger, I took the head shot. I could've hit him in the shoulder, the leg...but I didn't."

Leah turned in her chair to face Tillie. Gently, she reached out and touched her arm. "Do you believe in reincarnation?"

Tillie, reacting to the contact, twisted her head around to look at Leah. "Yeah, I think I do. Why?"

"One of the basic tenets of the philosophy is that we keep coming back here until we've learned our lessons. Whether there's a God, or whether all of the minds on Earth are interconnected, like the cells in our head, to form a giant brain, whatever has staged this series of impossible events to create this outcome, I think, is a lot more interested in whether we've learned the right lessons, than whether we ever made the mistakes in the first place."

Tillie dropped her feet loudly to the floor and spun to face Leah. "You think?"

"Of course I do. Who is less likely to do a bad thing...someone who did it before and had to suffer through the horrible consequences of it, or someone who has never experienced that?"

She turned to her husband. "And this applies to you, too. In your life, in the positions you've held, you've seen it all. You have witnessed the results of almost every action a person can take. You've watched individuals, as well as entire countries, make mistakes, and many times it's been up to you to clean up the mess afterward. Who better to know what choices to avoid than you?"

Elias thought back over his life and his career. Her words made sense.

"Elias, baby, in the coming months and years ahead, you are going to be a big part of it, an integral cog in the process that forms this reborn society. There will be hundreds of times you will be in some meeting, listening as someone proposes an idea which, to that person, is a brand-new concept, but to you will be *déjà vu* all over again.

It's going to be your job to make certain we avoid as many of those pitfalls, the ones which will lead us to disaster, as possible. In a sense, it'll be as if we are all going to be on a safari and you are the guide. You'll be the one who knows where the bad places are that we need to avoid."

"What you're saying makes sense as far as Elias is concerned, but what do I have to offer? I'm just broken. I'm not going to help anybody make the right decisions."

Before Leah could respond to Tillie, Elias said, "You're right."

His wife whirled around to stare at him, shocked. Tillie, stunned by his bluntness, had nothing to say as he continued, "You're an angry, bitter fool with nothing to offer anyone."

"Elias!" Leah exclaimed.

But he was not finished. "Your brother died and you decided that it was your fault, which, by the way, it was. You couldn't handle it, so you split. You ran away to Aegis. But you found out that Aegis was just another community...just another society...just like the one you ran away from, only smaller. So, instead of trying to fit in, you did what you do best; you hid in the ductwork, like a rat."

Tillie was staring at Elias, her face frozen.

"What a bitter irony this must now be for you. The society, which you thought you weren't good enough to live in, is dying. And the place where you came to hide, to commit a metaphorical suicide because you didn't have the guts to do it for real, has turned out to be the Ark. You keep trying to punish yourself, and God or fate, or whatever, keeps cheating you out of the punishment you know you deserve. Tillie, you were a worthless screw-up when you first came in here and you're still a worthless screw-up!"

Her hand flashed forward, slapping him hard across the face.

"How dare you call me that? I saved your ass! If it hadn't been for me, everybody in this place would be...."

She stopped. The furor on her face dissolved, softened. A single tear welled up at the corner of her eye.

"Dead?" Elias finished the sentence for her.

The tear broke loose and trailed down her cheek as she moved her head in a single nod. A second tear followed, then a third, until the dam burst and she was racked with sobs. She flew out of her chair, and throwing her arms around Elias, she broke down, holding him tightly. He put his arms around her, and Leah placed a hand gently on her shoulder.

"Hey!" someone shouted from the doorway before he noticed the scene that was being played out. "Oh, sorry."

Elias was able to turn his head enough to see that it was Crabill. "What is it, Jay?"

"We've...the radio's working. Uh, you should probably come and hear this."

Elias nodded. "We'll be right there."

Crabill left and Tillie loosened her grip on Elias, backing away and letting him go. Her eyes a bright red, her nose running, she dragged her sleeve across her face and sniffled loudly. After a few swallows, she said, "We should go listen."

"Anytime you're ready."

With another loud sniff, she stood up. "I'm ready. We can go."

Elias and Leah stood, and as they all walked toward the door, Tillie stopped abruptly. "I know you're expecting a 'thank you' or some other soppy thing...."

Elias began to deny that he was, when he was interrupted.

"But I'm gonna kick your butt for that." She finished the threat with a weak smile.

He broke into a relieved grin. "Better bring your lunch."

$$\odot$$

A twelve-volt power supply and some speakers had been located. The makeshift radio was on a small folding table which had been placed atop the elevated platform Pierce and Wilson had spoken from earlier. The group, scattered throughout the hall, edged forward, closer to the radio, many of the people sitting down on the floor at the base of the platform.

Crabill scanned the channels looking for a station. Finding one, he turned the volume up, moved to the edge of the platform, and sat down.

> "...that is all we know at this time. We have been completely unable to contact any authorities for a report or an update on the epidemic. Broadcast stations in our nation's capital are off the air. Cellular systems are so overwhelmed with people attempting calls that it has proved useless to try them. We have made repeated attempts to contact our sister station in Washington, D.C. using land lines. When we were able to get through, there was no answer other than voice mail.
>
> "There has also been no contact with other major cities, including New York, Boston, Philadelphia, Miami, Charlotte...the list is growing by the minute. We have not heard anything from Atlanta, the home city of the Center for Disease Control.
>
> "Some functionality still remains on the Internet, and we have been able to receive word that martial law has been declared by the governors of all states not yet affected by the epidemic, or pandemic, I guess. We have also been able to find

out from the Internet that cases have been reported overseas.
Illness, fatalities, and widespread panic are reported in France,
England, Germany, and the rest of Europe. At this time, the
Middle East, Asia, South America, and Australia have not
reported any outbreaks of the epidemic."

Elias looked around the room and watched the faces of the crowd. Everyone was listening silently, and he was certain that each was thinking about friends, family, and acquaintances on the outside, visualizing the horror that was spreading like a wildfire around the country and the entire Earth. He knew that all of them must be as dumbstruck as he, trying to comprehend the magnitude of the events.

The gathering continued their vigil into the night, with more arriving from other parts of Aegis. Everyone listened. No one spoke. At one point, Milton Pierce, helped by two others, brought food and drinks, distributing them individually, rather than placing the meal on a table, buffet-style, as he would have only hours ago. The rationing had begun.

Fours hours after the radio had been turned on, the station, which they had learned was based in Denver, abruptly went off the air with no explanation. Crabill jumped up and quickly found another station which was still broadcasting from South Dakota, and they continued listening as the news broadcasters, sounding more exhausted, more hopeless, and more terrified as the night went on, provided a litany of locations where the pathogen had struck.

When the final populated continent fell victim, Elias turned to Leah. "I don't think I can stand listening to this anymore."

She nodded and they both stood up, careful to not step on the strangers around them, many of whom were now lying down on the floor, loath to return to their quarters, craving the presence of others. Some of them were huddled against their neighbors. Some were curled up in almost fetal positions. Leah espied Tillie several feet away, lying on her side, sound asleep. Pierce had dimmed the lighting in the hall hours ago, so they were not able to locate Wilson, Sweezea, Lisa, or the others from their original group. The only other person they recognized was Crabill, now sitting on the platform near the radio, his back against the leg of the folding table, his eyes drooping from fatigue.

"Where do you want to go?" Leah asked in a whisper.

Elias surveyed the room filled with strangers, realizing that very soon he would know each and every one of them intimately.

"I need to get outside" was all he said, as he walked to the heap of clothing Pierce had piled against the wall near one of the exits, as a resource for the volunteers who were working on the roof. He grabbed two heavy parkas and some thick gloves and, with Leah following, left the meeting room which had become a site for a wake.

Twenty minutes later they were standing on the roof of Aegis, buffeted by the frigid winds and surrounded by the shaking and rattling heaps of debris. The salvage crews had cleared a passable trail from the hatch to the perimeter wall, which was where they now stood, clutching each other and staring off into semidarkness. To the left, in the direction of the now collapsed entrance, they could barely see, in the moonlit night, that the people outside the wall had pulled several of the abandoned vehicles into a tight semicircle as a windbreak.

Elias had heard earlier that the first supply of food, water, warm clothing, and blankets had been dropped, accompanied by a message from Pierce, explaining that he would continue to supply them outside until he was satisfied that they were not infected. Although Elias could not tell in the darkness, he guessed they were now all huddled inside the vehicles for warmth, most likely running the engines so the heaters would function. The rooftop around them was dark. The volunteer crews had quit for the night.

He felt Leah pressing hard against him, holding him tightly.

Looking at her profile in the moonlight, Elias was, once again, overwhelmed at his fortune in being reunited with her. In all of the thousands of hours since he first received the news of her demise, he had never thought for a moment that this would be possible. And yet, despite the almost mind-numbing series of events which had to happen to bring them together, they were.

She sensed his gaze and turned to him. Their eyes connected and they kissed, the cowls of the parkas forming a fur-lined tunnel around their faces. It was a consuming and passionate kiss, both of them trying to convey, with the contact, the intensity of their love for the other; both celebrating the fact that they were alive and with each other, right then, at that moment. Somehow, despite the fact that the entire world had been turned upside down, with all of the billions of pieces crashing into a jumbled heap, they were standing side by side, looking out over it all.

CHAPTER TWENTY-THREE

Wilson told all of us today that we each need to start keeping a journal. He said that someday, way in the future, people are going to want to know what it was like for us in Aegis. I think it's stupid and I told him that. But he wouldn't give up until I said I would do it. So here it is, all of you grandchildren of the grandchildren of the grandchildren of the grandchildren of the people who are in Aegis today, Mathilda's journal.

I woke up a few hours ago. I was sleeping on the floor in the big hall, where all of us listened to the radio last night. There was some station on – I don't know from where. A lot of people were still glued to it, but I couldn't stand listening, so I left and came back here, to my pad in the ductwork. Besides, Pierce and his sister were handing out rations and I've got my own stash.

Here I am, back at the pad again. Ate two bites from the sandwich I made and felt bad. So I packed up all my food and took it to Pierce to add to the communal food store. Dumb, huh?

It's later now. Hunted down Matthias today because we haven't really had a chance to talk since, well, you know. But he was busy up on the roof working with the other guys on the solar panels. Then I went looking for Wilson. But he was tied up with Pierce, having some kind of meeting.

Couldn't find Elias and Leah. They probably have a lot of catching up to do. After two years, I would think so. Sweezea, Hutson, and Crabill were all busy gathering up weapons. Right now they are only asking people for them. They'd better not start just taking them, at least mine.

This journal is ridiculous. I don't have anything to say. And I don't feel like reading right now. Maybe I'll go up on the roof and help those guys.

DAY 2

Didn't get back to writing this last night. I was so tired that I just crashed. Got up this morning and grabbed my ration and wolfed it down in like two minutes. If that's all the food I'm going to get for breakfast, I'm going to starve.

Bad news at breakfast. The supply drop to the poor people outside was still sitting where we dropped it, unopened. And nobody could see any people around. They might still be inside the cars and trucks out there, but it seems like they would have gotten out to grab the stuff. I hope they're okay.

I started marking my calendar. There are two "X" marks now. Who knows how many to go?

DAY 6

I apologize to all of you twenty-second-century folks who might be reading this, but I haven't had a chance to write a word in the journal for days. Sweezea was put in charge of our army. Everybody calls it the security team, but I like "army" better. I had a chance to talk to him on Day 2, and he asked me if I wanted to be on the team. Me! How cool is that? Today, flopped in my pad with every bone in my body hurting, I'm not sure it was such a dandy idea. He's gone nuts. Has us training all the time. And when we're not training, we're doing workouts. And when we're not doing either of those, he has us studying! Studying? Well, overall, it's not bad, so I'll hang in there. I am running circles around most of the guys on the team. Ha!

A bunch has happened since the last time I wrote in this thing. Let me see if I can remember it all. Wilson was real excited because one of the last-day newbies, actually two of them, if you want to count the blond, are meteorologists. One was on a TV station, the blond of course, before she came into Aegis. But the guy was the local head of the national weather office. They've been huddling up with Wilson, trying to figure out exactly how this downdraft works.

Milton Pierce seems to be doing a great job. He takes it so seriously. I thought he'd lost his mind, asking the Aegis people to vote in his sister as his second-in-command. I even had a chance to talk to him about it for a little bit. He said that she would be a good balance for him. Whatever that means! We'll see, I guess.

Elias and Leah are so cool together. They are never more than about five feet apart, and every time I look at him, he's staring at her with a sappy grin on his face. Other than that, he kind of bounces all over the place. One day he works with us on security. The next day he's on the roof with Matthias, helping the crew. He did get real jazzed the other day. It seems he was walking down one of the hallways and ran into two brothers he knew from the outside. He only told me that they were the Barton brothers and he met them on his trip here. He didn't tell me why they were here.

They've gotten three sections of the panels hooked up, so we are getting a trickle of electricity back into the batteries. They say it isn't enough yet, but it helps. I guess the wind has died down a little. Wilson said it got worse so that it was strong enough to knock down the entrance, and now it has eased off to the level needed to keep the bug away. This is all so strange. I don't know if I'm ready to really think about it yet.

I have been thinking a lot about how we all feel inside Aegis, and it is bizarre. Before the "event," as everybody calls it – I think they are all afraid to call it what it was – we were stuck in here, anyway. We weren't supposed to leave. Ever. And we had no communication with the outside world. Nothing's changed, not even a little bit. Well, that's not true. We did have incoming communication for a day or two, until the last station went off the air. Other than that, everything is the same as it was.

But, in all of our heads, everything has changed. I'm not just talking about the newbies, who aren't used to Aegis. I'm talking about the other people who have been here a long time, like me. They are all acting differently now. It's hard to describe.

Wilson says that before the event we were all in purgatory, killing time and waiting for the end. But now, he says, we are all in a womb, waiting for our lives to begin. Makes sense. I just wish I knew how long the pregnancy was going to last.

And that's part of the deal. Before, none of us ever paid any attention to the days. It didn't matter because we weren't ever getting out. But now, it has only been six days and everybody's getting a little stir-crazy. Sweezea tells me that's why we need the security team. We don't know if anyone's gonna freak out and we need to be ready.

Oh! I can't believe I didn't mention this first. Those poor people outside…I guess they didn't make it. Nobody ever came out of the cars and trucks. Since we're so high up, when we look down from the roof, we can't really tell if any people are in the vehicles, but where else would they be? Elias, Leah, Sam, and Lisa took it real hard. I think Wilson did, too. But it's not easy to tell with him.

Gotta go. Need to take a couple of aspirins and hit the sack. Sweezea has a run planned for tomorrow where we have to carry about a thousand pounds on our backs, so I need some rest.

Day 11

Milton Pierce finally had an opportunity to talk to all of the last-day newbies who flooded into Aegis right before the entrance collapsed. I think he was expecting all of them to tell him they had a visitation or a dream or something that told them to come to Aegis. It was weird. From what he told me, each of them had a different reason for coming. One guy said he was watching the news and just became disgusted with the politics. He couldn't stand it anymore, so he came here. Another one said that his business was failing and he was way deep in debt. So, instead of putting his family through losing everything and filing bankruptcy, he brought his wife and kids here. In other words, if two hundred newbies came – there were two hundred different reasons. As Wilson would say, another coincidence?

Matthias organized a painting party. Everyone in Aegis was invited. We painted over all the graffiti.

Day 15

Hello, future folks! I hope that the other people who are keeping journals are more conscientious about it than I am. I'm sure that Wilson's journal goes on for pages about each day. Well, what he has to say is a lot more important than my twitterings.

Anyway…you aren't going to believe this. Pierce, well, both Pierces actually, along with Wilson and Elias, decided that we needed to have a governing body. A group of Aegisites. Oh, by the way, there isn't a Madison anymore. And you probably know from reading your history books and other people's journals before mine, there already wasn't a Walden, even before the event. Everyone here is part of one group. There really wasn't a formal meeting or anything on this. One by one people started using the new name, coined by – guess who? You got it, me! I was calling us Aegisites on my own, and it just got picked up by everyone else.

As I was saying, the Pierces, Wilson, and Elias thought we should have a governing body. I screwed up and called it a committee and got one of those twenty-minute droning lectures from Pierce about how ineffective committees are. He calls it a board of governors. Every person in Aegis voted. It was all by write-in votes. There weren't any nominees or candidates and there wasn't any campaigning. We were called in, had it explained to us, and we voted, right then.

Guess who one of the new governors is? Me! The people here picked me! Is that cool, or what? They picked Wilson, of course, and Elias and Leah, Matthias, Sweezea, and Hutson. Crabill came close, but didn't quite make it. I don't think he wanted it, anyway.

We had our first meeting today. Appointed Pierce, Milton of course, as Chief of Staff. He likes that title.

I haven't mentioned Kreitzmann yet in this journal. He recovered just fine from his concussion and has been working with the rest of his old staff, and the Aegisites, putting together educational and training programs. I think the event changed him. We haven't had a chance to talk much, but he has told anyone who will listen to him how sorry he is for the way that he did his research and experiments in the past. Especially the "using babies" part. I suppose he is trying to take the best of what he learned before and apply it to this brave new world we're going to be starting. Some of it makes a lot of sense. The mind readers are a little spooky but sure come in handy sometimes. Not much use for the fast-talkers, but they are fitting in with our little society nicely. Seems they can slow it down if they want to. Not as slow as we talk, but we can understand them. All the adult Zippers, or Accelerants, as Kreitzmann calls them, died during the time leading up to the event. The younger ones are cool and also really come in handy. It's strange that Kreitzmann and his people and his subjects were picked to be a part of the surviving party. Maybe it's up to us to figure out why and how they all fit in if we leave here. I mean, when we leave here.

Oh, one more cool deal before I sign off for today. One of the Aegisites is a guy who studies the history and meaning of names. I met him today at lunch. He told me I had an interesting name, considering what had happened and where I was. I think it's embarrassing, so I'm not going to include it in this journal. He brought up the significance of Elias' first and last names, but I already knew that. Then he told me something I didn't know, and it blew me away. I am assuming that all of you future "history buffs" will be aware of the pre-event history of America. Otherwise, this won't make any sense to you. Wilson's name, John Chapman, was the name of a famous guy in the past. And with what's happening now, I think it's pretty profound. John Chapman was the real name of Johnny Appleseed.

Day 19

Had lunch with Kreitzmann. It wasn't my idea. I was sitting by myself and eating my rations when he plopped down in the chair next to me. He obviously wanted to talk because all it took from me was asking how he was, and, boy, off he went. At times he was almost like a born-again, explaining how much he now understands that he didn't before. Carrying on about the event out there making him see the one thing that he had forgotten, in his zeal to do his research – the value of a single human life. The rest of the talk was about how he was going to spend every waking minute trying to make things right. Whatever that means. We'll see, I guess. But, man, has he changed. It's kinda cool, actually. It made me think about what Leah said about how we were all picked because we've learned from our mistakes.

Day 31

I'm going to stop apologizing to you for the long gaps in my journal. You're probably getting tired of reading them, anyway. I write when I can and if I feel I have something to say. I'm sure you understand.

The winds are unchanged. We have enough solar panels working now to keep the batteries charged, the pumps running, and everything else working. We have all fallen into routines. Other than maintenance, there isn't much work to do here. To keep everyone occupied, Wilson and Mildred Pierce – by the way, I've gotten to like her quite a bit – have put together a formal program they call cross-training. They went through the entire population and found out what skills, training, and even hobbies people had before coming here, and put together a list. Now we attend classes taught by the other Aegisites so that we all learn about each other's knowledge and skills.

I'm enjoying it. One day it's woodworking, and the next it's psychology. Wilson thinks it's important that all of us know as much as possible before we leave here. Makes sense to me. If there is only one person on Earth who knows how to make a beautiful rabbeted-joint and something happens to him, that would be horrible.

Wilson, by the way, was carrying on today, as he so likes to do, about the coincidences in the list of knowledge and skills we have here. He was amazed at how many of the essential ones made it into Aegis before the event. I wonder when he's going to quit being so amazed and just accept what happened.

I moved out of the ductwork yesterday, and moved into one of the apartments. I thought it was about time I joined the human race. Elias and Leah are my neighbors. I'm glad I did it.

Day 35

We ran out of coffee today. There are a lot of grumpy people in Aegis.

Day 40

It's morning. I'm staring at the calendar I started marking on Day 1. I just put the fortieth "X" on it. I am so excited. Today will be the day. I'm sure of it. After all, Aegis is the Ark, and Noah and his group were able to leave after forty days. So should we.

You're probably wondering why we are waiting for the winds to stop. Well, if you are reading this, that means we were right and survived. If you're not, oh well. The board has had several meetings on this. We've also had open discussions with the Aegisites. Wilson has spent what seems like a thousand hours meeting with the meteorologists, the doctors, the biologists, and anyone else inside here who might have a fact he can use to fit into one of his mental jigsaw puzzles. We have all been trying to decide how we will know when it is safe to leave. Since there isn't anybody out there we can ask, we don't know.

Wilson has created several scenarios – making assumptions on what kind of pathogen they used, or how the monsters who created the bug would have made certain the world was safe for them to re-enter and resume their lives. The list seems endless. At times he has become something of a recluse, trying to crunch the numbers…trying to find the pattern which will give him the answer. I think the only thing all of his work has given him is a headache.

So, we decided that whoever or whatever saved us in the first place would let us know when it was safe to leave. And the way we would be notified was when the winds stopped. And, as I said earlier, I know for a fact that they will stop today. So there!

This experience inside Aegis for the last forty days has been awesome. I know that it has changed me. I think, for the better. But I'm ready to get out of here now. That's odd, isn't it? For almost the whole time I was in Aegis before the event, I knew how to get out through the overflow tunnel and I never wanted to leave. Not for a moment. But now…I am itching to get out there. I'm so glad that today is going to be it.

Day 41

It's still windy.

Day 50

The mood has really changed in Aegis. I think that most of the people, whether they admitted it or not, believed that we were going to be able to leave after forty days. At least it was a goal, a target. Now we have no idea how long we need to wait. And that is quite a bit more difficult.

Not that there are any problems with the Aegisites. That hasn't been the case. There haven't been any issues, any fights, not even any serious arguments. It feels, to everyone, as though we are all in this together, which we obviously are, and we need to make the best of it.

I've made some new friends in the past month, like Keith, the man who studies people's names. He enjoys playing chess, which I've never learned. He is teaching me, and so far, I like it. I've also become friends with Erin, the meteorologist from TV. She just knocked on my door one night because she wanted to talk. I guess we clicked, since she didn't go back to her apartment until after midnight.

Ever since the fortieth day came and went, I'm guessing that Wilson has become even more obsessed with figuring out the pattern of the bug. Other than the board meetings, I never see him. I miss the talks we used to have on the porch of his shack.

Day 63

Leah invited me to their apartment for dinner last night. Since we are all on rationing, I was a little surprised as I walked in – they had a big spread of food on the table. I know that neither one of them would ever steal from the stockpile, so I asked where they got it all. Elias told me that he and she had been planning to have me over for quite a while, and they had been cutting back on how much of their rations they were eating, saving some up for the feast. Okay, I'll admit to you future folks, it made me cry.

I have to tell you…we stuffed ourselves. It reminded me of how I used to feel as a kid after Thanksgiving dinner.

Afterward, the three of us sat around and talked. It was nice. The more I get to know Leah, the more I can see why Elias loves her so much. It's almost as if they are connected. They even finish each other's sentences. I keep trying to see the wispy little filament in the air between them, the line that ties them together. Last night, I think I caught a glimpse of it.

Even though most of the evening was just talk about pleasant things and fun things and silly things, at one point we talked about getting out and how long it would be. With the solar panels working, we are pumping all of the groundwater we need. The reservoirs are full. The rationing has been working about as well as Milton expected. We are around half of the way through the supply of food, although the items like fresh fruit and vegetables are long gone. We ate them first because, even with refrigerators, they would spoil pretty fast. So now we're down to the canned and frozen types. Elias told me they had to do that during World War II on the submarines. They would eat like kings right after they left port for a patrol, fresh fruits and vegetables with every meal, before that stuff went bad.

We figured out last night that we have enough food for about two more months. Wilson, according to Elias, who checked in on him recently, has no idea or theory or even a guess as to when we'll be able to leave. Elias said that our pal looked a little haggard. We think he needs a break. At this point I suppose it's anybody's guess when we can leave.

But what we talked about next made me feel a little uneasy. Leah asked Elias how we could know for sure that it would be safe to go out, even if the wind just stopped all of a sudden. There isn't anyone broadcasting over the satellite stations anymore. Hasn't been for a long time. I had wondered if the satellites were still working, but one of the techie guys we have here told me that they were self-sufficient up there in space, and unless something happened to take them out, they would keep orbiting, waiting for someone to bounce a signal off them. I guess nobody is.

The techie also said that, as long as some of the servers on the Internet were still running, there would be an Internet, even if no one was on it. The problem is that we never did have access to the Internet at Aegis. The phones that Faulk and his men brought in had access to the Web for a little while. We were able to get some news that way, but only for a few days. They think that the power to the cell tower closest to Aegis probably went out, because on about the third or fourth day, we couldn't get a signal. And then the batteries went dead on the phones and Faulk's team hadn't thought to bring their chargers in here with them. We could probably rig up a charger, but what's the point with no signal?

We went through all of this again last night and still didn't have an answer to Leah's question. Guess we'll just have to trust in the fact that the wind wouldn't be switched off unless it was safe to leave. And, of course, the next question was, what if the wind doesn't switch off and we run out of food? That was when the evening ended.

Day 75

Hello, future folks. I really wish I could be with you and know how this all turns out. It's about eleven o'clock at night. We just finished having an open board meeting, and people are getting a little edgy. I suppose that I can't blame them. I got up and spoke to the crowd – funny, I never would have been caught dead doing something like that a few months ago – and I talked about how it was before the event. Most of the people here now have been here for some time, but more than two hundred of our residents are last-day newbies. That's why I thought I should talk, since I was a first-dayer.

I tried to explain that everything is still the way it was, that we had been able to get along for years without any real problems, except for the riot and ZooCity, of course. So there wasn't any reason to start getting all itchy now. Someone stood up and said it was different, because we all had known there was a civilization out there. I didn't know what to say to that.

One man, one of the newbies, I think his name is Trent, wanted us to open the back door. He said he was convinced, I don't know how, that the bug was dead and that it would be okay to leave. I started to argue with him and then I stopped. His question made me ask myself a different one. Is Aegis a refuge or a prison? One of the things Milton Pierce talks about all the time is personal responsibility. Wouldn't that apply to this situation? Wouldn't Trent have a right to leave if he wants to go? He knows the facts. He knows that there's plenty of room here, and still plenty of food.

Those were all only my thoughts. Then I said them out loud. I asked the board and the people in the audience what they thought. Man, did we have a discussion! There were some in the group who believed that we had to stick together, that we had to make sure everybody stayed inside until we all left together, when we were certain it was safe to go. I didn't ask them how they would make sure nobody left.

Did they want to lock people up? I also didn't bring up my discussion with Elias and Leah about exactly how we would be certain, even after the wind stopped. I thought that would be too much for one night.

There were others who believed that it was Trent's choice. We never did take a vote. I'm beginning to understand much of what Milton carries on about. After all the folks had a chance to state their opinions on the subject, he got up and said the board would discuss the matter further and we would reconvene to share our consensus with the residents. I expected the people in the audience to get ticked off when he said it, but they didn't! I was watching their faces and they were glad. I don't know if it was because they all had a chance to be heard. I don't know if it was because they were glad not to be the ones making the decision. I don't know if it was because they wanted to be led, and trusted us to come to the right decision. If that's the case, then this whole governing thing just got a lot heavier on my shoulders.

Anyway, the meeting finally broke up and the board is meeting tomorrow to talk about it. I already know which way it's going to go. The board is going to decide to open the back door. That decision is the only one we can come to and remain consistent with everything else we've said and done so far.

I'm exhausted. Good night, future folks.

Day 76

We met. We voted. We open the back door in three days. We want to give Trent a chance to change his mind.

Day 79

Four people left today – Trent, his girlfriend, and another couple I don't really know all that well. They promised that they would come back in a few days and let us know it was all clear to leave. This probably isn't consistent with being a good governor, but I couldn't make myself see them off at the back door.

Day 83

Still no sign of Trent. People are taking turns up on the roof, in the cold, watching for them.

Day 89

None of us think they'll be coming back. They would have by now. The people who were going up to the roof to watch have stopped. No one else is talking about leaving. Jay welded the back door again.

Fewer and fewer people are showing up for the cross-training classes. I think that they don't believe we're going to get out of here.

I quit playing chess with Keith. I just couldn't concentrate on the game anymore.

Day 101

Milton took the board of governors on a tour of the food lockers today. It isn't looking good. At the current rate of consumption, we are going to run out in less than two weeks. After we looked at the small amounts left, we had a meeting in private, supposedly to discuss a contingency plan. But none of us had anything to suggest, not even Wilson. Seriously, what kind of a contingency plan can we come up with? It isn't as if we have any options. Milton had one of the medical staff join us and talk about how long people can last with no food. It was depressing.

Wilson suggested that we keep the status of the food a secret from everyone else. He couldn't see any benefit in telling. We voted on it and his suggestion won. I voted with him, but wasn't sure it was the right thing to do.

Day 102

I had a horrible nightmare last night, after our meeting about the food. In the nightmare, Milton suggested that we needed to prioritize the value of the residents at Aegis, in terms of how much they will contribute to the new society when we get out, with the most valuable at the top of the list, down to the least valuable at the bottom. Then we would kill the last one on the list and eat him. We would work our way up the list until the wind stopped. He was so cold, so pragmatic, in the dream, with flow charts and everything, showing us how much longer we would live under this system. I woke up right after I punched him in the face.

Day 111

Down to the last few days of food. The word got out. I don't know who talked, but everyone in Aegis knows that it's almost gone. Sweezea had the security team ready for something to happen. He put extra guards on the food around the clock. People freaked out at first. There were quite a few angry confrontations between the residents and the board. But all of the anger was because we didn't let them know before. To our surprise, after the initial blowup, everyone settled down and, I think, is handling it fairly well. No screaming mobs made a move on the food. Nothing like that. Guess we were wrong about not telling them sooner.

Day 112

The board is having daily meetings now. I'm not really sure why. We don't have anything new to say, but we all feel that we should be doing it. At today's, Elias and Leah dropped a bombshell on all of us. They want to pull a Trent and leave Aegis. I'm afraid I lost it when they told us. But I managed to calm down and listen to what they had to say. Elias said that maybe he and Leah could make a run to the closest place, maybe Yuma or even Tacna, and find some food to bring back.

I said that the wind hadn't stopped. We didn't have any reason to believe that the bug was gone from out there. He just looked at me and smiled that smile of his and said that if we didn't try something, we'd all be dead soon, anyway.

That's when I said I'd go. Sweezea said the same thing, at the same time. Wilson insisted that he should go since he was the oldest and didn't have as much life to live as Elias and Leah. By the time everyone was done shouting, every single person on the board had offered to go instead of Elias and Leah.

After we were all quiet, all of us staring at the two of them, Leah thanked us. I could swear that I saw a tear coming out of her eye. She said that they had made up their minds. They were going whether any of the rest of us went or not, so there was no reason for anyone else to go, since it wouldn't keep them here.

Nobody knew what to say for the longest time. I wanted to think of something…anything which would change their minds, but I couldn't. And even if I did, what difference would it make? Elias was right. If we didn't try something, we would all be dead soon, anyway.

If there are any future folks…and if you are reading this…I want all of you to know that each and every one of you is alive because of Elias and Leah Charon. Please don't ever forget that…ever. And, if no one ever reads this, then I guess what I'm saying doesn't matter.

Mathilda Tulley

CHAPTER
TWENTY-FOUR

Tillie and Wilson were standing at the corridor intersection near the exit door. There was no longer any sign of the damage from the exploded grenade. Clements, and the crew he had assembled from Aegis, had repaired the walls and repainted.

Tillie, her eyes fixed on the hallway in the direction Elias and Leah would soon appear, said quietly to Wilson, "This isn't right."

Wilson, much thinner than he had been a mere four months ago, gently placed his hand on her shoulder. "Elias is correct. We need to do something before we all starve."

"That's not what I mean."

"What do you mean?"

"Every step of the way things happened...things all designed to get us here, keep us here, save us from the bug. You've talked about all of the incredible coincidences which had to happen in precisely the right sequence, just to ensure that Aegis survived while the rest of the world died. After all of those, and I don't care if you want to call them coincidences or miracles, where is our rainbow...where is our dove with the olive branch? Why is it...after everything else has been so carefully orchestrated, that we are now out of food...that the damn wind hasn't stopped? Why haven't we gotten a signal, a message, that it is safe to leave? Why do Elias and Leah have to go out there, the way Trent and the others did, when we don't know if they'll come back?"

In a soft voice, Wilson answered, "I don't know."

She whirled around to face him, her face flush. "You *can't* say 'I don't know'! You *never* say 'I don't know'! Why *don't* you know?"

The moment the words left her lips, she wished she could take them back. She knew that Wilson had taken this question more seriously than any other he had ever tackled in his life. For weeks he had forsaken needed sleep and countless meals, as well as any casual interactions with his friends, to devote himself obsessively to finding the answer. She knew him better than anyone in Aegis...anyone alive, in fact...and she knew how hard it must have been for him to admit that he did not know the answer. His face, already worn and haggard, his eyes sunken, seemed to slump even further.

"Wilson, I'm sorry. I am. It's just that I can't stand to see the two of them walk out that door."

He stepped forward and held her. "I know, Tillie. I know." She allowed him to hold her for a moment, then backed away, too anxious to be confined.

More people began to arrive. She saw Sweezea, Matt, Lisa, Sam, Hutson, and even Kreitzmann come in with the others. The intersection was filling rapidly, backing up into the hallways in all directions. The mood was somber and subdued.

To her left, the crowd parted and, in a moment, Elias and Leah worked their way through to the front. As soon as she saw Leah, she ran forward, throwing her arms around her friend. Despite her earlier promise to herself, Tillie began to cry, her shoulders heaving with each sob. Leah responded in kind as Elias stood quietly to the side.

After a minute or two had passed, Tillie took a step back from Leah and looked at Elias, tears streaming freely down her face. Taking a deep breath, trying to calm the spasms in her diaphragm, she finally spoke. "I wanted to tell you...you're off the hook."

Elias, momentarily confused, answered, "Off the hook? What...?"

Dragging the sleeve of her shirt across her face, she explained, "Your promise. It's over and done. I'm releasing you from it."

"Tillie, I still don't understand."

Valiantly trying to put a smile on her face, she replied softly, "You don't have to try to be Bruce Willis anymore."

In his eyes, she could see that he was flashing back to that day, so long ago, in her den. He tried to speak but the effort was derailed by the quivering in his lower lip. Without waiting another moment, she rushed against him, wrapping her arms around his neck and holding him tightly. He held her in a bear hug.

They stood together for a long time, neither wanting to break the moment. When, at last, they parted, Elias reached up and held her face in his hands, finally finding his voice. "I will be back. I...I promise."

Tillie only nodded, afraid to say another word. Elias turned to Wilson and shook his hand. "I will see you soon, my friend."

"Be safe, Elias. Both of you."

Leah gave Wilson an emotional hug. As she did, she whispered in his ear, "Please keep an eye on our friend here, will you?"

Wilson nodded.

Elias and Leah moved toward the exit, which was now wide open, the frigid wind whipping into the enclosed space with a howl. As they proceeded, all of the friends they had made during their days in Aegis were lined up to shake their hands, hug them, and wish them luck. It seemed as if the entire population of Aegis was crowded into the hallway behind Wilson, having come to see them off.

When they reached the door, Crabill was standing in the wind, a forced grin on his face. "I went out to the parking lot and found the truck with the most gas and jumped the battery. She's running and all warmed up for you."

"Jay," Leah said, "you shouldn't have gone out there."

He shrugged and answered, "It's the least I could do. Besides, I didn't want the two of you wandering around in the cold, trying to get one started."

"You didn't go near the circle of vehicles the outside people used, did you?" asked Elias.

"No, sir. Just the parking lot."

Elias smiled at him. "Thanks. And stop that 'sir' stuff, will you?" They shook hands and Crabill moved back, pausing at the doorway. Tillie was jammed next to him in the tight opening, shivering in the cold and staring at her two friends, a look of profound sadness on her face.

Elias and Leah both waved. Tillie, and the others visible through the open door, returned the wave. The two turned and climbed into the yellow SUV parked near the door, its engine running.

Tillie stood clutching Crabill's arm, watching her two friends as they pulled the doors closed. She had to fight off the urge to run to the truck and jump into the back seat. She knew that if she did that, Elias would only make her get out. After a minute's hesitation, the truck pulled away, slowly skirting the perimeter of Aegis. She leaned out farther and farther from the door, watching the receding taillights for as long as she could, until they disappeared around the gradually bending arc of the wall.

She felt a hand on her shoulder and turned to see Wilson, standing behind her and gently trying to pull her inside so the door could be closed. Reluctantly, she gave in, not taking her eyes off the last point where they had been visible. Crabill closed the steel door with a loud slam, dropping the crossbar into the new saddles he had welded on the frame.

None of the gathering had yet dispersed. They were all standing as if rooted to their spots, unsure of what to do next. Tillie, in a daze, worked her way through the people. With a silent nod of her head, she accepted the occasional comment of reassurance that she would soon see Elias and Leah again. Once she cleared the back of the group, her pace quickened and she walked briskly. After putting another turn of the corridor behind her, she broke into a full run, dashing down one hallway and then another, until she reached the access ladder she was seeking. Almost flying up the rungs, she found herself in the mechanical system. Running again, she sprinted all the way to her old den...her, now empty, home for many years, where she collapsed to the floor, sobbing.

⊙

Tillie stood alone at the west end of the roof, her body pressed against the inside face of the parapet wall, which stopped at her shoulders, her eyes fixed on the distant point where the road from Aegis disappeared at the horizon. Before coming to the roof, she had added extra layers of clothing, and found some heavy gloves and a parka with a thick, furry hood; yet, the cold still penetrated, chilling her and making her shiver. With the constant roaring of the wind, she did not hear Sweezea approaching, startled when she felt a sudden touch on her arm. Turning, she saw him standing beside a fifty-five-gallon drum, which he had rolled to her spot on the roof using a hand truck.

"Hey, Tim." She had to shout to be heard.

"Brought you a present." He slid the flange of the hand truck out from under the barrel. Tillie glanced inside and saw that it was full of chunks of wood. It looked like dimensional lumber, rather than something simply cut from trees.

"Where did you get the wood?"

He smiled sheepishly. "I took apart a few pieces of furniture, mostly sofas, a couple of bookcases." As he spoke, he pulled what looked like an old-fashioned oilcan out of his jacket pocket, removed the rubber stopper, turned the can upside down over the barrel, and squirted a fluid onto the wood, soaking it. Setting the oilcan aside, he pulled out a book of matches he had been carrying from his last MRE, lit one match and tucked it into the rest, igniting the entire book, which he dropped onto the wood. In spite of the wind, flames leapt up instantly.

Sweezea gave a lopsided grin to Tillie. "I know we can't talk you into coming inside tonight, so we did the next best thing. Now you can warm up."

Before she could thank him, she saw Hutson approaching, doing an impersonation of Santa Claus, with a huge bundle over his shoulder.

Despite her mood, she managed a smile at her two friends as he dumped the bundle next to her feet, spilling out a mound of additional wood for the fire.

"Guys, thanks."

"Least we could do," Hutson shouted. "Sure you won't let one of us take a watch for you?"

She shook her head. "I'm sure."

"Suit yourself. This should hold you through the night."

She thanked them again and they retreated to the access hatch, rolling the empty hand truck with them. The metal side of the barrel was now radiating heat generously, and she stood as close as she dared, not wanting to ignite the fur on her parka. After she had absorbed enough of the warmth to stop her shivers, Tillie turned back to face the west, again remaining as close to the barrel as possible while keeping her vigil. She watched the sun set and the stars come out for the night, moving occasionally to capture a bit more of the heat from the fire on one side of her body, then the other.

Her wristwatch was under far too many layers of clothing to bother with, so she had no idea what time it was when she felt another tap on her shoulder, startling her once more. This time it was Wilson.

"Hi," she barked over the wind.

Leaning close to be heard, he shouted, "Hello, Tillie. The others told me you were up here. I don't understand why. You know that Elias and Leah won't come back sooner than twenty-four hours from their departure."

She shrugged. "I know. They want to give the bug time to kill them, if it's going to, before they come back. I was thinking they might change their minds, that's all. Anyway, it'll be twenty-four hours in the morning."

Wilson began to argue with her, then decided against it. He turned and gazed out to the west, resting his arms on the top of the parapet wall.

They both stood without speaking for several minutes before Tillie broke the silence. "They aren't coming back, are they?"

"Of course they are," he replied quickly, trying his best to sound sincere.

"Why? Why would you say that?"

"Elias and Leah are two of the most clever, resourceful, and adept people I've ever known. If there is a way to gather food from an uninfected origin and bring it back to us, they will find it."

She did not respond for quite some time. Finally, she said, "Thanks." With a single word she conveyed that she did not believe him for a moment.

Wilson fumbled to find something else to say, when she placed her hand on his arm. "Wilson, I'm fine. Okay? There isn't anything you can say that will make it any better. And there isn't anything you can say that will make me decide to come inside. Please understand, this is where I need to be. I tried it inside and I couldn't stand it. Looking at walls with no windows…knowing Elias and Leah might be driving up while I was in there and I wouldn't know about it the minute…the second it happened…was driving me crazy. Besides…what difference does it make, anyway?"

Wilson began to speak, but Tillie put a gloved finger to his lips. "Please don't. You might say something that'll turn on these water pumps behind my eyes again. And as cold as it is out here, I'd have icicles on my cheeks. So go back down where it's warm. I'll be fine."

Despite the fact that much of his face was covered, she could see the concern he had for her. She knew that he was desperately trying to think of the right thing to say that would change her mind. And she could see the exact moment he gave up. "Do you need anything?"

She shook her head to indicate that she did not.

"I'll check on you later."

Tillie nodded.

Resignedly, he squeezed her arm once and turned to walk away. She did not watch his retreating figure cross the roof back to the hatch. Instead, she bent over and picked up an armload of the wood piled at her feet and dumped it into the barrel, causing an explosion of glowing embers to burst from the top and swirl out into the night. Turning her back to the frigid, unceasing gale, Tillie resumed her vigil.

⊙

The day was warm. The sun was bright, casting its rays upon the gently rippling waters of the pond, and scattering them into a million sparkling pinpoints that seemed to caress her eyes instead of hurting them. She was wearing a yellow cotton top, navy blue shorts, and a pair of black Keds. Her tanned legs pumped up and down with each rise and fall of the foot pedals on the paddleboat, each push creating a soft whooshing sound as the paddles at the rear of the boat turned shallowly in the water, easing it forward. A steady, shrill *chirp...chirp...chirp* from an unseen bird almost synchronized with the motion of her legs and the pedals.

The air was filled with the smell of hamburgers grilling at the stand near the dock. And popcorn, its buttery aroma making her mouth water. Close to the shore, picnickers stoked their fires in anticipation of their own burgers soon to be cooked. The smoke from the barbeques wafted through the still air over the water and caused a not unpleasant sting in her nostrils.

Tillie looked at the seat to her right and saw Maxwell, now a towheaded teenager. Although he did not share her red hair, the familial connection provided him with a generous sprinkling of freckles. He was smiling broadly at her as he assisted with the chore of propelling them through the water.

A part of her mind was in another locale, a distant place, different from where she was now in every way. But the remaining part was not only engaged in this idyllic moment, but was relishing it, embracing it, devouring every aspect of her surroundings. She smiled at her brother and put her arm around his already firm and muscular shoulders. "I love you, Maxwell!"

He leaned into her, his hand sliding between her body and the seat back, and circling her waist, pulling her tightly to him. "I love you, too, Tee."

She tousled his blond hair. "What a perfect day! This is so wonderful."

The two continued pedaling across the pond. Tillie turned to face her brother. "Maxwell, do you forgive me?"

"I do, Tee. I always have." The smile left his face, replaced with a more serious expression. "What's important now is that you forgive yourself."

"I don't know if I can."

"You need to, Tee. You must. Tee, wake up! You have to wake up now!"

His words struck her like a hammer blow. She stared at Maxwell, looking deeply into his eyes, trying to understand what he meant and knowing it at the same time. Although her feet were still pushing the pedals down, the sound of the wheel splashing into the water no longer reached her ears. The smell of the hamburgers and popcorn was gone from the air.

Her feet slipped from the pedals which halted instantly. "This can't be," she said aloud, not comprehending why they would not continue their rotation under Maxwell's power.

Chirp…chirp…chirp!

The bird was singing its monotonous song, even louder now, although Tillie could still not see where it was perched. Turning her head to face the shore of the pond, she saw that it was now dense with the smoke from the picnickers' barbeque pits, the people and the grills no longer visible. Just the smoke. Thickening and moving lazily toward her across the water.

The sunlight on the bare skin of her legs and arms, only moments ago feeling warm and comforting, now seemed to bake her. She realized she was sweating.

"Let's find some shade," she said to Maxwell, turning back. The seat beside her was empty. She searched the water around the boat, unexplainable terror gripping her heart and kneading it as a baker would work a mound of dough on his table.

"MAXWELL! MAXWELL!"

Her shouts went unanswered. As she thrashed about in the seat wildly, her eyes swept over the water all around the boat, and she repeatedly yelled her brother's name. The thick smoke from the shore reached her, making her desperate search of the water's surface impossible, and burning her throat and eyes. Tillie's throat was so irritated she could no longer call out his name, uncontrollable coughing racking her.

Chirp…chirp…chirp!

Now completely enveloped in the heavy gray smoke, unable to speak and, in fact, unable to draw a breath without her throat clenching closed in reaction, she decided she must get off the boat and swim to the shore.

Maxwell is already there, she thought to herself. Able to see absolutely nothing around her but a gray curtain, Tillie moved, from memory, to dive off the paddleboat to her left. Twisting around and bracing her feet on the bottom, she pushed off. But rather than plunging into the cool water, she was stunned by an impact from her shoulder slamming into something metal and very hot.

Chirp…chirp…chirp!

Her shoulder blazing with pain from the jolt, and her eyes squeezed tightly shut to avoid the smoke, she tried to crawl over the side of the small boat, careful to avoid whatever it was she had crashed into a moment before. Confusion filled her mind as she crawled. The edge of the boat should have been mere inches from her, yet she was crawling and crawling but not reaching the side, not reaching the water.

Chirp…chirp…chirp!

Born of despair, her crawl became a scramble forward, her hands searching to avoid another obstacle. Risking a quick look, she opened her eyes and saw that the smoke was thinning. No longer attempting to understand or visualize her surroundings, she hurried forward. The smoke continued to lessen and she could see that she was on a flat, gray surface. To her right was a vertical concrete wall.

Chirp…chirp…chirp!

She followed the wall, scraping her knees on the rough texture beneath her, until she had gone far enough to escape the smoke completely and she was able to finally draw in a deep, purging breath. Her throat and lungs, still burning, rebelled at the influx of air and triggered another series of violent coughs. Tillie dropped to the surface and leaned against the wall, waiting for the coughing to stop.

Chirp…chirp…chirp!

When it finally subsided and she was able to draw several moderate breaths, her head cleared and she understood that she was on the roof of Aegis, not in a paddleboat floating on a pond somewhere else. Panting as she assimilated the details of her surroundings, she realized that the fire in the barrel must have gone out, and the charred wood at the bottom must have begun to smoke. She must have been asleep. The rest of it, the pond…the boat…Maxwell…the popcorn and hamburgers and the bird, had all been a part of her dream.

Chirp…chirp…chirp!

"Except the bird, I guess," she muttered to herself. Her mind, climbing the rest of the way out of the dreamworld she had created, reacted. "A BIRD?"

Jumping up, she looked in the direction of the sound. Perched on the parapet wall, not ten feet from her, was a wren, its head jerkily swiveling back and forth, its beak opening.

Chirp…chirp…chirp!

This mundane denizen of the desert might as well have been the mythical Phoenix. She stared at it, as if mesmerized, her mouth agape; she had not seen a bird…any bird…at Aegis in years. Not since the wind had begun.

Slowly, she pulled her eyes away from the sight of the bird, slipped off her hood, and tilted her head back, her eyes sweeping upward. The sun had risen and she saw a beautiful, clear blue sky. Still in disbelief, not trusting her senses, Tillie tore off her gloves, opening her hands wide, palms upward, and extending her arms as far as she could.

"It stopped! IT STOPPED!" The last, an exuberant shout, filled the glorious silence of the still air, her outburst startling the wren and causing it to fly upward and circle above her.

Her breath coming in quick and shallow gasps, her heart beating as rapidly as a trip-hammer, she lowered her gaze and looked across the massive roof of Aegis, no longer cluttered with debris. She now understood her other sudden discomfort in the dream. With the absence of the frigid downdraft, she was hot, sweating beneath the parka and layers of clothing she wore. The Arizona sun beat down upon her and upon the roof, warming the air over Aegis as it had not been in years. In the quiet, she could hear the structure beneath her feet popping and cracking, the sudden temperature change expanding the elements of the building.

Tillie stripped off the parka, tossing it down on the roof. She then shed the extra shirts and pants, until she was down to a single, regular layer of clothing. Although she was still very warm, she basked in the feeling of the sun on her face and arms. From the direction she had crawled, the fifty-five-gallon barrel was enshrouded in smoke from the smoldering fire, as there was no longer any wind to whisk it away.

Turning to the parapet, she looked out over the desert. Even though the sun was still fairly low in the sky, it was working its thermal magic on the desert air, producing a small dust devil in the distance to the west. She knew that she should head toward the hatch, go down below, and tell everyone that the wind had stopped. But she wanted just one more minute first.

Resting her arms on the top edge of the parapet wall, feeling the warmth from the sun already baked into the concrete, she laid her chin on the top of her arms and continued to watch the lazy progression of the dust devil as it drifted closer to Aegis.

Since she had not grown up in the desert, the mechanics of the slender tan funnels were unfamiliar to her. The few she had seen in the past had always looked more defined, more crisp. This one more closely resembled a broad column of dust, dissipating rapidly above the ground and leaving a trail in the air behind its path. And there was something odd at its base...at its leading edge, something she could not quite identify. She pressed harder against the wall, leaning her head farther forward and straining her eyes, when suddenly she was able to discern an object at ground level, moving toward her at what looked like a fast pace. Within another minute, the vague object clarified and a jolt of adrenaline electrified her.

"Oh, my God!" she gasped.

Unable to tear her eyes away for a moment, not even allowing herself to blink, she watched as the color of the object resolved to a bright yellow, the form itself emerging as an SUV. Her entire body tingling with excitement, she forced herself to watch the approaching vehicle long enough to be sure, to be absolutely certain that she was not imagining what she saw.

A minute passed, then another, before Tillie spun away from the wall and ran as she had not run in years, sprinting for the access hatch.

EPILOGUE

And so this band of survivors emerged from Aegis, much as travelers would step out of their craft onto the soil of a new and foreign planet: their minds filled with questions; their hearts torn between fear of what they would discover as they ventured forth from their sanctuary, and hope for the new world, the creation of which had fallen to each of them to accomplish.

In the days, weeks, and months ahead, this new core of humanity would bifurcate their time, their attention, and their efforts. To begin with, there was much that needed to be done. The monumental and the minuscule aspects of the idle infrastructure, which lay dormant, waited patiently for the touch of a human hand to bring them back to life...as if the members of a family were, at long last, returning to their shuttered home after an extended absence. Within their cohort, the group would learn that all of the knowledge and all of the skills, required to breathe artificial life back into the systems, devices, and machinery of the once pervasive population, were present within their ranks.

Still, while they applied their efforts to the repairing, cleaning, and reactivation of their old, yet new, home, not a day passed when they did not ponder and discuss the myriad questions raised by the cataclysm itself, and the innumerable incremental events which allowed for their very survival.

Some of the party were obsessed with finding the answer to one question: who had been responsible for the creation of the pathogen? A team, led by Elias and Leah, found their answer, and assembled a list of names which would then be vilified for generations. Having provided nothing other than the satisfaction of their curiosity, the list was put aside for posterity. They each concluded that there had existed a truly evil cabal on the Earth, a malignant assemblage who very nearly caused the extinction of mankind; however, none of them would ever know that, had some mysterious hand swept those vile men and women into the sea, others would have eagerly arisen, others with an identical nefarious goal. And the cataclysm, rather than being averted, would have merely been deferred.

The day-to-day efforts continued. Neighborhoods and communities were reclaimed and brought back to life, as the individuals among the band grappled with other questions. Most wondered why they were selected to live, while so many perished. The psychologists within the group repeatedly explained that they suffered from survivor's guilt, and eventually counseled them to a tacit acceptance.

Others believed that their presence within Aegis prior to the cataclysm was serendipity, a random, chance occurrence and nothing more, as was the collapse of the entrance to Aegis on the first day of the epidemic. Their friends argued the odds against the many coincidences, but to no avail as these individuals clung to their belief.

Some needed to understand the nature of the pathogen. Eventually, they uncovered only the mechanics of it, without ever ascertaining the recipe itself. That would remain unknown and unknowable for all time. Again, they stored away the details they possessed for study by future generations.

They asked if they were truly safe from the pathogen, whether it had been fully eradicated from the Earth. In time, that, too, was answered. The malignant organism was no more.

They queried as to why the vaccine did not protect the perpetrators as it had been designed to do, and then so thoroughly tested to guarantee its efficacy. The answer, they decided, was that a fluke mutation in the pathogen made it immune to the vaccine.

Furthermore, the group wondered if there were other survivors, other places like Aegis in the world, which had also been protected. They found that there were, that they were not alone.

As these survivors progressed in the re-establishment of a society outside the walls of Aegis, nearly all of their questions were, over time, answered. Would it be best if they were to remain together as a group, or should they scatter throughout the countryside? What must they do to ensure that another global calamity would not occur at some point in the distant future? What form of government was appropriate for them? Or was a government needed at all? Resources were once again abundant and there was such vast open space that conceivably all of the survivors on Earth could so disseminate that rarely, if ever, would they see another person, unless by choice. During darker moments, all of them asked whether they were worthy and deserving of this chance they had been given.

As the once overwhelming aggregation of questions was whittled down, the emphasis in the daily activities and thoughts of the survivors shifted to the immediate, the temporal, concerns of life. And yet, as they put behind themselves the queries and the quests for answers, and focused their attention on the future, one nagging question remained, one which could never be explained away as a fluke…a coincidence…a random act of nature…or a deliberate deed by man, and that was the wind: the cascading, tumbling avalanche of air from the bitterly cold regions of the upper atmosphere, the downdraft which held the pathogen at bay and protected this small and fragile group of men and women. For no matter how long they may wonder, how long they may search, the one answer they will never find is that the hand which begat this wind was mine.

John Wilson Chapman

If you enjoyed reading *The Aegis Solution* by John David Krygelski, you will be truly captivated by his previous novels.

The Harvest

Doctor Reese Johnson, a professor of psychology and anthropology, who specializes in theology and religion, is brought in to interview a stranger who claims to be God. Unsure what to expect, Reese is immediately surprised by the profound and insightful answers that the stranger provides him. He also witnesses something that might be a miracle. It is at this time Johnson discovers that the stranger prefers to be called *Elohim*. Being a religious scholar, Reese already knows that this name, in Hebrew, is the word for God. But he also knows that in some ancient cultures, it was used to describe the cadre of angels from whom Lucifer descended. In some, it was even used as the term for a group of aliens from another planet who came to colonize the Earth. Reese is now faced with the choice that the stranger is God, the devil, or an alien from another planet. Other experts are brought in to talk to Elohim and, as a result, word leaks out to the press, who announce prematurely that God is on Earth. People and governments react strongly to the news, and it is during this turmoil that Elohim reveals what he has come to do. It is a plan that will affect all of humanity, and the timetable is only five days. Reese is now in a race against the clock as he attempts to determine whether Elohim's plan will be a wonderful event for mankind, or something truly horrifying. Events and characters lead to a surprising and monumental climax that will answer all of your questions and leave you breathless.

Praise for John David Krygelski's debut novel – *The Harvest*

"It is, in one word, a masterpiece! The best book I've ever read, and I've read thousands."

"…this book was one of the most extraordinary books I have ever read. It touched me and made me examine my entire life. It is hard to believe that this is anyone's first book. Thank you for writing it."

"*The Harvest* is amazingly written, intriguing, very different and fascinating, deep…highly recommended reading."

"…this book is our lives; we are living it as we read it. Krygelski reached into my most inner thoughts and put them in words. *The Harvest* will have you questioning the very foundations of your beliefs."

"I have been reading nearly all of my 60 years. This is the most profound book I have ever read. I can't believe that this is the first novel of Mr. Krygelski."

"*The Harvest* had me completely enthralled from beginning to end. I never wanted to put the book down, being one of the most interesting reads I have ever had the pleasure to experience. I have difficulty expressing in words how much I truly loved this book."

"This dense and carefully plotted story involves a thoughtful look at religion. Reese Johnson, a professor at the University of Arizona, is teaching 'Religion Under Assault' when he suddenly finds himself investigating a man who calls himself 'the Creator.' For hopefuls everywhere looking for a second chance to create a better world, this is an intriguing novel." – J. C. Martin, *Arizona Daily Star*

"…congratulations on *The Harvest*…I appreciate the way you clarify some of my deepest beliefs. I think your book challenges the reader to look inward and think. Brilliant. I'm telling everyone I know to get *The Harvest*."

"…haunting characters and alarming events are interwoven with such artistry and precision they pop off the page, raising the hair on the back of one's neck…."

"I have really enjoyed *The Harvest*. It has been one of the best books I have read in a long time. I was even shocked to have found myself referring to certain passages in the book and looking more into the depth of the history in certain topics, and actually using a dictionary as well; no book lately in the past 5 years has accomplished such. I actually am reading it again for the second time. Thank you."